The GIRL *from the* PARADISE BALLROOM

The GIRL from the PARADISE BALLROOM

A Novel

ALISON LOVE

B\D\W\Y
Broadway Books • New York

This is a work of fiction. Names, characters, places, and incidents either are the product of the author's imagination or are used fictitiously. Any resemblance to actual persons, living or dead, events, or locales is entirely coincidental.

Published in the United States by Broadway Books, an imprint of the Crown Publishing Group, a division of Penguin Random House LLC, New York.
www.crownpublishing.com

Broadway Books and its logo, B \ D \ W \ Y, are trademarks of Penguin Random House LLC.

Originally published in hardcover in Great Britain by Quartet Books, in 2014.

Library of Congress Cataloging-in-Publication Data is available upon request.

ISBN 978-1-101-90451-0
eBook ISBN 978-1-101-90452-7

Printed in the United States of America

Book design by Lauren Dong
Cover design by: Tal Goretsky
Cover photography: (London skyline) Popperfoto/GettyImages; (Hawker Hurricanes) Print Collector/Getty Images; (ballroom dancers) ullstein bild/Getty Images
Title page photography: © Collage Photography/Veer

10 9 8 7 6 5 4 3 2 1

First American Paperback Edition

For Barry, with love

HISTORICAL NOTE

FROM THE NINETEENTH CENTURY THERE WAS A WELL-ESTABLISHED Italian community in Britain, working in many different professions: as glassblowers, knife grinders, artists' models, street musicians, ice-cream sellers, restaurateurs. When Mussolini came to power in 1922, the first of Europe's fascist dictators, he set out to gain the loyalty of these Italians abroad, who had been ignored by previous governments. His regime established new leisure and welfare programs, and local fascist headquarters became social and cultural centers for the Italian community. For many Italians, fascism restored a sense of pride in their own nationality: belonging to the Fascist Party was a simple gesture of patriotism.

With the rise of Hitler, tensions across Europe reached fever pitch, and British mistrust of foreign residents increased. The situation worsened in 1935 when Mussolini invaded Abyssinia—now Ethiopia—claiming it for his new Roman empire. As war approached, there were fears that Italy would forge a military alliance with Nazi Germany, and hostility toward Italians in Britain grew ever more intense.

JUNE 11, 1940

THEY CAME FOR HIM AT FIRST LIGHT, AS HE HAD KNOWN THEY would. There were two of them. They walked briskly but not hurriedly along the pavement, glancing up from time to time to check the house numbers.

Antonio stood at the bedroom window. The June morning was mild, almost milky. It seemed to him that if he stayed perfectly silent, perfectly still, they would pass the house and leave him be. And yet he knew that they would not. At any moment—in thirty seconds, in twenty, in ten—they would knock at the door. The knock would be loud and hollow: a drumbeat, a summons. There would be no anger in it, no private hatred. The men were doing their job, that's all.

In the street below, an errand boy was on his way to work, late and scowling. He kicked a fallen bottle from last night's riots. Someone in the crowd had tried to throw a bicycle through the window of Fortuna's, the Italian pharmacy, but it had bounced off the wall, the mudguard twisted.

I am calm, thought Antonio, I am prepared. I will not weep or tremble when they come for me. Even as he thought it, though, he watched the errand boy hurrying toward the lime trees of Soho Square, free to begin his ordinary day, and despair seized his throat. My life, he thought, my sweet promising life. What will become of it? The memories hurtled in a landslide through his mind, unstoppable: the dazzle of spotlights, the sway of the tango, a woman's soft fingers upon his neck, his own voice soaring, soaring.

And then the policemen knocked at the door.

AUTUMN 1937

CHAPTER 1

THEY WERE LOWERING THE GLITTER BALL IN THE PARADISE Ballroom when he arrived. The hall smelled of cigarettes and stale spilled beer. Below the dais the dance hostesses were killing time, tugging at their dress straps, poking at their hair. Their faces had the strained pallid look of nocturnal creatures who never see broad daylight.

"You're the stand-in for Victor, are you?" A man in a checked cap stepped from the stage, where he had been adjusting a gilt music stand.

Antonio bowed. "Yes, I am Antonio Trombetta."

"Eyetie, are you? Well, the girls will like that," said the man, without enthusiasm. "At least you're on time. Maurice hates it when his singers are late. You can leave your things backstage. Jeanie will show you the cloakroom, won't you?"

"Not half," said Jeanie, a bold-eyed girl with a crimped permanent wave. The other dance hostesses snickered amiably. Jeanie led Antonio through the baize door into a whitewashed corridor. He could hear the warble and squawk of a saxophone player, warming up.

"Well, you're a nice surprise, I must say." Jeanie pushed her way into a windowless room littered with coats and hats and furled umbrellas. "Usually when Victor's ill we get an oily little man from Orpington with wandering hands."

Antonio smiled. "Tell me, Jeanie, is Victor often sick?" he asked as he took off his overcoat. Underneath he was wearing an old dress suit, sponged and pressed to hide the shiny patches.

"Don't get your hopes up. He and Maurice are like that." Jeanie held out her index fingers side by side, then hooked them together with a suggestive wiggle. "Besides, Maurice is past it. Too much of what the Yanks call happy dust. The Paradise is the only place that'll have him now."

Turning to the mirror—a grubby mirror, smeared with pinkish powder—Antonio straightened his collar. His black hair was glossy with brilliantine. He touched it with his fingertips, gingerly, as if it belonged to someone else.

"Come and find me later," said Jeanie, as she turned to leave. "I'll give you a dance on the house. You'll love the way I foxtrot."

MAURICE GOODYEAR WAS in his forties, with a jaded, handsome face. From time to time he sniffed, raising his knuckles to his nose.

"Any of the songs you don't know?" He was not unfriendly, but he had seen a dozen singers come and go, and he no longer had the will to learn their names. "Well, I'll cue you in and after that you're on your own."

Antonio nodded. He knew his place: in bands like this it was the leader, not the vocalist, who was the star. The dancers were gathering around the stage now, the male hosts as well as the girls, eyeing him with curiosity. The lights dimmed. Antonio felt a flicker of stage fright as he stepped toward the microphone. It vanished, though, the moment he began to sing.

"*You and the night and the music . . .*"

The dancers' faces changed, a raised eyebrow here, a half-reluctant smile there. Jeanie, at the front of the hall, was grinning. Opening his throat, Antonio let his voice flood out. This is what I am for, he thought, this is what I was born to do.

Maurice Goodyear brought the band to a halt. "That will do,

gentlemen. Now, once through 'These Foolish Things,' and they can let in the great unwashed."

The hall began to fill the moment the doors were thrown open. Soon the air was shrouded in smoke. There was a hum of voices, the constant shuffling of feet. Antonio watched the professionals weave their way among the other dancers, their faces spattered with light from the glitter ball. Jeanie's partner was a gangling young man whose neck sloped like a giraffe's. Beside her a tall girl in silver lamé was dancing the tango, eyes fixed, one bare arm outstretched. There was something extraordinary about her face, though what it was Antonio couldn't tell.

"*The moon got in my eyes . . .* " He exaggerated his accent to make himself sound exotic: a cheap trick, but it meant that his listeners remembered him.

"You're doing well, my friend," murmured Maurice Goodyear, giving another sniff. "Go and wet your whistle. Back in ten minutes."

There was a crate of beer at the side of the stage. Antonio wanted fresh air after the fug of the dance hall, and passing through the baize door he made his way to the back entrance. It gave onto a small yard, lit by a single lamp. The night smelled of rain on dusty pavements.

Antonio raised the beer bottle to his mouth. He was about to drink when he heard a whimper. A girl was stooping beside the brick wall, one hand pressed against her stomach, the other to her lips. It was the tango dancer in the silver dress.

"What's wrong? Are you ill?"

The tango dancer did not answer, still holding her fingers to her mouth. Antonio touched her shoulder. Her skin felt clammy beneath the coarse metallic fabric of her dress. Crouching beside her, he handed her the bottle of beer. She lifted it and swallowed. Her face was very pale.

"Thank you," she said, and she passed the bottle back to him with a lopsided smile. Antonio drank. The beer was tepid and gassy against his dry throat.

"Olivia?" It was Jeanie, peering into the yard. "The manager's asking for you. They're playing another tango, he wants to know why you're not on the floor."

The girl in silver straightened up. As she did so her body was gripped by a spasm of pain, and she gasped. Antonio took her hand, which was cold as a mermaid's. From the dance hall there came the sway of a tango: "Dark Eyes," the old Russian song of love and ruin.

"She shouldn't be working," said Antonio, "she's not well."

Jeanie squinted as she made him out in the darkness. "Oh, she'll be all right. It's her own fault, after all. Oldest mistake in the book." She gave a shrug. "At least in a place like this the girls always know someone who can get you out of trouble."

It took Antonio an instant to realize what she meant. He dropped Olivia's hand as if it had scalded him.

"Dear God," he said, before he could stop himself. Olivia's chin reared fiercely upward in the lamplight. He could see her high cheekbones, her wide scarlet mouth.

"Yes, it's true. I've had an abortion. What are you going to do? Call the police?"

Antonio stared. "Of course not—"

"Don't look at me like that," said Olivia. "Who the hell do you think you are?" Her eyes flashed, daring him to pity her. Once again Antonio thought how extraordinary her face was. It's because she's so plain, he thought; and then, No, she's not plain, she's beautiful. The knowledge catapulted through his body, a revelation.

Olivia whisked at her silver skirt, and without looking at Antonio, she swept away toward the dance hall.

"Good riddance," said Jeanie cheerfully. "They'll be playing a foxtrot next, I'll give you that dance I promised." She inched closer, tilting her face invitingly upward. He could smell her violet perfume. "I suppose I've missed my chance, though. I suppose you've already got a sweetheart?"

"As a matter of fact," said Antonio, "I'm married. And my wife is expecting our first baby."

"Oh, lord," said Jeanie, "I've dropped a brick there, haven't I?"

Antonio did not stay to answer. He strode back inside, returning to his place on the stage. There was no sign of Olivia. For the rest of the night he looked for her in the crowd, trying to glimpse the pale line of her face, but it seemed that she had vanished.

IT WAS DRIZZLING when the Paradise Ballroom closed, the pavements greasy with rain. Antonio pulled his trilby over his forehead and set off toward Soho. He liked to walk home, even when the weather was bad. It gave him a breathing space between the two worlds he inhabited, the shabby glamour of the dance halls and the noisy, familiar, claustrophobic atmosphere of Frith Street, where the Trombettas lived. Antonio's father, Enrico, ran a kiosk in Leicester Square that sold sweets and cigarettes. During the day Antonio helped out there, and his other life as a singer seemed as improbable as a mirage.

In Soho one of the cafés, Ricci's, was open still. Antonio could hear the rise and fall of voices, punctuated by the twang of a mandolin. He thought of Maurice Goodyear's parchment face, of Jeanie's violet scent, of the way he had fluffed a high note in "Night and Day." He tried not to think about the tango dancer, and the terrible thing she had done to her own body.

When he reached the house he turned his key carefully in the lock. His wife, Danila, was a light sleeper. Slipping off his shoes, he went toward the kitchen for a glass of water, and saw to his surprise that the light was on. Filomena, his sister, was sitting at the table, wrapped in a dressing gown of fawn checked wool, her hair in a thick plait. She was frowning at a piece of paper in her hand. The moment she saw Antonio she swept the paper into her pocket.

"I thought you would be asleep," said Antonio.

Filomena did not answer. "Let me make you some warm milk, Antonio," she said, and crossing to the stove poked vigorously at the damped-down fire.

Antonio sank into a chair. He was fond of his sister, who was a kind, stolid girl. She worked as a laundress in Goodge Street, and there was always a pleasing aura of soap and starch about her.

"Was that a letter from Bruno?" Bruno was Filomena's *fidanzato*, her fiancé; he was also Danila's cousin. Like Antonio's, the marriage had been fixed by their families when they were young, thirteen or fourteen. Bruno had been working in one of the grand Mayfair hotels, but when Mussolini invaded Abyssinia he had joined the army in a surge of patriotism. Now, two years later, he was still in Africa with the occupying forces and nobody knew when he would return.

Filomena touched the pocket where she had put the piece of paper. "Yes. It was a letter from Bruno."

She took the enamel saucepan from the stove and poured the milk into a cup. Filomena was twenty, a year older than Danila. Bruno's departure had left her in limbo, an unmarried daughter when she should have been a wife.

"He will be home soon, Filomena." Antonio disagreed with Bruno's politics, but there was no doubt he would make a good husband: he was devoted to Filomena. "Do not fret."

Filomena put the cup of milk on the table, pushing aside a newspaper to make room. It was *L'Italia Nostra*, Antonio noticed, the weekly fascist paper. His younger brother, Valentino, must have brought it home. Valentino was a barman at the *fascio*, the Italian club where the Fascist Party had its headquarters; like Bruno, he was an ardent supporter of Mussolini. He had been desperate to go and fight in Abyssinia too, but his father had forbidden it. You're only seventeen, it's too young, Enrico had said, although the rest of the family knew that it was because Valentino was his favorite, and he did not want to lose him.

"Half of it's been torn out," said Antonio, turning over the paper. "There's only the advertisements left."

"I used it to light the stove. Why? Did you want to read it?" Filomena widened her eyes ironically at her brother, who smiled.

"Valentino will be furious."

Filomena flicked her plait over her shoulder. "I will go back to bed now," she said, stepping down into the scullery, where her mattress was laid out on the tiled floor. "Sleep well, Antonino."

THE TROMBETTAS RENTED the lower floors of the house in Frith Street, four rooms with a lavatory in the backyard. Above them lived a countryman from Lazio, Mauro Bonetti, with his niece Renata. The Trombettas felt sorry for the Bonettis, especially Mauro. He was lame from childhood polio, and the only job he could manage was washing dishes in the kitchens of the Savoy Hotel. He earns next to nothing, Enrico would say, stretching out his hands with an air of superiority. How can he ever make his way in the world?

The bedroom where Antonio slept overlooked Frith Street. Before the death of his mother, Mariana, it had belonged to his parents, and it was full of the huge elaborate Victorian furniture Mariana had insisted on buying from secondhand shops. As he stepped into the room Antonio barked his shins on the mahogany sideboard.

"Antonino? Is that you?"

"Of course it's me." He sat on the bed, sliding out of his braces. The light from the street lamp filtered hazily through the rose-patterned curtains. "I didn't mean to wake you."

Danila sat up, one arm cradling the bulge of her stomach. She was seven months pregnant. When they were first married she had been tiny and slender, her wrist bones as delicate as filigree. Now it was as if someone had gently smudged her beauty with a thumb, broadening not only her body but her face, turning her from a flower into a fruit.

"I wasn't asleep. I was waiting for you." There was a note of reproach in Danila's voice. "Were you talking to Filomena?"

Antonio hesitated. His wife and his sister did not see eye to eye. Danila was a sweet-tempered girl, but she liked to have her status as a married woman acknowledged, and it irked Filomena, who had been running the household since her mother's death.

"Yes. She made me some hot milk."

"Why was she awake? She has to go to work in the morning."

"She was reading a letter from your cousin Bruno." Antonio loosened the studs in his collar and slid them onto the bedside table.

"But there haven't been any letters from Bruno. Or if there have, she hasn't told me."

"Maybe she was re-reading an old one. She misses him, Danila, out in Africa."

Danila pulled a rueful face, and she put her arms about his neck, asking to be forgiven. The scent of her skin aroused Antonio. He slid his palm to her breast, which was taut and hot beneath her cotton nightdress. At once she stiffened. For the past few weeks she had been nervous about sex, afraid it would hurt the baby. He withdrew, and pulled his white shirt over his head.

"It is just that I am sleepy—"

"It's all right, my darling. You need your rest."

When he had undressed he slipped between the sheets beside her. She was snuffling against the pillow: an innocent sound, like a small pet animal. Antonio thought of their wedding day, and how Danila had gazed at him in the church, her huge eyes misty with rapture. That is love, he thought, reassurance flooding through him, that is true love. For an instant he remembered the girl from the Paradise Ballroom, with her fierce tragic face, but he pushed the thought out of his mind and fell asleep.

CHAPTER 2

OLIVIA LAY UPON THE LUMPY DIVAN IN HER BEDSIT IN Pimlico, staring at the yellowish plaster ceiling. A week had passed since her encounter with Antonio, and in that time she had not set foot outside her front door. She had stayed in bed first out of pain, then out of misery. The memories bobbed and surfaced like monstrous fish: the abortionist's flat with its reek of disinfectant, the tugging pain, the hot gouts of blood. She knew she would lose her job at the Paradise Ballroom, but she could not bring herself to move.

Olivia had been christened plain Olive Johnson, daughter of a bank clerk who was killed on the Somme at the age of twenty-three. There was a photograph of him on the mantelpiece, absurdly young, perpetually startled. Daisy, her mother, had been bred to be pretty, not clever, and it was a shock to have to earn her own living. She became a dressmaker, sewing party frocks for middle-class wives in Uckfield. Her chief ambition was for her two daughters to make decent marriages. With this in mind she sent them to elocution lessons and dancing classes, although the younger girl, pink-and-white Wilma, repaid her efforts far better than poor gawky Olive. Mrs. Johnson had great hopes of Wilma.

Both girls left school at fourteen. Wilma got a job in a haberdasher's, where she enchanted the customers with her cheeky smile. As for Olive, she worked with her mother, rolling the slippery hems of crêpe de Chine frocks, stitching sequins and bugle beads. The only time she came out of her shell was in the dance hall. Daisy had paid for Olive's dancing lessons mainly so that she could accompany Wilma, but she turned out to be unexpectedly good. The tango became her forte. She danced it as though she had hot Latin blood, her face set, her eyes wild.

"I don't think you ought to be doing that, Olive," Wilma said, as they were walking home one day. It was a fine autumn evening, and the air smelled sharply of their neighbor's conifer hedge.

"Doing what?"

"The tango. I don't think it's quite nice. Can't you stick to the other dances, the waltz and the quickstep? At least they're not vulgar."

Olive stopped walking. "You're jealous," she said, astonished. Nobody had ever been jealous of her before, certainly not her bewitching younger sister.

"Of course I'm not jealous. I think you look a bit of a fool, that's all."

The tears stung Olive's eyes. "You're horrible. That's a horrible thing to say. I wish you were dead."

"Don't care." Wilma swung her handbag at the dense green hedge. "I wish you were dead too, so there."

Two days later Wilma came home complaining of a sore throat. The next morning her tongue was as bright as a strawberry. It was scarlet fever. Olive caught it as well, and for three days the silver mercury in the thermometer soared. In the end, though, she recovered; Wilma did not.

The death of her favorite daughter was the last straw for Mrs. Johnson. Since the loss of her husband she had felt as if her real life had been stolen from her, and was unfolding somewhere else, behind a window in some stranger's house. She had a vague notion of what was happening in it—comfort, prosperity, the joys of a good marriage—but she had no idea how she could cross the glass to reach it. Now there no longer seemed any point in trying. Olive watched her mother's spirit leach away as the color fades from chintz curtains in south-facing rooms. She grew grayer, thinner, ceased to eat, ceased to talk, until one morning she was no longer there at all.

At the funeral an aunt who ran a boardinghouse in Croydon offered Olive a home, but Olive could see what the aunt thought of her: a hulking girl who would never marry, good for a lifetime of skivvying.

"No, thank you," she said. "That's very kind of you, but I've decided to move to London. And I'm going to change my name. From now on, I intend to be called Olivia."

IT WAS JEANIE who came to Olivia's rescue. She had betrayed her fellow dancer's secret out of pique, seeing the Italian singer take her hand, and she felt guilty, especially when Olivia failed to reappear at the Paradise Ballroom. At three o'clock on a gloomy October afternoon Jeanie made her way to the house in Pimlico, carrying a sixpenny bar of milk chocolate as a peace offering.

"This place is a mess," she said. "You're a mess too, if you don't mind my saying so."

Olivia did not argue, but lit the gas fire with a loud pop. Jeanie sat down in the chair closest to the fire; the room was very cold. It was not a bad room—Jeanie was a connoisseur of bedsits—but the furniture was filmed with dust and there was a bottle of sour milk on the table next to the gas ring. A damp towel and a pair of lisle stockings hung dejectedly over a wooden clotheshorse.

"I suppose I've lost my job at the Paradise?" Olivia said, hugging her knees to her chest.

"Mmn," said Jeanie, through a mouthful of milk chocolate, which she was eating herself since Olivia had shown no practical interest in it. She wanted to add, What did you expect? but she thought it might depress Olivia even more. "I've got good news, though, that's why I came. Some place in Kingly Street wants dance hostesses for a private party. A chap who plays the sax there told me about it. It's only for one night, but the tips'll be good."

"Oh, I don't know." Olivia stretched down lethargically and clasped her feet in their knitted bed socks. "When is it?"

"Tonight. For two pins I'd do it myself, but I've got a new regular who's the cat's pajamas. Steady job, pretty face, the works. I don't want one of the other girls poaching him."

A shadow of a smile crossed Olivia's face, as though she had remembered a joke that once, perhaps a year ago, she had found funny. "I don't know," she said again.

"Well, what do you think will happen if you don't give it a go? Do you want to slouch about here for the rest of your life? Some people would kill for the chance to earn a bob or two." Jeanie swallowed the last piece of chocolate. "Here's the address. Six o'clock sharp, ask for the manager. It's up to you now."

When Jeanie had gone Olivia picked up the tortoiseshell hand mirror that lay on her bedside table. It had been her mother's, and whenever she looked into it she half-expected to see Daisy's face, pinched and pretty and disappointed. This time though she saw not her mother, but Antonio Trombetta, his eyes stark with horror. How dare he judge me? she thought. Putting down the mirror she reached for her sponge bag, and set off to light the geyser in the mildewed bathroom.

CHAPTER 3

BERNARD RODWAY HAD NOT INTENDED TO GO TO THE PARTY in Kingly Street. It was to celebrate the first anniversary of *Carnival*, a gaudy magazine full of society gossip; not the kind of thing Bernard himself would ever pick up, except by accident. Nevertheless, he had an hour to kill before dinner, and he decided to call in for a drink. You could never tell whom you might meet in the strangest of places. Cheerfully he accepted one of the lurid cocktails from a tray, and surveyed the room for anyone he might recognize.

Bernard was always being invited to parties; the mantelpiece of the house he rented in Bedford Square was thick with embossed cards. He was a sociable, serious, plumply attractive man of thirty-two, who looked as though he might be someone important: when Bernard entered the room people instinctively turned their heads. He dabbled in journalism—poetry reviews, articles about the rise of fascism—and he sat on several committees concerned with the welfare of refugees. These activities gave him a pleasing, rather frantic feeling of achievement, but they could not erase the sense that he had not yet made his mark in the world.

"Rodway! Good to see you." It was John Allsopp, the editor of *Carnival*. He resembled a cynical, middle-aged leprechaun, dark and slight, with protuberant eyes. "Decent of you to slum it with us."

Bernard remembered, too late, that Allsopp's handshake was

limp and clammy. "Oh, it's a pleasure," he said. He wheezed a little when he spoke, a relic of childhood asthma, which gave his voice an unexpected charm. "This all looks very jolly. Dancing, too."

Allsopp glanced toward the parquet floor, where a small band was playing among the potted palms. Half a dozen girls in evening frocks were leading their partners in a foxtrot. The dance hostesses had been Allsopp's idea. He thought they would give the party some allure, and besides, in these hard times the girls might be grateful to him for the chance to earn a little extra. There was one that he particularly fancied, a blond creature called Florence with helpless eyes; just his type.

"So, Rodway," he said, in his bright facetious voice, "how are you? I've spotted your name in the *New Statesman* a couple of times. I like to keep an eye on the competition." He seized a cocktail from a passing waiter. "Glad they're keeping you busy. Though of course you don't have to worry about paying the rent, unlike the rest of us poor reptiles."

Bernard gave a tight-lipped smile. He did not like to be reminded that he had a private income. His family owned a silk manufacturing business in Macclesfield, weaving exquisite jacquard cloth in crimson and indigo.

"I wouldn't have thought the *New Statesman* would be competing for readers with something like *Carousel*," he remarked.

"*Carnival*," said Allsopp, rising to the bait; and then: "Of course, if you have any suggestions for improving the magazine, I'd be delighted to hear them."

Bernard knew that Allsopp was being sarcastic, but he gave a magisterial frown all the same. "You should be more critical of the dictators: Mussolini and that madman Hitler. Even if you just poke fun at them, it would be better than nothing. In fact, that would be an excellent strategy. Humor can debunk monsters where logical argument fails."

Allsopp sniffed. "We can't do that. Nobody else does."

"Precisely. All the national papers treat them with kid gloves for fear of offending them. It's time someone made a stand. Your readers will welcome it, even if the politicians don't."

"I don't think you're very familiar with the readers of *Carnival*," drawled Allsopp, annoyed by Bernard's moralizing. "They don't care about politics. In any case, not everyone thinks that Herr Hitler's such a bad thing. What's wrong with a powerful leader who inspires his people?"

Bernard opened his mouth to do battle. He thrived on political arguments. Just as he was about to speak, though, the band struck up a tango, strident and bittersweet, and automatically he turned to look. A tall young woman was sweeping across the floor. She wore a spangled black sheath dress, split to the thigh. It was Olivia.

"What an astonishing girl," said Bernard. Unlike Antonio Trombetta, he recognized at once that she was beautiful. "Who is she, do you know?"

Allsopp peered. He had not taken to Olivia, who seemed to him too clever by half, not a quality he admired in women.

"She looks like an exiled Russian countess," Bernard was saying. "And she's a wonderful dancer. Seriously, Allsopp, who is she?"

"Just a hostess I hired for the night. Nobody very distinguished. And now, Rodway, if you'll excuse me there are people I must see . . ."

Bernard looked at Olivia once more, this time with regret. An empty-headed creature, if Allsopp had picked her; that air of grandeur was a trick of the light. The tango came to an end. Bernard glanced at his wristwatch. Once around the room, he thought, and then I'll be off.

In the lobby the attendant gave him his coat and hat. Bernard was groping in his pocket for a tip when he heard a girl's shrill voice coming from the red-curtained cloakroom.

"Take your hands off me. I don't want to."

"Don't be a silly girl, Florence." That was Allsopp, nasal and peremptory. God, he's a slimy little shit, thought Bernard, and he snatched at the plush curtain.

It was Olivia who intervened, though. She had noticed Allsopp's pursuit of Florence, and although she thought Florence a foolish girl she did not see why he should get away with it. Seizing a canary-yellow cocktail from a tray, she upended it over Allsopp's head. Florence let out a giggle of shock as the cocktail ran stickily down his red, rather bulbous nose.

Allsopp rubbed his hand across his face, gasping. "You'll be sorry for that. I'm a very influential man. I tell you, you'll never work again."

"I don't believe you," said Olivia. Her voice was husky and pleasing, Bernard noticed.

"Bravo," he said, "well done."

Allsopp turned furiously toward him. "Lend me your handkerchief, Rodway, and don't be such a prig. Those girls are no angels, you can have any one you want for tuppence ha'penny. Don't pretend you don't know that."

Bernard pulled the handkerchief from his pocket and held it out disdainfully as if it, or Allsopp, or both, stank like a cesspit. Then he extended his arm in Olivia's direction.

"I wonder, my dear," he said, "if you would do me the honor of dancing with me?"

CHAPTER 4

THERE HAD BEEN TROMBETTAS IN LONDON FOR MORE THAN sixty years, migrating from their village just outside Rome. Antonio's grandfather Nino had arrived first, in 1870. He had been recruited in Lazio by his mother's cousin, who ran a flock of organ-grinders from his house in Clerkenwell. The organ-grinders were all boys, thirty of them, under contract for three years. Each morning they would go out into the streets with their barrel organs and their mischievous white-faced monkeys; each night they would return to the ramshackle house in Saffron Hill, hand over the cash they had gathered, and sit down to eat boiled rice and cabbage and bacon.

Nino was fortunate. Unlike some *padroni*, his mother's cousin was an honest man, who fed his boys properly and paid up at the end of their contracts. When he got his lump sum of eight pounds sterling Nino went home to Italy. He gave half the money to his father, to buy a small plot of land on the outskirts of the village; then he married his *fidanzata* in the plain stone church where his parents had been married. There was not enough work in Lazio to feed him, though, never mind keep a family, and six weeks after the wedding he returned to England.

By now organ-grinders had fallen from favor. Too many people complained that they were a nuisance, plaguing respectable passersby with their squalling. Nino, wise to the times, purchased a handcart and a brazier and sold roast chestnuts, imported each autumn from his homeland. The handcart was shaped like a Venetian gondola, prettily studded with mirrors. In the summer his young wife made ice cream, boiling up the milk and sugar in their little kitchen in Soho. The ice cream was pale and crystalline, scented with vanilla. It was served in small glasses, a penny a lick, sluiced out between customers in a tin bucket beneath the counter.

This was the business that Enrico, Antonio's father, inherited. When he was thirteen he came to London and learned to peddle his barrow along Piccadilly, trilling his hand organ as he went. Like his father, though, Enrico had a nose for change. More and more of his compatriots were abandoning their street traders' lives to set up proper establishments—cafés, boardinghouses, barbershops. Enrico wanted to be one of them. After Nino died from tuberculosis Enrico sold the barrow and persuaded his father-in-law to go shares on the lease of a sweet kiosk. It was in a convenient spot; working men and girls walked past each day, as well as plush West End couples in their top hats and fragile silk dresses. The right man could make good money from it.

Enrico worked hard, hefting boxes of wine gums and peppermints, smiling benignly when pimpled office boys accused him of shortchanging them. Half of what he earned he sent home to Lazio. It meant that his mother could purchase her own small house on the village's steep main street; it meant that his brothers did not have to live in poverty. Soon he felt confident enough to bring his wife, Mariana, to London. Antonio came too, a dark-eyed, curly-haired boy of three. Before long more children were born: two daughters, Paolina and Filomena, then Valentino, his youngest, the apple of his eye. The family took rooms in Frith Street, and Enrico smiled indulgently as his wife bought furniture, bric-a-brac, smart Sunday clothes for the children. There were trips to Italy every other year; more land was bought; marriages were arranged for Antonio and for Paolina, who joined her new husband in Lazio—one less mouth to feed. It was a good life, a settled life, and Enrico knew it. All the same, in the summer when day broke early, he would dream that he was back in Italy, in the village that he thought of unshakably as home. He would hear the jangling of the church bells, the shrilling of the cicadas, he would feel the heat reverberating from the earth, and his heart would sink like a stone to remember where he was: in a gray foreign country, a stranger.

"WILL YOU NEVER learn, Valentino? You will bring shame upon our family."

It was a cold, dark evening in November. Enrico was planted grimly in the Trombettas' kitchen, staring at his younger son.

"I am sorry, Papa," said Valentino. "It was only meant in fun—"

"What has happened?" asked Antonio. He was preparing for his night's engagement: not in a dance hall this time, but a local Italian restaurant, La Rondine, decorated with Chianti bottles and tinted photographs of Naples.

Enrico jabbed his hand toward Valentino. "Tell your brother the mischief you've caused."

Valentino bit his lower lip. He did not accept censure without a fight, which made it surprisingly easy for him to wriggle out of it.

"It was a flirtation, that is all. It is not my fault that Lucia's family have taken it to heart."

"What? Lucia from Ricci's café?" Antonio looked up from his accordion. He was wiping the keys with a chamois cloth, so the constant touch of his fingertips did not yellow the ivory.

Enrico's creased eyes were like chestnuts, hard with reproach. "Her father has packed her off to Italy, to be married to her cousin Federico. He is afraid that if she stays the story will get out, Federico will learn that she is damaged goods, and he will not have her."

"She is not damaged goods," said Valentino. "I told you: it was a bit of fun. Besides, the Riccis should have taken better care of her. Any man could flirt with her, working in that café."

"And that is another thing. Carlo Ricci will have to send for his niece, to take Lucia's place. There will be all the trouble of asking for a work permit. Long difficult forms to be written out in English, and no guarantee that the authorities will say yes. Carlo hates such things. It will make him sick with worry."

Valentino pushed back his chair scornfully. "These British. It is an outrage. They treat us like second-class citizens, when in truth we are Romans, with a heritage far more noble than theirs—"

"Don't change the subject. The customs of the British are neither here nor there. You must mend your ways, Valentino, do you hear? You are nearly twenty. You cannot play the fool forever."

Valentino's lips flickered like quicksilver, as if to say, Why not? He guessed that he had gone too far, though, and he bowed his head. "Yes, Papa. I am sorry."

Enrico contemplated his son. Nobody could stay angry with Valentino for long. He did not have Antonio's obvious good looks—he was lankier, with a thin, expressive mouth and a beaky nose—but there was a vitality about him that was irresistible. When you saw Valentino smile you felt glad to be alive.

"Well," said Enrico, "perhaps it was not entirely your fault. I did not say so to Carlo, but I have always thought Lucia a flighty girl. You must be careful all the same though, eh, my son?" He turned toward Antonio. "It is your responsibility too, Antonio. You should keep an eye on your brother, help him to stay out of trouble."

"Yes, Papa," said Antonio. He had been taking an oblique sort of blame for Valentino's antics ever since they were children. Like Filomena, Valentino had been born in London. He had been apprenticed as a waiter at Bertorelli's grand restaurant in Charlotte Street, but he was always getting up to mischief there: breaking plates, mimicking the chefs, folding the starched napkins into phalluses and waggling them behind the customers' backs. After six months the headwaiter told Enrico that it was no use, Valentino would never learn his trade. Enrico had been at his wits' end when Bruno, Filomena's *fidanzato*, had proposed Valentino for the barman's job at the *fascio*, the Italian club. Antonio was troubled by the plan, but Enrico overruled him. Fascism is the only thing your brother takes seriously, he had said. Who knows? Perhaps he will do well there.

Antonio watched as his father rinsed his hands at the scullery tap. Enrico himself had not joined the fascist party—he was not a political man, he said—but over the years he had grown to admire Mussolini. The *duce*'s practical achievements in Lazio impressed him: the draining of the Pontine marshes, so that they were no longer a breeding ground for malaria; the building of an orderly new city, Littoria, on the land that had been reclaimed. Lately he had begun to read the copies of *L'Italia Nostra* that Valentino brought home, and he would nod approvingly when his compatriots talked of how the *duce* had made them proud to be Italian once more.

"I am going to Ricci's," Enrico said now. "I will explain to Carlo that you have apologized, Valentino. He is a man of the world, he will be satisfied."

Antonio slid his accordion into its leather case. "If Carlo wishes, I will help him with his niece's work permit. I am used to these complicated British forms. They do not frighten me."

Enrico nodded and fastened the stud in his collar. Beneath his shirt he wore a gold chain with a crucifix and a coral horn, to guard against the evil eye. "Well, I will be off," he said. "Tell Filomena I will be back for supper."

WHEN HE HAD gone Antonio looked across at his brother. Valentino grinned, all pretense vanishing from his face.

"Don't give me the evil eye, Antonino. You've seen Lucia. Ripe as a plum. If it hadn't been me, it would have been another man. So why not me? I know what I am doing, after all."

"It was not just a flirtation then?"

Valentino shrugged. "She wanted me to speak to our father, ask him to arrange a match. Her cousin Federico is like a bear, she says, all rough and clumsy."

Lucia's face sprang into Antonio's mind. She was a docile young woman, not very clever. He felt sorry for her.

"There was no point my talking to Papa, though," Valentino said. "Lucia has been promised to Federico since she was twelve. Her father would never have agreed to a match with me, I'm not even from his village. And besides, I don't want a flirt for a wife. I want a sweet honest girl like your Danila. An Italian girl, brought up in Italy."

The door opened and Filomena came into the kitchen. Her thick dark hair was tied in a checkered scarf.

"Men's talk, Filomena," said Valentino. "Not for your ears."

Filomena pulled a face. Of all the family she was the most resistant to Valentino's charms. "Talk as much as you like," she said, taking her apron from its hook, "but if you don't want me to hear, you'd better go somewhere else. I've got to make the supper."

"Never mind Lucia Ricci," said Valentino, clicking his tongue, "it's Filomena who should be sent home to Italy, to learn some manners."

"Lucia Ricci's been sent home? Why?"

"None of your business." Valentino turned to Antonio. "I hope Bruno doesn't find out what a shrew our sister is until after they're married. We'll have her on our hands for the rest of her life."

"Tcha," said Filomena, clattering in the cupboards. She was a good cook but a noisy one, slamming the pots against the stove as though she wanted to punish them.

"Isn't Danila helping you with the supper?" asked Antonio.

Filomena whacked the kitchen knife through an onion. "She's resting. She says her feet have swollen up. To the size of watermelons, she says."

"What do you expect? She's pregnant. She needs to take care of her health." Valentino rose to his feet. He treated his brother's wife with reverence, as though she were set apart from other women. "You should have respect for that, Filomena. What higher destiny can a woman have, than to produce sons for the Italian empire? As the *duce* says, maternity is to the woman what war is to the man. Well, I'm off to work. Are you coming for a drink later, Antonio?"

"Not tonight. I'm singing at La Rondine tonight."

"You should come to the *fascio* more often. Mix with your compatriots, hear the news from Italy. It would do you good." On the threshold Valentino turned to Antonio with a smile. "I tell you, there's one thing I've learned from this business with Lucia Ricci. Don't meddle with young girls. From now on it's married women only."

FILOMENA HAD NOT been close friends with Lucia Ricci, but she was shocked by her banishment. As she set off for work the following morning she remembered how Lucia had arrived in Soho, a gauzy-cheeked girl of twelve. Many of the Italians brought their relatives to London when they were of school age so they did not have to apply for work permits. The ploy was not always successful: sometimes the British authorities sent the children back once they reached fourteen. Now Lucia was on the long train journey home, her eyes red and swollen. No doubt a brother or a nephew had been sent with her, a surly reminder of her fall from grace. Men can be so self-righteous, thought Filomena.

That morning Filomena was making the journey to Goodge Street alone. Generally she walked with Renata, the Trombettas' upstairs neighbor, who also worked at the laundry: a satisfactory arrangement, in their families' view, since the two girls could chaperone each other. Filomena did not mind Renata, but she wished she was not such an infernal chatterbox. Both her parents were dead, and nobody—certainly not her uncle Mauro—had taken the trouble to arrange a marriage for her. As a result she was constantly reviewing the single men in the community, asking

Filomena what she thought of this one or that, sighing to think she might never be a wife or mother. She had even cast her eye upon Valentino, although he snorted with laughter. She's a good sort, Renata, I admit, he said, but when I get married it won't be to a dumpy girl with a mustache.

Renata was particularly in awe of Filomena's status as Bruno's *fidanzata*. You are so lucky, she would say, Bruno is a fine man, and a patriot too. You must be so eager for him to come home from Abyssinia. At first Filomena had replied to these remarks, but she soon realized that Renata did not want to hear: she was imagining herself in Filomena's shoes, with a *fidanzato* who would come back any day to sweep her off her feet. This fantasy made Filomena uncomfortable. The truth was she did not think about Bruno very much. No doubt he would return from Africa, and no doubt they would be married, but there did not seem to be much point considering it until it happened. When she did picture Bruno's return it filled her with a curious blankness, as though a dark curtain were falling about her, and she pushed the thought away.

Filomena had reached the corner of Soho Square, where St. Patrick's church stood. St. Patrick's, consecrated in 1792, was the first Catholic church to be built in England after the Reformation, and it was huge and solid, with an elaborate white marble porch. The energetic priest, Padre Barbera, held services in Italian there and organized a host of activities besides: a youth club, and a mobile library that came to the church every Sunday. Filomena glanced up at the redbrick bell tower. It was Italian in style, as if to cheer her compatriots with memories of home. Her mother, Mariana, had been a devout Catholic who went to mass at least once a week, no matter how tired—or, in her last months, how ill—she was. Filomena had gone with her, but it was out of tenderness for her mother, not religious belief: her own faith had died, quietly, when she was fifteen. It seemed to her now that Mariana's remembered presence was slowly fading, as smoke fades from the air. Soon, thought Filomena, soon we will have forgotten all the small, important things about her: the sound of her voice, the powdery smell of her skin, the way she rolled her eyes behind Papa's back whenever he was ranting.

As she drew close to Oxford Street Filomena caught sight of a policeman, examining the frontage of a pawnshop. Her heart quickened.

"Miss Trombetta," said the policeman, in a gruff voice. He was a young man, wide faced and sturdy, with straw-colored hair.

"Constable Harker." Filomena inclined her head to acknowledge his greeting. She did not pause, though, but continued to walk in the direction of Goodge Street.

"Your friend is not with you today, I see," said the constable, falling into step with her.

"No," said Filomena, "not today."

After that they did not speak again, but walked in silence side by side, their strides perfectly matched.

CHAPTER 5

THE MORNING AFTER THE PARTY IN KINGLY STREET, BERNARD Rodway sent Olivia a huge quantity of dark red roses. They looked rather silly in her bedsit. She only possessed one vase, a chipped green jug purchased from a junk shop, and the rest of the flowers had to go in jam jars and empty Rowntree's cocoa tins. Olivia eyed them with a tired worldliness. She was quite sure that she understood Bernard's intentions toward her. Well, she thought, I'll be careful this time.

It was five years since Olivia had moved to London. That wide-eyed girl now seemed to her an entirely different person, made of a different element. On her arrival she had had a starry notion of becoming a dancer in the theater. That would show them, she thought, with a ferocity that she did not recognize as grief: the shrewd aunt in Croydon, the frail, self-centered ghosts of her mother and her sister. In her best hat and coat she marched around stage doors in the West End, asking in a refined voice if she could speak to the show's producer. The first two doormen laughed in her face; the third squeezed her bum and told her not to waste his time. It was the fourth man she saw, a tawny-haired stage manager at the Palace Theatre in Cambridge Circus, who finally, briskly, chucked her dreams into the dust.

"You girls," he said, shaking his head as though he had seen it all a dozen—no, a hundred—times before. "What makes you do it? You haven't trained, you're not a pro, you wouldn't survive for two hours onstage, never mind eight shows a week. I daresay you're a virgin too, aren't you? You'd do better to go back home to—where is it?—East Grinstead?"

"Uckfield," said Olivia. By this time she was footsoré and thirsty, and she could not help the tears springing to her eyes. The stage manager, whose name was Jimmy, sighed, and took her to the nearest café, where he bought her a currant bun and some milky coffee. Then he told her several rude, gossipy tales of life backstage, which made her laugh, and he advised her to look for a job as a dance hostess in one of the city's ballrooms.

A week later, in Jimmy's tiny room high above Romilly Street, Olivia lost her virginity, between the matinée and the evening performance. It seemed to her a bold thing to do, like coming to London and changing her name. Besides, she was disarmed by the fact that Jimmy appeared to want her. She could hear Wilma's astonished voice in her head. Are you sure, Olive? He's really quite attractive. Maybe he just feels sorry for you.

Sex was not in the least what Olivia had expected. She was startled by the animal strangeness of it, and yet it seemed that very strangeness created a bond between her and Jimmy, like sea voyagers who have survived a storm. She was beginning to wonder if, remarkably, this was love, when Jimmy announced that his wife was coming back, and they would have to call it a day. His wife was a bottle-blond dancer named Gloria, who had been touring the country in a production of *The Gay Divorce*.

"What did you expect?" Jimmy said as Olivia sat weeping in bed, the sheet pulled to her armpits in belated modesty. He said it with a harassed air, as though things like this were always happening to him and it really wasn't his fault. "Don't make a scene, there's a good girl. You know as well as I do that this was just a bit of fun."

The girls at the dance hall said the same thing, sitting in the smoke-fugged changing room. What did you expect, girlie? That's what men are like. Don't lose your heart, don't lose your head, and for gawd's sake don't get pregnant. One of them, a blowzy young woman with a mellow contralto voice, warbled a Sophie Tucker song: "*If your kisses can't hold the man you love, your tears won't bring him back.*"

Olivia listened in silence. The following week she agreed to go out for dinner with one of her dance partners, a commercial traveler from Cardiff, a freckled smiling man with a pencil mustache. They went to the Lyons Corner House in the Tottenham Court Road, where they had what the dance hostesses, always hungry, called a slap-up meal: lamb chops and gravy with a mound of mashed potato, followed by syrup sponge. While they ate, the commercial traveler talked without stopping, which was just as well because Olivia could not think of anything to say. I come to London every four weeks or so, he remarked in his lilting Welsh accent, implying that this could become a regular arrangement. Afterward they went to a drinking club for a couple of gin and Its, then to his hotel, a cheap one that smelled of gas and boiled cauliflower. Oh, well, thought Olivia, as listlessly she unrolled her stockings, it doesn't matter. None of it really matters at all.

FOR THEIR FIRST dinner, Bernard took Olivia to Quaglino's, near Piccadilly. It was plush and glamorous; no less a person than Hutch—Leslie Hutchinson, the handsome black cabaret star from Grenada—was singing at the piano. Olivia was astonished. She had expected a discreet restaurant in Soho where nobody would recognize Bernard, and the waiters would wink at him conspiratorially when they thought she wasn't looking.

"Do you like champagne?" Bernard asked. He was slouching in his chair as though he dined here every night.

"Of course," said Olivia, who had never tasted anything more exotic than sweet Moussec, brewed in Rickmansworth. She glanced at the menu, which was in French: *oeufs pochés piémontaise, paupiettes de veau.* She would have to point disdainfully and hope for the best.

"Oh, don't worry with the *carte,*" Bernard said, seeing her frown. (What in the world was bouillabaisse? Would she be able to swallow it?) "I never do. I just ask for what I want." Blithely he ordered Dover sole meunière and roast pheasant, and he turned back to Olivia. "Which of your parents was fond of *Twelfth Night*?"

"What?" said Olivia.

"Shakespeare's *Twelfth Night.* I imagine that's why they named you Olivia."

The champagne flush on Olivia's cheeks deepened. "As a matter of fact, I chose it myself. I was christened Olive: Olive Johnson. I decided to call myself Olivia when I came to London."

Bernard began to laugh. "Oh, how charming," he said. Olivia bridled, afraid of being patronized.

"I don't see why that's funny."

"No, no. That is not what I meant. I think it was a clever thing to do. To make a new start, to re-create yourself. I like it. It shows originality."

Olivia said nothing. She suspected him of humoring her, and she did not want him to think that he could flatter her into bed. If that was where the evening was destined to end—and quite probably it was—she intended do it with her eyes open, undeceived.

"We'd all like to be original," Bernard went on, as the waiter brought their fish on thin white china plates. "Not many of us can achieve it, though. I've been struggling with it since I was at Cambridge, but I fear I'm simply a Jack of all trades, master of none. The only thing in my favor is that I'm enthusiastic." Deftly he applied his fork to his fillet of sole. "And where did you live before you came to London?"

The sole was bathed in nut-brown butter, which tasted burned, yet strangely addictive. At the piano Hutch was singing "These Foolish Things." For an instant Olivia remembered the Italian singer at the Paradise Ballroom, with his big shocked eyes.

"Uckfield," she said, in an uncompromising voice.

Bernard laughed again, and reaching out he squeezed her hand. He did it in a friendly, natural way. "Don't look so fierce, my dear. I brought you here to have some fun, not to cross-examine you. Uckfield's in Sussex, isn't it? My uncle Dickie has a house in Sussex. Dickie Belvoir: you may have heard of him. He was a stage designer once upon a time. He worked with Sarah Bernhardt, Eleonora Duse, the Russian ballet, most of the great names. Of all my relations Dickie is my favorite. He and I are the black sheep of the family. The rest are dull dogs, though I say it myself."

Bernard's voice—relaxed, cultured, with a faint attractive wheezing—began to soothe Olivia. As he talked she ate: gamey pheasant, which, like the sauce meunière, was all the more exquisite for being so nearly unpleasant; a crème brûlée with its golden carapace of sugar; the chocolate truffles that arrived with the pungent coffee. This is how rich people live, Olivia thought. She wanted to mock—a free plate of sweets for well-fed diners?—but the deliciousness of it overwhelmed her.

"Would you like to dance?" Bernard asked. "I'd love it if you would, but I can see that it might be a busman's holiday."

On the floor he held her loosely; he did not use the pretext of dancing to paw her thigh, or to pull her suffocatingly close. Olivia found herself relaxing in the haze of champagne and music and wonderful food. I could grow accustomed to this, she thought.

"Time to go, I think," Bernard said, after their second dance. "There'll be plenty of taxis outside."

In the vestibule Olivia pulled on her gloves. They were wearing out, creased from molding themselves continually to the shape of her hands. Things could not go on being flexible forever, she thought giddily. It did not matter how well you cared for them, oiling and nourishing them, drying them gently when they got wet; sooner or later there were bound to be cracks.

Bernard clasped her by the elbow, steering her toward the door. They had just stepped into Bury Street when a stout man in a homburg, crossing from the far pavement, exclaimed: "Bernard! Fancy running into you."

Dismay crossed Bernard's face, but only for an instant. "Good lord. Lionel. I didn't know you were in London. You should have telephoned me."

"Oh, I'm only passing through," said Lionel. Close to, he bore a clear resemblance to Bernard, although Lionel was fatter and much redder in the face. "Don't worry, Bernard, I'm staying at my club, it's very convenient, much better than troubling you. And who's this?"

He fixed his stare upon Olivia: benignly, with curiosity rather than lust. All the same it made Olivia squirm. She might have been able to fake elegance in her evening dress, but her shop-bought outdoor clothes—the herringbone wool coat, the blue hat—looked shabby and garish.

"This is my friend Olivia Johnson." Bernard was still holding her elbow. "Olivia, my brother, Lionel. My older brother, down from Cheshire."

"Pleased to meet you," said Olivia, in her elocution-class accent. Lionel surveyed her once more.

"Well, I won't keep you. I'm sure you have plenty of exciting things to do. How does the song go? *The night is young, and you're so beautiful.* Bernard, a word with you, if you don't mind."

Olivia waited on the pavement, passive, excluded. She thought of how Bernard had said *friend*, making it sound like a subtle, man-to-man code. My friend Olivia. She remembered the paraphernalia she had stowed in her handbag, the rubber diaphragm, the tube of evil-smelling jelly. It is always like this, she thought, it won't be any different this time. Why did I think it might be?

When he had waved off his brother, Bernard hailed a taxi. He did it with an air of authority, as though all taxis were his of right, circling the London streets like gleaming wheeled servants, waiting to be summoned. Then he handed Olivia into the car, gave some cash to the driver and prepared to close the door.

"Oh," said Olivia, "but I thought—"

Bernard smiled. "I'll write to you in the morning," he said, and he blew her a kiss. "Sweet dreams, Olivia."

Baffled, Olivia gave the address of her bedsit in Pimlico. She had no idea what had happened. Had Bernard's brother said something to make him change his mind? Or had he changed his mind anyway, put off by—what?—Olivia's gaucheness? The realization that she was, after all, no more than a cheap dance hostess in a homemade frock?

In fact, what had happened was simple. Taking his brother aside, Lionel Rodway had whispered in his ear: "Really, Bernard, where do you find them? She's impossible. Why in the world can't you pick someone of your own class?" Olivia did not know that, though. Nor did she know—she could not conceivably have guessed—that in that moment Bernard Rodway had decided to marry her.

CHAPTER 6

IN NOVEMBER THE *FASCIO* OPENED ITS NEW PREMISES IN Charing Cross Road. The Casa d'Italia had taken a year to renovate, and it was large and imposing, with a vast atrium lined with marble.

Antonio accompanied his father and brother to the opening ceremony. As a rule he did not like going to the *fascio*. The sight of the men in their black shirts disturbed him. He was anxious that one of them would fix upon him, needling him into an argument, or else trying to convert him to the fascist cause. Tonight, though, was different. Plenty of people would be there out of curiosity, to see the new building. Besides, thought Antonio, if I show willing this time it will stop Valentino from nagging me for a month or two.

"It is a pity that Bruno cannot be here with us," Valentino said, as the three men were preparing to leave. "He would have been thrilled to witness this great day. At last the *fascio* will have a building worthy of our cause."

"Will you be long, Antonio?" asked Danila in a plaintive voice. She was sitting beside the stove with Filomena, her knitting needles click-clacking like an automaton. The day before her gait had changed, and she had begun to waddle, as though the bulge of her stomach was suddenly too great for her slender legs to bear. Antonio found her lumbering slowness infinitely touching.

"Not long, I promise." He stroked the hair from her forehead.

"Don't be afraid. If anything happens, Filomena will come and fetch me, won't you, Mena?"

Filomena nodded. She too was knitting, counting stitches furiously under her breath. Unlike Danila she was always making mistakes. Everything she finished had a hole here, a ragged edge there.

Valentino was already at the door, impatiently stamping his feet. "Nothing's going to happen, Antonio. Come along. It would be disrespectful to be late."

THE OPENING CEREMONY for the Casa d'Italia took place in the marble atrium, known as the Sala dell'Impero, the Empire Room. It was seething with people, mostly men, embracing, calling out, shuffling to get into position near the dais. Several greeted each other with the fascist salute, the raised fist that, according to the *duce*, had been used by the ancient Romans. On the edge of the balcony were embossed the words *Credere*, *Obbedire*, *Combattere:* Believe, Obey, Fight.

"Look!" Enrico pointed, an awestruck expression on his face. "There is the ambassador himself, there is Count Dino Grandi."

Dino Grandi had been Mussolini's ambassador in London since 1932. He had a spadelike beard and his dark hair was swept heroically back from his face. You could not have called him handsome, but he had about him the silky luster of power. He was surrounded by a cohort of burly, black-shirted men: his bodyguards. There were tales that he never went anywhere without these guards, even in London, ever since the communists had tried to murder him in 1920.

"He was converted to fascism by the *duce* himself," said Valentino. "As a young man he was seduced by the false doctrine of communism, but the moment he met the *duce* he saw the error of his ways."

"Mussolini is always right," said Antonio. "That's what they chalk on the walls in Rome, isn't it?"

His brother glanced at him doubtfully, suspecting irony, but Antonio's face was bland. "We should do this more often: the three of us, united in a single cause," Valentino said. "Alone we are weak, but together we can be strong. Isn't that so, Papa?"

Enrico nodded, stirred by the grandeur of the occasion. "Valentino is right. It is too easy for us to forget our national pride, while we scrape our living here in Britain. But we are Italians. We must always remember that." He said it half-accusingly, as though their failure to remember was somehow Antonio's fault.

All faces were turned to Dino Grandi now, high upon the dais. The air was electric. "To accept a revolution and regime is no longer enough," he was saying. "We must have the courage and the responsibility to bind our personal destiny, however great or small, to this revolution and to this regime."

Antonio glanced at his father. He did not like Enrico's burst of enthusiasm. If my mother were alive, he thought, she would put a stop to it. She would not argue, she would simply nod and be silent, and half an hour later Enrico would see his own foolishness. As he was thinking this he caught sight of a squat familiar figure, threading her way toward him. It was Renata Bonetti, their upstairs neighbor. Antonio's heart turned a somersault.

"What is it, Renata? What has happened?"

Renata was staring goggle-eyed at Count Dino Grandi, and it took her a moment to answer. "Your wife's gone into labor," she said at last. "Filomena sent me to tell you. The midwife's on her way."

Antonio pulled at Enrico's sleeve. Like Renata, he could not keep his eyes from the ambassador. The man held him in a trance, as a stoat holds a rabbit with its swaying lethal dance.

"I must go home, Papa. Danila will be wanting me."

"Don't be foolish," whispered Valentino. "It's women's business, we should stay out of it. Tell him, Papa."

Enrico shrugged, without shifting his gaze. "There will be nothing for you to do, my son, you will only be in the way. Go home when it is over."

"But if Danila asks for me—"

A couple of the black-shirted men hissed at him to be quiet. On the dais Count Dino Grandi was still speaking.

"We do not need the permission of Britain to be great. Our glorious victory in Africa has scotched that myth. We have challenged the dragon, and we are winning."

Valentino whooped and raised his fist high in the fascist salute. A moment later so did Enrico. Antonio closed his eyes. The roars about him echoed through his body, and he felt a flutter of panic, like the fear of drowning. Then he pushed his way out of the Sala dell'Impero.

Danila had been quarreling with Filomena when her labor began. They often quarreled when they were on their own, usually about trivial things, although they both knew that the struggle between them was not trivial at all: it was a battle for supremacy.

In the beginning Filomena had welcomed her new sister-in-law. She was glad to have another woman in a household packed with men, and she felt protective toward Danila, transplanted so abruptly from her home in Lazio to the seething foreign streets of Soho. Besides, it pleased her to think that Antonio, her favorite brother, had such a pretty wife. Filomena had no illusions about her own looks, her squared-off face, her strong, serviceable body. People told her that she had beautiful eyes, and she knew that it was true, but she also knew that they said it as consolation, not a true compliment. She would never be a beauty like Danila.

Little by little, though, she realized that beneath her air of sweetness Danila had a will like iron. Although she was supposed to help Filomena around the house she was always too tired, or, since her pregnancy, too sick. When she did come into the kitchen she insisted on doing things her way, taking over the cooking and expecting Filomena to clear up after her. Afterward when one of the men—usually Valentino—complimented her she would melt and blush as though she, not Filomena, had done all the work. If Filomena confronted her, her eyes would widen with injury. But I did make the *ricotta dolce*, she would say. I know that you mixed them, Filomena, but I did the frying, or most of it anyway, and that's the difficult part, everybody will tell you that.

That evening they had been arguing about the proper way to make *gnocchi alla Romana*, her cousin Bruno's favorite dish, according to Danila.

"I'm surprised you didn't know that, Mena," she said, comfortably patting the bulge of her stomach. "He always used to ask my mother to make it for him, back home in Lazio. With tomato sauce and a good pinch of black pepper."

"Papa likes it with nutmeg," said Filomena, as she hooked a dropped stitch from her knitting. Her sister-in-law was always talking about Bruno, how he liked this, how he thought that. It made Filomena feel trapped. She did not know if it was from annoyance with Danila for laying claim to Bruno, or another, more troubling fear: that one day her life would be governed by Bruno's wishes, Bruno's whims.

Danila's smooth forehead twisted into a knot. "I know you make it with nutmeg, Mena, but it's not really correct."

"Oh, Bruno will get used to it."

Filomena bundled up her knitting and stuck the needles through the ball of wool. Then she slid her hand into her cardigan pocket to touch Stan Harker's note. He had dropped it off at the laundry three days ago. Same time, same place next week, it said, in his skewed ugly handwriting. Cheerio till then.

"Don't you think you should learn to make it the way Bruno likes it?" Danila's voice was deliberately patient. "I'd be happy to show you how. You put the pepper in right at the end, so that it is still sharp when you eat the gnocchi."

Filomena did not answer, but began to clatter at the stove, opening the iron door to feed the fire. She was not listening to Danila: she was thinking about Constable Harker. She had first encountered him when he came to sort out a squabble between two of the women at the laundry. Now they met once a week, and if Renata was not with her they would walk together from Soho Square to Goodge Street. There was nothing wrong in their friendship, she was certain of that. It was not like Lucia Ricci's flirtation with Valentino. She and Stan did not even touch, except once when he had pulled her out of the way of an errand boy's hurtling bicycle. My conscience is clear, thought Filomena, jabbing the poker into the red and gray embers.

"There's no need to sulk." Danila pressed her fingers daintily to her lips. She was prone to wind now that she was in the ninth month of her pregnancy. "I am trying to be helpful."

Her voice to Filomena was like the buzzing of a gnat. She wished that Danila would be quiet and leave her free to daydream about Stan. She pictured his face, neutral, unruffled. It's my copper's face, he said. You acquire it, being in the force. It means you don't have to get involved. Whenever she thought of that face Filomena had the feeling that everything would be all right. She remembered how he had rescued her from the errand boy's bicycle, his arm quick and confident about her waist.

Danila was gazing at her reproachfully. Filomena straightened up from the stove. "I'm not sulking," she said, "but rest assured, I do know how to make *gnocchi alla Romana*. I've been feeding this family for the past eighteen months, ever since Mama died."

"I want to advise you, Filomena, that's all," said Danila. Her pretty mouth was quivering. "I may be younger than you, but I'm a married woman, I understand what it's like to have a husband. You have to learn their tastes. It is complicated. I wish you would let me explain."

"I do not need you to explain. I will find out soon enough, if I marry Bruno."

Danila frowned. "What do you mean, *if* you marry Bruno? You are engaged to him, he is your *fidanzato*."

Filomena realized that in her impatience she had gone too far.

"All I mean is that Africa is a long way off. The climate is not a healthy one, and there is fighting in Abyssinia still. Many things could happen—"

"Are you saying that you think my cousin will die?" Danila's eyes were like saucers.

"No, of course not," said Filomena. Then she stopped short. Bruno had gone to fight the Abyssinians. It was entirely possible that he might die. Why did they pretend otherwise?

Danila looked as if she had been hit but was too startled to feel any pain. Filomena crouched beside her chair, penitent.

"Do not be upset. Bruno will come home safely, and then of course I will marry him . . ."

Danila's rosebud mouth opened. The next moment she began to bellow. There was a puddle of water, tinged with blood, beneath the chair.

"Oh, lord," said Filomena. "Here, take my hand. Breathe, Danila. Deeply now."

"It's the baby," wailed Danila, "it's the baby, and Antonio is not here. It's the baby, and I'm all alone."

"You're not alone, you're with me. Let's go upstairs. You will be comfortable upstairs, I'll make you comfortable." Gently Filomena raised Danila to her feet. "And then I will send Renata to run for the midwife, as quick as she can."

THE MIDWIFE WAS a bossy woman from Tuscany. From the moment she arrived she took over the Trombetta house, demanding hot water, clean towels, cups of strong sugary coffee to keep her alert.

"Of course you can't see her," she said to Antonio, who had hurried all the way from the Casa d'Italia, his heart banging like a piston. "Don't be absurd. Men! What will they think of next?"

"But she wants me there. She'll be crying for me, I know she will."

"She'll be crying for her mother and half the blessed saints before the night is out, but we're hardly going to fetch them, are we? Now sit down like a good fellow, and let me get on with my work. Filomena, bring that basin of warm water, if you please."

Filomena gave him a gleaming smile as she followed the midwife upstairs. "Don't worry, Antonino," she whispered. "I will tell you what is happening."

His father and Valentino came home at midnight. Antonio heard them making their way along Frith Street, singing the "Giovinezza," the anthem of the National Fascist Party. Enrico sang softly but well, Valentino extremely badly. Their eyes glittered with grappa and with excitement.

"I told you there would be nothing for you to do." Enrico blinked at his son. Antonio was playing patience over and over, the cards bright and meaningless upon the kitchen table. "You should have stayed to hear the ambassador. He is such an inspiring orator, you can hear the *duce* himself speak through his lips."

"Who knows? Perhaps Antonio would have been moved to join the party too." Valentino clapped his father about the shoulders. "Today is a great day, Papa. I am proud of you."

A sheepish expression crossed Enrico's face. "Ah, well. Better to be on the winning side, eh, Valentino?" With persnickety care he took off his hat and coat and hung them on the peg. "And now we should go to bed. Someone will have to open the kiosk in the morning."

In the room above them Danila let out a shriek, instantly hushed by the midwife. Valentino glanced warily at the ceiling.

"Is she doing a lot of that?"

"It will be all right," said Enrico in a philosophical voice. "I slept through your birth, Valentino, I see no reason why I should not sleep through the birth of my grandson. Or granddaughter, if the child is destined to be a girl. As for you, Antonio, you would do well to get some rest. The midwife will call you soon enough if you're needed."

ANTONIO'S SON WAS born at four o'clock the next morning, in the dark still winter hours when it seems that day will never break. He was a small baby, but healthy, according to the midwife. It was Filomena who brought the news to her brother. She was wearing the coarse white apron she used for cooking, only now there was a watery streak of scarlet across the stains left by flour and egg and brown *ragù*.

"And Danila? Is she all right?"

Filomena nodded. They were waiting in the kitchen while the midwife prepared Danila to greet her husband. "Oh, yes. She is all right."

"You must be exhausted, Mena. And you have to go to work in a couple of hours."

Filomena pulled a face, half rueful, half satisfied. "I thought it would be useful knowledge: how a baby is born. You can never tell when you will need such knowledge."

Antonio felt a surge of respect for her. While their mother was dying Filomena had stayed at her bedside hour after hour, stroking her hair, spooning broth into her slack mouth, not minding the smell or the terrible, bone-aching boredom of it. He clasped his sister's hand.

"Well, it will be your turn before long. When Bruno returns you will soon have children of your own."

Filomena withdrew her hand. "Oh, yes," she said, "of course."

The midwife returned. Danila was ready to show her husband his firstborn son. As he climbed the stairs Antonio thought how odd this conspiracy of women was, to keep from him the pain and the disarray of childbirth. And yet if there is a war I will be expected to fight, as Bruno has been fighting in Africa. There will be more pain, worse disarray, only this time it is we men who will try to keep it from our womenfolk.

In the bedroom there was a smell of lavender, not quite masking the sweetish scent of blood. Danila sat upright against the pillows wearing a clean nightdress, her dark fine hair combed into a knot. There were shadows like bruises beneath her eyes, but on her face was an expression of triumph. The baby in her arms was wrapped in a white shawl, fine as lace, sent from Lazio by Danila's mother. He had the walnut face of an old, old man.

"Be careful," said Danila, as Antonio bent to lift his son, his fingers probing for warmth beneath the layers of wool. At once the baby began to cry. His crying was thin and high-pitched, like the tearing of cloth.

CHAPTER 7

Bernard Rodway had never had much in common with his older brother. Lionel was healthy, hearty, good at games; Bernard was a frail, dreamy boy, haunted by those desperate nights when he struggled for every breath. Both brothers were sent to Rugby, where predictably Lionel flourished, and Bernard—equally predictably—was bullied. Their mother, Penelope, wanted to withdraw Bernard from the school and send him somewhere more liberal, but Ernest, Bernard's father, shook his head. A self-made man, he did not want to cosset his children. Bernard needs toughening up, he said; if the bullying gets out of hand, well, his brother will defend him. Bernard, who knew that Lionel would rather be skinned alive than intervene on his behalf, went white-faced to weep in the lavatory beside the boot room. It had a high black cistern and a clanking chain. The bitter luxury of tears calmed him. I am not like other people, he thought, and the knowledge filled him with angry, consoling power.

After Rugby the brothers went to Cambridge, where again their paths diverged. Lionel took up rowing; he narrowly missed selection as a Cambridge blue, or so he claimed. Then he returned to Macclesfield, where he joined the family firm and married a wealthy, red-cheeked girl named Caroline whom he met at a hunt ball. As for Bernard, he fell in with an arty set who called one another "comrade." He bought a sheaf of jazz records and joined the Labour Party; he also played Laertes in a modern-dress production of *Hamlet*, wearing suede shoes and a Fair Isle sweater. His uncle Dickie Belvoir came to the show with a couple of London actors, and Bernard experienced the heady joy of reflected glory, watching all eyes turn as he led the glamorous newcomers into the pub.

At home in Cheshire there was an assumption, hardly discussed, that once he left Cambridge Bernard would follow his brother into the family firm, and all this socialist nonsense would be knocked out of him. The summer after his exams Bernard went to Europe: a last hurrah before the serious business of life claimed him. As he crossed the Alps he had the vague notion that he might write a travel book: the adventures of a clever young Englishman, living on his wits in Mussolini's Italy. He kept detailed notes of his journeys, the higgledy-piggledy beauty of the Ponte Vecchio, the serene purplish sunsets over the Tuscan hills, the hunchback in the Arezzo square whom everyone touched for luck. The pleasure of writing intoxicated him. On a thundery day in Rome, confined to his room by the weather, he realized that he could not possibly join the family business: it would eat up his soul from the inside. The following morning he went to Termini station and booked his ticket home to England.

His interview with his father took place not at the silk factory but in Ernest's den, a manly, leather-scented room that looked toward the sandstone ridge of Alderley Edge. Bernard thought it would be more tactful to break the news there, so that his father would not be obliged to put on a brave face afterward among his workers. He had rehearsed what he would say several times. I realize that you are disappointed, Father, but I have thought hard about this, and my decision is final. All the same, his throat was dry as he began to speak. There was an eagerness in his father's face that pained him, knowing that he was about to blight Ernest's hopes.

He had barely got through his first sentence when his father interrupted. "So, Bernard, you are saying that you do not wish to join the family firm?"

For an instant Bernard wavered. "No, Father. I mean, yes. That is what I am saying."

Ernest lifted his eyebrows; then he smiled. "Well, Bernard, you are twenty-two. Old enough to know your own mind. I do not believe that a man should be forced to work against his natural grain. Of course, I would have made a place for you in the firm. You know that. And I am sure that Lionel will do the same, if at some point in the future your circumstances change." He picked up the brass paper knife on his table and then set it down once more. "If that is all, Bernard, perhaps you will excuse me? I have this quarter's accounts to check."

Bernard's head was ringing with astonishment as he left the room. All the things he had not said weighed him down like obsolete currency. It was only the next day as he was traveling back to London, the perfume of Penelope's farewell kiss still upon his collar, that he realized his father had not been disappointed at all: he had been relieved.

This realization, which ought to have made Bernard happy, made him furious. It was one thing for him to reject the hidebound values of his father and his brother, quite another for them to reject him. He saw them as the sleek faces of the enemy, quietly closing ranks to shut him out, like Ishmael, like Cain, the slighted son cast into the wilderness. His sense of exclusion was compounded when, three years later, Ernest died from a heart attack. Under the provisions of his will, Lionel inherited the Macclesfield house and the family firm, while Bernard received a substantial income for life, or at least, for as long as the silk business thrived. It's a bribe, thought Bernard, listening to the stone-filled earth thrum upon his father's coffin, to prevent me encroaching on Lionel's domain; and then, No, it's not a bribe, it's worse than that. It's compensation. My father thought me a failure, who'd never fend for himself. Well, I'll prove him wrong, the bugger. You see if I don't.

After their dinner at Quaglino's Olivia had not expected to hear from Bernard again, and she was startled when a thick expensive card arrived, intimately signed with the letter B. Bernard also sent more flowers, white lilies this time, which made the bedsit in Pimlico look like the scene of an elaborate society funeral. They had another dinner, at the Café Royal; then they went to the ballet at Sadler's Wells Theatre in Islington. Olivia had never been to the ballet before—it was Arthur Bliss's *Checkmate*, simple but striking—and although she tried to look blasé she could not hide her rapture. Bernard was charmed. That night as he put her into her taxi he kissed her for the first time. His mustache was silky and unexpected against her mouth.

A week later he took her to meet his uncle Dickie. Dickie Belvoir lived in Chelsea, in a red mansion flat overlooking the Thames; they were going for a drink before dinner. As they waited on the doorstep, Olivia caught Bernard glancing across at her, at her black sheath dress, her evening bag beaded with poppies. It was an appraising look, rather like the one his brother, Lionel, had given her. She guessed that the visit was some kind of test.

Uncle Dickie was rotund and immaculate. He had perfectly groomed white hair, and he smoked Turkish cigarettes, extravagantly, from a long jade holder. His drawing room had heavy silk curtains and a great many of what he called *objects:* a word Olivia had always considered to mean something mundane, but which on Dickie's lips implied all that was rare and precious, a mother-of-pearl card case, a Japanese vase. Some of Dickie's stage designs were hung upon the walls, riotous as Léon Bakst paintings. There was a gallery of silver-framed photographs too, resembling the pages of a glossy magazine.

"Dickie knows everyone," said Bernard, as Olivia paused before a picture of his uncle with Noël Coward.

"Well, I used to," said Dickie in a self-deprecating voice. "It's harder to keep up these days. That's my sister Penelope, my dear. You can see the resemblance to Bernard, can't you?"

Like Bernard, the woman in the photograph was fair, with peachlike cheeks. She had an arch look about her, though, as if she kept one of her plucked eyebrows perpetually raised, like a character in a French farce. This artificiality made Olivia warm toward Bernard, with his simplicity, his enthusiasms.

"Yes and no," she said, glancing at the next picture, of an older woman, long nosed, who wore her dark hair severely parted in the center. "Who is that? She's very handsome."

Dickie's eyes grew filmy. "Oh, that's Katya. My late wife. She danced with Pavlova, you know."

"Oh," said Olivia, who had assumed that Uncle Dickie must be a bachelor, "I'm so sorry." The moment she said it she realized how foolish she sounded, and she blushed. Dickie patted her hand.

"Thank you, my dear. That is very sweet of you." Still grasping her hand he turned to Bernard. "I like her, Bernard. She has promise. Keep hold of this one, eh?"

"Oh, I intend to, Dickie," said Bernard lightly, as though this was a conversation they had had a dozen times, in a dozen places. He sat down, propping one expensively shod foot upon the opposite knee. "Well, and what do you think of the news from Rome? Do you still believe that Mussolini's fascists are no threat to democracy?"

Dickie crossed to his cocktail cabinet, a beautiful Art Deco affair lined with mirrors. Mussolini had just announced that Italy was withdrawing from the League of Nations, that hopeful blundering body intended to keep the peace in fractious Europe. There were fears that soon he would announce an alliance with Nazi Germany.

"You know I don't mind old Musso, Bernard," Dickie said, as he refilled Olivia's glass. He was giving them Negronis, which he mixed himself, fragrant with juniper and very strong. "He has fresh ideas, he understands that Italy must increase its efficiency, it cannot go on forever being picturesque. He has found a third way between the extremes of right and left. And you have to admire his handling of the newspapers. All those pictures of him sledging and driving tractors and looking heroic. He is not a desiccated snob like Baldwin or Chamberlain, he knows how to make himself popular." He passed her drink to Olivia. "What do you think of him, Miss Johnson?"

"I think he has mad eyes," said Olivia. At once the two men laughed—how like a woman, to make such a remark—then they both fell silent as they realized that she was right: Mussolini did have the eyes of a fanatic, wide and staring.

"He's an emotional fellow, I grant you," Dickie said, "but I believe that he will be a force for good. If nothing more, he's well placed to negotiate with Germany. And I agree with you there, Bernard: Hitler's a monster. Someone ought to shoot him." He took a decisive mouthful of gin and vermouth. "But enough of such gloomy things. My nephew tells me that you dance the tango quite wonderfully, Miss Johnson. I hope that one day I'll have the privilege of seeing you."

Bernard was smiling as they left, and Olivia knew that whatever the test might have been she had passed it. The taxi he hailed took them not to dinner but to Pimlico. Bernard had never been in a bedsit before, and to him it was exotic as a foreign country. They went at once to bed, among the rinsed-out tins of flowers. The Negronis she had drunk had gone to Olivia's head. As she embraced Bernard she felt, as if from a great distance, the dangerous flicker of hope.

SPRING 1938

CHAPTER 8

THE LETTER FROM BRUNO REACHED FRITH STREET ONE EVENING in March. It arrived unnoticed, while Valentino was lounging at the kitchen table after supper, talking about politics.

"I don't know what the fuss is about. Austria has always been part of Germany: it says so in *L'Italia Nostra*. Besides, the Austrians cheered Hitler's armies, they waved Nazi flags, they threw flowers. They would hardly have done that if they did not wish to become a part of the Third Reich."

Five days before, Adolf Hitler's soldiers had marched as conquerors through the streets of Vienna. The British government had protested, but in the end had concluded that the coup—the *Anschluss*, or unification, the Germans called it—was inevitable, short of declaring war.

"I suppose we should be grateful that no blood was shed," Antonio remarked. The news disturbed him. It was as though the weather had changed overnight; there was a heaviness in the air, presaging storms. In Piccadilly Circus some British Blackshirts had gathered to celebrate Hitler's success, raising their fists in the fascist salute.

"Don't be so lily-livered, Antonio. It is necessary, sooner or later, to shed blood. How will Italy regain its empire without it?" Valentino leaned back in his chair toward the scullery, where Filomena was washing up the supper things. "Be quiet in there, Filomena, will you? We men can't hear ourselves think."

In answer Filomena banged two pan lids together like cymbals. Valentino stubbed out his cigarette and made to get up, ready to box his sister's ears.

"Let her be," said Antonio. "She's nearly finished."

"But it's not respectful. She'll disturb Papa, and he needs some rest. He's not well, you know, Antonio."

Enrico had retired to bed, suffering from a chest cold. Every winter he caught some infection that refused to clear in the fog-drenched London air. Antonio would have to open the kiosk in the morning, although he was working late tonight, performing at La Rondine. The thought of rising at dawn made his flesh quake with exhaustion. He had not had an undisturbed night in the four months since his son was born. The baby had been christened Enrico: after his grandfather, according to the custom, but also in secret homage to Antonio's hero, the singer Enrico Caruso.

Valentino rose to his feet, pulling a comb from his trouser pocket. "Well, I will be on my way. No, I'm not going to the *fascio* tonight. I have other fish to fry." He winked at his brother, who groaned.

"Oh, God, Valentino. Who is it this time?"

"You don't expect me to reveal the lady's name, do you? What do you take me for, a cad?" Valentino ran the comb through his hair, which was slicked with scented oil. "All I will say is that her husband works late at Bianchi's restaurant, sometimes until one, two o'clock in the morning. The poor girl gets lonely and longs for company. Oh, how she longs for company. I cannot describe it to you, Antonio."

"I hope that you're being careful, that's all," Antonio was saying, when he heard the flurry of footsteps in the corridor. It was Danila, who had come downstairs after settling the baby. In one hand she waved the envelope she had picked up from the mat.

"It's from Bruno! I recognize his handwriting. Filomena, there's a letter from Bruno."

Filomena stepped from the scullery, wiping her hands on her

apron. She took the letter from Danila and stared. The envelope looked as though it had passed through many damp, weary hands on its journey from Africa.

"Open it," said Danila, so impatiently that Antonio thought she would snatch the letter from his sister.

"Perhaps Filomena would like to read it alone," he said.

Danila stuck out her lower lip. "Pouf! Why should she? Bruno is not one for writing love letters. It will be full of his news, that's all. If she wants to read it by herself she can do it afterward."

"Maybe he is breaking off our engagement," said Filomena, still without opening the letter.

"I do not believe so for an instant. He is an honorable man, my cousin Bruno. You should not even think such a thought, Filomena. It is not worthy of you."

"No, you should not," said Valentino, who like Danila was craning over his sister's shoulder, eager to see the letter. "Who else would have you, eh? Come on now, Filomena. Open it."

Inside the envelope was a single sheet of paper, covered in looped untidy handwriting.

"Well," said Danila, "what does he say?"

In silence Filomena handed her the letter. Danila had been right: there were no endearments in it, nothing that made it personal. It did not matter if the whole family read it.

"He is coming home! Why didn't you say so at once? He has been injured, although the injury is not great, and he is coming home. That is wonderful news. Isn't it, Valentino?"

"Wonderful," said Valentino, who was gazing at the sheet of paper with reverence: a letter from a fascist hero, sent from the furthest outpost of the new Roman empire.

Antonio looked at his sister. Her eyes met his for an instant, gravely.

"Aren't you happy, Filomena?" Danila said it warmly, but there was something needling in her voice all the same. "Bruno is coming home. You must be so glad."

"Yes, of course I'm glad." Filomena knotted the strings of her apron more tightly about her waist and took a papery brown onion from the basket. "And now I must make some soup for Papa, so that he has something nourishing for tomorrow, while I am at work."

"You don't sound glad," said Danila.

"Oh, there is no pleasing some people." Valentino put Bruno's letter on the table and reached for his hat. "Take no notice, Danila, she's always been a sourpuss. Well, I'm off. I'll see you in the morning, Antonino."

Danila was still staring at Filomena, a hurt expression on her face, when there was a chuntering wail from the room upstairs. The baby had woken. At once Danila forgot about Bruno's letter. The whole of her being was caught up in the baby, as though she were nourishing him with her soul as well as her flesh.

"I thought he was settled," she said, scurrying upstairs once more. "He cannot need changing, he must be hungry."

In the kitchen Filomena began to chop onions, the knife slamming against the board. Antonio heard her sniff.

"Don't cry," he said, "it will be all right."

"I am not crying. It's the onions."

"I daresay you have forgotten what Bruno is like, it has been so long, he is so far away."

"No," said Filomena, "I remember him well enough."

"You'll remember then that he is a decent fellow. You may not see eye to eye where politics are concerned, but he will be kind to you, you know that. Look at me, Mena. I am telling you the truth. You will learn to love him as a husband, I promise. And when we work so hard it is a relief, to have one thing in your life that is calm and settled."

Filomena's mouth gave a twist that in a man Antonio would have called sardonic. "Yes, I am sure that you are right."

She turned her back and began chopping again. Antonio felt annoyed. He had done his best for Filomena. What else could she expect? Most brothers would do what Valentino had done: tell her to stop being foolish and to count her blessings. Without speaking he went upstairs to fetch his accordion.

Danila was sitting on the bed, her blouse unbuttoned, the baby at her breast. His mouth was blind and greedy, like a newly hatched bird.

"So the child was hungry, then?" Antonio said, removing the cloth that covered his accordion, to protect it from the moist black grime of the city.

Danila frowned. "Your sister Filomena is a strange girl. Why isn't she overjoyed that Bruno is coming home? I do not think she loves him at all."

"She is anxious. It is a long time since Bruno went to Abyssinia. And it will be a great change in her life—"

"You should be stricter with her, Antonino." Lately Danila had become more assertive, especially where Filomena was concerned, as though motherhood had increased her authority. "Who does she think she is? I did not complain when our fathers agreed that we should marry."

"That is different—" began Antonio. Then he stopped to think about what Danila had said. *I did not complain.* Why would she complain? She had loved him, she had wanted to marry him. Surely she had wanted to marry him?

"It is because she was brought up in London, in my opinion. I am sure that your mother did her best, but it is not the same, it is never the same. I do not think that Filomena truly understands how Italian women should behave."

Danila cupped the baby's head in her hand. She did it confidently, as though she had been feeding infants all her life. Antonio watched her. Through the days of their courtship she had been shyly adoring, as if she could imagine no higher destiny than becoming his wife. He remembered her downcast eyes, her timid smiles. Had they been—not false, of course not false—but exaggerated, designed to flatter his vanity? Suddenly Antonio saw himself as perhaps Danila saw him, a forked hairy grasping creature, like a satyr.

"Danila," he said, blurting out the words, "do you still love me?"

Danila's eyes widened in surprise. "Don't be foolish. Of course I love you, you are my husband. I left my home to come and live with you." She clasped the child to her shoulder, while with her free hand she tried to button her blouse. "But we have a son now. It is a big responsibility, we cannot carry on exactly as we were. Pass me that towel, will you, Antonio?"

She was rubbing the baby's back now to wind him, her movements firm and deft. Her very competence seemed to Antonio to shut him out, just as he had been shut out when she was in labor. He laid the towel upon his wife's knee. Then he picked up his accordion and ran nimbly down the stairs.

LA RONDINE, THE restaurant where Antonio sang twice a week, was managed by a thick-necked bull of a man called Giuseppe, nicknamed Peppino, who came from Naples. He was a communist. He claimed to have fled Italy ten years before because of persecution by the *squadristi*, the fascist paramilitary gangs, although Antonio suspected that there was a more ignoble motive for his flight, a vendetta of some kind. Peppino was notorious for getting into fights. More than once Antonio had had to restrain him from throwing a punch, especially when the conversation turned to politics.

Tonight the restaurant was quiet. By ten o'clock only a pair of tables was occupied, one by a love-struck couple, the other by a group of Englishmen, scruffy but well-spoken, who were discussing the invasion of Austria in jagged excitable voices. Antonio knew that neither set of diners would welcome his warbling "Isle of Capri" in their ears.

"Perhaps I will go home," he said to Peppino, who was standing at the bar beneath a luridly tinted photograph of the Blue Grotto. "I do not suppose there will be any more customers this evening."

"Stay and have a drink." Peppino spoke mournfully, expecting a refusal. He lived in a state of perpetual homesickness. Unlike the Trombettas, he could not return to Italy for a summer's visit, and since so many of his countrymen supported Mussolini he got no pleasure from consorting with them. Even the Italian social clubs, the waiters' cooperative, the Dante Alighieri society, were barred to him. They all held their meetings at the Casa d'Italia now, and he would not step across the threshold of that accursed building.

Peppino's marmoset eyes touched Antonio. Besides, he did not want to go home yet. He took the grappa that Peppino gave him and swallowed it.

Peppino looked surprised. "That is not like you, my friend. What has happened? Are you grieving or celebrating?"

"You are not a married man, are you, Peppino?"

"That is the problem, is it?" Peppino reached for the bottle once more. "In that case, drink long, drink deep."

Antonio felt the grappa shimmer through his veins. Through its haze he remembered Danila on their wedding day, fragile and shining as a piece of Venetian glass. Then he thought of how she did not like to make love in the baby's presence, squirming in his arms, hushing him to silence. Was that how their life together would be from now on?

Behind the bar Peppino was polishing glasses with a linen cloth. For a man of his great size he had unexpectedly deft fingers. "Your wife is from Lazio too, is she?"

Antonio nodded. "She is a kind girl, a beautiful girl, I love her very much, but—I do not know—since our son was born she has changed. It is as though she thinks of herself as a mother first, and then as my wife."

"That is what happens," said Peppino sagely. "That is what women are like. I have heard the same story many times. You should take a mistress, my friend. English women like you. I have observed it. If I were not such a sweet-tempered man I should be jealous." He gave Antonio a wolfish smile, revealing his large pointed canines. "I would not mind finding an English woman for myself. A plump grateful one, with a nest egg to keep us both comfortable. I'd be happy to marry her. It would be no bad thing, in my opinion, to become a British citizen."

"What?" said Antonio. "You?"

"Why not? I cannot return to Italy. And if Mussolini continues licking Hitler's fascist arse we'll soon see the mood in Britain change. We Italians will no longer be harmless, friendly folk: we will be the enemy."

"But we belong here. My family has been in London for more than seventy years."

Peppino shrugged and drank his grappa with gloomy pleasure. "It will count for nothing, believe me. In dangerous times people favor their own kind."

The amorous young man beckoned then, asking for a song. Antonio adjusted the strap of his accordion and began an Italian love song with a yearning melody: "Tornerai," or "You Will Return." He could hear his voice reverberate in the half-empty restaurant. One of the Englishmen, a fair-haired man, older and more smartly dressed than the others, turned in his chair to listen while his fellow diners gabbled on.

"We are on the edge of a volcano. Think how quickly the Great War began. A fat archduke gets himself shot in Sarajevo, and the world blows up like a tinderbox. That is why, if we want peace, we have to rearm. We have to rearm at once."

THE LOVE-STRUCK COUPLE left after Antonio's song, but it was eleven o'clock before the table of Englishmen called for their bill. There seemed to be some confusion about paying: they began to slap their pockets, looking sheepish. In the end the fair man took charge. "I'll cover the damage," he said, shooing his friends toward the door. "Be off with you."

Antonio shouldered his accordion. Like it or not, it was time to go home to Frith Street. It was late; he would have to tiptoe into his cramped bedroom, so as not to waken Danila or the baby. He thought of the frowstiness of the room, the milky, faintly sour smell of the baby's crib.

"I enjoyed your singing," the Englishman said, as he thumbed out coins. "Your voice is exceptional. Who is your teacher?"

"I do not have a teacher, I am not a trained singer. I only perform in places like this, restaurants, dance halls—"

"Oh, but you should train. With the right teacher you would go far. I'm a well-connected fellow, I daresay I could get a recommendation for you."

His effusiveness unsettled Antonio. He did not want to have to explain to a stranger—a wealthy, educated, English stranger—that he had no money for singing lessons.

"Perhaps you would like another song, before you go?" he said, to change the subject.

"That would be a great pleasure. Do you know 'Core 'Ngrato'?"

"Of course," said Antonio. It was one of the tragic full-blooded Neapolitan ballads Peppino liked, that reminded him of home. He was just beginning the song when the door to La Rondine jangled open and two Italian men came in. One was in his thirties, a sallow swaggering fellow, the other a boy of about seventeen. Under their overcoats they wore black shirts.

"We're closed," said Peppino swiftly.

"I do not think so." The older of the two pointed contemptuously to the glasses on the bar. "Two grappas, if you please. We want to drink a toast to the *duce*."

Antonio guessed why they had come. Peppino's dislike of Mussolini was well-known in the Soho community. It was considered great sport—a rite of passage, almost—for young fascists to come and taunt him; Antonio had had to dissuade his brother, Valentino, from doing it. Sure enough the boy, lounging against the bar, began to sing the "Giovinezza," the fascist anthem.

"*Salve o popolo d'eroi, salve o patria immortale.*" His voice was loud and brassy. "Hail, nation of heroes, hail, immortal fatherland."

"Aren't you going to sing too?" said the other man, glancing at Antonio. "You were warbling like a canary when we came in."

Peppino let out a gruff cry, and seizing the two Blackshirts, he banged their heads together. The boy shouted in triumph; then he snatched up the grappa bottle, ready to smash it against the bar.

"Stop that!" said the Englishman, in a commanding voice. Rising from his chair he grasped the boy's arm. At once the boy jabbed his elbow backward. It struck the Englishman hard in the solar plexus, and he doubled up with a groan, his knees buckling beneath him.

"*Santa Madonna*," said the older Blackshirt. At once he put a weighty hand on the boy's shoulder and steered him rapidly from the restaurant, leaving the glass door ajar.

Antonio eased the fair man into a chair, where he slumped forward, wheezing. His face had turned cheesily pale.

"We should call the police." Peppino shut the restaurant door, flicking the sign belatedly to "Closed." "It is an assault upon an Englishman, they cannot dismiss it as foreigners squabbling."

"Forgive me," the fair man said, "but I am feeling rather giddy." His voice was unnaturally precise, as though he were trying to be heard above the roar of a hurricane. "Perhaps you could loosen this . . ."

Antonio undid his bow tie, then the studs of his collar. They were made of gold, small and disproportionately heavy. "You would be better off at home," he said. "Let us find you a taxi."

The fair man was still struggling for breath. After a moment he said: "I suffer from asthma, quite seriously sometimes. If you would not mind accompanying me—it is not far, and my wife will be at home to receive me. It would be a great kindness."

Peppino got the taxi, stepping into the street to hail it as if he were a constable arresting a particularly insolent felon. From the backseat Antonio watched the familiar lamp-lit streets spin past, Old Compton Street, Charing Cross Road, St. Giles Circus; then they were among the tall, dense, silent houses of Bloomsbury, set around their shadowy squares of lawn. High in the sky there was a crescent moon. Beside him the Englishman was breathing ponderously, as if he had only just learned how to do it and was afraid that if he paused, even for an instant, he might lose the knack.

The taxi drew to a halt. Antonio helped the Englishman from the car, supporting his elbow as they climbed to his door. The curtains were drawn back in one of the upper rooms, and Antonio could see light spilling upon a wrought-iron balcony. He rang the bell once, twice, three times. At last he heard the scuffle of feet, the creaking of hinges. The next moment the front door sprang open, and he came face-to-face with the girl from the Paradise Ballroom.

CHAPTER 9

OLIVIA RODWAY HAD SPENT THE EVENING IN THE UPstairs drawing room of her husband's house, trying to read *Anna Karenina*. It was on a list that Bernard had given her, of the books that any educated person ought to have read by the age of thirty. She was enjoying Anna's story but she found Levin—the character Bernard himself most admired—earnest and insufferable.

Rising from the silk-clad sofa she rang the servant's bell. She had been putting this off for the past half hour. Olivia was not accustomed to asking other people to make her pots of tea, bring her trays of supper. It seemed much easier to go to the kitchen and do it herself.

"Yes, madam?" said Avril, the housemaid. She was a gaunt young woman, all chin and elbows. Bernard had inherited her from his mother, who had trained the girl herself.

"I am ready for supper, Avril," Olivia said, in a lofty voice. She knew that Avril idolized Penelope, who was a proper lady—she had been a debutante, ostrich feathers and all, before the Great War—and that nothing she, Olivia, could do would win the same devotion. If she was firm, Avril would call her snooty; if she was friendly the maid would despise her as weak.

At least I look the part, thought Olivia when Avril had gone, throwing herself onto the sofa once more. She was wearing dark yellow evening pajamas with a tobacco-colored cashmere wrap, an engagement present from Bernard, and her hair had been very expensively cut, which made the sharp lines of her face look distinguished rather than gawky. All of Bernard's friends admired her: the poets, the journalists, even the earnest young socialists with their pipes and their corduroy trousers, who did not generally notice women. I told you, Olivia, her husband had said triumphantly: you're an original. And it's I who discovered you. We should both be very proud of ourselves.

OLIVIA HAD MARRIED Bernard in January, two months after their first meeting. The wedding took place in a registry office. The only guest was Uncle Dickie, who bought them lunch afterward at the Ivy. Olivia had considered inviting her aunt from Croydon, but she knew that it would be from the worst of all motives, and she thought such pettiness might put a curse on her own good fortune. Once upon a time Olivia had wished her sister dead; she was nervous about curses.

For their honeymoon Bernard took Olivia on a winter cruise to the Caribbean. She had not believed it was possible to be so happy. They drank champagne cocktails among the potted palms, they watched flickering Hollywood films in the ship's cinema, they danced the tango and the foxtrot in the green and ivory ballroom. They also spent a great deal of time in their mahogany-paneled cabin; specifically, in their large double bed with its cool Egyptian cotton sheets and its Vi-Spring mattress. More than once they arrived late and flushed for dinner, and the other passengers would look at them with a spellbound mixture of indulgence and envy.

AVRIL BROUGHT IN her tray of supper and laid it on the table. "I'll close the curtains, madam," she said, bustling toward the tall window that overlooked the square. It was twilight; a fingernail of moon was turning from chalk to silver.

"No," said Olivia, "leave them, thank you. And that will be all, Avril, if you wish to go to bed."

Avril raised her eyebrows. Olivia could hear what she was thinking. It is not for you to dismiss me, what if the master needs me when he comes home? She did not say anything, though, but bobbed in acknowledgment and left the room.

Olivia ate a mouthful of cold chicken, piquant with thyme. Of course, their life was different now that they were back in London. She could not expect her honeymoon to last forever, Bernard had work to do. Every morning after breakfast he would shut himself in his study, hammering away on his Remington Noiseless typewriter. He was writing a novel, he confessed to Olivia, a novel about the very nature of society, set in the future; soon he would let her read it. Then, after lunch, there were meetings of one or other of his committees. The refugee associations were especially busy, preparing for a flood of arrivals from Austria. In the evenings they would dine out or go to the theater, and sometimes they went to parties, but often, as tonight, Bernard had commitments that did not include Olivia. Have an evening at home, darling, he had said as he dressed, struggling before the mirror with his collar studs. It's only drinks with a couple of journalists, and then a Labour Party meeting. Not much fun for you. I'm sorry I'm so hectic at the moment. It will quieten down, I promise.

Well, thought Olivia peaceably, drinking Scotch and soda, I am glad that he cares about such things. I would not change him, even if I could. She picked up her book once more. She had reached the place where Anna gives in to her lover, Vronsky: a scene she had been anticipating with a shivery, half-erotic thrill. When she came to it, though, it filled her with unease. Anna's surrender was raddled with guilt; there was no joy or defiance in it. Olivia fingered the pages of the book. They were thin as cigarette papers, edged in gold. She remembered how, on her honeymoon cruise, one of their fellow passengers had asked her to dance. He was a flashy businessman of about forty, and there was a glint in his eye that

Olivia recognized. She glanced at Bernard, hoping he would forbid it, but of course he did not.

"It will be a pleasure. I love watching you dance, my sweet, and I can't do it when you're in my arms."

The dance was a tango, and once she was on the floor Olivia could not help showing off, twisting her slim satin hip, spinning upon her heel. She knew that all eyes were upon her. Bernard's gaze was crooked, as though he could not look at her for fear of being dazzled.

When the tango was over the businessman's wife, who had fair curls and a pretty, sulky mouth, commented rather pointedly on her skill.

"I used to be a professional," Olivia said, calmly accepting the cocktail that Bernard gave her.

The businessman's face broke into a smile. His forehead was beaded with perspiration. "So you're a woman of the world, eh? I thought so."

Olivia drank. She had the feeling that she was skating on thin ice. In a facetious Marlene Dietrich accent she said: "Oh, yes, my friend. It took more than one man to change my name to Shanghai Lily."

The businessman's wife gave a squeak of shock. Olivia felt Bernard seize her wrist. "Come, Olivia. I've just remembered, I told them to take some champagne to our cabin."

As he pulled her through the door she thought that he must be furious, but the moment they got into the cabin she realized it was not rage at all. Oh, no; it was a different passion entirely. Bernard could not wait for her to take off her green silk dress, to unfasten the warm pearls about her neck, could not wait for her to undo the buckles of her high-heeled shoes.

Afterward, though, as they lay in a slippery tangle on the cabin floor, he said: "I wouldn't talk too much about your past if I were you. Not with people like that, anyway. Strangers."

"I'm not ashamed of the way I used to live, Bernard," said Olivia.

"Of course not, my darling." Bernard kissed her neck, just above the collarbone. "It's one of the many things that has made you the remarkable woman you are. But it's over and done with. You're my wife now, remember."

In bed, when Bernard had fallen asleep, Olivia lay awake in the beautiful darkness. The ship's engines hummed like a persistent drum roll as the ship plied its way south toward Barbados, where, the following day, they would be driven at a stately pace through field after field of white-plumed sugarcane. Olivia thought of the commercial traveler from Cardiff, she thought of the abortionist's flat, she thought of the horror she had glimpsed in the Italian singer's eyes. Bernard might claim to understand, he might describe her old life as *interesting* and *colorful*, but she had never told him about any of those things. Would he forgive her, would he still love her, if he knew?

THAT FEAR RETURNED to Olivia now as she sat on the sofa, blankly gazing at *Anna Karenina*. To quell it she crossed to the gramophone. One delight of living with Bernard was the sheer quantity of things he owned: books, pictures, records, clothes. Since her pinched genteel childhood Olivia had always had to choose, knowing that if you had this you could not have that, until your pleasure was corroded by doubt. Luxuriantly she fingered the black shellac discs in Bernard's collection: Caruso singing Italian arias, Dinu Lipatti playing Chopin, the Hot Club de France. How can you die, she thought, when there are such solid exquisite things in the world? She put on some Django Reinhardt, dizzy and invigorating. Sliding off her shoes she began to dance about the room, the treacle-colored floorboards smooth beneath her toes.

The music was so loud that at first she did not hear the doorbell. Remembering that she had sent Avril to bed she ran down the stairs and pulled open the front door. On the porch stood Bernard. He was leaning upon the arm of Antonio Trombetta. She recognized the singer at once, and a shock ran through her, sudden as electricity. Then she saw that Bernard's face was white and sweating, as if he were about to faint. Behind her Avril, wrapped in a flannel dressing gown, let out a squeal of dismay.

"Bernard!" said Olivia. "What's happened?"

"He had an accident." Antonio's eyes were fixed upon her face. He remembers me too, thought Olivia. "In the restaurant where I work—"

"Don't caterwaul, Avril," said Olivia, unfairly since after that first squeal Avril had been silent. "Well, thank you for your trouble. He is safely home now." She reached out to draw her husband indoors, away from the interloper.

Bernard took a careful breath. "Take the taxi, if you wish, my friend." His arm flailed in the direction of the cab, which was still waiting in the square. Antonio hesitated, and Olivia guessed that Bernard had not yet paid the fare.

"You had better step indoors," she said. "Bernard, give me your wallet."

Olivia paid the cab driver, who looked askance at her naked feet. Antonio, his hand still cupped about Bernard's elbow, hovered in the black and white tiled hallway.

"The master's having an asthma attack, madam." Avril tightened the cord of her dressing gown in a businesslike way. "He needs a bowl of steaming water, to help him breathe."

"All right," said Olivia. "You'd better fetch one, then, Avril. Come, Bernard."

As they climbed the stairs Antonio tried to tell her what had happened, but it sounded like gibberish, some tale of Italian fascists fighting in a restaurant.

"Why on earth would Bernard get into a quarrel with a Blackshirt?" she was asking when Avril came in with the hot water.

"I've put in some Friar's Balsam." Avril set down the basin, a beige Mason Cash mixing bowl, and flicked a towel from her shoulder. "That's what Mrs. Rodway told me to use. It works wonders."

"Well, it smells nasty enough. Thank you, Avril, I can manage." Olivia threw the towel over Bernard's head, settling him above the basin. Then, her hand proprietorially between her husband's shoulder blades, she glanced at Antonio. "Sit down, since you are here. Would you like a drink? Avril, bring some ice."

"There is no need . . ." began Antonio.

His diffidence, as he lingered there beside the grand piano, annoyed Olivia. He must know he is not wanted, why doesn't he have the wit to leave? "You have done a great service to my husband," she said. "The least that I can do is to offer you a drink."

At the frostiness in her voice Bernard's head reared up. "Antonio is a singer," he said, pushing the towel aside. "He has one of the most beautiful voices I have ever heard. I am going to find him a teacher, so he can make the most of his talent—"

"Breathe, Bernard." Olivia slid her hand to the nape of his neck. "Don't chatter, breathe. God, that water reeks."

Antonio cleared his throat. "I should go home. My family—my wife—will be expecting me."

Once again Bernard tried to grope his way from under the towel. "Olivia, darling, write down his address. I will call on you, Antonio, to thank you properly. And I mean it about finding you a teacher—"

He paused, wheezing above the basin. Olivia rose to her feet. She and Antonio Trombetta looked at one another. It was a long, candid look. They both knew that she had no intention of taking down his address.

"Do not be afraid," murmured Antonio, as he preceded her down the stairs. "I will not say anything. Even if we do meet again—"

Olivia's lips tightened. "You can say what you like. I have no secrets from my husband. He knows everything about me."

CHAPTER 10

FILOMENA REALIZED THAT SOONER OR LATER SHE WOULD have to tell Stan Harker she was going to be married, and that their friendship would have to end. She kept putting it off, though. First Renata was ill with a head cold and it seemed a shame to spoil such unlooked-for privacy; then the March weather improved, which meant she and Stan could linger and enjoy the walk between Goodge Street and Soho Square. Stan had begun to meet her after work whenever he was off duty. He would stand discreetly at the street corner, the *Daily Herald* open in his hand, and as soon as he saw that the coast was clear he would slip forward to join her.

It was a mild afternoon, its brightness hinting that spring was just within reach. As they fell comfortably into step Filomena remembered their first encounter at the laundry. Two of the Italian women had been squabbling over a torn shirt, each insisting the other had caused the damage. Filomena had watched Stan going about his business, asking questions, making notes with his stubby pencil, eyeing the quarreling women with a placid air. It was as if he had seen it all before, but instead of making him weary it had made him wise.

Stan lived south of the Thames in Bermondsey, with his parents. His father had been a docker, but he had lost an eye in an accident five years ago, and Stan was the breadwinner now, he told Filomena. Like all their conversations this exchange took place not only in public but on the move. As long as they were walking

Filomena felt she was beyond reproach. Once Stan had suggested that they sit and chat beneath the lime trees in Soho Square, and she had squawked with horror. Anyone might see them, coming in and out of St. Patrick's church. Why, the priest himself might spot her, zealous Padre Barbera, and who knew what chatter he would spread? If her father, if her brothers, heard about it she would be in terrible trouble. Stan had opened his mouth to argue, but then had thought better of it, and was silent.

"And how is your father?" he asked now, as they strode along Newman Street. "Is his cough better?"

Filomena shook her head. "Antonio told him he should see one of the doctors at the Italian hospital, but he will not do it."

"He does not want to admit that he is ill," said Stan. "We men are like that. We make believe we are invincible."

"Besides, the hospital reminds him of my mother. The smell of it, the doctors' long faces. He will do anything to avoid going there."

"And the baby? How is the baby?"

"Oh, the baby is thriving. He grows plumper by the day. But my brother Antonio is in disgrace with his wife. The other day he didn't get home till after midnight. He says there was an accident with a customer at La Rondine, but Danila says he came to bed stinking of grappa, and she has been sulking ever since."

Stan gave a smile. Filomena had never admitted her dislike for Danila but she knew that he understood it. She felt a stab of sorrow. Did she really have to tell him about Bruno's return? We are doing nobody any harm, she thought. Why can't we go on like this, walking together, talking? Why can't we go on like this forever?

They had reached Oxford Street. A young bootblack sat on the pavement, with his wooden step and his tins of shoe polish. Filomena glanced at the boy's grubby, resigned face. Soon it would be too late, they would be in Soho, at risk of being seen, they would have to go their separate ways. She took a breath.

"I have had a letter from Bruno, my *fidanzato*. My fiancé, the man I'm going to marry. He has been injured in Africa, and they are sending him home." The normality of her own voice encouraged her. "He wants us to be married at once, as soon as he returns to London. And of course I'll have to leave my job at the laundry."

Stan stopped dead on the pavement. "Well, then," he said, "that's that."

A sense of fear gripped Filomena. "What do you mean?" she asked.

Stanley's expression was serene, still faintly smiling. "Don't look so tragic. I mean, that is the end of this hole and corner business. You will have to talk to your father now."

"Talk to my father?" said Filomena. "Why?"

"Oh, Filomena," said Stan. "You know why."

Filomena gaped. In a single, competent movement Stan lifted her by the arms and shunted her into the nearest doorway. The speed of it made her heart thump.

"What else are we going to do?" Stan had his back to the street, shielding her from sight. "We'll have to tell your father sooner or later, if we're going to get engaged."

"Engaged?" said Filomena.

"What? Did you think this was just tomfoolery? A bit of fun to pass the time? I'm serious about you, Filomena. I want you to meet my family, I want us to be married. But first we have to ask your father's permission. It wouldn't be right otherwise."

"Oh, Stan," said Filomena, and she who never cried, who prided herself on never crying, burst into tears. Stan put his arms about her.

"Well, I don't know. What kind of girl cries when her young man proposes? And I thought you were so levelheaded."

"I am—it is not—" Filomena managed to say. "I am not crying because of that. I am crying because it is impossible."

"It's not impossible." Stan put out his hand and lifted her chin. His face was closer to hers than it had ever been. "All you have to do is tell your father the truth. Tell him that I love you and I want to marry you. I can come with you. We can do it now, if you want."

"No!" said Filomena.

"No?" said Stan, and without warning he kissed her. It was a short, emphatic kiss, like the last word in an argument.

Filomena's hand flew to her lips. "How could you, Stan?" she said, pulling away. "How *could* you?"

She saw Stan's face fall. He has disgraced me, she thought, I am damaged goods, I can never marry Bruno now. And then, even as she stared at him, she began to laugh, and leaning forward she returned his kiss, touching his hair, tasting his mouth, as though her own disgrace had freed her for life.

SINCE OLIVIA HAD not written down Antonio's address Bernard went back to the restaurant in Soho to look for him. He was irritated by her failure—it was a simple task; Avril would have managed it—but he did not feel he could reprove her. I was worried about you, Bernard, she said, fixing those beautiful serious eyes upon him. It put everything else from my mind. Well, he thought, as he strolled along Old Compton Street, a man should not complain about his wife's devotion.

At La Rondine Peppino slapped him enthusiastically on the back. "So you did not die, my friend?" he said, with his wolfish smile, uncorking a bottle of Marsala. "Good, I am glad. If you are looking for Antonio you are in luck. He has come by to collect a cherry preserve that our cook makes. His father is not well, and Antonio is hoping that the taste of cherries will remind him of home. I will call him for you."

Antonio was disconcerted to find Bernard sitting in the restaurant. By day he looked more fine-spun than ever, an elegant man in expensive clothes, incongruous among the cheap red and white gingham tablecloths.

"Mr. Rodway," said Antonio, putting out his hand, "I am pleased to see that you have recovered."

"Oh, yes. These attacks are dramatic, but they do not last long." Bernard took an amber mouthful of Marsala. "I've discovered a singing teacher for you, Antonio. His name's Konrad Fischer. He's a composer from Vienna, he worked with the singers at the opera house. You can come to my house for lessons. Herr Fischer is seeing several pupils there."

Antonio licked his lips. "That is very kind of you, but I cannot afford—"

"Don't worry about the cost. My uncle Dickie is paying Herr Fischer's bills until he settles. He will be glad of the distraction. He had to leave his sister behind in Austria and he is worried about her."

There was something overwhelming about Bernard, for all his sauntering charm. He is so sure, Antonio thought, that the world belongs to him, and he can dispose of everything within it just as he chooses.

"It is not only the money, Mr. Rodway. My family runs a cigarette kiosk in Leicester Square. I work there during the day. My time is not my own."

"*Kiosk*," said Bernard. "Now there's an interesting word. It comes from the Persian, did you know that? It means an object that creates shade. There are many words like that, which have been absorbed into our English language so entirely that we forget their origins." He took another sip of Marsala. "Surely somebody else can do your job. Selling cigarettes is not exactly a skilled task."

Antonio thought of what his father would say. When he was fourteen a music teacher at the Italian school had offered him lessons at special rates for a *paesano*, a fellow countryman. Enrico had refused, barely glancing up from his game of cards. And then what, Antonino? he had said. Can you support a wife and children by singing? Better to keep it for pleasure.

Peppino stepped forward to refill Bernard's glass. "You should do it, Antonio. You have a talent: something that is not given to many of us. This is an opportunity to nourish it."

"Peppino is right," said Bernard. "You have a great talent. Who can tell where it may lead?"

A wave of defiance swept through Antonio. Why shouldn't I have ambition? he thought. Why shouldn't I have hope?

"Thank you, Mr. Rodway, sir," he said. "I accept your generous offer."

"Excellent." Bernard got briskly to his feet. "Shall we say next Wednesday at half past two? I will let Herr Fischer know."

It was only later, as he was walking home with the jar of cherries in his hand, that Antonio remembered Olivia. He thought of how she had declined to write down his address, how she had shooed him imperiously out of the house. She did not want her husband to find me, he thought; she hoped that I would vanish into the darkness, never to be seen again. Is it because I discovered her secret, that night at the Paradise Ballroom? Antonio pictured her fierce extraordinary face. Olivia had claimed that Bernard knew everything about her. Well, he thought, I cannot help it if she is lying. I told her I would not say anything. It is not my fault if she does not believe me.

Antonio was turning into Frith Street now. As he did so he saw a young man escorting his girl around the corner from Soho Square. He was a stocky young man, English from the look of him, with hair the color of straw. At the corner the couple paused to say good-bye. They did it silently, touching hands but not faces, not lips. Something about their formality moved Antonio. They seemed to him like figures in a medieval fresco, their love expressed by scant solemn gestures. Then the girl turned away, and he saw that it was his sister Filomena.

CHAPTER 11

"You should have expected it, Bernard," said Dickie, as he reached for the porcelain bowl of whipped cream. "Your mother doesn't like Lionel's wife either."

"That's different," said Bernard. He and Dickie had been to a meeting of the refugee association of which they were both members, and they were having afternoon tea in Claridge's, sitting in brown leather chairs beside the fire. "She thinks Caroline's boring, and of course she's right. But I thought she would take to Olivia."

"I can't think why." Lovingly Dickie added a spoonful of blackcurrant jam to the cream daubed on his scone. "Penelope's jealous. Secretly she'd prefer it if you were homosexual, so that she could be the only woman in your life."

Bernard squirmed. He was not prejudiced against homosexuals—of course not, he had plenty of friends who preferred men—but he did not like the idea that anyone might think he was one himself.

"What about Lionel?" Dickie dabbed jam from his cherub's lips. "Was he scandalized by poor Olivia?"

"Oh," said Bernard airily, "I don't give a damn what Lionel thinks."

The previous weekend Bernard had taken Olivia to Cheshire to meet his family. He had had a clear, delicious vision of what he expected to happen: Lionel's red-faced outrage, his mother's delight. It had not been like that at all, though. True, Lionel's jaw dropped when he realized that Bernard's wife was none other than the impossible woman from Quaglino's, but he recovered swiftly from the shock, and thereafter was all politeness. As for Penelope, she greeted Olivia graciously, with a sweeping up-and-down look; then she ignored her and devoted her attention to Bernard, stroking his hand at dinner, laughing at all his remarks.

Olivia's behavior had disappointed Bernard, too. He wanted her to be funny and outrageous, telling risqué tales of her life in the dance halls, how this bandleader snorted cocaine, how that suave singer tried to fondle the girls' bums. Instead she was thoughtful, even demure, tilting her head encouragingly as Caroline chattered about her children and her dogs. The following day, to Bernard's annoyance, she asked to see the silk factory. She listened as Lionel explained the workings of the jacquard looms: how it could take as long as a fortnight to thread the machine, how once it was done the loom could be kept running day and night, pretty much forever. When Lionel showed her the weaving cards, intricately punched with holes, she compared them to the white music rolls of a pianola, and Bernard saw his brother's face change as he recognized Olivia's intelligence.

"Well, she's no Vere de Vere," Lionel murmured to his brother afterward, "but she has something about her. Maybe it won't be such a disaster after all, old fellow."

His brother's approval irritated Bernard more than ever. He glowered silently all the way back to London in their first-class carriage; then, at home in Bedford Square, he and Olivia had their first serious argument.

"I don't know why you're angry," Olivia said. "When we were on our honeymoon you told me I shouldn't talk about my old life. That's why I was so careful. I guessed that it might shock your family, especially your brother."

"And so you decided to make eyes at him instead, like some ridiculous shopgirl?"

Olivia crossed toward him, her feet almost touching his. "I

wanted your family to like me," she said in a simple voice. "What is wrong with that? I mean it, Bernard. If it was the wrong thing to do, please tell me why."

Bernard stared, trapped by her candor. "Ouf," he said, flinging away, "if you don't understand how can I possibly explain?"

He thought of the argument now as he poured himself more tea. It was Lapsang souchong tea, the swollen blackish leaves like iron filings in the cup. He and Olivia had made it up—he smiled, remembering it—but there was something tarnishing about a first quarrel. It was like the first scratch on a new record, the first smudged mark on a freshly painted wall. Nothing would ever be quite the same again.

"And I hear you have a new protégé, Bernard." Dickie had laid down his napkin but he was eyeing a meringue upon the three-tiered silver cake stand. "An Italian waiter, I believe, with a voice like an angel."

"Not a waiter. He works, rather absurdly, in a cigarette kiosk in Leicester Square. But yes, he does have the voice of an angel. Almost as good as Caruso, Herr Fischer says."

Dickie reached for the meringue. "I know I shouldn't," he said complacently, "but these little cakes are as light as air. Is he handsome?"

"Come and see for yourself. More to the point, come and hear him. He's having a lesson with Herr Fischer tomorrow. Why don't you call in for a drink?"

"Excellent," said Dickie, picking shards of meringue from his plate with a meticulous fingertip, "and while I'm there I can have a nice juicy gossip with Olivia about her weekend in Cheshire."

"Oh, you won't see Olivia," said Bernard. "She makes herself scarce when Herr Fischer gives his lessons. Goes shopping, or to a matinée."

"That's considerate of her, don't you think?"

Bernard took a mouthful of tea. He had let it brew too long, and it tasted nastily of kippers. "Pah," he said, stretching out his tongue against its bitterness. "I daresay you're right, Dickie. It's only—well, I'd rather she stayed at home."

"Don't you like her gallivanting?"

"It isn't that. There's a skill to becoming a good hostess: making other people feel comfortable, bringing them out of themselves. I want Olivia to learn it."

Dickie smiled. "I adore Olivia, you know that. I won't hear a word against her. And remember, Bernard, she was working before she married you, she's used to having an occupation. Maybe you should send her to art school, or get her involved in one of your committees. She's cleverer than half those middle-aged literary types. The ones who think it's bourgeois to comb their hair. Or wash."

"I can't see Olivia stomaching a committee. She wouldn't have the patience. Besides, being my wife should be occupation enough, don't you think?"

Dickie was silent as he picked the last fragment of meringue from the little china plate. "Perhaps," he said, "perhaps. But you married an unusual girl, Bernard, remember. Don't turn her into an ordinary one."

THE FOLLOWING DAY, while Dickie was listening to Antonio sing, Olivia sat in the cinema, wrapped in a caramel musquash jacket Bernard had given her. She liked going to the cinema alone. She enjoyed the darkness, the anonymity, the sense that she had stolen a sliver of time from the real world. Besides, there was nobody to accompany her. She had lost touch with Jeanie and the other girls from the dance hall, and although a handful of the women in Bernard's circle had asked her to lunch, the invitations had not led to new friendships. The single women were inclined to be jealous of her, while with the married ones she felt shy and awkward. Bernard himself was much too busy to fritter away an afternoon like this. In any case, when he went to the cinema it was to see highbrow films, usually in French, Jean Renoir or Marcel Carné, not Fred Astaire and Ginger Rogers.

Although Olivia claimed that she went out so as not to make Herr Fischer feel uncomfortable, the truth was that she did not like being in the house with Antonio Trombetta. His presence made her feel unsteady, as though the ground below her might give way at any time. She wished that she had told Bernard about her first meeting with Antonio. At the time the shock had been too great, seeing the singer's face, knowing what he knew. It was too late now, Bernard was bound to be suspicious, to wonder why she had not mentioned it before.

On the screen, in luminous black and white, Fred Astaire danced his way through a throng of masked girls, hopelessly seeking the face of his beloved. Olivia burrowed in her seat. She had been proud of her behavior in the Rodways' house in Macclesfield. She thought she had managed a difficult situation cleverly, and she had expected Bernard to congratulate her on her deftness. Their argument had taken her entirely by surprise. She had never seen Bernard sulk before, and she did not know that it was possible for her civilized husband to become so suddenly peevish. He had flounced—was that really the word?—into his study and slammed the door.

Few of Olivia's previous affairs had survived arguments; she had no idea what would happen next. She did not even know what to say when Avril asked about serving dinner, and she felt the housemaid's eyes probe humiliatingly. It was possible that in an hour the old smiling Bernard would emerge, offering to mix her a pink gin, suggesting they eat at Quaglino's, as if they had never quarreled. It was also possible, in Olivia's opinion, that he would announce that their marriage was over, he had ceased to love her, she had better pack her things and move out.

Olivia could not bear the suspense. She did the only thing that she could think of doing, which was to seduce her husband. From the back of her wardrobe she dug out the black spangled dress in which he had first seen her, slit to the thigh for dancing. It looked cheap and brash next to the elegant clothes she now wore, but that did not matter, Olivia thought. It might even be a good thing. She put "Dark Eyes" on the gramophone, as loud as the machine would go. Her heart was like a hammer as she inched open the door to Bernard's study.

Bernard was sitting at his desk, and he looked up in blank astonishment. Olivia was afraid that the next moment he would ask, snubbingly, What on earth do you think you're doing? Don't be such a fool. Fixing her eyes smokily upon him she took a step forward, a precise exaggerated dancer's step, so that her leg slithered from her dress.

Bernard smiled. "Well, well," he said, pushing back his chair, "and what have we got here?"

The music was still wafting along the corridor. Bernard took her in his arms. She could tell he was aroused. Together they danced a few steps of the tango, their hands clasped, their thighs aligning. Then, hooking his arm beneath her silken knee, he kicked shut the door and steered her toward the velvet chaise longue. It's going to be all right, thought Olivia, as triumph turned her limbs to jelly. Deep down, though, she felt the icy whisper of disdain, that her husband should fall for something so obvious.

what she had said to Stan, the day he kissed her. I am crying because it is impossible.

Antonio came to sit beside her. His shirt smelled of the kiosk, a mixture of sugar and tobacco. "Mena, you must see that I am right. Promise me that you will give him up. Promise me that you will not see him again."

His hand was upon her arm. It was warm but insistent. Filomena took a breath. "I promise," she said, so low that he could scarcely hear her. Antonio got to his feet.

"I will speak to this man, this Stanley Harker. It is better if he knows this can never happen. It is better if he understands that from now on he has to leave you alone."

THE POLICE STATION in Bow Street was a gray imposing building, ornate and watchful in the bustle of Covent Garden. Hundreds had passed through its doors. Some were famous—Oscar Wilde, Dr. Crippen, Emmeline Pankhurst; many were doomed, to hard labor or the gallows. Antonio felt a frisson of unease as he entered. Faced with bland implacable British justice he knew himself to be a foreigner. He decided to emulate Bernard Rodway, that consummate Englishman, and he sauntered toward the desk clerk as though he had a perfect right to be there.

The clerk was not to be hoodwinked. He cocked an eyebrow, scanning Antonio's face as if to memorize it. Then, more genially, he said: "Well, you're in luck. That's Constable Harker over there. Stan! An Eyetie to see you."

Stan Harker, on his way out to the street, turned. "Can I help you, sir?" he said.

"My name is Trombetta. I am Filomena's brother: Antonio Trombetta."

At the name a flicker of relief, hardly perceptible, crossed the policeman's face. He was afraid I might be Valentino, thought Antonio. Filomena must have told him everything about us.

CHAPTER 12

IT WAS FILOMENA'S HALF DAY, AND SHE WAS SITTING AT THE sewing machine, a black and gold Singer that had been her mother's. She was performing a housewifely task called sides-to-middle, where you cut a worn sheet in half and stitched the far edges together. It left an uncomfortable seam in the center which irked you when you couldn't sleep, but it put off the day when you had to dig into your purse to buy new linen.

The bobbin of thread rattled and whirred. Two weeks had passed since the momentous afternoon when Stan had kissed her. In that time Filomena had seen him only once, when he walked her home from Goodge Street. He had wanted to discuss their plans. When should they approach Enrico? Should Filomena broach the subject alone, or should they speak to him together? If all else failed, would Filomena up sticks and go to live with his family in Bermondsey? Filomena scarcely heard any of it. She was in a glorious whirlwind of joy and novelty. The very touch of Stan's fingers upon her wrist, guiding her past a puddle, had filled her with rapture.

She was smiling now to think of it when the door opened and Antonio came in, dragging his rain-drenched jacket from his shoulders. Filomena looked up in surprise.

"I did not expect you home, Antonio. I thought you would be working all day."

Antonio did not answer, but crossed to the scullery and, rolling up his shirtsleeves, rinsed his hands under the tap. "Is Danila upstairs?" he asked.

"Yes. She went to feed the baby after lunch. I daresay she is resting now."

"Ah," said Antonio.

Filomena began to pump at the treadle, feeding the white flannel through the machine. The needle jabbed noisily up and down.

"Tell me, Filomena. Who is he?" Antonio's voice was soft, almost casual. Filomena lifted her foot.

"What do you mean?"

"You cannot fool me, Filomena. I saw you together, on the corner of Frith Street. Is he a *paesano*? He did not look like one."

Filomena stared at her brother. "No, he is not a *paesano*. He is English. His name is Stanley Harker. He is a policeman, he works at Bow Street station." Now that she had spoken Stan's name there seemed no reason why she should not keep talking, why she should not talk about him forever. "I met him at the laundry. There was a disturbance, a couple of the women quarreling over a torn shirt. I helped Stanley to quieten them. We became friends—"

"Friends?"

Filomena nodded. Then she thought of the salty unfamiliar taste of Stan's mouth, and her cheeks flooded crimson.

"I see," said Antonio, his lips twisting.

"It is not like that, Antonino. Stan wants to marry me. He wants to speak to Papa—"

"Oh, Filomena. I thought you were cleverer than that. Did you really fall for such moonshine?"

The disdain in his voice annoyed Filomena. "You don't know what you are talking about. You have not met Stan. He is a serious man. He means it."

"And Bruno?" said Antonio. "What about Bruno? You are engaged to be married, Filomena. Or had you forgotten?"

Filomena fell silent. She had been trying not to think about Bruno.

"You know what will happen, don't you, if Papa finds out? He will pack you off to Lazio, just like Lucia Ricci. He will send you to live with our sister, Paolina, and hope that nobody gets wind of your disgrace."

"He can't do that," said Filomena. Her sister, Paolina, lived in a ramshackle stone house on the edge of the village, with no running water and three squalling children. "I was born in London, I have the rights of an Englishwoman."

"And that won't be the worst of it," Antonio went on. "If Valentino catches a whiff of what you've been playing at he will kill this Englishman of yours. He'll gather a squad of his Blackshirt friends, they'll get their sticks and their knives, and they'll slaughter him."

"But Stan is a policeman. They'll be hanged . . ."

Antonio shrugged, as if to say, Yes, they'll be hanged. Filomena gazed at her hands, brown creased competent hands, now useless and trembling in her lap.

"You will not tell them, will you, Antonino?" she whispered.

For a moment Antonio did not speak. His face was impassive. At last he said: "No, I will not tell them, Filomena. You are my sister, I do not want to cause you pain. But you have to give him up. How can I keep this secret, if you do not give him up?"

I love him, Filomena wanted to say, I cannot give him up, but the words would not come out.

"Think, Filomena," Antonio said, more gently. "What will your life be like, if you marry this man? Papa will never forgive you, he will disown you as if you had never been born. And what of your husband's family? They won't like him marrying a foreigner. Everything that goes wrong will be your fault. They'll complain about your cooking, they won't let you speak Italian to your children. You will be an outsider in your own home."

"It won't be like that—" Filomena was saying when she had a vision of Stanley's mother, her face just like his, a copper's face, giving nothing away. And underneath it perhaps she would be hating Filomena. You never knew with English people. She remembered

"Filomena is not ill, I hope?" said Stan Harker.

"No. My sister is perfectly well."

There was a silence. Stan Harker glanced behind him at the desk clerk, who was watching them, unabashed.

"I'm on my way to Malet Street. I have to talk to the foreman at a building site there. Part of the university, as it happens, the new Senate House. They are finishing the interior and there have been reports of pilfering—tiles, lead piping, that kind of caper. If you like, you could walk with me."

Antonio nodded. He had expected a rogue, a sly charmer who had bewitched his poor sister, and he was disconcerted by this pale solid young man.

Outside Stan pointed to the lamp above the stone steps. "Do you know, this is the only police station in the country that has a white lamp? Queen Victoria didn't like blue, apparently. Prince Albert died in a blue room, and every time she came to the opera the station lamp reminded her of it."

"And so they changed it?"

"Well," said Stan Harker, "she was the queen. Queen of the United Kingdom of Great Britain and Ireland, Empress of India." They fell into step, crossing Long Acre, walking north along Endell Street. "So Filomena has told you about me?"

Antonio nodded. "She says that you have a friendship."

"A friendship?" Stan's mouth contracted for a moment. "Yes."

"You must see that now she is to be married, my sister cannot continue such friendships. She was foolish to permit it in the first place. We are a close-knit community. Word gets about. If her *fidanzato*, Bruno, finds out, Filomena will be in disgrace."

They were approaching the Senate House. It was a grandly designed structure with its looming tower of pure white stone; across the London skyscape only St. Paul's Cathedral was taller.

"A handsome building," Antonio said, without enthusiasm. "It reminds me of Littoria, the new city Mussolini is constructing upon the Pontine marshes. I saw it on my last trip home to Italy."

"Yes," said Stan Harker, "it is a very handsome building. Much of the work has been done by your countrymen, Signor Trombetta. The marble tiles and so forth. All to a very high standard."

Antonio stiffened. "Tile makers come from Friuli, they could almost be described as Austrians. We are from Lazio, my family and I. Do not laugh, Constable Harker. You live in Bermondsey, I believe. I do not think that you would like it if I confused you with a man from Liverpool, or even from Islington."

Stan Harker's smile broadened. "Fair point," he said, and he turned once more to the Senate House, studying its clean cold lines, its blind windows. "I have heard that if the fascists come to power in Britain they will hold their parliament here. That is what Sir Oswald Mosley, the fascist leader, says."

The two men exchanged a look. Stan's eyes were blue and opaque. For an instant Antonio felt sorry that he would never have him as a brother-in-law.

"I suppose you have encountered Sir Oswald Mosley's men in the course of your work," he said.

"I was on duty at the battle of Cable Street, yes. I know what Mosley's fellows can do." Stan paused. "My intentions toward your sister are entirely serious. I wish to marry her. And I think—I am sure—that she wishes to marry me. I have good prospects, I'm in line for promotion. I can provide for your sister, just as I've provided for my parents these last years."

Antonio lifted his shoulders. "It is not possible. Filomena has known Bruno all her life, they were betrothed when she was fourteen. It is how we do things in my country."

"But we are not in your country," Stan said mildly.

"We might as well be, as far as Filomena is concerned. Everything has been arranged according to our customs. And our father has set his heart upon the match. It would be a kind of violence to break it off." Antonio sensed that by explaining this to Stan he was being drawn into a quagmire of disloyalty. I have to stop this conversation, he thought: firmly, crisply, now. "It is no use, Constable

Harker. You must end your friendship with my sister. If it continues—if you try to see her again—you will do her great harm. That is what I came to tell you."

Stan was silent, gazing at the white tower of the Senate House. Then he put out his hand to shake Antonio's.

"I would never willingly harm Filomena. But I will not forget her, Antonio. It is only fair to tell you that."

Antonio did not answer. What in the world could he say? Touching his hat he nodded good-bye to Stan and he turned aside, along the dust-blown street toward Tottenham Court Road.

CHAPTER 13

BRUNO CAME BACK IN APRIL, AND THE TROMBETTAS WELcomed him with a celebratory dinner. After all, said Valentino, they were the closest to family that he had in London: he would soon be a son, a brother, as well as Danila's cousin. Their upstairs neighbor Mauro had agreed to take him in, shifting Renata to a camp bed in the kitchen so that the returning soldier could sleep in comfort.

It was Danila who took charge of preparing the dinner. Filomena did as she was told, stirring the bubbling pan of milk and semolina, dipping finely sliced lamb's liver in seasoned flour, folding candied fruit into snowy, grainy heaps of ricotta. Bruno's favorites, Danila said knowingly, and Filomena nodded, without attempting to contradict her. It gave Antonio a pang to see his sister so downtrodden, but there was no help for it. She will be happier once Bruno is home, he thought, as he went upstairs to change. She will have the status of a bride, she will have a new life to plan, this business with the Englishman will seem a moment of madness.

Antonio was feeling cheerful. His singing lessons were opening for him a gilded new world of possibilities. His teacher, Herr Fischer, was rather formal, and at first Antonio had found him sternly persnickety. Little by little, though, he had come to learn the deep pleasure of self-improvement, hearing his own voice grow stronger and more supple. A week ago Mr. Rodway's uncle Dickie had been enraptured by his singing. He had offered to mention Antonio to one of his friends who ran a nightclub in Piccadilly. It would be a far more profitable engagement than La Rondine, and more prestigious too. As Dickie himself said, wafting smoke from his green cigarette holder, who knows where it might lead?

Danila was standing at the wardrobe, wearing a faded pink petticoat of rayon. Since the baby's birth there was a trim solidity to her, in the curve of her thighs, the weight of her breasts. She would never again be fragile as glass, as she had been on their wedding day. In his crib beside their bed, the baby was sleeping, his eyes closed beneath his fringe of black hair. Antonio felt an impulse to embrace him: his son, the flesh of his flesh.

"Don't," said Danila, as he touched the white honeycombed blanket. "He's only been asleep for five minutes."

Antonio looked at his son's skin with its pure delicious bloom. Once, surely, his father Enrico's skin had been just as unspoiled, just as flowerlike, and now it was leathery with the long years of hard labor. That will never happen to my child, thought Antonio, I swear it. I will succeed, I will prosper, I will shield him from the demons of poverty.

From the wardrobe Danila pulled a cherry-colored dress with a full skirt. "I am so proud of my cousin Bruno. I am surprised Filomena does not boast about him more. She will be marrying a war hero, after all."

"You know Filomena." Antonio was still gazing at his son. "She does not wear her heart upon her sleeve."

"That's not true, Antonio. In many ways your sister can be extremely emotional. But she does not show much enthusiasm for our victory in Africa, or so it seems to me."

"Filomena is not alone. There are many people—Italians as well as British—who believe the *duce* has done our country no good by invading Abyssinia."

"But we have the right to an empire. We were cheated by Britain and France after the war. We were on the winning side, and they did not treat us with the honor our nation deserves. They kept all the spoils for themselves."

Antonio looked up, surprised. His wife did not generally mention politics. "Have you been talking to Valentino?"

"No. Well, yes, but only a little. I have been reading *L'Italia Nostra*. Women should read the newspaper, Antonio. We should have the knowledge to challenge the propaganda against us, especially here in Britain, where Italy has so many enemies."

There was something so undigested about this speech that Antonio could not help smiling. At once tears sprang to Danila's eyes.

"You do not take me seriously, Antonio. You think I am not capable of understanding these things. Now I am a mother I have to know about the world we live in, I have to know the dangers that my son will face." Danila clutched at the bright red wool of her dress. "Yes, I do talk to Valentino, but that is because Valentino explains it to me: how we must put Italy first, or we will lose a part of our soul. And how we should not trust the British, they want only to humiliate us. Nobody understands the art of humiliating foreigners better than the British, Valentino says."

"Oh, Danila," said Antonio, sitting down on the bed, "it is not so simple. You shouldn't swallow everything my brother tells you as if it were gospel truth."

Danila slipped the cherry-colored dress over her head. "Valentino told me that you would not like it," she said, patting the skirt where it draped her hips. "He told me that you would try to change my mind. It is because you mix with outsiders, he says, Englishmen and Jews, not your fellow countrymen."

"Well," said Antonio drily, "if my behavior troubles Valentino perhaps he should be addressing his remarks to me instead of you."

Danila did not answer. She was studying her reflection in the glass, a faint self-absorbed smile on her lips. Antonio watched her scoop up the mass of her hair, ready to wind it into a knot. The nape of her neck was tender and beautiful. Rising to his feet he pressed his lips just below the downy lobe of her ear.

"Don't let's argue, Danila," he whispered, and he slid both his hands about her waist. Danila, her eyes still on the mirror, gave a discouraging flick of her haunches.

"Not now, Antonio."

"But the baby's asleep." Antonio's hands tightened into the yielding warmth of her stomach. Her dress smelled of rose cologne and tantalizingly of her own sweat. "I'll be quiet, I promise, I won't wake him. And I'm sure Filomena can do without you in the kitchen for half an hour."

For a moment Danila stiffened, and he thought she was going to whisk herself from his grasp. Then she relented, turning in his arms to face him.

"Oh, Antonio," she said. Her expression was sweet and rather shy, but there was something coquettish about it, which reminded Antonio of the first blissful days—and nights—of his marriage. It filled him with delight as he bent to kiss her peony mouth.

"THEY ARE NOT a bad people." Bruno waved his glass of prosecco in the air. "Some rotten apples, of course, but you find that in any society, even our own. No, the Abyssinians are not a bad people. They are a more primitive race than ours, that is all. They need a civilizing influence to guide them."

Valentino's eyes glittered with hero worship. He and Bruno had gone to the *fascio* before dinner, so that Bruno could see the Casa d'Italia. Afterward two of Bruno's friends had accompanied them back to Frith Street, confident young Blackshirts with neatly oiled hair. They were squeezed around the makeshift trestle in the Trombettas' kitchen while the women—Danila, Filomena, Renata—hovered about them, clearing plates, refilling glasses.

Antonio spooned up a portion of gnocchi, smeared with tomato sauce. Danila had poured the thick yellow porridge onto the tabletop, just as they did in Lazio, and the men were now helping themselves. He had remembered Bruno, in his absence, as a wiry attractive fellow, and he had been disconcerted to see the real man step through the door. Bruno was short—an inch or so taller than Filomena, no more—and his sunburned skin gave him a wizened look. If Filomena was disappointed by the sight of her *fidanzato* she did not show it but stepped demurely forward to greet him.

"And how were you injured, Bruno? Was it in a battle?" That was their neighbor Mauro, peering eagerly from the end of the table. Bruno took a gulp of wine.

"They do not fight battles, the Abyssinians. They are too cowardly. They lie in wait by the roadside, hidden by the vegetation, taking aim at braver men. That is what happened to me." He slapped his chest on the right, below his collarbone. "The bullet went clean through. I was fortunate; otherwise Filomena here would have no father for her unborn children."

The men all turned toward Filomena, who was carrying the dirty semolina pot into the scullery.

"But the wound is healed now?" Antonio said.

"Oh, yes, it is healed." Bruno raised his empty glass, and Danila ran smiling to fill it, the prosecco foaming from the dark green bottle. "I am not as quick as I should be with my rifle, though, and that is why my commanding officer chose to discharge me. With honor, of course."

"Of course," said one of the Blackshirts. He tried to rise and give the fascist salute, but his chair had no room to budge, and by the time his neighbors had scraped their own chairs sideways the moment had passed; Renata in her best yellow dress was bustling about, clearing the table for the next course.

"I hear that you have joined us in the Fascist Party, Enrico?" Bruno glanced courteously toward the older man. "Valentino tells me that you were inspired by Count Dino Grandi on the night the

Casa d'Italia was opened. What a magnificent building that is. A testament to the patriotism of our community here in London."

"Indeed," said Enrico, who still looked sheepish whenever his membership in the party was mentioned. "There is so much happening there. I would go more often, only it is so expensive for poorer members. Last month Beniamino Gigli, the *duce*'s favorite singer, gave a recital in the Sala dell'Impero. Even Antonio was persuaded to come and hear him."

"Ah, yes," said Bruno. "Are you still singing in your spare time, Antonino?"

"It is more than that, Bruno. I am making good money from my singing engagements. And I have a patron, an Englishman, who has great hopes for the future . . ."

Bruno was not paying attention. "Well, perhaps you will give us a song later? I would love to hear you sing the 'Giovinezza.'"

At the name of the fascist anthem Filomena, who was carrying a dish of fried liver from the stove, put down the plate with a bang. Valentino opened his mouth to rebuke his sister, but thought better of it, and gestured to Renata for more prosecco.

"I have brought you a gift, Filomena," Bruno said, swallowing the last of his wine. "I bought it in Egypt, on my journey home. It is in my kit bag, in the hall. Fetch it for me, will you, Danila?"

The parcel was a soft oblong, wrapped in tissue paper. Filomena took it as though it might burn her. She was standing in the doorway to the scullery, all eyes upon her.

"Don't you want to see what's inside?" said Bruno. For the first time Antonio saw him look shy. He was eager to please Filomena, he just did not want it to show here, in front of the other men. It will be all right, thought Antonio, watching his sister as slowly she undid the string. They will manage well enough, once they are on their own.

In the parcel there was a silk shawl, patterned in lilac, with a long cream fringe. Valentino whistled. "That must have cost you a fortune, Bruno."

"It's not bad, is it?" Complacently Bruno lit a cigarette. "I haggled for it of course, as you do in Cairo. But nothing is too good for my *fidanzata*. Do you like it, Mena?"

Filomena said nothing. The shawl was draped across her hands, and her eyes were devouring it, as if its loveliness pained her. Danila let out a shivering sigh of envy. "Put it on, Filomena," she said.

Lifting one hand Filomena stroked the hair from her forehead. Then she unfolded the shawl and threw it over her head. The colors lightened the sallow tinge of her cheeks, made her eyes deeper and darker than ever.

"You look lovely, Filomena," Antonio said, in a grave voice. His sister lifted her face toward him. Her mouth was trembling. The next moment she let out a wail, and flung the shawl to the ground.

"I cannot do it. I cannot marry you, Bruno. It is no use."

"What?" said Bruno. His cigarette was poised in midair.

"I have tried—believe me, I have done my best. But I cannot do it. You are a kind man, an honorable man, but I do not love you . . ."

Enrico leaped to his feet. "What do you mean, you will not marry him?" he bellowed. "You will do as you are told, Filomena. It is my wish, it was your mother's wish. Who are you to defy the living and the dead?"

"I do not care." There was a flash of red upon Filomena's cheeks. "I cannot do it, you cannot make me do it. It would be death to me to marry Bruno—" She crammed her hand against her lips, as if it were the only way to stop the words flooding out. Then she ran from the room, pushing gawping Renata out of the way.

"Come back," Enrico shouted, "come back at once." The veins at his temple were distended with rage. Filomena had gone, though, her heels clacking like castanets upon the linoleum stair.

Bruno looked from one end of the table to the other, bewildered. "What does she mean, she cannot marry me?"

Enrico turned toward Antonio. "Do you know anything about this, Antonio, my son?" Antonio shook his head, so that he did not have to speak.

"What has happened, in the name of God?" There was a note of accusation in Bruno's voice now. "You are her family, you have been living side by side with her. Something must have happened."

Danila started to cry, lifting her checked apron to her face. "It is not my fault. Truly, Bruno, it is not my fault."

At once Valentino put his arm about her. "Do not blame Danila. She is a mother, she has had other duties, she is not responsible for our sister. I told Papa he should send Filomena home to Lazio after our mother died, I knew she would get foolish ideas, but he would not hear of it—"

"Don't tell me how to manage my own family, Valentino," snapped Enrico. "I am the head of this household, and don't you forget it. If I had wanted to send Mena home to Lazio I would have done it without advice from you."

Valentino grasped Bruno by the elbow. "Come, Bruno. Do not stay here to be insulted. We will go back to the *fascio*. In the *fascio* they have respect for the dignity of men."

Bruno's face was stunned, but he allowed Valentino to pull him upright and sweep him along the corridor. The two Blackshirts looked at each other; then, pushing back their chairs, they followed. One of them sketched a fascist salute as he went.

Enrico put his head in his hands. Through his fingers he said, helplessly: "What are we going to do, Antonino? She has to marry Bruno, it has been agreed since she was fourteen. Our honor is at stake."

"It is nerves, I daresay," said Antonio. "She has not seen Bruno for so long. And she has grown used to her independence."

"You mean, you think she will see sense and change her mind?"

Antonio thought of Stan Harker's pale blue eyes, his unruffled face. "I do not know, Papa," he said.

His father groaned. "Valentino is right. I should have sent her home to Lazio to live with her sister, Paolina. Perhaps we should send her now, right away, before word of this gets out."

Renata, forgotten in the corner, gave a squeak of excitement. Her uncle Mauro scowled, annoyed at her for drawing attention to their presence. He did not often sit down to so good a dinner, and he had been hoping surreptitiously to polish off at least one helping of fried liver before anyone noticed.

"We had better go upstairs, Renata," he said. "It is not polite to stay. Do you know if Bruno will be sleeping with us after all? We went to a great deal of trouble . . ."

Nobody answered. Enrico had buried his face in his hands once more. Antonio looked across at Danila. She had stopped crying, and her pretty mouth was pursed in satisfaction: the peculiar intense satisfaction of one whose worst expectations have been fulfilled. Clicking her tongue she bent to gather the lilac shawl from the floor.

"If Filomena does not want Bruno's present, I will take it. He brought it all the way from Egypt. It would be a shame if it got spoiled."

SUMMER 1938

CHAPTER 14

"YOU'VE NEVER HEARD THE DIVINE ANTONIO SING, HAVE you, my angel?" Dickie asked, as they stepped into the plushly carpeted lobby of the Golden Slipper Club. Olivia unfastened the clasp of her evening cloak.

"Only through the drawing room door," she said.

Dickie handed the cloak to a hovering attendant. "Well, you have a great treat before you. Doesn't she, Herr Fischer?"

Herr Fischer nodded. He was a balding man of fifty, with mournful eyes. On the tip of his long nose was a tuft of hair which gave him the look of a woodland creature from a children's story: a bear, perhaps, or a wise badger. He had the kind of elegant, fussy manners that Olivia thought of as continental, bowing to her, calling her *gnädige Frau*.

"Indeed," he said, "Signor Trombetta is a gifted young man. You will enjoy his singing, I think, Mrs. Rodway."

"Well, come along." Bernard shooed them forward. "Let's find our table. We're late already. I couldn't get Olivia out of the bath."

Olivia dipped her head, embarrassed. She still could not resist the bliss of wallowing in unlimited hot water. It seemed to her the pinnacle of luxury after the penny-in-the-slot geyser in her shared Pimlico bathroom: a decent bath for two pennies, a sumptuous one for three.

"Perhaps she's really a mermaid," Dickie said, sliding his hand about Olivia's elbow. "I must say, she's looking very alluring tonight. Aren't you proud of her, Bernard?"

Bernard glanced at his wife. She was wearing a damson satin dress, bias-cut and snug around the hips, with a dozen bracelets on each slender arm. "I'm always proud of her," he said. "Now, come along. I want to order drinks before Antonio appears."

Silently Olivia followed her husband into the nightclub. That afternoon they had had another argument. He had returned from his lunch engagement with a bottle of scent, wrapped in gilt paper. The moment Olivia took out the stopper she recognized it. It was the powdery floral perfume that Penelope Rodway wore—gallons of it in Olivia's opinion, so that it preceded her when she entered a room, and lingered there long after she had gone.

"But I like that scent," Bernard said, baffled as a schoolboy, when she objected. "It reminds me of home." Then his face closed up, as it always did when arguments did not go his way. He removed the bottle from Olivia's dressing table and placed three five-pound notes there instead. "In that case, you'd better choose something for yourself. Don't mind about what I'd like, it's got nothing to do with me."

Olivia stared at the five-pound notes, large and white, with their portentous black lettering. Bernard paid a monthly allowance into her bank account, but he had never given her cash before. She felt like the elf bride from the folktale, who marries a mortal on condition that he never touches her skin with iron. Well, Bernard had touched her with iron now. She sat frozen before her looking glass. In the story the elf bride throws her husband one last reproachful look and vanishes forever beneath the Welsh hills. Olivia grimaced. Vanishing is all very fine, she thought, but where do you vanish to? There is always going to be another part of the story, unless—until—you die. Folding up the banknotes she tucked them at the back of her drawer, as if they were love letters from another man.

The interior of the Golden Slipper Club was expensively decorated in bronze and gilt. There were chairs with ornate metal backs—beautiful, though not very comfortable—and the lamps on the round tables had pleated shades of yellow Fortuny silk. With a flick of his fingers Bernard summoned the waiter to bring them champagne.

Olivia turned to Herr Fischer, who was sitting beside her, stiffly upright in wing-collared evening dress.

"Have you had any news yet of your sister, Herr Fischer?" she asked. She was afraid that this might be a tactless question, but she could not think of anything else to say, and Bernard liked her to make conversation with their guests. It is a courtesy, my sweet, he said, a note of impatience in his voice. He did not say, It is your job, but she could tell that was what he meant.

"No, nothing." Herr Fischer shook his head. "I have written many times, I have asked friends to write to their friends, but there is nothing."

"Surely it is possible to get out of Austria? Bernard was telling me that Dr. Freud the psychoanalyst and his family have left Vienna. They are living here in London, in Hampstead. It is Hampstead, isn't it, Bernard?"

Herr Fischer gave a small sad smile. "My sister Brigitta did not want to abandon our apartment. She has all her little things there, her china, her furniture. And she thought—she thinks—that I exaggerate the danger of the Nazis. She says that the laws against Jews are aimed only at the wealthy. Ordinary people can have nothing to fear."

"Well," said Olivia, "let us hope that she is right."

"But she is not right, *gnädige Frau*." Herr Fischer fixed his sorrowful eyes intently upon her. "She is terribly wrong. She has become a stateless person in her own homeland, and who knows what will follow? The great powers—Britain, France, the United States of America—have made it clear that they will not intervene."

"Absolutely. It's disgusting," Bernard chimed in, turning from the waiter with his silver ice bucket. "We may hold grand international conferences on the refugee problem, but none of our illustrious politicians dares condemn Hitler's persecution of the Jews. Pure cowardice."

The master of ceremonies appeared, surrounded by an oval pool of brightness, and the room fell murmuringly quiet. Olivia gazed at her champagne glass with its winding threads of bubbles. She felt suddenly nervous on Antonio's account, afraid he might make a fool of himself. When he stepped out, though, she hardly knew him as the down-at-heel singer from the Paradise Ballroom. There was a poise about him, the plane of his face perfectly tilted to catch the light. Then he opened his mouth, and at once she remembered that soaring swooning voice. He was singing an Italian love song, "Tornerai," pitching each line to captivate his audience. It reminded Olivia of how, when she danced, she would focus her whole being upon the angle of her knee, the twist of her head. There was something enthralling about watching a gifted man display his powers; against her will Olivia felt a tremor of admiration.

When Antonio had left the stage Bernard called for more champagne. "A triumph," he said, "no doubt about it. You must be pleased with your pupil, Herr Fischer."

"He has done very well." Cautiously Herr Fischer ran the tip of his tongue over his lips. "He has done even better than I hoped."

"It isn't just his voice," said Dickie, "it's those looks of his. Ravishingly handsome, don't you think, Olivia?"

"I suppose so," said Olivia, "in an obvious way."

"Oh, my angel, you're so sophisticated. The rest of us have simpler tastes. You know, it wouldn't surprise me if Antonio got himself a society mistress, like Hutch. Everyone says Hutch is sleeping with Edwina Mountbatten." Dickie took an appreciative mouthful of champagne. "It's terribly hush-hush. She has to sneak him in by the tradesmen's entrance, so to speak."

A young woman in a polka-dot silk dress was approaching their table. She had pale, rather glaucous eyes and a halo of yellowish hair.

"Hallo, Bernard," she said in a languid voice. She looked, Olivia thought, like the kind of thin-skinned girl who got excused from school netball in winter because her lips had turned blue.

"Iris. How are you?" There was a deliberate heartiness in Bernard's greeting, which made Olivia suspect that once upon a time he had slept with Iris. She occasionally had this impression when she met her husband's female friends, although she never said anything about it, and neither did he.

"Well, and how did you like our friend Antonio? Marvelous, wasn't he?"

"Oh, you *know* him, do you? How exciting."

"I discovered him," Bernard said, preening. "I heard him singing in a scruffy little restaurant in Soho, earning threepenny bits for his pains. He's been having lessons at my house with Herr Fischer here."

Iris studied the Austrian dispassionately for a moment and then turned back to Bernard. "Would you introduce me? I'm throwing an anniversary party for the aged parents next month, and Mummy would adore him."

"Of course. He's coming to join us later. Sit down, have some champagne. Unless you have to go back to your own table?"

"No, the people I came with are so dull, I'd rather stay here." Iris sat in one of the uncomfortable bronze chairs. "This is your wife, is it, Bernard? I heard on the grapevine that you'd got married. None of us thought you'd actually take the plunge."

She said it in a frank, cheerful way, as though it was such common knowledge that he could not possibly be offended. Bernard laid his hand upon Olivia's wrist. "Ah, but I did take the plunge, you see. This is Olivia. My wife, as you correctly surmise."

Olivia extended her arm. Her bracelets click-clacked noisily. "Delighted to meet you," she said, in the voice of a duchess.

"You're English." Iris sounded disappointed. "I thought you were a continental of some sort. That's what I'd heard: that Bernard had married a refugee. Someone exotic."

"Olivia *is* quite exotic, my dear," said Dickie, "though she's also deliciously English. Ah, here comes Antonio. Our bright particular star. Bernie, call the waiter to bring another glass."

ANTONIO, EMERGING INTO the smoke-filled nightclub, felt slack and dazed with relief. Stray glances flickered toward him and lingered as he moved between the tables: a clear sign of success.

Both Bernard and Dickie stood to welcome him, clapping their hands.

"Bravo," said Dickie, "*bravissimo*, Antonio. That was quite wonderful."

Antonio smiled, tugging at his collar. He was wearing a new suit; his ancient one, so carefully pressed by Filomena, was far too shabby for an engagement like this. Beneath it his skin was damp and hot.

"And you, maestro?" He turned with deference to Herr Fischer. "What did you think?"

"Very good." Herr Fischer cleared his throat. "Not perfect, of course, nobody is ever quite perfect. But we will talk about that at your next lesson."

"Would you like some champagne, Signor Trombetta?" It was Olivia. Antonio had seen her a couple of times in Bedford Square, but not like this, in damson satin and war paint, and once again he was struck by the beauty of her face. There was a stillness about her, at once deep and watchful. He had the sense that it had taken a great effort of will to achieve it.

"Just a little, thank you," he said. "I have to sing again in an hour."

"Oh, goody." Iris put out her hand to introduce herself. She did it imperiously, as if she expected him to bow like a gigolo and kiss her fingers. "I thought you were splendid. In fact, I wanted to ask if you'll sing at a party I'm holding next month."

"You should do it, Antonio," Bernard said, rubbing his finger and thumb together in a jocular mime of wealth. He made no attempt to hide the gesture from Iris, who laughed as she rattled off time, date, place. She was staring at Antonio with a wide-eyed, greedy expression.

"I will be delighted to sing for you," he said, "if I can find the time. I have a family wedding that day. My wife and I are the *compari d'anello:* the guardians of the ring. Best man and bridesmaid, I suppose you'd call it."

His mention of a wife did not perturb Iris. "I'm sure you'll manage it. I must say, I've set my heart on having you there."

"You can't cross Iris, Antonio," Bernard said in a teasing voice. "She's like a cat. One minute all lazy and purring, and then she pounces, and you're done for."

"Well, you should know, darling," Iris said, without rancor. There was a silence, rather awkward. Dickie wiped his forehead with his silk handkerchief.

"It's stifling in here," he said, and indeed his round, childlike face was mottled with crimson. "Isn't it ridiculous that even in midsummer we men have to wear the full regalia, dinner jackets and white waistcoats and lord knows what, while women are allowed to go half-naked?"

"Ah, but in winter it's the other way round," Olivia said. "In winter we're shivering and you can be as cozy as you please."

Dickie smiled. "You're quite right, my angel. What a logical young woman you are." The band struck up a quickstep, brisk and inviting. "You young people should dance. Don't mind Herr Fischer and me, we're happy to sit and chatter about music. Antonio, dance with Mrs. Rodway. She's a perfectly marvelous dancer."

Antonio hesitated. Olivia's limbs would be cool and immaculate, she would feel the dampness of his skin, it would be mortifying. All the same he was about to speak when Bernard intervened.

"Forgive me, Antonio. I know it's your night of triumph, but every so often a man wants the privilege of dancing with his own wife. Especially when she's the most beautiful woman in the room."

An expression of startled pleasure lit Olivia's face. Antonio watched as Bernard spun her across the floor. He had no right to feel aggrieved—he had not even wanted to dance with her—and yet he felt a pang of loss, to have that opportunity snatched from him.

His disappointment must have shown in his expression because Iris put her hand consolingly upon his wrist. "Never mind, Signor Trombetta," she said. "You can dance with me. I know a girl shouldn't blow her own trumpet, but the fact is I'm a perfectly marvelous dancer too."

CHAPTER 15

AT THE END OF JULY PENELOPE RODWAY CAME TO LONDON, and Bernard took her to lunch at the Savoy. Penelope liked the Savoy. It reminded her of elaborate five-course dinners before the Great War, when she was a sweet-faced debutante and the world was still a settled place. She was in London to fulfill a string of pleasurable errands: visiting the hairdresser and the corsetiere, having her face healthily pummeled by Mrs. Gladys Furlonger, the Canadian masseuse who had treated Mrs. Simpson's poor complexion.

Penelope's eyes darted to and fro across the restaurant; she was disappointed not to see anyone she recognized, or, more to the point, anyone who might recognize her. What she wanted was a trio of men, at least, to leap up from their tables, crying, Penelope! How wonderful to see you! You haven't changed at all.

"Lionel is so dull," she complained, poking at a shrimp soufflé with her fork. Penelope's taste was for light, expensive food—oysters, Scottish salmon, out-of-season fruit—which she pushed fastidiously around her plate as though its function were to be judged, not eaten. "All he talks about is the risk of war. I don't want to think about war, Bernie. I lived through it once, I don't see why I should go through it again. Politicians can always avoid it if they want to, can't they?"

"They can, yes, but it depends at what price," said Bernard, who tolerated a much higher level of political naivety in his mother than in anybody else, including Olivia. "Does Lionel think that we should be doing more to stop Hitler?"

"Oh, I've stopped listening to what he says. It gets on my nerves." Penelope thrust out her chin in a not very good impression of Lionel. "It's a serious matter, you know, Mother. We could be at war with Germany before the year is out." She lit a cigarette and blew smoke effusively over her shoulder. "Now, tell me, darling: why didn't you bring Olivia with you? Don't tell me that you've quarreled already."

"Of course not. I wanted to have you to myself, that's all." In fact Bernard had decided not to tell Olivia about the lunch. Since their visit to Cheshire his wife and his mother had met two or three times. On those occasions Penelope had been deliberately, remorselessly *kind* to Olivia, who as a consequence disliked her more than ever.

Penelope laid her free hand upon his sleeve. "You've always been such a generous boy, Bernie. A boy who thinks about others. I can say this to you now, but with those endless refugees of yours, I was afraid that you'd end up marrying a foreigner. A noisy red-faced Czech girl or one of those irritating Russians who insists they have royal blood. Or even—I'm sorry, Bernie, I know this will offend you, but I can't help how I feel—even a Jew."

"I know that Lionel thinks Olivia is impossible," Bernard said, with satisfaction. Penelope did not answer.

"I blame Dickie. He encourages you to be Bohemian, and it doesn't suit you." Taking her hand from his sleeve she pushed at the lock of fair hair falling over his forehead. "I hope you're not going to wait too long before you have children, Bernie."

"Oh . . ." Bernard shifted his weight from one buttock to the other. He had always imagined that one day he and Olivia would have children, but the prospect lay vaguely in the future, not to be considered now. In the meantime he had no intention of discussing his sex life with his mother.

"Well, I don't want my only grandchildren to be Lionel's. At least Olivia's a looker. She doesn't have the absurd modern view, does she, that children ruin your figure? It's nonsense, you only have to look at me. My waist's as small as it was when I was twenty-two. And it's good for a woman to have children. It gives her a purpose in life."

Bernard smiled. Well, perhaps she's right, he thought. Children would settle Olivia, she would have an occupation, she wouldn't be so restless. And I would be a wonderful father, I am sure of it; so much kinder than my own father.

Penelope was looking pensive now, head on one side, birdlike. "Does she make you happy, Bernie? Olivia, I mean?"

"Of course," said Bernard. "That is, as happy as it is possible for any thinking man to be. Look, Mother, here comes the waiter. Why don't you have *omelette surprise* for pudding? You know how much you love ice cream."

On the night before Bruno's wedding all the men went to drink at the *fascio*. Antonio accompanied them, dressed in his expensive new suit; he had to sing at the Golden Slipper later that evening.

Bruno's engagement to Renata had been announced in June. He told Enrico first, in private, out of courtesy to the man who should have been his father-in-law. They would be married in London: a simple wedding, without fuss.

"I cannot travel to Lazio, so soon after returning to my job at the hotel," Bruno said. "It would be asking for trouble, and besides . . ."

A silence, cloudy with disappointment, hung in the air. Magnanimously Enrico embraced Bruno, as if he were indeed his son-in-law. His chagrin he kept to himself until he was at home, in the Trombettas' kitchen.

"Well, Filomena," he said, leveling his eyes upon his daughter, "you have lost the love of a good man. You have squandered it as if it were nothing, spitting it out like the pips from an apple. I hope that you are pleased with your conduct."

Filomena was at the stove, cooking some fritters of onion and minced meat. Her face flushed, but she did not speak.

"You're a fool, Filomena." Valentino looked up from his copy of *L'Italia Nostra*, which he was reading at the table. "You'll never find a husband now."

Filomena spun round from the stove, mouth open. For a moment Antonio thought she was going to snap, and reveal her secret. She thought better of it, though, and turned back to her frying pan, scraping and prodding ferociously at the fritters.

"Bruno's engagement won't make any difference, Mena," he said, when they were alone. "You know that, don't you? Papa would never agree to let you marry an Englishman."

"Yes," breathed Filomena, "I know that. I am not a fool."

"Have you been in touch with Constable Harker? Have you told him what has happened?"

Filomena let out another breath. Then, so quietly that he could scarcely hear her, she said: "I made you a promise, Antonio. Do you think that I won't keep it?"

IN THE BAR of the *fascio* Valentino was playing cards with a couple of Blackshirts. It was a game called *scopa* that he liked because you left your tricks on the table, to show that you were winning.

"Well, good luck to you, Bruno, my boy." Enrico's cough had improved during the summer, but his skin had taken on a sallow look, like a crumpled sheet of newspaper. "I wish you every happiness. We all wish you happiness, don't we, Antonio?"

Bruno was leaning against the bar without saying much. His eyes were as wide as an owl's.

"It will be a fresh start for you," Enrico went on. "A new wife, a new home. You are pleased with your lodgings, I hope?"

Bruno nodded. Now that he was to be married he had moved from his cramped quarters at Mauro's to a room in Maddox Street, not far from the hotel where he worked. He had managed to get his job back after his return from Africa; a piece of good fortune, since Renata would leave the laundry in Goodge Street after the wedding. It was not right, Bruno declared, for his wife to continue slaving in another man's service. If he could not afford to keep her, well, he should not be getting married.

In the corner Valentino gave a whoop of triumph as he won the game of *scopa*. "I am invincible, I am like the *duce*'s army, I cannot be beaten. Time to pay your dues, oh vanquished ones."

The men were reaching into their pockets, disgruntled, when the door from the marble Sala dell'Impero was flung open. It was the secretary of the London *fascio*, Bernardo Patrizi. He toured the Casa d'Italia most evenings to greet the club's members, accompanied by a couple of officials. The men stood to attention and gave the fascist salute—even Antonio, to avoid attracting attention, although he did it halfheartedly.

From the doorway Signor Patrizi gazed benignly at Bruno. "I hear that you are to be married, my friend. I wish you happiness, and many children. The new Roman empire needs the sons of good fascists."

Bruno opened his mouth and closed it again, like a fish. "You do me a great honor, sir," he managed to say, but it was too late: Signor Patrizi had turned back toward the Sala dell'Impero. The official behind him gave a compassionate smile, as if he understood that Bruno's awe had struck him dumb. He was a handsome man in his thirties, with piercing blue eyes.

"Times are hard for honest Italians," he said, sliding a coin into Bruno's palm. "We in the *fascio* recognize that. If you find yourself struggling, my friend, remember that we are here to help."

Bruno held the money in the hollow of his hand, staring. The official cast his bright blue glance about the room.

"Ah, Valentino. Even off duty it seems the *fascio* is a second home to you. Excellent. And this as I recall is your father? I'm glad to see you here. We must draw strength from our fellow Romans. It will help us to walk among our enemies with our heads held high."

"It is a pleasure—" Enrico began, but the official had moved on, fixing his eyes upon Antonio.

"And who is this? I do not think I have encountered you before."

"It is my son Antonio," Enrico said. "He works with me in our kiosk—"

"But not enrolled within the *fascio*, I believe? I do not think you have paid your twelve lire to be one of us, have you, my friend?" There was a glassy jollity about the official's face.

"No," said Antonio, "I have not."

The official held his gaze, searchingly; then, still smiling, he looked away. "I hope that in due course you will recognize your duty to the fatherland, Antonio. The time is coming, you know, when we must stand up and be counted. Better then to be among patriots."

THE DRINKING WENT on until past nine o'clock. Bruno's eyes grew wider and more owl-like than ever. Valentino won three further games of *scopa* before one of the Blackshirts, irked by his jubilance, led him off to play billiards instead.

"I must go to work," said Antonio to his father, whose eyelids were beginning crêpily to droop. "I'll walk you home first though, Papa. You're looking tired."

At once Enrico straightened in his chair. "No," he hissed, "honor demands that I stay. Bruno must know that there is no bad blood between us. He must know that we forgive him for his marriage."

At the word *marriage* Bruno looked up blearily. There was an air of bewilderment about him, as if the events of his own life had moved too fast for him and he could not keep up.

"Antonio," he said, reaching out his hand, "my friend. My brother."

Hardly your brother now, Antonio thought, but he accepted Bruno's hand. He felt sorry for him. After the first triumph of his return nobody had showed much interest in Bruno's adventures in Africa. There was greater excitement about the Italians leaving for Spain, to support General Franco's army. Besides, there were other men who had fought in Abyssinia, with more glorious tales of war than Bruno's; louder voices too.

"You hoped that in spite of everything I would marry your sister, Antonino." Bruno spoke with the slurred precision of a very drunk man, mortally determined to make himself clear. "Don't pretend, I know you did. I loved Filomena, I believed she would be my wife, I thought about her all the time I was in Africa. But after that night—"

"It is all right, Bruno. You do not have to explain."

Bruno's grip tightened upon Antonio's hand. "No, you don't understand. When she threw my present to the floor—"

"I know," said Antonio. "I do not blame you, Bruno."

"But you don't understand what it was *like*. In front of her family, Antonio. In front of my cousin Danila, in front of my comrades from the *fascio*. How could I forget? It is too much to ask." Bruno looked at his glass, found it empty, and looked again, to be quite sure. Then he said: "Renata is a good girl. She will be a good mother to my children. And I do not wish to be a bachelor all my life. No, I will be happy with Renata. I am certain of it."

CHAPTER 16

THE SIGHT OF THE SOUTH DOWNS, GLIMPSED THROUGH THE carriage window, gave Olivia a thrill of recognition. It was the first time she had seen that curved green horizon since she left for London, and she had not realized how clearly it was etched upon her mind, deeper than any conscious memory. She closed her eyes for a moment. It made her throat ache to think of her lonely, thwarted childhood.

Olivia was spending the weekend in Sussex with Uncle Dickie. You've never seen my pretty house, have you, my angel? Dickie had said, while they were having dinner in his tiny, Pompeii-red dining room in Chelsea. Yes, Bernard, I know you're too busy to leave London, but there's no reason why Olivia shouldn't have a trip to the country. You'll just have to manage without her.

The train slowed as it drew into Haywards Heath. A couple of smartly dressed women, on their way home from shopping in London, gathered up their bags to alight. They inclined their heads politely to Olivia, in her silk blouse, her beautiful amber suit, her ivory kid gloves. These were the kind of women for whom, once upon a time, Olivia's mother, Daisy, had made clothes, kneeling before them with pins in her mouth, pretending it was her mistake when their waistbands were too tight. Graciously Olivia returned the women's smiles. Oh, I am a fraud, she thought.

She stretched out her gloved hand for the newspaper she had bought for the journey. There was another crisis in Eastern Europe, some standoff with Hitler over German nationals living in Czechoslovakia, and Olivia was trying to understand what it meant. Bernard had told her about it, of course, but the way he explained these things made her mind switch off. It was partly his tone of voice, patient, but with a note of exasperation; it was also that he talked for too long. Just when Olivia had grasped the point he would add another fact, another theory, and she would lose the thread once more.

A string of names leaped from the black newsprint: Bohemia, Moravia, Silesia. Magical names, Olivia thought. They conjured up pictures of turreted castles and tumbling russet-leaved woods, and yet she knew there was something ugly about the whole business, it was a rattling of sabers, an excuse for war. Where will it end? Bernard had said, throwing up his hands in despair. We should have stood firm sooner, first on the Rhineland, then on Austria. That is what you do with bullies: you stand firm.

Olivia tried to settle herself more comfortably in the cushioned seat. She was bleeding. Her period had come on two days before, painfully; after lunch she had gone to bed with some aspirin. A few minutes later Bernard appeared, bringing a hot water bottle.

"Did you know," he said, "the rubber hot water bottle was invented by a Croat from Austria-Hungary, a man named Eduard Penkala? He called it the Termofor." Bernard gave a nervous grin, dallying beside the window. "His invention didn't do him much good, though. He died of pneumonia when he was fifty."

Olivia thought he must be gabbling because he was embarrassed: Bernard, sisterless, was in awe of menstruation. She settled the hot water bottle on her stomach and waited for him to go. Instead he sat down on the edge of the bed.

"Poor darling," he said, taking her hand. "I had hoped that maybe this month—well, you know."

Olivia stared. She and Bernard had ceased to use contraception soon after their marriage, but it had been in a casual, don't-let's-bother way; they had never talked about starting a family.

"Penelope is looking forward to having grandchildren," Bernard said. "That is, she's looking forward to our grandchildren. She thinks they'll be more interesting than Lionel's brood, and she wants to enjoy them before she's old and gaga." He chafed at Olivia's fingers, which in spite of the hot water bottle were cold. "That's a good sign, don't you think, darling? It shows that she's accepted you into the family."

The words ran silently through Olivia's head. I thought you didn't want them to accept me, I thought you married me to defy them: your outrageous misfit wife.

"Well, you have a nice long sleep. I've got to go out, there's a meeting this afternoon to talk about the Czech crisis, but Avril will bring you anything you need." Leaning forward Bernard kissed her on the forehead. "Maybe we'll have better luck next month, eh?"

Olivia wriggled down beneath the brown silk eiderdown. The pain shimmered from her pelvis to her spine. It echoed that other pain, bent double in the mildewed lavatory in Pimlico. My miscalculation, she thought, and a tide of misery rose within her.

WHAT OLIVIA CALLED her miscalculation had happened, as these things do, when she least expected it. She had been a dance hostess for nearly five years and she had grown used to that twilight world, sleeping until noon, counting her tips, rinsing her stockings. The commercial traveler from Cardiff had moved on, but there had been others, three or four of them, whom Olivia had learned to treat with a salty detachment. The younger girls asked advice from her now, instead of the other way about. He claims he's serious, but I think there's a fiancée at home in Essex, they would say mournfully, and Olivia would smile, elegant, contemptuous. Oh, there's always a fiancée at home in Essex, she said.

She had thought herself pretty much fireproof when, queuing for the cinema on her evening off, she heard a familiar voice.

"Olivia? Good lord. It is you, isn't it?"

Olivia glanced up with the haughty air she employed to quell wandering hands on the dance floor. It was Jimmy, the stage manager from the Palace Theatre: her first lover. He looked older but he had not lost his rumpled tawny charm, and he seemed delighted to see her. They went for a drink at the Coach and Horses in Greek Street. The girls in the pub stole surreptitious glances at Jimmy, but for once he had eyes only for Olivia.

"I'm going to buy you a Guinness, you need fattening up. No, actually, it suits you. It makes you look *très distinguée.* All tits and cheekbones. You've really grown up, darling, haven't you?"

Jimmy's attention brought back memories of her younger, innocent self, startled to find herself the object of desire. Between this nostalgia and two glasses of Guinness it seemed natural—pleasurable, even—to go back to his flat in Romilly Street. Just once, she thought woozily, for old times' sake. It can't do any harm.

They were already naked when Jimmy, reaching to his bedside table, said: "Damn it, I was sure I'd got a condom. I don't suppose you . . ."

Olivia shook her head. "I haven't got anything with me. It's probably all right, though. I'm due to get the curse next week."

Jimmy looked at her admiringly. "My, my. You have changed, my darling. I must say, I rather adore you like this. You used to be a bit of a dozy Dora." He slid back into the bed. "Well, I'll be careful anyway, I promise."

It did not take long for Olivia to realize what had happened. She tried to keep it from the other girls, but of course word got out; she could tell from the way they looked at her. How are the mighty fallen, their glances said. Jimmy would probably have given her the money to help her out, handing it over with that hard-done-by look of his, but Olivia was too proud to ask. Instead she sold the last bits of jewelry she had inherited from her mother: her wedding ring, a silver locket, a cameo brooch with a Medusa's head upon it.

The abortionist was a former doctor, pallid with a smattering of gingery hair. The fact that he had been struck off for misconduct did not hamper his sense of superiority. He peered at Olivia through round metal spectacles, as if it demeaned him to be breaking the law on her account.

"Will I—will it stop me from ever having children?" asked Olivia, as she lay on the narrow couch, knees raised, staring at the cream distempered ceiling. The smell of antiseptic, which should have been reassuring, filled her with horror. She wanted to ask, Will it hurt? but she was afraid of what the answer might be.

The doctor was sterilizing his hooks and knives in a pan of boiling water. "It's possible," he said. "To be frank with you, young lady, you should have thought of that before."

DICKIE'S HOUSE WAS a sprawling, flint-clad cottage just below Firle Beacon. As he had said, it was very pretty, with a garden full of cornflowers and pink rambling roses, leading to a small orchard. They sat upon the sunlit terrace drinking Dickie's favorite, Negronis.

"A barman in Florence taught me how to mix them. He claimed that he used to make them for the Count de Negroni himself, although I suspect it was a fib." Dickie handed Olivia her glass with its clinking ice and its twist of orange. "Katya liked Negronis too, you know."

"I'm not surprised, if you made them like this." Olivia felt strangely joyful. Perhaps it is because I am in the country, she thought, perhaps this is where I belong, not in London at all. She did not want to believe, even for a moment, that she was happy because she was away from Bernard.

Dickie was watching the gardener, a ruddy-faced boy in a collarless shirt, cross the lawn from the orchard. When the boy came within earshot he called: "Plums, Fred?"

"Greengages." Fred held out his trug with a sweet lazy smile. "Ripe as you like."

Dickie took one of the green and gold plums and bit into it. "Pure nectar," he said, catching the juice from his chin with his little finger. "Olivia? No? Go on, then, Fred. Take them through to Mrs. Gander in the kitchen."

"It's so beautiful here." Olivia stretched out her long legs. Above her loomed the snub-nosed mass of Firle Beacon, like a benign watchful spirit. It seemed to her that the very beat of her heart was slower, calmer. "I'm astonished you can ever bring yourself to leave and go back to Chelsea."

"Oh, it's a rural idyll. Hills, sunlight, wood smoke, plum trees, boys. What could be more like paradise? You and Bernard should find a place in the country. Except, of course, Bernard would never go there. He would be full of the best intentions but there would always be something new to keep him in London: one of his committees, one of his protégés." Dickie fitted a cigarette into his jade holder. "Is he neglecting you, my angel?"

"No. What Bernard does is important, I admire him for it. It is only—"

"You wish that he would spend some time with you, instead of rushing madly from one enthusiasm to the next. I'm afraid that is Bernard, my sweet. I love my nephew very much, he is a clever man, a generous man, but you could not commend him for his staying power. None of his passions last long."

"Including his passion for me?" Olivia said. Dickie paused, breathing a blue scented plume of smoke into the air. Then he reached for Olivia's hand and kissed it. She knew that he was searching for a diplomatic way of saying, Yes, including you.

"That will be different," he managed at last. "In my experience the best marriages are never built on passion."

"It is all right, Dickie," said Olivia. "You don't have to be tactful. I've learned what Bernard is like. He didn't fall in love with me: he fell in love with the idea of me." Even as she spoke Olivia recognized, for the first time, that this was true. It gave her a frisson of satisfaction, to have at last named the thing that had been troubling her.

"Of course he did. We only ever fall in love with ideas." Dickie flicked a gray worm of ash from his cigarette. "Reality would send us screaming to the madhouse. But Bernard does it more than most. He's a born romantic. The trouble is, he doesn't realize it. As that great connoisseur of human nature William Shakespeare would say, he hath ever but slenderly known himself."

They sat in silence, gazing at the dappled lawn, the plum trees, the curve of the South Downs. What would happen, Olivia thought, if I confided in Dickie? What would happen if I said, Once upon a time I had an abortion, and now I am afraid that I will never have children? She looked at Dickie's face, wise and faintly waspish, and she opened her mouth to speak.

Before she could say anything Dickie stubbed out his cigarette and patted her briskly on the knee.

"Come on now, drink up, my angel. It's time to get dressed for dinner. We're having duck with damson sauce, and plum tart for pudding. Mrs. Gander makes the most wonderful pastry, you can taste the butter in it. My mouth's watering already."

CHAPTER 17

As summer ended the tension in London grew. After months of rumbling thunder it seemed the storm was now, at last, about to break. Trenches were hacked out in the parks to provide makeshift bomb shelters, scarring the grass with their deep zigzag lines; there were calls for air raid wardens and auxiliary firemen to join the civil defense forces. Wherever you went you heard whispers. Nazi bombs would pulverize the city within hours, the government had a secret cache of sixty thousand coffins, there would be chaos in the streets as London panicked beneath the onslaught.

In September loudspeakers across the city called on residents to queue for their gas masks. Danila, who had just returned from mass in St. Patrick's church, refused to go.

"It is nonsense. The authorities are trying to frighten us, to turn us against the fascist cause. There isn't going to be a war, the *duce* will intervene personally to prevent it. That is what Valentino says."

"And I suppose if there is a war the *duce* will intervene personally to prevent our son from being gassed?" Antonio said in exasperation, as he put on his coat to join the queue. He was feeling tired and anxious. The night before he had performed at a society party: a subdued affair despite the champagne and the glittering dresses, overshadowed by talk of Czechoslovakia. "Come, Danila. It is foolish to risk the child's life."

Danila's mouth pursed into a sullen rosebud, but she went upstairs to fetch the baby. He was a stout child now, nearly a year old, dressed in white piqué leggings and a bonnet that Danila had made herself. He wriggled in his mother's arms, fractious at being woken.

"I will carry him, Danila, if you like," said Filomena. "He is getting too heavy for you." She and Enrico were waiting in the hall, ready to set off. As for Valentino, he was still in bed. He had come home in the small hours of the morning—out carousing, Enrico said indulgently—and nothing could waken him, not even the loudspeakers calling from Soho Square.

"No, thank you." Danila struggled to hoist the child to her shoulder. She did not like Filomena handling her baby. It was as though she feared he might soak up some rebellious influence through his aunt's touch.

The queue for gas masks was, like most London queues, grumbling but obedient. As he shepherded his family toward the hall, Antonio heard the disgruntled word *Eyeties* once or twice, but to his face everyone was polite. A couple of people stepped aside to give Danila and her child more room, and one man, a leather-cheeked fellow in a tweed cap, offered Enrico a Fisherman's Friend to ease his cough.

"It won't be long, Papa," said Antonio. He could smell eucalyptus from the lozenge that Enrico had, after some hesitation, accepted. Behind them a man was complaining that it was a quarrel between foreigners, nothing to do with Britain, we ought to keep our noses out. Someone else shushed him swiftly.

At last the queue snaked inside the hall, where three air raid wardens were doling out masks in square cardboard boxes. A small girl with pigtails was chortling gleefully over hers, with its red rubber face and its long blue snout.

"Well, one happy customer," said the warden, a plump woman in overalls and scarlet lipstick. Reaching forward she scooped the baby from Danila's arms. "Now, my little princess, let's see what we can find for you."

"He's a boy," said Antonio. He could feel Danila bridling.

She had understood what the warden had said, although her English was not good enough to answer back. Doubtfully the plump woman poked at the baby's lacy bonnet. Antonio laid his hand upon Danila's arm, to stop her from snatching her child away.

"You have special masks for babies, don't you?" he said.

The air raid warden pulled out a khaki and black contraption, with a concertina-shaped tube on one side. "Pop the little cherub in this. You have to strap him in, and then operate the air pump here—do you see?—so he doesn't breathe in the gas." She spoke very fast, demonstrating flaps and buckles as she spoke. Danila threw Antonio a furious uncomprehending look.

"I'll show you," said the air raid warden, and she slid the rubber hood over the baby's head. At once he began to shriek, in loud peals of fear and rage. The warden smiled.

"He'll get used to it, they all do," she was saying when Danila seized the baby. Dragging him free of the khaki rubber, she threw the mask to the floor.

"It's horrible!" she screamed, in Italian. "How can you do this to your own wife, your own child? I'd rather die, Antonio. I'd rather choke to death."

The baby's face was wet and crimson. Clasping him to her shoulder Danila pushed her way through the queues and ran into the street. Several heads turned to watch her. There was the complacent sound of tongues clicking in disapproval.

"That's Eyeties for you," the air raid warden said serenely. "Screaming and wailing at the first sign of trouble. Let's hope that if there is a war, they'll be on the first boat home."

DANILA SULKED FOR the rest of the afternoon, sitting on the bed with the baby in her arms. Antonio did his best to persuade her to return for her gas mask but she was immovable.

"You cannot ask me, Antonio, it is not fair to ask me. If we were in Italy we would not need these things, these masks. We would be safe, there would not be all this stupid talk of gas and bombs. And I would have my mother to help me with the baby, instead of being alone like this . . ." She began to cry, her tears dripping upon the baby's white bonnet.

"Danila, you're not alone. You have me, you have Filomena. We are your family now." Antonio reached out to comfort her, but she threw him off, clutching at the child with a noisy sob. He gave a sigh, and went downstairs. Better to leave her in peace, he thought, until she had calmed down.

Valentino was in the yard, sprawled on the black metal fire escape, lazily smoking a cigarette.

"I wish you wouldn't talk to my wife about politics, Valentino," said Antonio. "It makes her obstinate."

Valentino's crumpled face was the picture of innocence. "But why shouldn't I? She has a right to understand what is happening. You can't keep her shut away like a doll."

"I don't want her to be shut away. I want her to know the truth, that's all, not some moonshine you've heard in the *fascio*. And the truth is that this country could be at war before the month is out."

"Nonsense. There isn't going to be a war. In a week or two Hitler will turn to the *duce* for help. He will realize that on his own he cannot persuade Britain and France to back down, and he will ask our great leader to step in and broker an agreement."

"I don't see why. Hitler has made it clear that he intends to march into Czechoslovakia, and no threat of war can stop him."

Valentino blew a smoke ring across the yard, where it dissolved in the autumn sunshine. "He's bluffing. He's not prepared to fight, he wants the Sudetenland without coming to blows. And Mussolini is the only man who can arrange it. Nobody else has any influence over Hitler. The *duce* holds the balance of power in Europe. Everyone trusts him."

"I am not sure that *trust* is the word," said Antonio. He did not really believe Valentino, and yet he found his brother's confidence perversely reassuring.

"It will be good for Italy," Valentino went on. "Hitler will be grateful, Britain and France will have more respect for the *duce*, we will be well placed to regain our empire." He ground out his spent cigarette beneath his heel. "And now that I have explained the political situation to you, Antonio, my brother, I must go. I have an assignation with a beautiful woman, and it would be churlish to turn up late."

"I thought Claudia's husband was at home on Sundays."

"Oh, it's not Claudia. I'm tired of Claudia, she's too clingy, she does nothing but weep and whine. And she's lost her looks anyway now that she's pregnant." Valentino sighed. "The baby's due in the spring. Claudia's terrified that something will go wrong, that God will punish her for being an unfaithful wife. It's very boring. Women, ha?"

"It is her husband's child, I presume?" said Antonio in a dry voice.

"Who can tell? I'm not sure Claudia knows herself. I tried to be careful, but there's a limit to what a man can do. It won't matter, though." Valentino grinned and ran his index finger along his beaky profile. "Her husband Pasquale's got a big nose too."

In Bedford Square Olivia watched Konrad Fischer cradle a cup of nearly cold tea. He had started to linger after his singing lessons as though he could not bear to return to his lodgings in Riding House Street. There had still been no word from his sister in Vienna.

"We have to reach an agreement with Germany," Bernard said. He had just returned from a Labour Party meeting, to discuss what would happen in case of war. "A clear agreement to show Hitler once and for all that we are serious, we will not allow him to expand his territory willy-nilly. Perhaps that will call a halt to his ambitions."

"But it will not," said Herr Fischer, in a mournful, singsong voice. "Once he has the Sudetenland he will swallow up the rest of Czechoslovakia, and then he will turn his greedy eyes upon Poland. He will be like a German Napoléon, stretching his grip across Europe. In the meantime, wherever he goes he will persecute the Jewish people. Your excellent welfare societies, Mr. Rodway, will be overwhelmed by refugees, homeless people who have lost everything. And they will be the lucky ones."

Olivia leaned attentively forward. She wished that Herr Fischer would finish his cold tea and go. She and Bernard were meeting Dickie for the first night of a new play, and it was already past six o'clock; if he did not leave soon there would be no time to bathe and dress. The thought made her feel guilty. It was unkind to shoo away a lonely, troubled man so that they would not be late for cocktails; her husband would be ashamed of her if he knew what she was thinking.

"What is the alternative, though?" Bernard was saying. "I too believe that Hitler is a monster, that the fascist cause is evil, but anything, surely, is better than war."

"Is it? It will come to war sooner or later, Mr. Rodway. Better sooner, in my opinion. More lives will be saved."

"At least if we reach an agreement with Hitler now we will be buying time," said Olivia, who had heard Dickie say this. "We can prepare ourselves for war: rearm, improve our civil defense."

Herr Fischer gave a shrug. "So can the Germans. It makes no difference, *gnädige Frau*." At last he drank his tea, and carefully setting his cup upon the saucer he rose to his feet. "But I must go. I am sure that you have many things to occupy you, I do not wish to overstay my welcome."

Bernard threw a sharp look at Olivia, as though she had somehow precipitated Herr Fischer's departure. She flushed. "Please stay," she said. "Let us offer you a glass of sherry . . ."

She was too late, though. Herr Fischer had already reached the door, his music case in his hand. For an instant he paused and then, with a prim desolate bow, he left the room.

IN THE THEATER the audience was restless. Nobody could settle to the play, which was a gentle family comedy: *Dear Octopus* by Dodie Smith, with Marie Tempest and John Gielgud in it.

"Oh, dear," said Dickie at the interval, fanning his round pink face with his program, "it's going to be a disaster, they're hardly laughing at all. The woman in the seat next to me is so fidgety, you'd think she had ants in her pants."

Bernard was not paying attention. He could hear a man's voice, talking excitably, on the far side of the room. "Hush," he said, "there's some news. Listen."

The whisper gradually spread through the crowd in the theater foyer. Hitler had invited the prime minister, Neville Chamberlain, for talks in his mountain retreat in Berchtesgaden, and Chamberlain had accepted; he would fly to Bavaria the following day. Little by little the taut elegant faces eased. Nobody dared to raise a glass, but the atmosphere lightened. The word *peace* began to bubble through the Queen's Theatre like an underground spring.

During the second act the audience relaxed, determined to have fun. In the darkness of the auditorium Bernard gazed at the stage: a dinner scene, candlelit, the family reunited while handsome John Gielgud proposed a toast. Bernard's own family had never been like that. Nevertheless he felt a joyous nostalgia, a sense of rightness, as though this was something to which they could all belong. Impulsively he reached for Olivia's hand.

"I love you, my darling," he murmured. "You mustn't doubt that. You're my wife, I'll take care of you. Everything will be all right, I promise."

Olivia turned to him in astonishment, but he had looked away once more, smiling as he watched the golden stage lights bathe the perfect image before him.

SPRING 1939

CHAPTER 18

THE RELIEF OF THE MUNICH AGREEMENT DID NOT LAST. IN March 1939 Hitler, without argument, claimed the rest of Czechoslovakia; his lust for territory had not, it seemed, been satisfied. Half incredulous, half fatalistic, London prepared for war. The trenches in Hyde Park, crumbling and waterlogged, had been abandoned; now there was talk of building air raid shelters in back gardens, and shoring up church crypts to withstand the force of German bombs.

"I might volunteer as an air raid warden," Dickie said, standing at the window of his flat in Chelsea. In the distance you could see the silver barrage balloons, nicknamed Flossie and Blossom, that had been launched to prevent German planes flying low across the city. "I'm sure the most ghastly thing about an air raid will be the boredom. Better by far to have something to do. Don't you think, Bernard?"

Bernard poured himself some whisky. He was feeling disconsolate. That morning his chosen publisher—an urbane, clubbable man, whom Bernard had always considered a friend—had turned down his novel, gracefully but emphatically. Bernard did not lack talent, he said, but perhaps fiction was not the best way for him to express it. He should stick to journalism, where he was having some success. Then he had hinted that if Bernard really wished to see the book in print he might do it at his own expense, a remark Bernard considered nothing short of an insult.

"I've been meaning to tell you, I've had a marvelous idea." Dickie crossed toward the sofa, gently straightening one or two of his framed photographs as he did so. "It's Olivia's birthday in May. Why don't we throw a costume ball in her honor? We can hold it at Bedford Square, there's more space than I have here. The weather may even be fine enough to use the garden."

"Oh," said Bernard, "yes. Why not?"

Bernard was glad that he had not told Olivia about his meeting with the publisher. She would have asked him about it when he got home, confident, as he had been confident, of success. Bernard could not bear his humiliations to be witnessed, especially by those close to him. He preferred to drag them into a corner, as a dog drags a bone, and chew over them until he could make them acceptable to himself.

"I'll design it, of course," Dickie went on, blithely. "And we can ask Herr Fischer to write a song for her. Antonio can sing it. Perhaps it will lift Herr Fischer's spirits, to hear his own work in public once more."

Bernard drank some of his whisky. "I'm not sure that anything can lift Konrad's spirits. I took him to see *The Bartered Bride* at Covent Garden last week, thinking it might cheer him up, but it was no good. They put on the performance especially, to show solidarity with the Czechs. Of course, it didn't help that they sang it in German."

"Ha," said Dickie, "we do that in this country. We have the best intentions but somehow we fail in the execution. Well, Olivia will be thrilled, anyway. I don't suppose anyone has given a party in her honor before."

"No," said Bernard, "I don't suppose they have." He looked at his uncle, who was affectionately contemplating Olivia's photograph. The picture had been taken on their honeymoon; in the background you could see the potted palms of the green and ivory ballroom.

"You don't sound enthusiastic, Bernard," said Dickie.

"Oh . . ." Bernard stretched out his hands in a vague dismissive gesture. A curious thing had happened in the past months. He had ceased to desire his wife. As the weeks went by and still Olivia did not conceive, making love had become a means to an end, not a pleasure at all. Bernard had expected this feeling to pass, but it had not passed; if anything, it had become more acute. He could not help thinking that this was somehow Olivia's fault. Other women, surely, managed the transition from mistress to wife to mother without quenching their husbands' sexual appetites. What flaw was there in Olivia—in her nature, in her background—that prevented her from doing it?

Aloud he said: "You don't think that it's tempting fate, to have a party? Fiddling while Rome burns?"

Dickie shook his head. "No, Bernie, no. Life must go on. Another gaudy night, and all that." He set down Olivia's photograph, positioning it with care. "Besides, war is not inevitable, even now. With luck it will not happen; or at least, not in my lifetime."

IN THE TINY backstage dressing room at the Golden Slipper, Antonio was waiting for his second performance of the evening. While he waited he studied the song Herr Fischer had written for Olivia's birthday. The text, chosen by Dickie, was from *Romeo and Juliet*, and the first line was a tongue-twister: *Oh, she doth teach the torches to burn bright*. Antonio mouthed the words silently, trying to get the phrasing right.

The night before he and Danila had had a quarrel, hissing at each other in the darkness of their bedroom. Ever since the incident with the gas masks Danila had turned against their life in Britain; or perhaps, thought Antonio, she had always been against it, but now she felt justified in saying so. She talked endlessly about returning to Italy. It was unfair to their son to grow up in exile, not hearing his own beautiful language in the streets. Besides, if there was a war Hitler would bomb London to smithereens. They would be much safer in Italy, the *duce*'s regime would protect them, there would be no bombs, no poison gas in Lazio.

Antonio tried to answer her calmly. That winter Enrico had been ill again, and someone had to share the burden of running the kiosk. Besides, he was earning good money from his singing now. It would be folly to jeopardize his promising career, and for what? He would be lucky to find work of any kind in Lazio, never mind work that paid so well. As usual the moment he disagreed with her Danila began to cry, her sweet kitten's face contorted with distress. You care more about your singing than you do about me, she said. If you loved me, if you loved our child, you would take us home to Italy.

The bitterness in her voice haunted Antonio. To blot it out he concentrated upon Herr Fischer's score. My best work, the Austrian had said, eyeing the manuscript on Bernard's glossy black piano. A man from the BBC whom Dickie knew was coming to the party to hear it. He will adore it, Dickie had said, lavishly waving his jade cigarette holder. It could be the most marvelous opportunity for you both.

There was a knock on the dressing room door. Antonio thought it must be the call boy summoning him onstage, but when the door opened he saw that it was Bernard's friend Iris. Over the winter she had drifted out of view, but lately she had begun to visit the Golden Slipper once more. She would sit at a table close to the stage, watching intently as he sang. It stirred Antonio's vanity in spite of himself: a society beauty, making eyes at him. That would never happen to me working in the fields in Lazio, he thought.

"Hallo there," Iris said. "I came to say, don't rush off when you've finished. My escort tonight has got pots of money. If you come over to our table I'm sure I can persuade him to hire you for one of his parties."

Antonio rose to greet her. The room was so small that when he stood he was almost touching her. She wore a flimsy yellow dress with a halter neck that revealed small round breasts. "Thank you, Iris," he said. "That's very kind of you."

"Are you learning a new song?" Inquisitively she leaned over his shoulder to peer at the score upon the dressing table. "Oh, dear. Shakespeare. Very highbrow. You're not going to sing it here, are you?"

"No, it's for the party Mr. Rodway's giving next month. My teacher, Herr Fischer, wrote the music."

Iris straightened up. Her face was suddenly level with his. She had a wide-eyed expression, not bold now, but unguarded.

"Antonio . . . ," she breathed.

It seemed oddly natural to kiss her. Her mouth tasted of crème de menthe, her hair smelled of vanilla. I could have her if I wanted, thought Antonio. I could have her here, now. The violence of the thought shocked him and he pulled away.

"No, Iris. We mustn't—"

"Is it because of Bernard's wife?" Iris demanded. "I've always thought you liked her."

"What? No. It's got nothing to do with Olivia."

"Olivia, eh?" said Iris, exaggerating the name. "That sounds very chummy. Have I stumbled on a secret passion?"

"Of course not," said Antonio. He did not want to talk about Olivia. There was something too private, too complicated, about his knowledge of her. "I'm a married man, remember, Iris."

"I know," said Iris, "but it's an arranged marriage, isn't it? You don't actually love her."

"Of course I love her, she's my wife, she's the mother of my child." The words tumbled out like a catechism, unquestioned. "That was a mistake, Iris, I shouldn't have kissed you."

"I wanted you to kiss me." Iris fixed her filmy blue eyes upon him. At that moment there was a rap on the door, and the call boy put his head into the room.

"Five minutes, Mr. Trombetta."

Iris pulled a rueful face. "Saved by the bell," she said, and she began to rearrange her neckline, pulling up her shoulder straps, tidying her breasts. "I'm glad that you're not having an affair with Bernard's wife, anyway. She can't stand me. Bernard wanted to invite me to this party of his, but she wouldn't let him."

"I'm sure that's not true," Antonio said.

"Oh, I don't care. There are plenty of women in London who don't like me. It's never stopped me from doing what I want." Iris glanced down at his lap, a glint of satisfaction on her face. "You might want to wait awhile before you go and sing in public."

Antonio felt his cheeks redden. He had not realized that his state of arousal was so obvious. He thought fleetingly of Olivia and then, with a pang of guilt, of Danila.

"Well," said Iris, "it's nice to know you're not entirely immune to my charms." From the doorway she blew him a kiss. "Just you remember what dear stuffy old Bernard said. Once I pounce you're done for."

When she had gone Antonio sank into the dressing room chair once more. I could have her, he thought again, coolly this time. It would be very discreet, nobody need find out. My brother, Valentino, would do it without a backward glance. He felt a frisson of disgust. I am not like my brother, I could not sleep with a woman I do not love. He pictured Danila, the tender curve of her neck, her pretty peony mouth, the softness of her thighs as he entered her. Perhaps she will be sorry that we argued, he thought, perhaps she will be eager to make up. Sometimes a quarrel can clear the air. Tonight, when I go home, I will talk to her. Tonight I will woo my wife, and together we can make a new start.

CHAPTER 19

ON THE EVENING OF HER BIRTHDAY PARTY OLIVIA SAT before the glass examining her face for signs of age. She had the sense that thousands of women had done this over the years, and thousands would do it in the future, tracing the creased circlets about their necks, eyeing the first silver threads at their temples. She felt a flicker of pity for those vain battalions of women. Beauty is our currency, she thought, how would we—how will we—live without it?

The costume she was wearing had been designed by Dickie. It was green, to give her the air of a mermaid, with a fishtail hem and a slit skirt so that she could dance. Dickie loved watching Olivia dance; he said that it reminded him of Katya. Downstairs, the Bedford Square house and garden had been transformed. The hallway had been hung with swathes of colored silk, like a caliph's tent, while outside there were red and gold Chinese lanterns swaying upon the trees. They could be glimpsed through the windows, as though out of doors the tales of the Arabian nights were slowly, enticingly unfolding. Olivia could hear the musicians tuning their instruments, jagged runs and swells rising up the stairs. And there is a surprise, Dickie had said. No, I won't tell you. It's a secret.

Olivia reached for her vast powder puff. She looked paler than ever tonight, her skin white and luminous. And it is two months, one week and four days, she thought, since my husband last made love to me.

In the beginning Olivia had not noticed Bernard's waning enthusiasm for sex. She was too worried about her own body, waiting to see if this month she would bleed. Little by little, though, she realized that her husband had altered. When he made love to her he went about it briskly, no longer kissing her breasts or running his tongue along her thigh, no longer gasping *I love you* as he reached orgasm. Then he began to avoid her. He would stay out late, not returning until one, two in the morning when he could be sure that she was asleep. Even when he was at home he would sit till midnight reading or preparing papers for one of his committees, frowning by lamplight over his desk. You go to bed, my darling, he would say, when Olivia knocked on the door. I'll be with you in a minute or two. Ten minutes at the most.

Olivia touched one of the silver hairs at her temple. It seemed coarser than the rest, as though it had achieved strength by sacrificing color. She knew she ought to speak to Bernard but she had no idea how to do it. When she tried, her mind went blank, and underneath that blankness was a terrible fear. What would she find, if she lifted the stone slab of Bernard's indifference?

Just as she thought this the door opened and Bernard came in. Dickie had designed his costume too: Neptune, to accompany Olivia's mermaid. He wore a pair of wide Turkish trousers, which like Olivia's were encrusted with sequins to resemble fish scales, and a loose robe of green gauze. It revealed half his chest, his hair fair and curling like the golden fleece. On his head there was a verdigris coronet, in which he looked handsome but sheepish.

"I've left my trident on the landing," he said, with a smile. "We should go downstairs. People have started arriving. Dickie and my mother are holding the fort."

Olivia sprayed perfume along the arc of her throat. It was a spicy, rather masculine perfume that Dickie had helped her to choose. Bernard had never told her whether he liked it or not.

"Your mother's here already, then?"

"Yes. I asked her to come early, in case we needed her to play hostess." Bernard watched as she rose from the brocaded stool. "You look beautiful."

"It isn't very comfortable," said Olivia. "And I'm cold."

"Well, pride must suffer pain. You'll soon get warm downstairs." Bernard hitched up his green gauze robe and took her hand. "Besides, it's authentic. Mermaids are meant to be cold-blooded, aren't they? That's why they find it so easy to lure men to their doom."

"Just as I lured you," said Olivia. She said it teasingly, before she could stop herself. Bernard did not hear, though, or else he decided to take no notice of the remark, because he turned his head aside, tucked her arm beneath his and led her toward the stairs.

In the drawing room Dickie was holding court. He had dressed himself as a Persian caliph, in a grandiose outfit filched from an ancient production of James Elroy Flecker's *Hassan*. It smelled strongly of mothballs when you got close to him. On the mosaic table before him was a hookah, the water bubbling as he drew upon the pipe. The costumes of the party guests were less coherent. Some wore Harlequin and Columbine outfits, others Venetian masks. Most of the women had made a token gesture to the party's theme, with marabou on their frocks or silken turbans wound about their heads, but several of the men had made no effort at all, and wore their accustomed evening dress, or rumpled corduroys. Beside the piano a cluster of musicians was playing "Smoke Gets in Your Eyes."

"Perfect," said Dickie, when he saw Olivia and Bernard. Bernard had collected his trident—verdigris like his coronet, wound with a green satin ribbon to resemble seaweed—and was brandishing it with his free hand. "Who says that the things you imagine cannot be achieved? I am not disappointed in you *at all*."

"What is my surprise?" Olivia said. "I'm longing to know."

Dickie patted her cold hand fondly. "Possess your soul in patience, my sweet. It won't be much longer. Bernard, come and talk to Charles Connor. My friend from the BBC."

Olivia, left alone, looked around the room. It might have been her party, but she scarcely knew anybody, and those she did know she did not much like. She had a sudden desire to see Jeanie strut through the door, with her cheap scent and her crimped hair, flagrantly eyeing up the men. That would rattle them, thought Olivia with bleak glee. A photographer was prowling the room, his flashbulbs popping at unexpected moments. In the corner she could see Konrad Fischer in eighteenth-century knee breeches, talking to a man from one of Bernard's refugee associations. Beside him Penelope Rodway was pirouetting happily, a cigarette in one hand, a glass of champagne in the other. She wore a gold lamé gown that revealed her crumpled cleavage. She was supposed to be Cleopatra, but she had turned up her nose at the heavy horsehair wig Dickie had provided. Don't be ridiculous, she had said, I'm not going to put on that smelly old thing. Not when I've spent a fortune at the hairdresser's.

"Oh, that is quite the wrong idea," she was saying to a solemn young man in a Fair Isle sweater. "I don't care what the fashion is, there is no place for politics in poetry. It makes everything so ugly. Give me Keats or Shelley any day."

"But Shelley was a revolutionary, you know," the solemn young man broke in. "A democrat at a time when democracy was as maligned as Bolshevism is today . . ."

Penelope's eyes glazed over; in a moment she would look around for someone else to talk to. Olivia, afraid it might be her, ducked from the room with a vague unhappy plan of going into the garden. She had reached the top of the stairs when she saw Antonio Trombetta ascending. There was a bright, deliberate expression on his face. It was the expression of one who has to give pleasure at all times, who does not dare show sullenness or boredom; Olivia recognized it from her own reflection.

"Your costume is very beautiful, Mrs. Rodway," he said, looking at her gravely.

"Thank you," Olivia said, and then, on impulse: "You are right, it is beautiful but—well, I worked as a dressmaker when I was a girl. All I can think of is how sewing sequins hurts your fingers. So much pricking and scratching. Mine feel sore just to look at this dress."

A smile crossed Antonio's mouth. "It is like that after a day selling sweets in our kiosk. Sometimes I think I will never get the smell of coins from my hands."

"Olivia?" It was Dickie, plump and splendid in his Persian robes. "You're the guest of honor, you can't run off like that." He positioned her by the balcony, pooling her green mermaid's train at her feet. Then he glanced at Herr Fischer, who flicked aside the tails of his blue brocade coat and sat at the piano.

"Antonio?" said Dickie. "Where are you? 'Tis time, descend, be stone no more, approach."

Antonio stood in the glossy curve of the piano. He tilted his head toward Olivia; then, as Herr Fischer struck up the rich opening chords, he squared his shoulders to sing.

"*Oh, she doth teach the torches to burn bright . . .* " The moment he opened his lips the air in the room seemed to alter. It resonated with his voice, and with the sudden rapt attention of his listeners. Olivia looked for Bernard. Surely he should be at her side for this performance, her devoted husband? He was on the far side of the room, though, next to Penelope, who murmured in his ear from time to time. He did not turn his eyes in her direction at all.

"*Beauty too rich for use, for earth too dear . . .*"

At the piano Herr Fischer played a fading tremolo, and the song ended. There was a moment of silence before the applause began. The photographer's flashbulb burst pale and fierce as lightning, capturing Antonio. Then he and Herr Fischer were engulfed by a surge of people: Bernard, Penelope, Charles the BBC man.

"That was your surprise." Dickie's round face glowed with the heat of the room. "Herr Fischer composed it, of course, but I chose the text."

"Oh," said Olivia, "I thought it might have been Bernard."

Dickie pouted, caught between duty to his nephew and the urge to claim credit. "Well, I chose it *for* Bernard. *Did my heart love till now? Forswear it, sight!* We've been rehearsing it for days. Over in Chelsea, so you did not find out. You did like it, darling, didn't you?"

"It was wonderful," said Olivia, who realized that she had hardly listened to the song. She had been too busy watching Bernard, waiting to see if he would look at her.

"Listen, my angel, I have to buttonhole Charles Connor. I'm hoping he'll find a nice little spot on the radio for our musical friends." Dickie kissed Olivia on the cheek. "You enjoy your party, darling."

FOR THE NEXT hour or two Olivia drifted like a green-clad ghost about her own house, trying not to drink too much, dipping in and out of conversations she did not understand, or which did not amend themselves to include her. It was nearly midnight when Dickie came bustling toward her once more. The band had begun Ravel's *Bolero*, played as a tango.

"Olivia, my sweet, you have to dance, you haven't danced all evening."

"But I can't interrupt Bernard. He hates it when I interrupt him."

Bernard, clutching his incongruous gauze robe, was surrounded by a group of eager, talkative young men. He was holding forth on the threat facing Poland from Hitler's lust for *Lebensraum*.

"Really, darling. By what law are you obliged to dance with your husband? Look, Antonio's still here. He'll dance with you, won't you, Antonio?"

Antonio had been a huge success at the party. All evening he had been surrounded by women, flirting, gazing, making excuses to touch his arm or squeeze his hand. What better way to demonstrate her own status, thought Olivia, than by dancing with him now?

"I do not know the tango very well," said Antonio rather anxiously, as he took her arm.

"Don't worry." Olivia gave his fingers a reassuring pinch. "I'll make sure you don't look foolish."

In the center of the room she placed his palm upon her waist and threw back her head. At once the glorious skill of it returned to her, the way you could hint with your body, controlling the dance by a touch here, a twist there. "Good," she murmured. "Now turn and look me in the eyes. *Good.*"

The floor had cleared. Everyone in the room was watching, Olivia knew, even Bernard. Especially Bernard. She curled her fingers about the nape of Antonio's neck. She could feel the place where his hair began, warm and soft.

"No, not like that. Keep your feet still." Olivia went spinning across the room, her mermaid's skirt swirling about her knees. The music flared and sharpened. Olivia could tell that the band smelled danger, they were thrilled by her dancing.

"I'm going to fall against your arm now," she whispered. "Don't bloody drop me."

The saxophone rose to a shimmering peak of sound. Olivia spun one last time before she let her body curve and dip backward, her hair brushing the floor.

"Bravo," said Dickie, clapping noisily. "Olivia darling, I've never seen you dance with such fire. You must have inspired her, Antonio. That was marvelous."

"*Meraviglioso,*" Bernard put in, in a jocular voice. His eyes were skewed as he approached Olivia, sliding his hand along her wrist. He desires me, she thought. He sees me in another man's arms and suddenly he wants me again.

"Let's go upstairs." Bernard's face was so close she could feel his breath upon her cheek. "Nobody will miss us."

Olivia glanced over her shoulder. Now that she was being taken from the party it seemed gaudy and enthralling. Penelope was flirting with Charles Connor. She looked the worse for wear, her hair wilting like an overdressed lettuce. Then Olivia saw Dickie. Something strange had happened to his face. One side had crumpled, and the corner of his mouth was drooping wetly. The next moment his glass thudded to the floor.

Antonio sprang forward, catching Dickie as he fell. "Mr. Rodway! Sir!" he called.

"What is it?" Bernard was still grasping Olivia's wrist. The briskness in his voice stopped just short of irritation. Releasing Olivia, he pushed his way toward his uncle. Dickie was sprawled on the carpet, Antonio's arm about his shoulders. He was trying to speak.

"Dickie," said Bernard, "Uncle Dickie. Don't be afraid, everything will be all right."

Dickie was still mouthing silence, his lips shaping a desperate O.

"I believe that he wants your wife," said Antonio.

"Olivia? Where are you?" Bernard retrieved Dickie's cigarette holder, which was smoldering on the Turkish carpet. "Stay with him, will you? I'm going to telephone for an ambulance. I think he's had a stroke."

Olivia crouched beside Dickie. "I'm here," she said, taking his hand in both of hers, "I'm here, Dickie."

Charles Connor had begun tactfully to shift party guests out to the garden. Dickie's breathing was shallow. Olivia felt the pressure of his hand. Neither of them spoke, or tried to speak. For one long moment they gazed serenely at one another; then Dickie turned his head, let out the whisper of a sigh and closed his eyes.

"Dickie!" Penelope dropped to her knees, nearly toppling Olivia. "Oh, Dickie, darling . . ."

Bernard had come back into the room. "It's all right, Mother," he said in an authoritative voice. "An ambulance is on its way."

Olivia, ousted, was struggling to her feet. The green sequins scraped against her thighs. In silence Antonio put out his hand to help her.

"He's dead," she murmured, "isn't he?"

Antonio did not answer. Instead he slid the jacket from his shoulders and wrapped it about her. He did it carefully, you might say tenderly. Until that moment Olivia had not known it, but she was trembling; trembling uncontrollably, as though the nugget of ice deep within her had at last claimed her for its own.

CHAPTER 20

"DON'T PESTER ME, VALENTINO." ENRICO FLICKED THAT week's *L'Italia Nostra* onto the kitchen table. "In three months' time we have to renew our lease upon the kiosk. We need every penny we can find. If you want to buy extravagant presents you should have saved some of your earnings."

"But it is a question of honor, Papa. The christening will be a grand affair. I do not want Pasquale to think that we are paupers."

"I do not understand why you have been invited in any case. We don't know this Pasquale. He is not from Lazio, is he?"

"He is a friend of Bruno's," said Valentino, "and a good fascist."

Enrico threw a look of appeal at Antonio. Frequently his older son came to his aid on these occasions, justifying his decisions in a way that made Enrico seem not harsh, but reasonable. Tonight, though, Antonio was in a world of his own. He had an English newspaper open before him, and he was staring at a grainy photograph. The *Stage* had published a long obituary of Dickie Belvoir, with a picture of Dickie as a young man, sleek and sprightly.

"I thought you were friendly with the wife, not the husband, Valentino," said Filomena from the scullery, in an ingenuous voice. "Claudia. Isn't that her name?"

Valentino flushed, but he did not dare quarrel with his sister in front of Enrico. "I have met Claudia once or twice, yes. Pasquale sometimes brings her to concerts at the *fascio*. She is a devoted wife. She goes to mass at St. Patrick's three times a week, just like our dear mama."

He crossed himself reverentially at the mention of his mother. Enrico did not respond. "It is no use, Valentino," he said. "You must learn to live within your means. I have worked hard for our money, so has Antonio, so has Filomena. I am not squandering it upon a stranger's son." Standing up, he took his hat from the peg and jammed it decisively upon his head. "That is my last word on the matter."

Antonio glanced up from his newspaper. "What is the child's name, Valentino?"

"Riccardo, after his grandfather. He is a fine boy, a handsome boy." Valentino lit a cigarette. "I want to show respect, that is all."

"Ah," said Antonio. He did not need to ask, So you think the child is yours?

In silence he turned to the paper once more. In his memory Olivia's party had acquired a lurid glamour, too fierce, too bright, like the photographer's dazzling flashbulbs. He thought of how she had pinched his fingers in reassurance, how she had touched the nape of his neck as they danced. He thought of Dickie's face, skewed and sweating. He thought of how he had raised Olivia from the floor and wrapped his jacket about her. That was when it had happened, between one gesture and the next.

"What are you looking at?" Valentino's voice was peevish, resenting the way his brother's attention had shifted from his own affairs.

"It is about Dickie Belvoir, Mr. Rodway's uncle. He was a famous stage designer."

Valentino glanced at the photograph. "Pah! He looks like a *busone*. A queer."

"Don't be absurd. He was married, his wife was a Russian dancer. And he adored Mrs. Rodway—"

"I wish you would not mix with such decadent people, Antonino.

Homosexuals. Jews. They will corrupt you." Valentino's eyes were wide and zealous. "I sometimes fear you have been corrupted already."

Perhaps I have always loved her, thought Antonio, perhaps I fell in love that first night at the Paradise Ballroom. It is just that I did not realize it until now. He had not seen Olivia since the night of Dickie's death; the Rodways would not want intruders at such a time. How could he show his face in Bedford Square?

"I am sure that Danila does not like you spending your time with these people," Valentino was saying. "In fact, I know she does not, she has told me so."

"What?" said Antonio. He did not want to think about his wife; not now, with the knowledge of his love for Olivia burning in his veins. He and Danila had been living in an uneasy state of truce, neither daring to say anything that might start another quarrel. When he made love to her she did not push him away, but lay quite still, quite silent beneath him.

"She believes these people, these Rodways, are a bad influence upon you," Valentino went on, in a self-righteous voice. "She believes you should be mixing with your fellow Italians, as I do."

"Pah," said Antonio irritably, "it has nothing to do with Danila," and pushing back his chair he stalked out of the room.

The following night Filomena was sitting in the kitchen with Danila and Renata. The men had gone out—Enrico and Valentino to the *fascio*, Antonio to the Golden Slipper—and they had the place to themselves, to gossip and drink coffee and eat macaroons. Renata visited Frith Street twice a week, partly to see her uncle Mauro, but chiefly, thought Filomena, to gloat. She did not mind the gloating, which was so blatant it was almost comical. What infuriated Filomena was the new alliance between Renata and Danila. You wouldn't understand, Mena, they seemed to say, tilting their heads knowingly, you're not married.

"Of course, I make a point of buying fruit and vegetables from Italy," Renata was saying, sliding a macaroon into her mouth. "Bruno says that if all the forty thousand Italians in Britain did the same, our homeland would be richer by a thousand pounds a day."

Danila nodded in approval. Although she was no longer breast-feeding she still occupied the most comfortable chair, close to the stove, a trim neat-faced matriarch. She was knitting a jersey for the baby in powder-blue wool.

"My cousin Bruno is right. It is a shame that every Italian woman does not follow his advice." Danila threw a sidelong glance at Filomena, who bought whatever was cheap and plentiful, regardless of its provenance. Filomena thought of pointing out that patriotism was a luxury you could not afford when you had six mouths to feed, but she did not have the energy to start an argument.

"And has Bruno gained the promotion the hotel promised?" she asked instead.

A shadow crossed Renata's face. "It is not easy at the present time, especially for patriots like Bruno. His employers are British, they do not trust Italians. He was warned the other day for reading *L'Italia Nostra*. Imagine!"

"Tcha," said Danila, "the sooner we return to Lazio the better. Does my cousin not think so?"

"He would like to return, but it is not possible, at least not yet. He earns more in London than ever he could in Italy."

"That is what Antonio says, but I do not believe him." Complacently Danila looped the blue wool about her tiny knitting needles. "It would be safer for the child in Lazio. If war comes Britain will be crushed by Germany. The fascists are so much stronger, they have conviction on their side."

This remark exasperated Filomena. "You do not know that, Danila. Valentino may say so, but that does not make it true. Besides, Antonio is doing so well here in London, you cannot want to spoil his success—"

She was interrupted by a banging at the front door. It was loud and urgent, as if someone were hitting the panels with a stick. The three women looked at each other. There was fear in Danila's eyes, shadowy as a fish in deep brown waters. Filomena stood up.

"I will find out who it is," she said.

There was another thwack at the door. A man's voice bawled: "Valentino! Valentino Trombetta! Come out like a man!"

Mauro's anxious wizened face was hanging over the banister. "What is it? What is happening?"

Filomena did not answer, but threw open the door. Three men stood outside, all carrying rounders bats. The man in front was black haired and muscular. He had a clipped mustache beneath a large beaky nose.

"What do you want?" said Filomena in stern Italian. "My brother is not at home."

The black-haired man hesitated, nonplussed by the sight of Filomena. Then he said: "I do not believe you. Valentino is there, I know it. Hiding behind your skirts like the coward he is. Let me enter . . ."

Filomena planted her feet squarely upon the ceramic tiles of the hall. The posture filled her with a sense of power. This is why men fight, she thought, because they feel strong, they feel they can win. "What? You want to terrorize women and children in their own home? And yet you call my brother Valentino a coward."

"Your brother has defiled my wife!" the man cried, and the men shoved their way past Filomena, clubs raised. Renata began to squeal.

"Fetch a policeman," said Filomena to Mauro. "Don't argue with me, go."

Pasquale, the black-haired man, was standing in the kitchen, jerking his club to and fro. One of the other men had gone into the scullery and was poking at Filomena's bedding, stored in the corner.

"We are just women," clucked Renata, "please don't hurt us."

She was guarding Danila's chair, as though Danila, being the most beautiful, was bound to be the most at risk.

Pasquale took no notice. "He is here, I am sure that he is here. Giovanni, go and search upstairs."

"You will not," said Filomena. "My nephew is sleeping. I will not have him disturbed. He is only a baby . . ."

At the word *baby* Pasquale's mouth twisted like a terrible rope. Filomena thought of the damage her brother had done. That damage would haunt Pasquale and his family forever. How could he love his son, knowing what he knew? How could he trust his wife?

"Believe me," she said more gently, "Valentino is not at home—"

There was a clatter of footsteps behind her. It was Mauro, accompanied by a police constable, an awkward young man with a spray of pimples upon his cheeks. At the sight of his uniform Filomena's heart gave a leap, instantly suppressed.

"What's happening here, then? I've been told there's a disturbance." The young policeman stuck out his chin as though the gesture would, against the odds, give him authority.

Pasquale relaxed his grip upon his club. "It is a misunderstanding," he said in English. "We intended to play a joke on a *paesano*, a compatriot, but we came to the wrong house. We did not mean to frighten these ladies."

The policeman looked doubtfully around the kitchen, at Mauro, at Renata, at Danila rigid in her chair. When he spoke, though, it was to Filomena.

"Have these fellows been threatening you, miss?"

"I have explained, Constable," said Pasquale smoothly. Filomena remembered that he was a waiter at Bianchi's, accustomed to dealing with the high and mighty. "It was a joke, a mistake. We are leaving now."

"Miss?" said the policeman, his eyes still upon Filomena. She wavered for a moment and then shook her head.

"No, they have not been threatening us. We were startled, that is all."

"Well, I'll see them off the premises," the policeman said. "Come on then, let's be having you."

Filomena saw Pasquale's fist tighten on his wooden club, but he thought better of it and followed the policeman to the open door. At the last moment he turned to Filomena.

"I will find your brother," he hissed. "I will not rest until I find him. And when I find him I will kill him, even if I hang for it. You tell your brother that."

FILOMENA THOUGHT THAT Valentino would laugh off Pasquale's threat, but he did not. When Mauro fetched him home from the *fascio* his face was as pale as the tablecloths that arrived daily at the Goodge Street laundry.

"How many men were with him? Two? And they had clubs, you say?"

"Rounders bats," said Filomena, who could not help feeling a glimmer of satisfaction, to see her swaggering brother so rattled.

"Claudia must have told her husband." Valentino's hands were shaking; he could scarcely hold the cigarette to his lips. "She was afraid that she would go to hell if she did not confess the truth—"

"So the child is yours?" said Enrico. His eyes, fixed upon his favorite son, were like granite.

Valentino shrugged. "I do not know. He could be mine. Nobody will ever be certain, not me, not Pasquale, not Claudia herself."

Or the child, thought Filomena. What would it be like for that child, never to know his own parentage?

At the table Enrico put his head in his hands. "Oh, Valentino, my son," he said. There was despair, not reproach, in his voice now.

"Do not be angry with me, Papa." Valentino crouched beside his father's chair like a chastened schoolboy. "It is not my fault, Claudia was willing, she tempted me . . ."

Reaching down, Enrico caressed his son's black tangled hair. Then he said: "You had better leave the room, Filomena. This is no conversation for an unmarried woman to hear."

"I don't see why," said Filomena stoutly. "I understand what has happened. And I am the one who dealt with Pasquale."

"Yes, by calling in the British authorities." There was a zest in Valentino's bitterness, as he seized the chance to divert blame. "It is dishonorable, it is not how we Italians do these things, we settle our affairs within our own community—"

"Filomena did what she thought best," said Antonio, who had been silent until now. "She had my wife and child to protect. The question is, what should we do next? This man Pasquale is serious, Valentino. Next time you may not be so fortunate."

Valentino let out a whimper. "There, there, my son," said Enrico. "We will think of something. Antonio will think of something." He looked eagerly across the room. "Can we talk to this Pasquale, do you suppose, Antonio? I could speak to him. It will be better coming from an older man, from a father. I persuaded Carlo Ricci to forgive Valentino after that business with Lucia."

"That was different," said Antonio. "Lucia's father chose to be deceived, you know that, Papa. Pasquale will not be mollified so easily. You will have to lie low for a while, Valentino. Leave Soho, leave London for six months, maybe a year."

"But where will I go?" wailed Valentino. "I do not want to leave my home, my family . . ."

All eyes were upon Antonio now, part in appeal, part in fear. "You should go to Italy," he said. "Back to Lazio, back to the village. Pasquale is not from our region, he has no friends or relations there, he cannot pursue you."

A mutinous expression crossed Valentino's face. "I do not want to take flight like a coward. It would be shameful."

"It is not cowardice, Valentino. It is wisdom." Antonio paused. He guessed that what he was about to say would change his life, and yet when the words came out they sounded casual, reasonable, not dramatic at all.

"Danila wants to return to her parents' house in Lazio, she thinks it will be safer for our son. She cannot travel alone, and I cannot go with her. I cannot leave Papa, I cannot leave my work. You will not be taking flight, you will be protecting your sister-in-law. What is shameful about that?"

CHAPTER 21

FOUR DAYS LATER DANILA AND THE BABY LEFT FOR ITALY, escorted by Valentino. They took the train from Victoria, as once the children of loyal fascists had done, gleefully gathering for their summer camps while Ambassador Grandi doled out sweets.

Antonio accompanied the travelers to the station. Enrico had hoped to go too, to catch the last possible glimpse of his favorite son, but his breathing had grown worse and he was confined to bed in Frith Street.

"Courage, Valentino," said Antonio to his brother, who was weeping as the bus trundled inexorably along Piccadilly. "Papa will travel to Lazio soon. This summer, perhaps. It is not as though you will never see him again."

"If the war comes it may be impossible to travel," Danila said in a flat voice. She was in the seat behind the two brothers, beautifully dressed in a fawn coat and a yellow-ocher hat. Her sleeping child was cradled in her lap. She had cried when Antonio first told her he was not coming with her to Italy. For the rest of the night she had wheedled and wept and caressed him, trying to persuade him to change his mind. Once she realized, though, that he would not, it seemed to Antonio that she hardened, becoming brisk and organized. During those last days she showed no sign of intimacy or regret.

"We will find a way," said Antonio. He did not want to think about the future. All his concentration was fixed upon the task ahead. Farewells were muddled, awkward affairs; you could be tormented afterward by your own clumsiness. He was hoping that he would manage the departure of his wife and son cleanly, decently.

The platforms at Victoria were busy with day-trippers to the south coast. Antonio hauled Danila's suitcases toward the train. Most of the things she had packed were for the baby, christening gifts, the soft mass of jerseys she had knitted. Antonio knew that his son would not need so many warm clothes in Lazio—Danila would have to find him cooler things, of cotton or linen, to survive the Italian summer—but, like so much, the words had gone unsaid.

He turned to watch his wife follow him demurely along the platform. Last night, in the darkness, he had taken her in his arms, sliding his hand along her thigh to give notice of his intention to make love to her. Danila did not move. Antonio raised the hem of her white cotton nightdress, then let it fall once more. I do not want a wife who submits, he thought, I want a wife who desires me. He patted her knee—a peacemaking gesture, as if to say, It is all right, I will not insist—and he slid to the far edge of the mattress, where he lay awake until the room grew light.

On the platform the baby was chuntering irritably, his chubby limbs eeling from Danila's grasp. Soon he would be too big for her to carry. When I see him next, Antonio thought, he will not recognize me, and who knows? Perhaps I will not recognize him, for all that he is my flesh and blood. Putting down the valises he threw open the carriage door. Danila stepped forward to embrace him. For a moment he remembered the early days of their marriage, when she had nestled against him like a trustful bird.

"Oh, my love," he said, softening. At that moment the baby began to cry, pushing furiously against his father.

"Mama," he said, seizing a black lock of Antonio's hair, "Mama."

"Hush." Danila's attention turned to the child, uncurling his plump fingers. "We had better get him settled, Antonio. He will howl all the way to Dover otherwise."

And that is how it is, thought Antonio, as he helped his wife into the railway carriage. That is how it will always be.

"Take care of them, Valentino," he said, throwing his arms about his brother. "I am trusting them to you. Do not let any harm come to them, on the journey or in Lazio."

Valentino rubbed his eyes with the back of his hand. "Of course, Antonino. You can count on me." He gripped his brother once more, fiercely. "And promise me that you will look after Papa?"

"It will be my greatest care, Valentino. Keep your spirits up. We will see each other soon."

The whistle was blowing now. There was a frantic slamming of doors; then, like a pantomime dragon, the train began to huff and puff out of the station, gathering speed. Valentino leaned from the window, waving, but of Danila there was no sign. Antonio watched until the guard's brown van had disappeared along the track. Once the train was out of sight he walked back through the platform gates into the ornate brick ticket hall. A sense of unfamiliar lightness swept through him; he could almost taste it at the back of his throat. It was only when he had stepped into the sunlit street that he recognized it as freedom.

AT HOME IN Frith Street Filomena was stewing an oxtail for Enrico's supper. She was humming one of the songs she had heard Antonio practice. Unlike her brother, Filomena knew that she was happy: knew it straightforwardly, without shame. She had often imagined a home from which Danila and Valentino were absent, but she had never dreamed that it could be achieved so easily. Joyful vistas opened before her. She would be able to come and go without sniping or grumbling; nobody would complain that she was late home from the laundry, or that she had put too much nutmeg in the gnocchi.

"*These foolish things . . .* " sang Filomena, not very tunefully, as she poked at the oxtail in the pan. There was a rap upon the front door: a loud rap, full of bravado. Filomena wiped her steam-damp hands upon her apron. If it is Pasquale, she thought, I will tell him that he is too late, Valentino has gone, he will never find him. I will not be afraid, I will take pleasure in telling him.

It was not Pasquale, though: it was Stanley Harker, in his blue high-buttoned uniform. His copper's face was screwed up in a determined expression.

"I heard there'd been some trouble here," he said. "I wanted to make sure you were all right."

Filomena stared. Then in a matter-of-fact voice she said: "You had better come inside. Be quiet, though. My father is asleep."

Stan wiped his stout boots carefully on the mat. Once they were in the kitchen Filomena closed the door, so they could not be heard.

"Salty told me that he'd been here." Stan was looking around the kitchen, at the well-scrubbed table, at the black stove: all the things Filomena had described, in their walks between Goodge Street and Frith Street, but which until now he had never seen. "Constable Sellers, I mean. Salty's his nickname, that's what we call him down at the station. He said there'd been some trouble, a gang of men with clubs. It bothered me."

Filomena stood beside the table with her arms folded. She knew she ought to offer Stan something—coffee, a bottle of beer—but to do so would compromise her. It would confirm once and for all that Stan had been present, in her home; she would never be able to deny it.

"It was my brother Valentino. He caused offense to one of our countrymen. But it is all right now. My father has sent Valentino to Lazio, out of harm's way. He has gone with Danila and the baby."

"But you did not go too?"

"Of course not. Papa is ill, his chest is weak still, he needs nursing. And someone has to keep house for Antonio."

"Ah," said Stan, and then: "Is that the scullery where you sleep?"

There was an incredulous note in his voice that annoyed Filomena. How dare he criticize her family's arrangements?

"Yes," she said fiercely.

Stan gave a faint smile. "You did not send me word, Filomena. I thought that I would hear from you, but there was nothing. Even though you did not marry this fiancé of yours, this Bruno."

Filomena lowered her head. She could feel the blood burn in her cheeks. "I promised Antonio that I would not see you again. He said that he would not tell my father about you—about our friendship—as long as I gave him my promise—"

"And you agreed?"

The words crowded to Filomena's lips. I told you it was impossible, my father would have packed me off to Lazio, what in the world did you expect me to do? She did not say any of them. She stood silent, her head still bowed.

"I have another reason for coming," said Stan, after a moment. "I'm joining up. My father died at Christmas, so there's one less mouth to feed. And I want to do my bit against Hitler when the time comes."

Filomena looked at him then. "I'm sorry about your father," she said. "Does it mean that you'll be leaving London?"

"Yes. I'll be off for basic training in a couple of weeks. I'm going to Catterick, in Yorkshire." Stan paused. He was gazing at Filomena. A quite other dialogue was taking place within that gaze. "I've never been so far north before. Never been further than King's Cross, if truth be known."

He is going to kiss me, thought Filomena. The memory of their last kiss, sudden and thirsty, swept through her.

"Will you write to me?" she said abruptly, twisting sideways. It wrong-footed Stan.

"What? But won't your family find out?"

"You can send letters to the post office in Charing Cross Road, I'll collect them there. It will be easier now that Danila and Valentino have gone. I will have more freedom."

Their eyes met once more, as they each registered what Filomena's new freedom might mean. For an instant everything hung in the balance. Then, from the floor above, Enrico called out.

"Mena! Where are you, Mena?" It was a sick man's querulous voice, and it brought Filomena to herself.

"It's my father." She put out her hands, as though she could shoo Stan from the house without actually touching him. "You had better go, Stan."

Stan held his ground a moment longer, doggedly. "If I do write, Filomena, will you write back?"

"Of course I will. Only you must go now, Stan. Please, before my father hears you."

CHAPTER 22

DICKIE'S FUNERAL WAS HUGE AND GLAMOROUS. BERNARD ORganized it in a weeklong frenzy of efficiency, although it was Penelope who styled herself as chief mourner. She was draped in acres of black chiffon as she followed the coffin into the church, supported by her two sons. Olivia walked behind them, wearing a very simple, very severe coat and skirt that Dickie had always admired. Only you can get away with that, my angel, he had said, any other woman would look like a prison warder. The lump in Olivia's throat swelled. The church was crammed with people whom she did not recognize. For a moment she hoped she might see Antonio Trombetta's face—comforting, familiar—but there was no sign of him.

After the funeral, Dickie's solicitor read his will to the family, sitting in the drawing room at Bedford Square. Dickie had left money to the refugee association, and some of his objects—the more opulent ones—to Penelope. Everything else was divided between the two Rodway brothers apart from the house in Sussex, which Dickie had bequeathed to Olivia.

"How extraordinary," said Lionel, with a snort half of outrage, half of disbelief. "Are you sure you've read it correctly?"

Penelope gave Olivia a shrewd, rather accusing look. "It's a new will, isn't it? He made it only a few months ago. Do you think he was in his right wits?"

"Don't be absurd, Mother," Bernard said. "There's nothing

suspicious about it. Uncle Dickie was very fond of Olivia, he wanted to give her something."

"But a *house*," said Penelope. "He could have left her some jewelry, or maybe a picture. Far more suitable."

Olivia cleared her throat. "I stayed there with Dickie last year. He knew how much I loved the place. I grew up in Sussex, you know—"

"It's not a valuable house, in any case," Bernard put in impatiently. "It's a typical ramshackle country cottage. I daresay the upkeep will cost me more than the damn place is worth. Let's drop it, shall we? The rest of the will seems perfectly fair."

"Do you mind about the house?" Olivia asked Bernard later, when they were alone. They had both changed out of their constricting funeral clothes and were having a whisky before bed.

"Of course I don't mind. It would be churlish to mind. I don't understand why he did it, that's all. I think he was being mischievous. He guessed that it would annoy Lionel and my mother. And you can see their point, it is an eccentric thing to do. I know Dickie wanted you to enjoy the house, but he could just as well have left it to me on your behalf."

Olivia was silent. She had the feeling that Bernard cared far more about the bequest than he would admit. He had not talked at all about his grief for Dickie, or the sudden, shocking circumstances of his death. When he spoke of his uncle it was as though he were still alive and simply, for the moment, absent from the room.

"I could refuse to accept it," she said. "I could say that I wanted the house to be in your name." Even as she spoke she felt the kick of rebellion in her stomach. Dickie left the house to me, why should I give it up?

Bernard shrugged. "What's the point? We'd have to pay the lawyers to arrange it, it would complicate the whole business. Besides, it's clear that Dickie wanted you to have the place. We ought to abide by his wishes." He sluiced the last of his whisky about the glass and swallowed it. "You look worn out, my darling, you go on up to bed. I've got a mountain of paperwork in my study. Now the funeral's over I'd better start tackling it."

LIONEL CAUGHT THE train to Macclesfield the morning after the funeral; Penelope stayed for three more days before returning home. On her last night in London Bernard took her to dinner at the Ivy.

"Should we be going out so soon after Dickie's death?" Olivia said as she and Bernard were dressing. "You don't think it's disrespectful?"

Bernard was fastening the pearls about her neck, and he glanced up in irritation. "Of course it's not disrespectful. Don't be petit bourgeois. Dickie wouldn't have wanted us to weep and wail and shut ourselves away. You ought to know that, Olivia."

He clicked shut the clasp of her necklace. Usually he would bend and kiss her shoulder afterward, but this time he turned snubbingly away to put on his waistcoat.

At the Ivy they ate salmon and roast duck and caramel profiteroles, which Penelope as usual poked and prodded with an air of dissatisfaction. She managed to eat it all, though, Olivia noticed.

"I thought we'd go to the Golden Slipper afterward, if you're not too tired, Mother?" Bernard said. "Antonio's singing there tonight. You remember him, he sang at Olivia's party."

"The Italian? Yes, I remember him. Rather an exotic young man." Penelope sniffed as she stirred her coffee. "No, I'm not too tired, Bernie. As a matter of fact I'd welcome a little fun. This week's been such an ordeal for me."

The Golden Slipper was crowded, but the manager, recognizing Bernard, showed them to a table close to the stage.

"Look, there's Iris," said Bernard as he held one of the uncomfortable bronze chairs for Penelope. "Apparently she's a great fan of Antonio's. I've heard she comes here every week."

He raised his hand to Iris, who waved languidly back. Olivia was afraid that he would ask her to join them but before he could do it the master of ceremonies announced Antonio. A shiver of anticipation ran through the room; evidently Iris was not the only person who came each week to hear him.

"He's very good, isn't he?" Penelope said with a judicious air, as Antonio began to sing "Tornerai." "What do the words mean, Bernie?"

"It's Italian for 'you will return.' The tune's based on the 'Humming Chorus' in *Madame Butterfly*. Now hush, Mother. Listen."

She's smitten, thought Olivia. A handsome face and a heavenly voice, and dear snobbish Penelope is smitten. At that moment Antonio glanced toward them. Olivia saw recognition flare in his eyes. She remembered how solicitously he had wrapped his coat about her shoulders after Dickie's death. The memory brought hot tears to her eyes. I can talk to Antonio, she thought. Antonio will understand.

ANTONIO HAD NOT expected the Rodways to appear so soon after Dickie's funeral, and the sight of Olivia's face, pale above the silk-shaded lamp, took his breath away; for an instant he lost control of the phrase he was singing. Afterward, as he threaded his way toward their table, he could feel his heart thump.

It was Bernard who greeted him, slapping his arm, calling for the waiter to fetch him a drink.

"How good to see you, Antonio. And you're doing so well here, I'm impressed, you've clearly got a horde of devoted fans. My uncle would have been thrilled." Antonio opened his mouth to offer condolences, but Bernard overrode him, a bluff cheerful juggernaut. "By the way, I haven't forgotten about Dickie's BBC friend. I'm planning to telephone him in the next few days, to remind him about you and Herr Fischer. It's just that I've been preoccupied by my uncle's affairs. Well, you can imagine."

"Of course. Family business is always demanding. My wife went back to Italy three days ago, and there was so much to be done—"

"I thought that your family was settled in Soho?" Olivia said. She was wearing a dress of dark blue moiré, iridescent in the glimmer of the nightclub. There were dark shadows beneath her eyes, as though she had not slept. It made her look at once fragile and untouchable.

"Danila—my wife—wanted to go home to Lazio," Antonio said. "She was afraid for our son. She thinks he will be in danger if there is a war."

"*When* there is a war," said Bernard. "There can be no doubt about that now. I'm sorry, Mother, I know you don't want to believe it but it's true . . ."

Penelope was not listening. Her lacquered head was tilted toward the band, which was playing a waltz: Irving Berlin's "What'll I Do?"

"Oh, Bernie, my favorite. Can we dance, do you think?"

"Of course, Mother, if you'd like to. Will you excuse us, Antonio?"

Antonio turned toward Olivia. "Would you like to dance, Mrs. Rodway?"

Olivia shook her head. "No, not really," she said, and then, making an effort: "I am sorry about your wife, Antonio. You must miss her very much."

"Oh, yes," said Antonio. In fact he was ashamed by how little he missed Danila. In her absence his life had become much easier, without the quarrels, without the sleepless nights. "And it is strange not to see my son every day. I am afraid that when we next meet he will not know me at all."

Olivia nodded, but she did not answer. Instead she said: "I thought that perhaps you might have been at Mr. Belvoir's funeral."

The remark surprised Antonio. It had not occurred to him that he would be welcome at so grand an event. "But there must have been dozens of people there," he said. "If I had gone you would never have noticed me—"

Olivia made a fluttering movement with her left hand. It resembled a casual gesture of denial until she pressed her fingers to her lips, and he realized that she was on the brink of tears.

"Nobody talks about him, Antonio. Nobody talks about Dickie. They talk about the will, and how Dickie would have liked this or wanted that, but nobody talks about his death. It is as though it never happened. And yet we were all there—"

Her voice cracked. Antonio reached out and took her hand. "I know," he said. "I was there too, I saw it."

"I cannot bear it. It makes Dickie feel like a stranger—"

"It was you Mr. Belvoir wanted when he was dying," said Antonio. "Nobody else. Remember that, Mrs. Rodway."

Olivia's eyes widened with a kind of rapture. Before she could speak, though, Bernard returned from the dance floor.

"Penelope's just recognized an old acquaintance, she's gone to say hallo," he was saying when he noticed his wife's tears, and his voice sharpened. "For goodness' sake, Olivia, control yourself. You're embarrassing Antonio."

Olivia's face closed at once, like a door. It shocked Antonio to see how quickly it happened. She must have been doing it for so long, he thought, learning to hide her desolations, her pleasures.

"Forgive me," she said, and seizing her silvery evening bag she strode off toward the ladies' room. Bernard stretched out his legs and emptied his glass.

"Ach," he said, "women. There's no comprehending them."

For the first time Antonio felt dislike for Bernard's camaraderie, his carefree assumption that any sensible fellow must share his views. He rose to his feet. "I had better go and prepare for my next performance," he said. "Thank you for the drink, Mr. Rodway."

"It's a pleasure, Antonio. And we'll see you next week, shall we? Herr Fischer is giving lessons at my house once more, he will be expecting you. We should continue our normal lives for as long as we can, don't you agree?"

When Antonio got to the tiny dressing room he found Iris there, perched on the edge of the table. Through the slit in her black dress she was displaying a long golden expanse of thigh. His heart sank. He did not have the will, the energy, to deal with Iris now.

"I'm sulking. Why did you go and talk to dreary old Bernard instead of me?" Iris slipped her arms around his waist, under his jacket. "I think I deserve a long erotic kiss as compensation. Come on, don't be prudish, Antonio. You're practically a bachelor now your wife's left you."

"She hasn't left me," said Antonio, "she's gone back to Italy."

Iris stuck out her lower lip. "If that's not leaving you, what is?" she said, parting her knees to draw him closer. Before he could pull away Antonio heard the door open. It was Olivia. For a moment she looked shocked; then a smile crossed her face, a mocking smile, not a comfortable one.

"Oh! Signor Trombetta. I'm so sorry to have disturbed you," she said, and with a whisk of her dark blue dress she disappeared.

AUTUMN 1939

CHAPTER 23

THE SUMMER OF 1939 WAS STRANGE AND ELECTRIC; A SLEEP-walking summer, thought Olivia. War's imminence stalked the city like the certainty of death: you knew that sooner or later it must come, and sometimes that knowledge blinded, deafened you, but you could not think about it all the time, it was impossible: you had to pay the grocery bills, you had to get your shoes mended, you had to sit in your sunlit drawing room and pour tea smilingly for visitors.

During that summer Olivia spent as much time as she could at Dickie's house—now her house—in Sussex. She went alone, since Bernard was always occupied in London. Besides, he thought her visits unnecessary and told her so, irritably. The Ganders are looking after the place, he would say, seeing her stuff blouses and stockings and silk petticoats into her overnight bag, there is no need for you to go. If you'll only wait a week or so I can come with you. Olivia did not argue but she went all the same, catching the glossy malachite train at Victoria, taking a taxi to the house from Lewes station. Once she was there she sat among Dickie's pictures in his sage-green drawing room, she watched the plums ripen in his orchard, she tried to mix Negronis as he had mixed them. Her own solitude, her own freedom, delighted her, consoling her for the fact that Bernard was—or at least, Bernard seemed—too busy now to take her dancing. Olivia had not danced the tango since the night of her birthday party. She did not complain, though. She was afraid that her husband would think her shallow, to care about such a thing at such a time.

Bernard meanwhile had thrown his energies into civil defense preparations. He was agitating for a change in the strategy on air raid shelters. Londoners would need more protection than trenches or steel huts, or the shored-up crypts of churches. Why was the government refusing to open the underground stations, which would provide deep shelter for thousands? It was a scandal, a typical example of the few ignoring the many, and Bernard said so at every opportunity. Remembering Dickie's intentions—and his fear of boredom during air raids—he also joined the ARP. Bernard had exactly the right qualities for an air raid warden: natural authority, along with the bonhomie to chivvy without giving offense. He was especially deft at jollying sullen householders into acquiring sandbags and stuffing up cracks to make good their blackout.

In this purposeful flurry Bernard was able, most of the time, to bury his grief over his uncle's death. Olivia had been right. Bernard was hurt by Dickie's decision to leave her the house in Sussex. He felt that Dickie was criticizing his behavior toward Olivia—unfairly, since it was too late now for Bernard to justify it. Deep down he felt the subterranean heave of jealousy. Perhaps his uncle had preferred Olivia, perhaps he had loved her more than he loved Bernard. That fear haunted him, tainting his memories of Dickie with the tang of betrayal. He would never have prevented his wife from taking possession of her property. Apart from anything else he had no appetite for the recriminations, the bald truths that would follow. Nevertheless, he felt a perverse and childish—but of course childish—pleasure, to think how the war would soon end her forays to Sussex. He pictured Olivia as a migrant bird, high crested, brightly plumed, strutting restlessly between the four brick walls of the Bedford Square drawing room. Well, she can stay there, he thought, as he pulled on his regulation ARP boots, ready to begin his long evening's work.

On the morning of September 3 Filomena sat with her brother in the kitchen, listening to the radio. Unusually for a Sunday the BBC was playing light music, a selection of tunes by Sir Arthur Sullivan. It had been announced that the prime minister, Neville Chamberlain, was intending to broadcast to the nation at a quarter past eleven.

"I wish that he would speak and get it over with," said Filomena, fidgeting. She wanted something to occupy her, an onion to chop, a sock to darn, but it seemed disrespectful, out of keeping with the solemnity of the moment. In her dress pocket was the latest of the letters she had received from Stan. There had been three or four of them since he left London, robust cheerful letters, not very long; Filomena had the impression that he had struggled to write them.

"It won't be long," said Antonio. "It's already five minutes to eleven."

"Do you think we should wake Papa, to hear the broadcast?"

Antonio shook his head. "Let him sleep. He will find out soon enough."

Two days before, Antonio had taken his father to the Italian hospital in Queen Square. The doctor, a clever overworked young man from Verona, diagnosed a chronic inflammation of the lungs. He needs rest, he said, his own eyes crumpled from lack of sleep. They both knew that the cure he proposed was impossible: at six the next morning Enrico would be in Leicester Square, opening the kiosk.

"This is horrible music," said Filomena, and then: "What does your Mr. Rodway say about the war? Does he think that Mussolini will side with Germany?"

"Oh, the *duce* will do nothing. He will stay out of it until he sees who is winning. We will have to watch our step, though, Mena. Remember when Italy invaded Abyssinia, and people in the street called us traitors? It will be even worse this time."

"But I was born here," said Filomena, "I have lived here all my life."

Antonio shrugged as if to say, It will make no difference.

Filomena felt the crackle of Stan's letter against her hip. He had known that war was coming soon, but he had no idea where he would be sent. The letter was signed, Your friend, Stanley Harker.

On the radio the music drew to a close. There was a brief, fraught, heavy silence. Filomena pushed back her chair.

"I can't stand this," she said, and she ran out through the scullery into the yard. The sun was shining. From the open windows about her she could hear Neville Chamberlain's voice seep mournfully into the air. Filomena could not make out the words but she knew that they spelled the end of the familiar world.

"I DON'T UNDERSTAND," said Antonio. "Surely Mrs. Rodway is accustomed to traveling alone?"

"Oh, yes," said Bernard, "but it is different now. You never know what may happen."

They were sitting at the Lyons Corner House in Coventry Street, while a waitress in a stiff black dress brought them high tea. It was early in October, and still it seemed that the war had not yet begun. The theaters and cinemas were closed, and in the Regent's Park zoo the poisonous snakes had been killed with chloroform in case they escaped during a raid, but there had been no bombs, no choking clouds of mustard gas.

"I would go myself," Bernard went on, slicing across the white-filmed yolk of his poached egg, "but Herr Fischer has been summoned before a Home Office tribunal and I have promised to help him prepare."

As soon as war was declared the home secretary, Sir John Anderson, had announced plans for dealing with enemy aliens. Tribunals would be set up across the country to assess whether or not they were a threat to Britain. Category A, the most dangerous, would be interned; the rest would be left at liberty, though some—the doubtful cases—would be kept under watch, their movements restricted.

"Surely nobody can believe that Herr Fischer is dangerous?" Antonio said. "He's a refugee."

"Oh, it is a formality. Konrad is nervous, though. The hearings are held in secret, which is bound to put a man on edge. And the tribunal members will be the usual starched shirts: barristers, justices of the peace. The kind of Briton who thinks you can never trust a foreigner. You are fortunate, Antonio, that your great leader has declared his neutrality."

"For the present," said Antonio drily.

Bernard grinned and ate another luscious mouthful of toast and egg and butter. "Of course, there is no need for Olivia to go to Sussex, we employ a local family to look after the house. But you know what women are like. She insists that there are things only she can do. And I do not want her wandering the country alone. If there is an invasion the Germans could come smack through Newhaven. You would not have sent your own wife to Italy, would you, without the protection of your brother." He pushed a plate of tea cakes toward Antonio. "Eat something, please, Antonio. You're making me feel like a hog."

Politely Antonio bit into one of the tea cakes, which he found bland and stodgy. "There must be other—more suitable people to escort Mrs. Rodway to Sussex," he said. Someone of your own class, was what he meant. The thought of being alone with Olivia filled him with agitation. He had the feeling that he ought to do whatever he could to prevent it.

"Well, possibly," said Bernard, "but Olivia likes you, Antonio. At least, she doesn't dislike you, which appears to be the case with many of my friends." He sighed, and drew the tip of his knife delicately across his second poached egg, allowing the bright orange yolk to flood out. "And it will only be for one night. I know your father is not in the best of health, but surely he can manage without you for one night?"

OLIVIA WAS INFURIATED by her husband's maneuver. This might be her last chance to spend time alone in Dickie's house, and she could see that pleasure being snatched from her by Bernard's controlling hand.

She was also piqued by his choice of chaperone. She had been shocked to find Antonio in the arms of feckless flighty Iris. It was not only the discovery that her confidant, the man she had thought understood her, was a philanderer. She remembered the outrage in his eyes that night in the Paradise Ballroom, and how ashamed he had made her feel. He's nothing but a hypocrite, she thought. One rule for himself, a quite different one for me.

Antonio, sitting opposite her in the carriage—they were traveling first class, in plush antimacassared seats—could tell that she was fizzing with anger, although he did not comprehend why. She was wearing a dark purple suit and a small hat with a veil; a frivolous hat, although it did not look frivolous on Olivia, with her thunderclap face.

The October sun, streaming dustily through the glass, was unseasonably warm. As the train drew south of Croydon Olivia got up to open the window.

"Let me," said Antonio, "please, Mrs. Rodway."

"Why? I'm perfectly capable of doing it." Olivia tugged at the leather strap to pull the window down. "You are as bad as Bernard. He thinks that women can do nothing practical. I'm used to shifting for myself. I was living in a bedsit when he met me. A person who has lived in a bedsit can do anything."

She sat down once more, staring at him with wide provocative eyes. Antonio had no idea how he was going to survive the next thirty-six hours in her company. He thought of her mocking smile when she had found him with Iris in his arms. Was that why she was so angry? Surely not; surely nothing he did could matter that much to Olivia. All the same Antonio felt an intense compulsion to justify himself, to set the record straight.

"I ought to tell you, Mrs. Rodway," he said, licking his lips, "that there is nothing between me and Iris. There never has been—"

Olivia held up her gloved hand to silence him. "You don't have to explain yourself, Signor Trombetta. Your canoodlings are none of my business. Your wife's business, perhaps, but not mine." She picked up the magazine on her lap. "And now I'd like to continue the journey in peace. You're here because my husband asked you to keep watch on me. He may even have paid you, I don't know. But don't let's pretend that we're traveling together from choice."

THEY ARRIVED AT Lewes late in the afternoon. The station was solid and handsome, redbrick with whitewashed metal awnings. As they stepped from the carriage, porters sprang up to seize Olivia's bags and escort her to the taxi rank. Antonio fumbled the business of tipping them, and was annoyed to see Olivia suppress a smile. The money for the tips had come from Bernard, of course, handed over with the discreet grace that Antonio lacked. His own clumsiness gnawed at him as the taxi swept through the quaint streets of Lewes. It was ten minutes before he became aware that they were in the countryside, green curved beautiful countryside, cut through in places where quarrymen had been tunneling for chalk. The sight flooded Antonio with an unlooked-for calm. He was not accustomed to so much sky, pale but luminous, after the tall narrow canyon that was Frith Street.

He sensed a change in Olivia too. The rage ebbed from her, leaving her cleansed and calm in the seat beside him. "I love it here," she said quite suddenly. "I am sorry that I was rude to you, Antonio. I was angry with my husband, that's all."

The taxi drew up beside Dickie's flint-walled house. Olivia did not wait for Antonio to pay the driver; she hurried toward the porch, a large iron key in her hand.

"Mrs. Gander?" he heard her call. "Are you there?"

When he had dealt with the taxi Antonio followed her through the hall into a low-ceilinged room, painted a powdery sage green. Olivia was staring at the hearth, which was littered with soot and broken mortar. The debris had spilled onto the Persian carpet beside the gilt fender. She frowned. "It must have been a brick, falling down the chimney."

Antonio pointed to the leather of the chesterfield, spattered with dirty whitish streaks. "No, it's a bird. There is a bird in the house."

Briskly he crossed toward the window and shook the russet velvet curtains. At once a creature flew up, beating against the lead-lighted panes. It was a crow, its black feathers smeared with chimney dust. There was something dazed and terrible about it.

"Get it out." Olivia pressed her hands to her face. "Oh, please, get it out."

"But you lived in a bedsit," said Antonio. "A person who has lived in a bedsit can do anything."

When he looked at her, though, he saw that she was transfixed by horror, and he reached for the curlicued metal handle to open the window. "*Vai!*" he yelled, clapping his hands. "*Vai, cretino!*"

The crow, in a frenzy, thrashed hopelessly against the wooden sill. Antonio was afraid of seizing it in case he damaged its wings. Grasping the velvet curtain he whisked it to and fro to drive the creature out, still shouting. For half a minute the bird swooped and fluttered before at last it tumbled through the open window.

"Tcha," said Antonio, with satisfaction. He leaned out to make certain that the crow was not injured and then he closed the window. "We had better clean up, that mess will stain. Show me where the kitchen is, Mrs. Rodway. I will light the stove for hot water."

Olivia did not answer. She was standing beside the fireplace, a silver photograph frame in one hand. "That was horrible. Like a lost soul, trapped in the house. And the more it struggles, the worse it becomes . . ."

"The creature has escaped now. It is quite safe. You are quite safe."

Olivia shivered. "It's a bad omen, though. Degrading." She turned the silver frame to show him. It was a photograph of Olivia herself, serene and haughty in a gleaming oyster-colored dress. The glass was spattered with thick gray droppings. "Dickie loved this picture, he had a copy of it in Chelsea too. It was taken on my honeymoon with Bernard. We went on an Atlantic cruise. I had never seen such luxury. I felt that I was living someone else's life, someone luckier than me, someone more deserving . . ."

There were some decanters on the sideboard, elegant Art Deco decanters tipped with chrome. Antonio poured some brandy from one of them into a glass.

"You're upset. Sit down, drink this."

Olivia swallowed the brandy. Then she strode toward the window, still clutching the photograph. "I suppose you think that I married Bernard for his money," she said. "Well, perhaps I did. Money can be very glamorous. It wasn't wealth I wanted, though, it was opportunity. I thought that Bernard would open up my life like some wonderful book. I'm not a greedy woman, I don't care about furs or jewelry. All I wanted was the chance to do things, to see things. I didn't think of it as being about money. Is that naïve?"

"I do not know," said Antonio. He could not keep his eyes from her as she paced across the floor, talking, talking.

"You think you can escape your origins, but you can't. Bernard thought that he could transform me, that I would be wax in his hands, and in a way he did, and I was. But the real me shines through, and the real me isn't what poor Bernard wants at all."

The discontent in her face was like the eerie light of a storm. I love her, thought Antonio. I have never loved anyone as I love her. He tried to conjure the memory of his wife—Danila on their wedding day, sweet and shining—but her image seemed as artificial as a painted plaster saint. It had no power to protect him.

"Besides, I cannot have his children. I destroyed all that, you know how." Olivia's eyes flared at him for an instant. "Bernard does not realize it, I have never told him, he would not forgive me if he knew, he would never forgive me—"

"Hush," said Antonio, "hush." Crossing toward her he prised the silver frame from her fingers. Then he took out his handkerchief and wiped the glass until all the stains and smears had gone. Olivia watched him do it.

"I thought you must despise me," she said. "A scarlet woman, a gold digger. I was afraid you would betray me, and tell Bernard my secret."

Antonio stared at the photograph: Olivia, inscrutable in her oyster silk dress. The words burned unspoken on his lips. How could I betray you? I love you.

"No," he said aloud, "I have never despised you."

"The fact is, we are alike, you and I. We're both impostors. We do not belong here, we are outsiders, we belong in the yard of the Paradise Ballroom." Olivia gave a skewed grin. "Do you remember, Antonio? You gave me your bottle of beer."

Antonio did not answer. I cannot bear this, he thought. He replaced the photograph on the mantelpiece, running his fingertips across the frame's edge. His face felt rigid as a mask with the need to keep silent.

"Antonio," said Olivia, "is something wrong?"

"No, nothing is wrong. It is only—I do not think I ought to spend the night here. Perhaps there is a place in the village where I can stay?"

"Don't be absurd," said Olivia. "My husband knows you're with me, it was his idea. There's nothing scandalous about it—"

"I'm in love with you, Mrs. Rodway." The words rang in Antonio's ears as though someone else had spoken them. They sounded brusque, almost angry. "It is hopeless, I realize that, I've always realized that, but it's the truth."

Olivia did not move. Her eyes were wide as saucers. "Antonio," she said gently, "you cannot be in love with me. You have a wife, a child."

"Yes, I know, I am a married man." Antonio grimaced. "It makes no difference, though. It does not stop me from loving you. I am not a philanderer, Mrs. Rodway, I do not make a habit of seducing women. But I do not think I can stay here tonight . . ."

In silence Olivia crossed to the sideboard and poured herself more brandy. "Do you know," she said, in a conversational voice, "Bernard hasn't laid a finger on me for six months? That's how much my husband loves me."

She looked across at Antonio. There was a defiant expression on her face. It took Antonio's breath away. "Olivia . . . ," he said, stepping toward her. At once she crumbled, burying her cheeks in her hands.

"Oh, you are right, it is hopeless. Perhaps you should leave after all, Antonio. Perhaps it would be safer."

"Safer?" said Antonio.

Olivia lowered her head. Her voice was so soft he could scarcely hear. "I want you too. I have wanted you since I first saw you, that night at the Paradise Ballroom. I pretended I did not, I told myself it was nothing, but all the time, Antonio—"

He could not stop himself. He pulled her into his arms. She stiffened for an instant, startled, before she pressed herself fiercely against him. His lips were on her neck, her fingers were in his hair. He could feel the heat of her breasts. I would die for her, thought Antonio, and then: But this is betrayal, this is mortal sin. At once he lurched away.

Olivia drew back at exactly the same time. Her eyes were wild and terrified. He knew they were the mirror image of his own.

"Oh, Antonio. We cannot, we must not," she said, and before he could stop her—before he could speak—she fled from the room, running up the stairs into the dark unknown depths of the house.

CHAPTER 24

KONRAD FISCHER'S HEARING TOOK PLACE IN THE CLASSROOM of a dour redbrick Victorian school. The smell of the room reminded Bernard of his days at Rugby. It was a mixture of chalk and sweaty blazers along with an acrid scent—part boredom, part fear. Bernard felt a twang of indignation, that after all he had already suffered Herr Fischer was forced to undergo this examination.

"Don't be anxious," he murmured as they sat on hard upright chairs. "It will be all right, I promise."

Herr Fischer licked his lips without listening. He was carrying a sheaf of documents in a brown leather music case, letters vouching for his respectability from members of the refugee association, and from Charles Connor, Dickie's friend from the BBC.

The chair of the tribunal was a retired bank manager named Reginald Whitworth, now a justice of the peace. "Herr Konrad Fischer?" he said, eyeing them above his gilt half-moon spectacles. "And this is?"

"My name is Bernard Rodway. Herr Fischer was told that he could be accompanied by a friend, although regrettably he is not allowed the support of a lawyer."

Whitworth glanced at him before shifting his gaze deliberately to Herr Fischer. He had a port drinker's nose, Bernard noticed, red veined and bulbous.

"You do not need a lawyer, Herr Fischer. We wish only to determine whether you may present a threat to this country now we are at war. I am sure you understand that. You are an Austrian citizen, I believe? And you arrived in London eighteen months ago, in the spring of 1938. Do you have any family remaining in Austria?"

Herr Fischer tried to answer, but the words stuck in his throat like sand.

"Speak up, Herr Fischer," said Whitworth, not unkindly.

"My sister. My sister, Brigitta. If she is still alive . . ."

The desolation in his voice put Bernard in a fury. "I presume you know, Mr. Chairman, that Herr Fischer is a refugee? He was forced to abandon a prestigious musical career in Vienna on account of Hitler's persecution. Now that he has found shelter here he is hardly likely to offer comfort to the enemy."

Reginald Whitworth studied him. "What did you say your name was? Rodway? I thought that I recognized it. Don't you write for the *New Statesman*?"

"Sometimes," said Bernard, "yes."

Whitworth's eyes lit up, uncanny as marsh gas. "So you take the view that this country would be better off if we were ruled by Bolsheviks?"

Bernard hesitated. In fact he disliked the *New Statesman*'s reluctance to criticize Stalin, but he was not going to give this Colonel Blimp the satisfaction of admitting it. "In my opinion, our fear of communism has blinded us to the true evil in our midst. If we had been less inclined to regard Hitler as a useful buffer against the Reds we would not be at war today."

"A dangerous view. The Nazis and the Soviets are allies now. Let us not forget that."

Bernard was about to argue back when one of the other tribunal members, an elderly, mild-looking fellow, interrupted. "We are not here to debate your political views, Mr. Rodway. We are here to consider the position of Herr Fischer."

"Indeed," said Reginald Whitworth, displeased at being reminded of his own function. The atmosphere in the room grew still more awkward. "May I ask how you support yourself, Herr Fischer? Have you found employment here in London?"

"I teach. Singing and so forth. And I have some work in the theater. I have letters here vouching for me—"

"But it is all theatrical work?" the elderly gentleman remarked, with an air of disappointment. "Precarious in wartime, Herr Fischer. Most of our theaters have been closed."

"Music is Herr Fischer's profession," Bernard put in. "What else would you expect him to do? And it is not so precarious as you may think. Soon we will be thirsting for music to lift our spirits. Besides, Herr Fischer can call on my support at any time."

Reginald Whitworth glanced across as though he did not consider Bernard's support to be much of a recommendation. The panel members murmured among themselves. The elderly man appeared to be disagreeing, politely, with his chairman. At last Whitworth indicated to the tribunal's clerk that they had reached a decision.

"We recognize, Herr Fischer, that you are a refugee from Nazi oppression, and that fact will be recorded in your file. In our judgment, you present no immediate danger to this country, but we would like to keep abreast of your movements. For that reason, we are placing you in category B."

Herr Fischer frowned. "What does that mean?"

"Certain restrictions will be placed upon you, that is all. You should not travel more than five miles from your home, and you are forbidden from owning a motorcar or a camera. Nothing that could be called draconian." The chairman looked up with a brisk, you-can-go-now smile. "My advice is to find yourself a steady job, Herr Fischer, and perhaps we will reconsider your case."

Herr Fischer looked first at Reginald Whitworth, then at Bernard. There was a bewildered expression on his face. Bernard opened his mouth to protest, but thought better of it. Sheltering Herr Fischer with his arm he escorted him in silence from the schoolroom.

~

OLIVIA WAS SHOCKED by the outcome of Herr Fischer's hearing. She had assumed that Bernard, with his charm, his confidence, would easily persuade the tribunal that the Austrian could do no harm.

"Didn't you explain that he was a refugee?" she said. They were sitting in the drawing room in Bedford Square, she and Bernard. It was an afternoon when Herr Fischer normally gave lessons, but he had sent a message to say he was not well.

"Of course I explained. They did not want to hear, that is all." Bernard squirted soda into his inch of whisky. "The chairman was an archetypal pigheaded Tory. Tried to get me into an argument about communism, but I wouldn't bite."

Something about Bernard's nonchalance made Olivia guess that he was lying. She had a sudden glimpse of what had really happened at the tribunal.

Bernard switched on the radio, to forestall further discussion. The news was on: a German U-boat had managed to enter the British naval base at Scapa Flow. It had torpedoed a battleship, the *Royal Oak*, sinking it with the loss of nearly a thousand lives.

"Horrible," said Olivia, shivering.

"Well," said Bernard, "we had better grow accustomed to it. Those deaths won't be the last." He was rising to refill his whisky glass when the doorbell jangled. "Dear God, it's Antonio. Didn't you send to him, to tell him that Herr Fischer was ill?"

Olivia's heart leaped. She had not seen Antonio since their return from Sussex, and she could not tell if what she felt was joy or stomach-wrenching fear.

"I did not think," she said. "I assumed that you—"

"Can't you get anything right, Olivia? I'm a busy man, I had Herr Fischer's tribunal, I have my ARP shifts. The least you can do is to manage our lives with a modicum of efficiency." Bernard clicked off the radio. "You'll have to deal with him, that's all. My shift starts in half an hour."

Antonio, shown into the room by Avril, was bright eyed and composed. "I suppose it is not so bad," he said when Bernard told him about Herr Fischer. "At least they have not locked him up."

"Yes, that would have put paid to your singing lessons," said Bernard, and then, realizing how offensive he sounded: "Antonio, forgive me, I know that is not what you meant. This damned phony war is getting on everyone's nerves. And now I'm afraid I must leave you. I have an air raid warden's shift tonight. No, don't go. Olivia has nothing to do, she can entertain you." He shook Antonio's hand, glancing over his shoulder at his wife. "Don't wait up, Olivia. You know I will be late."

Olivia, on the sofa, raised her head and looked at Antonio. Their eyes locked. Neither of them spoke. Five, ten, twenty seconds passed. The front door closed with a thud. For another ten seconds they stared. Then Antonio crossed the room, and they were in each other's arms, and it was as though their bodies were one flesh, reunited after a long drought.

"I cannot stop thinking about you," Antonio mumbled into her hair. One palm was sliding upward along her leg, to the place where her smooth silk stocking gave way to her smooth silken thigh. Olivia stiffened.

"Not in this house," she said fiercely, "never in this house."

"Where, then?" Antonio's hand was still on her thigh. Olivia groaned and buried her face in his neck. His skin smelled of soap and hair oil and, faintly, of the confectionery he had been selling. It was a real scent, thought Olivia, a delicious scent, complicated and personal.

"Oh, my love," she said. "It will not be long, it cannot be long. I will find a way for us to be together. I promise I will find a way."

AS HE WALKED home in the darkness Antonio's nerves, his very sinews, fizzed and burned. The October sky was clear, with a pockmarked wedge of moon. He felt that his passion for Olivia was branded upon his forehead, visible to all, like the bands of white painted on the lampposts to guide wanderers through the black-out.

When he arrived in Frith Street his father was sitting at the kitchen table, smoking. His face was clay colored, and the ashtray was brimming with cigarette butts.

"What is it, Papa?" Antonio's head was seething. It took a peculiar effort to sound calm. "Is something wrong?"

"I am glad you are home, Antonio. I need to speak to you." Enrico drew on his cigarette and breathed out the smoke. "Next week the payment for our lease on the kiosk is due."

"Yes, I remember." Antonio crossed to the scullery and ran himself a glass of cold water. "Why does that trouble you, Papa? We have got the money. We set it aside months ago."

"You are right, we did. But circumstances change, Antonio, my son. There may be other demands—more urgent demands—on a man's purse—"

"What are you saying, Papa? That we don't have the money after all?"

Enrico stubbed out his cigarette. He did it meticulously, as though it were a dangerous object that might otherwise do harm. "It was hard for your brother, Valentino, to return to Lazio. He talks passionately of his fatherland, but the truth is that he has lived all his life here in London. He is not accustomed to working with his hands, as the men in our village do. It will take him time to settle . . ."

He looked across at his son. At first Antonio could not take in what that pleading expression meant. When he realized it was with a thud of disbelief.

"You gave the money for the lease to Valentino?"

"Not all of it," said Enrico. "Only half."

Antonio sat down, winded. "But it is our livelihood, Papa. I make money from singing, I know, and there are Filomena's wages, but without the kiosk—"

"We can borrow, Antonino." Enrico's voice was at once injured and eager. "It will not be for long. We will make economies and pay off the debt."

"Who will lend to us, Papa? There is a war on, people do not take risks with their money. Especially lending to foreigners."

Enrico cleared his throat. "I wondered—this English friend of yours, this Mr. Rodway, is a wealthy man. And he seems fond of you. Is it possible you might ask him to lend you the money?"

"No!" said Antonio at once. "Do not ask me to do that, Papa. Never ask me to do that."

Enrico's eyes widened, startled by the violence of his reply. "Well, there is another possibility, although you will not like it, Antonio. The *fascio* will lend funds to loyal Italians. The terms are favorable, too. Better than going to a moneylender."

"Oh, Papa," said Antonio, and he put his head in his hands.

"I spoke to one of the officials this afternoon, to see how the land lies. Signor Follini, his name is. You may remember him, he called in at Bruno's bachelor party. He asked after your brother, Valentino, very warmly I thought." Enrico paused before he went on, doggedly: "There is only one condition. I am an old man, you know that, I am not in good health. Signor Follini wants you to guarantee the loan, in case anything happens to me."

"What?" said Antonio, looking up. His father's gaze was fixed upon him, anxious, beseeching.

"You will have to sign a paper, Antonino, that is all, promising to repay the money. You do not have to join the *fascio*, they do not ask that."

"They do not ask that yet," said Antonio. "But what if we are late with our payments, eh, Papa? What will happen then?" He pictured Signor Follini, with his cold bright blue eyes. This is how it starts, he thought. They will reel me in like a hooked fish.

"We will not be late," said Enrico. "We will work hard, Antonio, we will find the money, I promise on my life."

Another scene ran through Antonio's head: of himself, asking Bernard Rodway for the loan. He imagined Bernard reaching comfortably for his wallet, just as he had done in the Lyons Corner House, and peeling off the white five-pound notes. Of course, it is a pleasure. Why didn't you ask me before? He let out a groan.

"Well, Papa," he said, "it seems that I have no choice."

Enrico's face broke into a smile. Reaching out he squeezed Antonio's forearm. "It is your name upon a piece of paper, nothing more. You are a good son to me, Antonino. I knew that I could rely upon you."

SPRING 1940

CHAPTER 25

THE FIRST WINTER OF THE WAR WAS A COLD ONE. PETROL WAS rationed; so were bacon and butter, and there were whispers that sugar would be next. Coal was hard to come by, and Filomena struggled to keep the stove alight in Frith Street. As the icy months passed Enrico was dwindling before her eyes. In February he was admitted to the Italian hospital in Queen Square with pneumonia, although there was not much that they could do for him, according to the tired young doctor from Verona.

"He needs a warmer climate," he said, when Filomena arrived to fetch her father home.

"Well, and I am afraid he works every day," said Filomena. "He will not stay at home in bed."

"You must try harder to persuade him, *signorina*." There was a restlessness about the doctor, as though there were a dozen, a hundred, other cases to which he should have been giving his attention, and every moment spent with Filomena was stolen from someone else. It made her wish perversely to extend the conversation. At the same time she was sorry for the doctor, who must feel that he had never truly finished his day's work.

A month later, in March, Bruno lost his job. Prejudice against Italians, he said bitterly. It is the fault of the newspapers, whipping up hatred toward us. No other hotels were hiring staff, and at Antonio's suggestion Bruno began to help in the kiosk. It eased the burden upon Enrico, so that Antonio could continue his singing engagements.

After the first stunned shock of war it seemed that everyone in London was desperate to go dancing. The Golden Slipper had reopened, and Antonio found himself in demand in dance halls from Victoria to Tottenham Court Road, standing in for singers who had joined up. He no longer exaggerated his accent now, but tried to sound as English as possible.

Meanwhile Bruno and Renata moved back to Frith Street, to live with Uncle Mauro. It was cheaper, and since Renata was expecting their first child she wanted company. She had been frightened by the shift in Bruno's fortunes. There was no question of her gloating over her status; it was Filomena who was in the ascendant once more. Her hours at the laundry had been reduced, with so many people gone from London, but she was still earning, and in Danila's absence she ruled the roost in the Trombettas' kitchen. For all the hardships of war, for all her fears over Enrico, she felt herself to be that fine thing: a strong, resourceful woman.

And she had a secret, which filled every day with a sweet, solid joy. Over the months the letters she and Stan exchanged had grown longer, warmer, more expansive. She wrote to him every week, wearing a cardigan and gloves as well as her dressing gown to avoid burning coal. His letters arrived more erratically at the post office in Charing Cross Road. He wrote carefully to avoid the pages being sliced by the censor. His division was still in Britain, kicking its heels, waiting to be sent to France or perhaps to Finland, which was under attack from the Soviet Union. He described the friends he had made, and the boredom. I miss the force, he wrote, there was always something happening in the force. He did not say, And I miss you too, but his letters ended, Chin up, keep smiling, from your loving Stanley. Filomena hoarded them like jewels, tucked in her drawer beneath her badly darned stockings.

⁂

Early in April, as the phony war continued, the prime minister, Neville Chamberlain, declared triumphally that Hitler had missed the bus: there would be no invasion now. Four days later they began to put out the deck chairs in the scarred landscape that was Hyde Park. Olivia watched them do it, wrapped in a thick white towel, from a high window overlooking the park.

"What are you doing?" Antonio raised his head from the pillow. He always fell asleep as soon as they had made love, plummeting into a deep short-lived chasm of unconsciousness.

Olivia looked over her shoulder. "I have to go, my darling. Lionel—Bernard's brother—is staying with us tonight."

Even as she spoke she crossed toward the bed once more. The peach-colored carpet was cloyingly soft beneath her bare feet. They were in an apartment overlooking the park, a grand apartment where half the furniture was eerily swathed in dust sheets. It belonged to a friend of Penelope Rodway's, a wealthy dowager who had quit London in a panic as soon as war was declared. The dowager was too mean or else too mistrustful to install a servant, and Penelope had volunteered Bernard's help in keeping an eye on the flat. I'll do it, Olivia had said when he complained, languidly putting out her hand for the keys. I can call in once a week, to make sure the place hasn't been looted. You have far too much to do already, Bernard.

"Can't you stay a little longer?" With one fingertip Antonio touched the pleat of the towel where she had tucked it between her breasts. "Bruno is at the kiosk this afternoon. They all think that I am meeting a bandleader in Pimlico, to talk about a job."

"Oh," said Olivia, "we are such liars."

"I know. I have never been a liar before, I have always told the truth. Does it trouble you?"

"Yes," said Olivia, as she let slip the towel and climbed back into the bed. She smelled of the soap she had brought with her to the apartment, the same soap that she used in her bathroom at Bedford Square. She bathed scrupulously every time they made love, so that no hint of Antonio, his sweat, his sperm, could be scented on her body.

Antonio put one hand upon her breast, running the other down to the fork of her thighs. These were all things Danila had never permitted him to do. He could kiss her, yes, and nuzzle her throat, and when the moment came he could lift her nightdress and enter her, but if he tried to caress her she would squirm out of his grasp, as though it were forbidden. He had never seen his wife entirely naked.

"We do not lie to each other, though," he said. "We have never lied to each other."

Olivia gazed up at him. "I could not lie to you. Even that first night, the night we met, when I was bleeding—I wanted to hide the truth from you, and I could not do it. I can hide nothing from you."

The sun inched between the curtains, not an intruder, but a witness. The war seemed more than ever like a phantasm, a bad collective dream that would not come to pass.

"WE SHOULD NOT be lulled into a false sense of security." Lionel Rodway cradled a glass of claret between his plump fingers. Like every man in England he had a clear opinion about what would happen next in the war. "If Hitler does attack, the French will send him packing, they have the strongest army in Europe. But we should be braced nevertheless."

They were having dinner at Bertorelli's in Charlotte Street. Olivia would have preferred to dine at home—she wanted to dazzle Lionel with her skills as a hostess—but Bernard had insisted on eating out. Meat rationing, introduced in March, did not yet apply to restaurants—a source of much grumbling about the privileges of the wealthy. It's unfair, I know, Bernard said, but let's face it, we'll get a better dinner if we go out. And he was right, Olivia thought grudgingly, as she tasted her veal cutlet, the sauce delicately flavored with tarragon. She had been late returning home—she had had to bathe again before leaving the apartment in Hyde Park—and she was out of breath from the scramble to get ready, climbing into her slippery red satin dress, twisting up her hair into a knot. She remembered what she had said to Antonio, in bed this afternoon: We are such liars.

Bernard dabbed his lips with his napkin. "Oh, I think we're pretty well prepared. Here in London everyone takes the blackout damn seriously." In fact two days before he had complained that householders had grown far too cocky about showing a light, but he liked on principle to disagree with his brother.

"And we have to be on guard against the enemy within," Lionel went on, as if Bernard had not spoken. "There are so many foreigners now, especially in our cities, Glasgow and Manchester and so forth. Many of them claim to be refugees—"

"Many of them *are* refugees, Lionel," said Bernard. "Our friend Konrad Fischer for one. He is a gifted musician who had to flee Vienna, leaving everything behind. And how do we treat him? We forbid him to travel more than five miles from his home, and we require him to register with the police like a common thief."

"Ah, but, Bernard. We cannot be too careful. What better device for the Nazis to plant spies among us, knowing how we always help the underdog? I am not saying that these fellows are dangerous necessarily, only that we do not know. It is the same with the Italians." Lionel gestured airily toward the dark-haired maître d'hôtel at the restaurant door. "Whose side will they be on, if Mussolini declares war?"

"Actually, the proprietors here are British citizens," Olivia remarked. "Their sons have just joined the army." Bernard laid his hand approvingly upon her wrist. All through dinner he had been making gestures like this, displaying their marital harmony as a peacock flaunts its green and blue tail. He had touched her more this evening, Olivia thought, than at any time in the last six months.

The remark, or perhaps the gesture, irritated Lionel. He found Olivia disconcerting: you never knew what she was thinking, damn it.

"Well, that may be so," he said, "but you take my point. We are too soft on the Italians. We think them charming, but that is just a smokescreen. In their way they are as great a menace as the Germans, especially as there are so many of them here. Café owners in Soho, ice-cream men in Glasgow. We should be locking up the whole crew."

"What?" said Olivia. "All of them?"

"Better safe than sorry, Olivia. Our friend Musso is a treacherous fellow. He could throw in his lot with Hitler at any time. And if we wait until he does it will be too late, half the fascists in Britain will have slipped through our fingers." Lionel, who had been loading his fork with steak and fried potatoes, filled his mouth with an air of finality.

"Don't worry, my sweet," said Bernard, his hand still clasping Olivia's wrist. "Antonio will be all right. He's not a fascist."

Neither is Herr Fischer, Olivia wanted to say, but the thought of Antonio's arrest made her stomach cave in, and she was afraid that if she said any more she would give herself away. Dispassionately she watched Lionel eat. As she watched, she imagined his padded frame swelling like a balloon, his face growing redder and damper, until he gave a last desperate gasp and burst.

CHAPTER 26

THE FOLLOWING MORNING THE NEWS BROKE: HITLER HAD INvaded neutral Norway. Within a day Oslo had fallen. The war had begun in earnest.

The British were incredulous, especially Churchill, who as first lord of the Admiralty had declared that the Germans were incapable of landing in Scandinavia. A week later, wrong-footed, British troops arrived in central Norway. Their transport ships were too bulky for the narrow fjords; men were decanted into destroyers to reach the port of Namsos, losing half their kit in the process. From there they headed south toward Trondheim, without skis or snowshoes, weighed down by their heavy lambskin coats. The engines of the planes that should have given them air cover froze in the Arctic night. There was nothing to stop the Luftwaffe bombarding them as they struggled onward through the snowdrifts, frostbitten, snow-blind.

Among those soldiers was Stan Harker, although Filomena did not know that. She knew only that his letters had ceased. Now when she went to the post office in Charing Cross Road the clerk would check the pigeonholes and shake his head briskly. She saw him do the same with other women, women she had begun, over the months, to recognize. Some were young girls who, like Filomena, were not meant to be writing to their sweethearts; others were older women, unacknowledged mistresses or faithless wives. None of them looked at each other. Late in April one of the women, a freckled creature in her thirties, began to weep when the clerk told her she had no letters. Filomena, seeing the tears drip from her chin, stepped instinctively toward her. The woman turned away at once, hiding her wet face beneath the brim of her hat. Well, thought Filomena, perhaps it is for the best. Perhaps we should keep our own secrets, after all.

A week later Bernard Rodway was strolling through Bloomsbury to buy a newspaper when he saw Antonio on the far side of the street. His trilby was pulled low over his forehead, but it did not occur to Bernard that he might wish to be left alone.

"Antonio!" he called. "Hallo there, stranger! Where are you going?"

Antonio looked up. He could see that it would be impossible to avoid Bernard. "I am on my way to Queen Square, to the Italian hospital. My father was admitted two days ago, I'm going to visit him."

"In that case I'll walk with you." Amiably Bernard fell into step as they strode east along Montague Place. "We've missed you, Antonio. I can't remember the last time you came to Bedford Square for a singing lesson. Konrad keeps asking what has become of you." The image of Herr Fischer's face sprang into Bernard's mind. Since his appearance before the Home Office tribunal he had grown more lugubrious than ever, his eyes lightless, his jowls drooping.

"I am sorry. There is so much to do, with my father in hospital, and my singing engagements. I will try to come this week, or maybe next."

There was a newsstand on the corner of Malet Street. Bernard paused to buy a couple of papers, reaching into his pocket for small change. He read the news as avidly as a schoolboy reads comics.

"Pah," he said as he examined the front pages. "I hate the newspapers when they're in a moral frenzy. Have you seen them? They insist that Norway was betrayed from within by Nazi sympathizers. According to them we ought to learn the lesson and clamp down on enemy aliens. The only one to talk sense is the *Daily Express*, and that's just because Beaverbrook has a Jewish mistress."

Antonio nodded without speaking. These days he could think of nothing except those rare gilded hours in the abandoned flat beside Hyde Park; the rest of the time it seemed he was only half alive. Even his father's illness, even the progress of the war, appeared as distant as the gray grainy images upon a newsreel.

Bernard gave a grim chuckle at his paper; then, registering Antonio's silence, he glanced up from the page.

"Don't let me detain you, Antonio. I can see that you're anxious about your father." He laid a comradely hand upon Antonio's shoulder. "These are difficult times, with so much uncertainty. You will tell me, won't you, if there is anything that I can do to help?"

LATE IN APRIL the British forces in Norway were diverted north, to join the offensive against the Arctic port of Narvik. Still Filomena had no news of Stan. She called at the post office every day now, and she detected a wariness in the clerk's expression when he saw her, fearing hysteria or rage. It is no good, Filomena thought, this is going to drive me mad. Any day now I will do something foolish. I have to take action.

The next day she was not expected at the laundry. After breakfast, as soon as Antonio had left to open the kiosk, she put on her best hat and coat, and set off for Bermondsey. She had the Harkers' address, but she had never been to Bermondsey before and as she got off the bus the unfamiliarity of the streets made them seem menacing. She walked the pavement stiffly, eyes straight ahead, trying to look as though she knew exactly where she was going.

At the street corner a woman was mopping her front step, a blowzy-looking woman with her hair tied in a yellow scarf. She straightened with a groan when Filomena spoke to her.

"I'm looking for Mrs. Harker," she said, holding out the paper with Stan's address on it. The blowzy woman gave her a searching look, full of self-confidence. It reminded Filomena that she might speak perfect English but she still looked like a foreigner. The woman glanced at the paper, and gestured with her thumb to the next left turn, before she doused her mop in the gray tin bucket once more.

The house was narrow, built of red Victorian brick, with thin curtains pulled shut over the sash windows. Filomena hesitated. Now that she was here she had no idea how to introduce herself. Acquaintance? Friend? Girlfriend? If she stopped to think, though, she would lose her nerve. She rapped on the door with the tarnished knocker. In the neighboring house a girl of about twelve put out her head from an upstairs window and watched her, without speaking. Like the woman on the doorstep she did it as though she had a perfect right to stare.

There were slow footsteps in the hall, and the door creaked open. Stanley's mother had the same wide, pale face as her son. She was wearing a cotton overall and her eyes—blue like Stan's—were bloodshot. The sight of her, so like and so unlike Stan, made Filomena's heart turn over.

"Mrs. Harker?" she said.

Stan's mother lifted her chin. "Who's asking?"

"My name is Filomena Trombetta. I am a friend of your son Stanley—"

"Ah, you're the Eyetie girl, aren't you? You look like an Eyetie."

"Yes, my family is Italian, although I was born here in London—"

"I've got your letters," Mrs. Harker went on, in the same blank, dogged voice. "The letters you wrote to Stan. That's how I know who you are. They sent them to us, with his things."

There was a cold ringing in Filomena's head. "What?" she said.

Mrs. Harker, seeing the shock on her face, smiled. "Oh, yes. The telegram came a fortnight ago." She looked Filomena up and down. "If he hadn't been messing with a foreigner he'd have got married. I know my Stan, he liked to be sure of things. And plenty of girls would have been glad to marry him. He might even have had a kid by now, a grandson maybe, to carry on the family name."

Filomena gripped the doorjamb. She could not seem to catch her breath. "But what did the telegram say? Is he dead?"

The smile was still on Mrs. Harker's lips. She waited, as though by prolonging Filomena's anguish she could somehow, temporarily, relieve her own.

"Missing," she said at last. "Missing, believed killed. In Norway, near Trondheim. So you won't get your man after all, missy."

Filomena gave a cry; then she pressed her gloved hands to her mouth. A vision came to her of Stan, lying abandoned in a wasteland of ice, his face turned empty to the moon.

"I suppose you'd like your letters back?" Mrs. Harker's blank blue eyes softened for an instant. "No, don't come in. I don't want you crossing my doorstep, thank you very much. You've done enough harm to my family. I'll fetch them."

She disappeared into the house, wiping her hands on her overalled hips. Filomena took a step back, away from the door. The sallow girl next door was still hanging inquisitively from her window.

Stan's mother came back with a Huntley and Palmers tin in her hands. The tin was green, decorated with pictures of King George and Queen Elizabeth. As she approached the doorway she pulled off the lid, angling it so that Filomena could not see inside.

"There," she said, "there are your precious letters," and swinging the tin she let its contents fly, sluicing them across the doorstep, out into the street. The letters had been torn into fragments. They fell about Filomena like confetti, or fallen petals, or black-stained flakes of snow.

STANLEY HARKER WAS not the only man to be destroyed by the Norwegian campaign. It brought down Neville Chamberlain, blamed by Parliament for its failure. By November he would be dead from cancer, his achievements eclipsed by that tainted word *appeasement.* In France he would always be known, scathingly, as Monsieur J'aime Berlin.

The new prime minister—Churchill—came to power on May 10. On the same day Hitler launched his long-feared, long-awaited offensive against Western Europe. British troops in Norway were shipped to France, to strengthen Allied forces there. Not that it made much difference: the Western Front tumbled like a house of cards, first Luxembourg, then the Netherlands. It was rumored that when German paratroopers landed in Holland they carried death lists of Allied sympathizers, supplied by the network of Nazis within the country.

"Belgium will be next," Bernard said grimly to Olivia over breakfast, "and after that France. What was it that numbskull Lionel said? The French have the strongest army in Europe? Ha!"

Olivia took a halfhearted mouthful of toast, smeared with yellowish margarine. She had given her weekly ration of bacon (four ounces) and eggs (two) to Bernard, to stoke up his energy for his ARP shifts. They had begun to sleep in separate bedrooms, she in their room, he on the chaise longue in his study. I don't want to disturb you when I come in late, he had said, and the truth is, darling, it's only going to get worse.

"What do you think Mussolini will do?" asked Olivia.

"Unless there's a miracle he'll come in on Hitler's side." Bernard sliced the top from his boiled egg. He did it casually, with no acknowledgment that it was by right Olivia's. "What would you do, in his place? If he doesn't act soon he'll miss out on the spoils of war. And he'll find it harder to defend his own German-speaking territories from Hitler's grasp."

"So Antonio will become an enemy alien," Olivia said, "just like poor Herr Fischer."

For a moment Bernard did not speak; then he said: "I am afraid so. There will be more tribunals, more internments. Churchill, I fear, will be a man for grand gestures. I will do what I can for Antonio, of course I will, but you must see that the situation has changed. We are ourselves in danger now. I don't mean you and me, I mean Britain, the way we live, our whole democracy. If France falls—*when* France falls—we will be the last line of defense against the Nazis."

There was a note of pride in his voice. Olivia looked at him in surprise. "You think it's exciting, don't you, Bernard?"

"Of course I don't. That's an appalling thing to say. We have the barbarians at our gates. How could I be excited?" Bernard's face had flushed to a dark wine-red. "Let me remind you, Olivia, that they've raised the age of conscription to thirty-six. I could be called up at any time. I could be facing the enemy within months."

"You won't be called up, though, surely? You'll be exempt on health grounds. Your asthma."

"We cannot be sure of that. We can no longer be sure of anything. That is what I am trying to tell you." Bernard pushed back his chair, abandoning his half-eaten breakfast. "And thank you for reminding me of my physical weakness. It is always so delicious when a wife has confidence in her husband."

THE FALL OF the Netherlands persuaded the government that stronger action was needed against the enemy within. Two days later the home secretary quietly gave the order that all category B aliens be interned.

The police arrested Konrad Fischer the next morning, knocking half-apologetically at his landlady's door in Riding House Street. Herr Fischer did not argue, but asked for time to pack some belongings: shaving tackle; a framed photograph of his sister,

Brigitta, smiling toothily beside the Danube; the score of the song he had written for Olivia. When he was ready to leave he raised his Tyrolean hat to his landlady and bowed from the waist.

"Thank you for your kind hospitality, *gnädige Frau*. I hope that my presence here has not caused you any embarrassment. If you could do me one last service I should be grateful. Send, if you please, to Mr. Rodway and tell him I will no longer be able to give singing lessons at his house."

CHAPTER 27

FILOMENA WAS SITTING IN THE KITCHEN WITH RENATA WHEN they heard that Mussolini had joined the war. He made the announcement at four o'clock on June 10, standing on the balcony of the Palazzo Vecchio in Rome. An hour appointed by destiny has struck in the heavens of our fatherland, he proclaimed, to loud and enthusiastic cheers. In private he believed the war would be a short one. I only need a few thousand dead, he said to Marshal Badoglio, his army chief of staff, so that I can sit at the peace conference as a man who has fought.

The past weeks had altered Filomena. She had told nobody about Stan's death. It seemed to her that she had swallowed all her grief, and now it was spreading through her like embalming fluid, transforming her into some inert resilient substance: rubber, perhaps, or nylon. The change unnerved her but it made her feel better able to face the future.

"What does it mean?" Renata turned her bulging rabbit's eyes upon Filomena. Pregnancy did not suit Renata. She was sick so often that there was always a sour whiff about her clothes.

"It means that we have become the enemy." Filomena switched off the radio with a click. Bruno had taken charge of the kiosk that afternoon, so that Antonio could visit his father in hospital. She felt an overpowering urge to be with her menfolk, to see their faces, to touch their sleeves. Briskly she began to put on her coat.

Renata let out a cry of dismay. "Don't leave me on my own. What if the baby comes early, like Danila's?"

"Don't be silly. The baby's not due for months. Anyway, your uncle will be home soon. So will Bruno, he won't keep the kiosk open now."

"But Bruno said he was going to the *fascio* after work," wailed Renata, "to hear the latest news."

"Well, then, he'll know to hurry back quickly. I can't stay, Renata, I have to make sure that Papa is all right. You'll be quite safe. Lock the door and don't open it to anyone."

When Filomena reached the hospital she found it in chaos. Nurses with frightened faces were scurrying along the corridors, and high in the building she could hear shouting. As soon as she entered the ward she saw that Enrico's bed was empty. The sheets were idly pushed back as though he had disappeared, just for the moment, to the bathroom or the lobby. Then she realized that there were two policeman at the end of the room. They were waiting as one of the patients, a gaunt young man with a yellowish complexion, climbed into his clothes, his fingers all thumbs. Beside them the doctor from Verona hovered, fierce and ineffectual.

"The fellow is ill," he said in English. "He has the jaundice, can't you see? You cannot arrest him. It is an outrage."

"His name's on the list, I'm afraid." The police sergeant tapped the piece of paper in his hand. "Collar the lot: that's what old Winston says. I'm sorry, my friend, but I have to do what I'm told."

The jaundiced man was dressed now. As the policemen turned to escort him to the door Filomena recognized Constable Sellers, with his acned cheeks and his face too young for uniform. Salty, Stan had called him, Salty Sellers.

"Constable!" she called out. "Constable Sellers!"

Sellers took a diffident step toward her. "You heard about Stan, did you? Rotten luck. I'd go home, miss, if I were you. There could be riots in Soho tonight."

"I'm looking for my father. Enrico Trombetta. He was here in the hospital. In that bed over there."

As she pointed, the constable's face closed up, and Filomena knew that Enrico's name had been on the list. She seized his arm, the blue serge coarse beneath her fingers. "Do you know where they have taken him? My father's not well, he has an inflammation of the lungs."

"Wait until morning, Miss Trombetta, that's my advice. You can ask at the police station tomorrow. Nobody knows anything right now." Sellers glanced swiftly about and then hissed in her ear: "And be prepared. We'll be arresting another batch tomorrow."

"Come on, Sellers," the sergeant shouted. "Get a move on."

"But they won't arrest my brother Antonio, he's not a fascist," said Filomena. The constable did not answer; he only shook his head, and disappeared along the ward.

Antonio had not visited his father in hospital that afternoon. He had gone to the apartment in Hyde Park, where Olivia was waiting for him, naked beneath an indigo silk kimono. He did not know of Mussolini's announcement until six o'clock, when he switched on the walnut-veneered radio in the living room.

"Oh my God," he said, as the newscaster's voice boomed soberly across the thick carpet, the brocade curtains, the vast beige sofas.

"What is it, my darling? What's wrong?" Olivia was coming out of the bathroom. Her hair had got wet in the bath, and her head was wrapped in a white towel.

"Italy has declared war on Britain. It happened this afternoon, in Rome." Antonio was climbing into his discarded shirt, struggling with his inside-out sleeves. "I must go home at once. I must make sure that my father is safe."

"But he is in no danger tonight, surely—"

"I do not know," Antonio said. He felt sick with the knowledge of his own lie. "Herr Fischer was arrested without warning. God knows what they will do."

Olivia rubbed at the damp mass of her hair and let fall the towel. "I'm coming with you," she said, as she reached for her own clothes, pulling on her silk knickers, hooking up her ivory brassiere.

"Olivia, you can't. How would I explain it?"

"I don't care." Olivia stood firm and straight in her underclothes, her eyes burning. "We belong together, Antonio. We always have. I'm coming with you. We can go to the house in Sussex, Bernard can't stop me, I don't suppose he'll want to stop me, he'll be glad to have me gone. We can start our lives all over again . . ."

Antonio fumbled with his shirt buttons. He dared not stop dressing, even for a moment. "Oh, my love, I can't. You know I can't. I'm not a free man. I don't mean Danila, I mean my family, my father, my sister—"

"We'll take them with us. There's plenty of room."

"Olivia." Antonio had fastened his shirt and was dragging his braces over his shoulders. "My love, we don't have time. We don't have time to talk about this. They could be arresting Italians at this moment. I must go home. I lied, Olivia, I said I was going to see Papa in the hospital. I must find out if he is safe."

Olivia stared. He remembered how he had first seen her face, across the floor of the Paradise Ballroom, that pale beautiful desolate face. It stirred him now as it had stirred him then.

"How will I know what has happened to you?"

"I will meet you," said Antonio. "There is a café in Old Compton Street, Ricci's it's called. Go there at eleven, tomorrow or the next day. I will meet you if I can."

"But what if they lock you up? What if we can never find each other?"

"Of course we will find each other. I would do anything on earth to find you, you must know that." Antonio took her in his arms, not as a lover this time but as a comforter. Her eyes were huge and terrible, like Medusa's. The sight made him shudder. Sensing it, Olivia rallied.

"I am behaving like a fool," she said. "I am making it worse for you. You are right. Of course we will find each other, the world is not so large a place." She pressed her head against his shoulder once, very hard; then she stepped away from him, twisting her tumbled hair into a knot. Her face had closed up once more. "No, don't kiss me. I'll die if you kiss me. Just go, my darling. Go."

WITHIN TWO HOURS of Mussolini's declaration eighty Italians had been arrested in London. They included Bruno, who was scooped up at the Casa d'Italia in the act of helping to destroy a heap of the *fascio*'s records. He had no opportunity to let Renata know, and by the time Filomena returned to Frith Street she was in hysterics.

"Calm yourself, Renata," said Filomena, as she hung her coat upon the peg. "You are not the only one in this position."

Uncle Mauro was eyeing his niece from a distance, as if he were afraid she might bite him. Nobody had attempted to arrest Mauro. Despite his enthusiasm for Mussolini he had never possessed the twelve lire necessary to join the *fascio*. "I've told her that," he said, "but she won't listen."

Renata gave a high-pitched yowl, and buried her head in her hands. Filomena contemplated her for a moment, coldly. "Go to Fortuna's, Mauro. See if they have something that will pacify her."

Fortuna's was the Italian pharmacy in Frith Street, a few doors away. Mauro shook his head. "It is shut. Ricci's café is shut too. Someone threw a brick through the window, and now they're all hiding upstairs, under the beds. How is your father? Is he shocked by the news?"

Filomena did not answer. She knew that if Renata heard about Enrico's arrest she would scream the house down. Opening one of the kitchen drawers she took out a bottle of aspirin. "Take Renata upstairs, Mauro, give her a couple of these. I don't suppose there will be any news of Bruno until the morning."

Mauro screwed up his wizened face as if he guessed that Filomena was concealing the truth, but he had the sense not to argue, and taking the bottle of aspirin he led the whimpering Renata away.

IT WAS PAST seven o'clock before Antonio reached his home. He did not dare take a bus for fear of being trapped by an avenging crowd. It was broad daylight, it would be light for hours yet, and anyone could see that he was Italian. Instead he made his way by foot from Hyde Park, ducking to and fro to avoid the angry knots of people on the streets. The words that floated in the summer air were ugly words: *Eyeties, cowards, stab in the back*. Once, as he drew close to Soho, he heard the splintering of glass.

Filomena screamed when he walked into the house. "Where were you? You said you were visiting Papa."

Guilt swept through Antonio, cold as nausea. "Why? What has happened?"

"They've arrested him at the hospital. I went to find him, but I was too late—" Antonio moved to touch her but Filomena threw him off. "There is a list. They are rounding up all Italians whose names are on the list. Bruno has vanished too. They must have arrested him at the *fascio*."

"Perhaps they will be together," said Antonio, "perhaps Bruno will take care of Papa."

"You lied, Antonio. You said that you were going to visit Papa. If you had been there—"

"What could I have done? Tell me that, Filomena. Could I have rescued him from the police? I do not think so."

His reply quelled Filomena. She sat at the table, staring at the palms of her hands: wide, capable hands, the skin coarsened by her years working in the laundry.

"I saw Constable Sellers at the hospital," she said. "He used to work with Stan—with Constable Harker. He told me they would be making more arrests in the morning. They won't come for you, though, Antonino, will they? Your name won't be on that list?"

Antonio was silent. He remembered how he had signed the loan document beneath the blue satisfied glitter of Signor Follini's eyes. That document, that signature, would be there in the *fascio*'s records; more than enough to put the authorities on his trail.

"Yes, Mena," he said at last, "it is very likely that they will come for me. I cannot explain, it is something I had to do for Papa. You will be all right, though. They are not arresting women, and besides, you were born in this country, you are a British citizen."

"Much good may it do me," mumbled Filomena. "And the kiosk? What about the kiosk?"

"I fear you will have to close it, at least for a few days. People will be avoiding Italian businesses now." Antonio sat at the table beside her. He felt a peculiar sense of comfort that it was his shrewd calm sister taking charge, not his brother, not his wife. "Whatever happens I will let you know, Filomena. As soon as I can, I will send you word. And when I do, will you tell Mr. Rodway? I will write down his address. They will want to know where I am, he and his wife."

As he said it Antonio felt a terrible desire to speak Olivia's name, to taste it in his mouth as two hours ago he had tasted her skin. I could tell Filomena, he thought, she would understand, she would not judge me. Instead he said, impulsively: "I was wrong to stop you marrying your Englishman. I liked him, he is a good man. He would have made you a good husband."

He thought that Filomena would weep with a kind of delayed gratitude, but she did not. Her mouth twisted into a bitter little smile, and she got to her feet.

"Well, it is too late for that now." She slid her apron over her head. "Stan will never be a good husband, not to me, not to anyone. He was killed last month in Norway. I had the news from his mother."

"Mena! And you told nobody?"

Filomena's mouth gave another twist. "Who was there to tell? You? Papa?" She took her knife and her chopping board from the drawer. "And now I am going to make the supper."

"That is kind of you, Mena, but I do not think I can swallow anything—"

"Neither can I," said Filomena, slicing through an onion with savage precision, "but when you do not know what the future holds, Antonio, it is better to greet it with a full stomach."

CHAPTER 28

THEY CAME FOR ANTONIO AT FIRST LIGHT ON THAT MILD JUNE morning, just as Constable Sellers had warned. Their booted footsteps in the corridor woke Renata, who, remembering Bruno's disappearance, began to howl.

Antonio picked up the suitcase he had packed the night before. It was an old suitcase, bought in Rome twenty years ago, the metal corners scuffed from a history of quaysides and luggage racks and station platforms. In it he had put a warm jersey for Enrico and a snapshot of Valentino.

"I've prepared some food," said Filomena. "Bread and cheese, and a few slices of sausage."

She could see the policemen eyeing her, unnerved by Renata's monstrous wailing. Their wariness sparked Filomena's pride. She was not a hysteric, she knew how to conduct herself. Tightening her lips she embraced Antonio, awkwardly because he had his suitcase in one hand.

Antonio patted her on the shoulder. The night had been hard and sleepless; now that the men had come he felt easier, as though the trial before him had begun. "Where are you taking me?" he asked.

The men exchanged glances before one of them said: "To the police station first. Then there are collection points, while the authorities check who's who. You will be well treated, my friend. Don't be afraid."

"I'm not afraid. I want to find my father, that is all. He was arrested in the Italian hospital last night." He smiled at Filomena. "Don't fret, Mena. I will write as soon as I can. You had better go and comfort Renata. Stop her wailing fit to wake the dead."

Filomena did not trust herself to speak. She clasped her brother in her arms for a long charged moment; then she turned away, so that she would not see the policemen lead him from the house.

Antonio spent the day in the police station, herded with the others who had been arrested in the dawn raids. The cell was so crowded they had to stand, jostling one another for half inches of space. The next morning they were moved to the Brompton Oratory School in Chelsea. As Antonio entered the building he remembered taking the bus to Dickie Belvoir's flat beside the river, to rehearse Olivia's song. *Oh, she doth teach the torches to burn bright.* He pushed the memory away. If he once allowed himself to think about Olivia he would be lost.

In the school hall he found Bruno, sitting cross-legged on the parquet floor. There was a nervous look about him, the look of a man who would jump at a car backfiring, not the bold patriot who had fought in Abyssinia. He had not seen Enrico, either in the police station or elsewhere in the school.

"What are they going to do with us, Antonino?" he asked. Antonio shrugged.

"I don't know. I don't think they know themselves. They can't hold tribunals, there are too many of us. I daresay they'll move us on once they've found somewhere to put us."

Antonio was right. Three days later they found themselves on a train with fifty or so other men. The nameplates had been removed from the stations they passed—a precaution against invasion—but Antonio had the impression that they were traveling north. He looked through the black-smeared window at the fields bowling past, moist and green in the June sunshine, studded with graceful ancient trees. Then the fields gave way to factories and dense brick houses, blocked as far as the horizon, and a pungent smell of smoke seeped into the carriage.

The camp where they were heading was a disused cotton mill, not far from Liverpool. Warth Mills had been commandeered hastily, and rusty machinery and cotton waste still littered the floors. The cracked skylights let in the cold and rain—for it was raining now, inexorable English drizzle, not warm and drama laden like the storms of Lazio. Antonio and Bruno were given a pair of blankets each; then they went to queue for their evening meal, bread and a small hunk of cheese.

"And no friendly glass of grappa to wash it down, alas," a voice said in Antonio's ear. It was Peppino, the waiter from La Rondine.

"Peppino! But you hate the *duce*. Why have they arrested you?"

"I am a communist, my friend. There are powers in this country that, much as they fear Hitler and Mussolini, fear the Russians even more." Peppino gave his wolfish smile, displaying his long white canines. "Meanwhile you will observe that we have been herded together with Nazis as well as refugees. There's a whole troop of sleek young Germans from one of Hitler's merchant ships. They do not care, these British. We are foreigners, that's what counts, and all foreigners are the same."

"They are disorganized, that is all. Disorganized and frightened."

"You are too trusting, my friend," said Peppino. "You always were." Contemptuously he held out his metal cup for some tea, thin and over-brewed. "By the way, Antonio, you know that your father is here, don't you?"

Antonio found Enrico wedged into a corner beneath one of the cracked skylights, wrapped in a gray blanket. The crucifix and the coral horn about his neck quivered as he struggled for breath. When he saw his son his eyes filled with tears.

"Oh, Papa," said Antonio, crouching beside his father on the damp floorboards, "I have been praying that I would find you."

Enrico's hand was leathery and familiar, a hand that he had touched all his life, a hand he remembered from walking through the village in Lazio, with the foam of oleanders upon the trees and the shriek of crickets. "Everything will be all right. Bruno is here, my friend Peppino is here. We will take care of you now."

Enrico did not speak. He leaned his cheek against Antonio's shoulder as though he no longer had the strength to remain separate, but had to rely on the heartbeat of his son to keep him alive.

That night, as Antonio lay listening to the scuttle of rats, he heard a crash in the darkness. Nobody could see what had happened but next morning one of the Nazis—a sailor from the captured merchant ship—appeared with a black eye. Later, as he was fetching water for Enrico, Antonio saw that Peppino's knuckles were red and bruised. There was a gleam in his eyes, though, as if it had been worth it.

There was a strange normality about Old Compton Street the day after Mussolini's declaration of war. In some places the pavement was scattered with glass and splintered wood, but most of the shops had opened, and there were people milling peaceably in and out as if nothing had changed. Olivia picked her way along the street, looking for Ricci's café. It was only half past ten, but she had been awake half the night and when dawn broke she had not been able to sit still anywhere in the house. Every room was like a cage, hemming her in. Bernard was asleep in his study when she left. He had come home at three in the morning; she had heard him clatter into the drawing room to pour himself a whisky. Her first instinct was to run to him and beg him to protect Antonio, but she stopped herself. He will guess the truth, she thought, I will not be able to hide it, not now, not tonight. Better to wait and find out what has happened.

She passed a men's clothing shop, with white starched collars on display. Outside the spaghetti house next door, a man in overalls was sweeping broken glass from the curb. He touched his cap politely to Olivia. All I want is to see Antonio, she thought. We do not have to speak, we do not have to touch. One glimpse of him, that is all, to know that he is safe. Her face felt stiff from lack of sleep, as though her skull was too large for her skin, stretching it like a canvas over her forehead.

At last she caught sight of the sign—Ricci's—and her heart leaped. Then she saw that the café was closed. The front window had been smashed, cracks radiating from a jagged hole in the glass. It was boarded up, clumsily, so that it was difficult to see inside. Olivia took a breath. Well, it does not matter, she thought, I can wait for him. It is not yet eleven. That's what he said: eleven o'clock, tomorrow or the next day. He knows I will be here; sooner or later he will come.

She turned toward Charing Cross Road. "The battle of Soho," a billboard on the corner proclaimed. A cluster of men huddled there, brandishing a newspaper, arguing. One of them glanced at Olivia, incongruous in her smart expensive clothes. Perhaps he thinks I'm a spy, she thought. The idea gave her a salty irrational pleasure. Somewhere in Soho a clock struck eleven. Olivia looked back at Ricci's café. It was still closed, still silent. He is late, that is all, she thought. He may be with his father in hospital, it may be that the police are questioning him. There are a dozen reasons why he has not yet arrived. I have to be patient.

The man with the newspaper was eyeing her again. It was wartime, nobody's business was private, you could be cautioned for all kinds of suspicious behavior, taking photographs, loitering. She wished there were an inconspicuous place where she could sit. As she thought this, she saw a figure moving in the depths of the café, a slim girl, dressed in black. Olivia did not hesitate. She ran across the pavement and began to rattle at the locked door.

"Hallo?" she called. "Hallo?"

Nothing happened; the figure beside the counter did not move. Olivia rattled again. At last a dark-haired girl, no more than sixteen, inched open the door. Her eyes were swollen and she had a bewildered expression on her face.

"We're closed," she said, with a strong Italian accent.

"Yes, I can see that, but I wondered—I have arranged to meet someone here. His name is Trombetta, Antonio Trombetta, you may know him—"

"Antonio? No, I have not seen him. I cannot help you, I am sorry." The girl made to close the door. Olivia sprang forward, grasping the frame with her gloved hand.

"He will be here soon, I am sure of it. If I could come in and wait—"

"Please go away. My aunt is not well, we do not want to be disturbed. My uncle Carlo was arrested last night. The police came and took him. They have taken all the men."

"Where?" said Olivia. "Where have they taken them?"

The girl shook her head. "We do not know. They are gone, that is all. Now please, whoever you are, leave us in peace."

CHAPTER 29

The mass arrest of foreigners was causing difficulties for the British government. All the internment camps were overcrowded, and there were fears of what would happen in an invasion. The Germans had marched into Paris on June 14; soon there would be nothing to prevent Hitler from turning the full power of the Wehrmacht on Britain. Who knew what damage these enemy aliens might do, rising up to welcome their fellow fascists? Dark visions of Quisling and his Norwegian traitors, of the Dutch Nazis with their death lists, haunted the war cabinet. Churchill wanted to deport all internees from the United Kingdom. Several destinations were proposed—Newfoundland, perhaps, or St. Helena. In the end the Canadian government was pressed into accepting four thousand men. The first ships—passenger liners commandeered by the army—were made ready in Liverpool docks.

At Warth Mills, Antonio was absorbed in caring for his father. Enrico could not stir now without straining for breath. He lay on his blanket beneath the cracked skylight, cradling the photograph of Valentino. The only time his face lit up was when Antonio talked to him of Valentino: tales of his brother's mischievous childhood, fantasies of what he might be doing at this moment in Lazio. He will be eating his supper in my sister Paolina's kitchen, Papa, slurping his spaghetti to make the children laugh. He will be smoking a cigarette beside the fountain in the square, surrounded by the young men from the village. You know what Valentino is like, he makes friends wherever he goes.

When Enrico was sleeping Antonio spent his time with Bruno and Peppino, playing cards or walking in the dilapidated mill yard. The building was encircled by two barbed wire fences; in between you could see the guards on patrol. As bored as we are, Antonio thought, and probably as edgy, not knowing what will happen next.

The rumors began slowly, trickling through the camp. Peppino got the story from one of the orderlies, a fellow communist named Charlie who slipped him extra rations.

"We're moving on," he whispered to Antonio. "Charlie doesn't know where, but there's a batch of men going. Maybe as soon as tomorrow."

"They can't move Papa tomorrow," said Antonio. "He won't be well enough." Peppino gave the vaguest of shrugs. They both knew that all the time in the world would not improve Enrico's condition.

The following morning guards began to march decisively through the camp, calling out names from a list. When the men answered, they were handed papers and ordered to gather their belongings.

Peppino was one of the first to be picked out. "And what, may I ask, will our destination be?" he asked, showing his teeth. "Should I pack my winter or my summer wardrobe?"

The guard pretended not to hear. Examining his list he pronounced Bruno's name in a loud flat voice. Bruno let out a whimper.

"Courage," said Antonio, "courage, my friend. You will not be going far."

Bruno began to weep, wiping his face clumsily with the back of one hand. With the other he was struggling to unfasten his suitcase. "It is my son. I am afraid that I will never see my son. Antonio, I should have married your sister, I should have married Filomena. Renata is a foolish woman, she will get something wrong—"

"Of course you will see your child. We will soon be free again, this cursed war cannot last forever—"

"Hush, Antonio." Peppino gripped him by the shoulder. "Listen."

The guard's voice was tinged with impatience. He was calling Enrico's name. The old man looked up as eagerly as an infant who wants to please.

"I am here," he said. "I am Enrico Trombetta."

Antonio sprang to his feet. "You cannot take my father, he is not well enough. Look at him. He can barely stand."

The guard glanced stonily at Enrico. "His name is on the list," he said, brandishing a sheet of paper, too quickly and too far off for Antonio to see. "Help him get his things together. We'll be setting off in the next hour."

"What about me? My name is also Trombetta: Antonio Trombetta. Am I on the list too?"

The guard hesitated before looking at the paper. From the subtle change in his expression Antonio guessed that his own name was not there.

"But I have to go with him. My father cannot travel alone, he will not survive—"

"Nothing doing, I'm afraid. We've been told to pick out these men and no more." The guard relented, and in a gentler voice he said: "I'd pack some warm clothes for your father if I were you. He's got a long journey ahead."

Antonio sank to his knees. For the first time since his arrest, despair overwhelmed him.

"Where are we going, Antonino?" asked Enrico. "Where are they sending us now?"

"I do not know, Papa." The words were like ashes in Antonio's mouth. His father gave him a trusting smile.

"Do not be unhappy. We will be all right. You will be with me, won't you, my son?"

They were beginning to round up the chosen men, chivvying them toward the yard. Peppino tried to linger, but the guards could see that he had packed his belongings, and they moved him on. Antonio threw open the suitcase he had brought from Frith Street and flung everything he could see into it, shirts, jerseys, underclothes, the photograph of Valentino. His eyes were half-blind with tears.

"Let's be having you," one of the guards said, lifting Enrico by the elbow. "There's a train to be caught, we can't wait all day."

A bewildered expression crossed Enrico's face as the guard pulled him away. "Antonino! Where are you? Aren't you coming too?"

Panic seized Antonio. He saw Bruno bend to lift his suitcase, and reaching out he grasped his arm.

"Bruno, my old friend, my countryman. Do me a kindness. Papa cannot go alone, it will destroy him. Change places with me."

"But we will be punished . . . ," said Bruno.

"They will not find out, there are too many of us." Antonio's fingers were tight on his wrist now. "Give me your papers, Bruno, for God's sake. Give me your papers, and let me go in your place."

THE INTERNEES WERE taken by rail to the Liverpool docks, drab and breezy in the June afternoon. Enrico leaned against Antonio's shoulder. He was silent except for the hiss in his throat as he struggled for breath.

"Perhaps they are taking us to the Isle of Man," Antonio said to Peppino, as they were marched toward the quayside. "That is where my old singing teacher, Herr Fischer, has been interned."

He adjusted the jersey his father was wearing, to shield him against the biting wind from the sea. The jersey had been knitted by Filomena, and the ribbing at the neck was loose and uneven. At least in a proper camp we can settle, he thought. We do not need much, we have never needed much, we can build a life for ourselves anywhere. He did not say, even to himself, And Papa will be able to die in peace, but the thought was a shadow on the edges of his mind.

They had reached the quayside. Berthed there was a passenger liner, its funnels painted gray, its portholes a dark, opaque blue. There were two guns mounted on its decks, one a cannon, the other an antiaircraft gun. Scores of men were trailing up the gangplank past the barbed wire barricades. On the vast side of the ship Antonio could see its name: *Arandora Star.*

Peppino grimaced. "That is an oceangoing liner. It must be at least fifteen thousand tons. I fear, Antonio my friend, that we are going a little further than the Isle of Man."

CHAPTER 30

BERNARD VISITED FRITH STREET AT THE END OF JUNE. HE had intended to go much sooner—Olivia had asked him to do it days ago—but he had been engulfed by the demands on his time. As the Nazis advanced there was a deluge of refugees from Belgium and the Netherlands. They spilled out from grimy, overcrowded trains at Victoria, clutching parcels and suitcases, and accommodation had to be found for them all. It was not easy. Londoners might welcome the soldiers who were arriving in the capital, the Polish and the Free French, but they were more grudging about civilians, those needy bewildered creatures with their foreign habits.

"I'm seeing a hotel manager in Paddington at twelve, to see if they can take a dozen families, but I'll go to Soho first," Bernard said. "I know you've been anxious about Antonio, darling. I have too, of course. I expect he is all right, but it would set my mind at rest to know where they've sent him."

Olivia was kneeling upright on the bedroom floor, sorting out blouses and warm cardigans to give to the refugees. She looked peaky, Bernard thought, through the haze of his exhaustion. Her face was hollow and even paler than usual.

"I should have gone," she said. "I could still go, if you don't have time."

"No, no. Much better for me to do it. I've already told you, I don't want you traipsing about Soho on your own, not after those riots. Besides, we don't know what Antonio's sister is like. She may be one of those hysterical girls who panics at the sight of strangers. I'm used to that, I'll know how to deal with it."

Olivia was folding a blouse of brushed yellow cotton. She paused, her hands in her lap. "You will do it today, Bernard, won't you?"

"Of course I will. I've said I will. For heaven's sake, Olivia." Bernard turned toward the door. "Oh, and I won't be home for lunch today. In fact, I have no idea what time I'll be back. You'd better tell Avril to leave me some supper on a tray."

It was Filomena who answered when he knocked at the house in Frith Street. Bernard's first impression was one of disappointment. He had imagined that perhaps she would share Antonio's good looks, but she was a plain, solid woman in a faded blue dress. She was not going to be hysterical, though; he could see that at a glance. She greeted him calmly and showed him into the kitchen: a dim, shabby space, smelling of fried onions and damp.

"Can I offer you something, Mr. Rodway? Coffee, perhaps?"

"That is kind of you, but no, thank you," said Bernard. "I came to ask if you have any news of Antonio."

Filomena shook her head. "No, I have heard nothing. The police took him three weeks ago. Since then there has been nothing, no letter, no message. My father was arrested too, at the Italian hospital." Her mouth trembled for a moment but she pressed her lips together. "Antonio said he would write to me, he asked me to tell you his news. And I would have done, but . . ."

Her voice trailed into silence. Bernard could tell that she was desperate not to cry, especially in a stranger's presence.

"There is no reason to be anxious, Filomena." He said it briskly because he knew that kindness would only make matters worse. "The authorities are overwhelmed, that's all. They have rounded up all these people and now they have no idea what to do with them. I don't suppose that Antonio is particularly comfortable, but wherever he is I expect he's safe."

Filomena did not speak for a moment, her face still taut. Then she said: "It is the not knowing. That is what makes it difficult to bear." Her mouth twisted into a smile. "And the fact that it is so pointless. Antonio has never been a fascist, he would do nobody any harm. This war has made everyone mad."

Her wryness took Bernard by surprise. "You are right, Filomena. The whole business is absurd." He reached into his pocket for his card. "When you do hear from him, please will you tell me? My wife and I are very fond of Antonio. We would do anything we can to help him."

Filomena lifted her head to look at him. She had beautiful eyes, Bernard noticed, deep and expressive. "Of course," she said, "of course. My brother is lucky to have such friends."

ON BOARD THE *Arandora Star* the Italians were divided into two. Antonio's group was sent to A deck, the lowest in the vessel, stinking of oil and of sweat. When the ship's doctor saw Enrico, though, he had them moved to the ship's great ballroom, closer to the main deck.

"The sleeping arrangements are not so comfortable, but he'll have more air," the doctor said. He was an elderly man, white haired, his face a deeply wrinkled brown.

"Is my father dying?" asked Antonio. The old doctor looked at him for a moment. In his eye there was the somber glint of candor. "Not yet," he said.

The ballroom was vast, with a honey-colored wooden floor, the walls decorated in green and ivory. As he helped Enrico through the door Antonio remembered how Olivia had talked about her honeymoon, that night in Sussex. *We went on an Atlantic cruise. I had never seen such luxury.* All at once the memories Antonio had been suppressing flooded through him: the taste of Olivia's mouth, her spicy perfume, the way her pale breasts spilled sideways as she lay on the bed. Perhaps she had sailed on this same ship, perhaps her feet had touched this very floor, dancing the tango in new expensive shoes. The bitterness of it made him groan aloud. Nobody heard him, though. The men were too busy seizing their places, putting down their sleeping bags, staking their claims for space. They had all been given life jackets made of cork, which they kept close at hand with their other belongings.

Peppino managed to secure a corner of the bandstand, where one of the potted palms still stood, its fronds brown and shriveled.

"You should feel at home here, Antonio," he said, as he surveyed the ballroom from the platform's edge.

"Home," Enrico said, hungrily catching the word. "We're going home, aren't we, Antonio? Will Valentino be there to meet us?"

THE *ARANDORA STAR* left Liverpool at four the next morning, zigzagging across the Irish Sea. From the deck you could see the coast of Wales, then the Isle of Man, as the ship headed north toward the Atlantic.

Down below Antonio's spirits lifted. The onward movement of the ship gave him the illusion of progress. Even Enrico was calmer, nestled upon the dais in his badly knitted jersey, Valentino's photograph in his hand.

"I think it is very kind of the British government to send us on a cruise to Canada," Peppino said. He had just asked one of the ship's amenable stewards to bring them a drink, and the man had returned with pink gin on a tray. "Here's to them. And bugger the *duce*."

Across the ballroom a knot of young Germans, the sailors from the captured merchant ship, began a ragged chorus of the Hitler Youth anthem. "*For today Germany belongs to us, and tomorrow the whole world.*"

"Just listen to those bastards," said Peppino. "You sing, Antonio. If you sing you can drown them out. Sing 'Tornerai.' It will cheer your father, it will cheer us all."

Antonio stood at the front of the dais. His father was watching him with an eager, peaceful expression. For an instant, as he opened his throat, he feared the sound would be lost in the clatter of the ballroom. Then his own voice soared, swelling through the air like a sirocco. Slowly the faces turned toward him: not only the Italians but the stewards, the British soldiers, the refugees, the Nazis. Little by little the Hitler Youth anthem died away. Antonio was filled with hope, and a sense of rightness. This is what I am for, he thought. This is what I was born to do.

At dawn on July 2 the sea was calm, beneath a damp, cloudy sky. The *Arandora Star* was steaming due west when it was spotted by a U-boat on its way home to Germany. U-47 was under the command of Gunther Prien, the bold young Nazi who had penetrated Scapa Flow and sunk the *Royal Oak*. On his latest mission he had destroyed eight British ships in three weeks. Through his periscope he examined the *Arandora Star*, with its cannon on the stern, its antiaircraft gun on the bow. The zigzag course of the ship identified it as an enemy. Gunther Prien had one torpedo remaining. Just before seven o'clock he fired it.

CHAPTER 31

AFTER HIS VISIT TO FRITH STREET BERNARD TRIED WITH-out success to find out where Antonio was. The civil servants whom he knew talked in harassed voices about emergency camps in Manchester and Liverpool, but they had no lists of names, and he soon realized it was pointless to keep asking; he would use up goodwill that he might need later, in a greater crisis.

Meanwhile a complaining letter arrived from Penelope. With so much riffraff flooding into London her dowager friend was anxious about the apartment in Hyde Park—worried sick, Penelope said, and she had heard nothing from the Rodways for weeks.

"Tcha!" Bernard flicked the letter down upon the lunch table. "It would serve the old trout right if I installed eight homeless families in her flat. God knows it's big enough. When did you last go there, Olivia?"

Olivia was eating pea and ham soup, or rather, not eating it, but turning the spoon over and over in the flecked green broth. She had not set foot in the Hyde Park apartment since the day she said good-bye to Antonio.

"I can't remember," she said, untruthfully. She raised her spoon and tried to swallow a mouthful of soup. It filled her with nausea. She had been sick once already today. "I can go this afternoon, if you want."

"Well, why not? If you don't mind, darling. I know it's a chore."

The weather was cloudy and stiflingly warm. Olivia felt a sense of oppression as she climbed the curved stairway to the Hyde Park flat. Like most women in these early days of war she wore sober clothes, a cream silk blouse, a tobacco linen suit. Her heart was thumping in her throat. She dreaded stepping through the door of the apartment.

Inside the brocade curtains were drawn, just as she had left them. She did not open them, nor put on the lights, but crossed toward the bedroom in the half-dark. Her blue kimono and a discarded towel were sprawled on the carpet. Olivia sat upon the unmade bed. The crumpled sheets smelled faintly of Antonio, of his skin, of his sweat. I should have come sooner, she thought, the scent of him is already fading.

Nudging off her beige kidskin shoes she climbed into the bed. As she lay there she remembered how when her mother died, the warmth in her body had so quickly evaporated, leaving her rigid, a stranger. She thought of poor disappointed Daisy, of her lost sister, Wilma, of Uncle Dickie. She thought of the phantom child she had flushed away in the mildewed lavatory in Pimlico. They clustered about her, drifting silvery figures, half threatening, half reproachful. She buried her face in the mattress, trying to conjure the touch of Antonio's fingers, the friction of his cheek against her neck. What was it that he had said? *I would do anything on earth to find you.* Olivia breathed in the scent of the sheets, but the smell of Antonio's skin had vanished.

ANTONIO WAS HELPING his father to dress when the torpedo struck. It hit the starboard engine room with a low deep crash, exploding the generators. The *Arandora Star* was plunged at once into darkness.

"Holy mother of God," said Peppino, "it must be a mine."

There was the acrid stink of burning. The ship juddered to a halt. Half the internees were scrambling up, grabbing their belongings, crying out to one another. Antonio could hear the German sailors repeat *torpedo* in rapid urgent voices. It took him a moment to recognize the word.

"It's not a mine," he said, "we're under attack. What should we do, Peppino? Wait for instructions?"

"There won't be instructions." Peppino, still in pajamas, seized his cork life jacket. "It's every man for himself. Let's follow those Nazi bastards. They know what they're doing."

The merchant sailors had formed a line behind their leader and were making their way out of the ballroom toward the deck. The ship tilted. There was an unearthly creaking from the lower decks, and the sound of men screaming. Antonio hauled his father to his feet.

"My photograph," said Enrico, resisting, his hand outstretched, "my picture of Valentino. I can't find it."

"Leave it, Papa. Nothing matters now."

Peppino helped to carry Enrico along the gangway, up toward the deck. The morning light was densely gray. A lifeboat, chock full with men, was being lowered from the davits. Above them a man was climbing toward another lifeboat on the top deck, impeded by the coils of barbed wire. A couple of others were hurling furniture overboard, deck chairs, benches, empty barrels, anything that would float in the oil-drenched water.

"Here, let me tie your father's life jacket." It was the steward who, the night before, had brought them the tray of pink gin. "If it's not tight it'll ride up when you hit the water. Could break your neck."

The German sailors had stripped naked and were lining up to dive into the sea, fifty feet below. The arc of their bodies was white and graceful as they fell. The water below teemed with men. Some were hanging on to debris from the ship, others were swimming toward the crowded lifeboats. Even as Antonio watched a man was pulled onto one of the rafts, his feet still dangling in the water.

"We're in a shipping lane," the steward said. "That's the good news. It won't be long before we get picked up. Just try and jump as far from the ship as you can."

Antonio stared as he realized what the steward meant. "We could wait for another lifeboat—" he began.

"No," said Peppino, "if we wait we'll die. Let's jump. I'll help you with your father."

They clambered to the ship's side. Peppino seized a rope from one of the davits, to help them swing out from the deck. It felt as though they were plummeting from the sky. As they hit the water Enrico's weight dragged Antonio under. There was oil and salt in his mouth, burning like swallowed fire. Just as he thought his lungs would burst they surfaced, buoyed by their cork life jackets. A wooden bench, floating among the debris, struck Antonio on the shoulder. He seized it, pushing his father toward it.

"Here, Papa, hold on. You'll be safe if you hold on."

Antonio encircled his father with both arms, pinning Enrico to the bench. A few yards away he could see Peppino swimming for a life raft; then the ocean swelled, and Peppino disappeared from view. On the deck of the *Arandora Star* stood a row of men, Italians mostly, staring down at the crowded water. Some were holding suitcases. They had struggled up from the lower decks, too late for the lifeboats, too frightened to jump. The great ship hissed and swayed, its stern dipping obliquely.

"Oh, my son," said Enrico, "oh, Valentino—"

A wave surged from the heaving ship, knocking Antonio sideways. As he sank he felt his father slide from his grasp. The old man slid away easily, almost willfully, without resisting. Antonio flailed and snatched but his arms closed upon nothing. And then the dark water was over his head, and he was struggling for breath, kicking and fighting his way to the surface. He managed to grab at the wooden bench once more, allowing it to support him. Enrico had vanished beneath the oil-black shimmer of the sea. Antonio tried to call out, to cry, Papa!, but his throat was still burning and the words would not come out.

A dead man floated past, his skewed head bobbing above his life jacket. Antonio gripped the bench. His fingers were numb and slow, as if they belonged to someone else, and he could not get the hang of using them. Perhaps it is for the best, he thought, that Papa mistook me for Valentino. Perhaps it helped him to go in peace. He wondered, quite calmly, how much longer he would be able to hold on. The last thing he heard was a high-pitched whistle like birdsong. He did not recognize it as the sound of men drowning.

CHAPTER 32

News of the sinking of the *Arandora Star* reached London the following day. By the next morning, it was in all the English papers. Filomena saw the billboards as she was going to Leicester Square, to check on the closed-up kiosk. Her first thought was to go to the police station, and demand to know what had happened to her brother. Then she remembered what Bernard Rodway had said. *I would do anything I can to help Antonio.* She had only the vaguest notion of what Bernard did but he had struck her as a powerful man. At any rate, she thought, he is wealthy, and where there is wealth there is always a kind of power. I will go and see Mr. Rodway.

Bedford Square, like the rest of London, appeared unclouded, blithely innocent of the risk that, any day now, German ships might appear in the Channel, German planes might appear in the sky. A gaunt young woman in a maid's uniform opened the door to Filomena. "Yes?" she said unpromisingly.

"I have come to see Mr. Rodway. He is—he was—a friend of my brother's." *Friend*, Filomena knew, was not the right word, and her doubt made her falter. The gaunt young woman pursed her lips, angling the door more sharply.

"Mr. Rodway is out. If you wish to leave your card—"

"Can't I wait for him?" said Filomena. The maid hesitated. As she did so a pale-faced woman in blue appeared on the stairs.

"Who is it, Avril?"

"A visitor for Mr. Rodway. She says that the master knows her brother . . ."

The woman's face changed at once. To Filomena's surprise she ran down the stairs and grasped both her hands.

"Filomena," she said, "you must be Filomena." She drew Filomena indoors, still holding her hands. "Have you heard from Antonio? Is he safe?"

"I do not know," said Filomena. "I have heard nothing."

Olivia's eyes, which were fixed upon Filomena, welled abruptly with tears. For a moment she was unable to speak. Then she said: "Come up to the drawing room, Miss Trombetta. Avril, would you bring us some coffee?"

Filomena gazed about her at the Rodways' drawing room, with its wrought iron balcony, its silken sofas, the glossy dark piano in the corner. She had never been in so large or so lavish a room before; even the smell of it was expensive, a mixture of wax polish and some kind of spicy perfume, Olivia's perhaps.

"This is where Antonio used to have his singing lessons," Olivia said, glancing toward the piano. There was a hunger in her voice that baffled Filomena. "So you have had no word from him?"

Filomena shook her head. "Nothing. I do not even know where they have taken him. Or my father, who is a sick man. And there is the news today, about the sinking of that ship . . ."

Olivia's eyes brimmed once again. "We heard the news too. Mr. Rodway—my husband—has gone to find out more. But there is no reason, is there, to believe that Antonio was on the ship?" Reaching out she grasped both Filomena's hands once more. Her grip was tight and desperate. In that moment Filomena realized that it was not a question of receiving comfort from her brother's friends; she would have to offer it instead.

"No," she said, to this curious, beautiful, intensely demanding woman, "no, there is no reason at all to believe it."

Bernard spent the next days bullying and cajoling to find out what had happened upon the *Arandora Star*. Nobody knew the death toll from the catastrophe, or who exactly had died. Already there were tales of men who had swapped papers to sail, or not sail, upon the doomed ship. The Red Cross tried to get accurate casualty figures but the government claimed that a complete list was impossible.

As the investigation continued two further batches of internees were dispatched to Canada. In Liverpool the SS *Dunera* was made ready to transport yet more men to Australia. Meanwhile in Ireland and in Scotland bloated oil-streaked bodies washed up on the shingle beaches, one after another. They were gathered up and quietly buried in the nearest cemeteries, their graves unmarked.

After a fortnight Bernard's chivvying bore fruit. He was grudgingly given sight of the embarkation list for the *Arandora Star*, which the government was about to lodge in the House of Commons library. In the few moments that he was allowed, Bernard spotted Enrico's name, and that of another man from the same address, Bruno Montisi. Both were recorded as lost. Of Antonio's name there was no sign.

Bernard's first sensation was one of relief. Then he thought of what this information would mean for Filomena. He had been touched by the way she had come to seek his help; it reflected the self he most liked to be, kindly and influential. He had been touched, too, by the sight of his wife holding Filomena's hands, consoling her. In these last months he had forgotten what tenderness looked like upon Olivia's face. I will go and tell Filomena what I have discovered, he thought. At least I have some good news for her, as well as bad.

Filomena was sitting in the kitchen in Frith Street, her hands flat upon the table. Beside her lay a sheet of paper, covered in looped untidy handwriting.

"I am afraid there is bad news, Filomena," said Bernard, standing gravely in the doorway, his hat clasped against his chest. "It is about your father—"

"I know. He is dead. A telegram came this morning."

"I am sorry, Filomena. He was an old man, I know, but he deserved a peaceful death. That is what any child wishes for their parent. And at least there is hope for your brother. It seems that your neighbor Bruno Montisi sailed on the *Arandora Star*, and he too is missing, but Antonio was not on the ship. I have seen the embarkation list. His name was not there."

Filomena grimaced. It was a strange, savage expression; Bernard thought that she dared not express joy, so soon after learning of her father's death. Then, gently, she laid her hand upon the paper beside her, running her fingertips across it like a blind woman reading Braille.

"He changed places with Bruno," she said. "They swapped papers so that Antonio could go with our father. Bruno wrote to tell me, he asked one of the camp guards to smuggle out the letter. You are wrong, Mr. Rodway, there is no hope for Antonio. He is lost."

Olivia sat at her dressing table, flouring her swollen eyes with powder. When Bernard had told her the news she had sunk to the sofa, too shocked to make a sound. Bernard did not notice. He was pacing the drawing room, on fire with indignation.

"It is an outrage, we should be ashamed of ourselves. I'm going to a meeting, we're going to put pressure on the government, we're going to stop these cursed deportations. At least that will mean Antonio has not died in vain." He looked at Olivia, white faced, ramrod stiff. "My poor sweet. You were fond of Antonio, weren't you? Do you remember how he sang at your birthday party? What a gifted young man he was."

Gently Bernard kissed her hair, and he left the house. After he had gone Olivia sent Avril out to buy meat, tea and butter. She would be a long time, Olivia knew; you had to queue for everything now. Once she was alone, she knelt on the bedroom floor, put her forehead upon the Turkish carpet and howled. She howled like a banshee, like a soul in hell. The noise echoed through the elegant spaces of the house in Bedford Square, primitive, unprecedented.

The sound, at last, of a key in the front door silenced her. It was Avril, returning from her errands. Olivia looked at her wet red face in the mirror. Then she laid both hands against her stomach, to feel their encouraging warmth upon her flesh. And so we live on, she thought, we do not die, we find new ways to survive.

Opening her wardrobe she leafed through her clothes, the expensive silks and satins faintly clammy against her fingertips, until, right at the back, she found the black spangled dress she had worn on the night she met Bernard. It looked shabbier than ever, limp from its long confinement in the dark. For an instant Olivia wavered. Its magic had worked before, but would it succeed this time? I have to try, thought Olivia. What else can I do? She laid the dress upon the bed, its silvered sequins catching the light; then, lifting her head, she began to sketch out the steps of the tango as she awaited her husband's return.

WINTER 1941

CHAPTER 33

A COLD FEBRUARY WIND WAS GUSTING THROUGH EUSTON station as Bernard walked along the platform. He was in the dreamily exhilarated state of one who has not had enough sleep for a long, long time.

The blitz had begun in September 1940. Bernard had stepped out of Sadler's Wells Theatre, where he and Olivia had been watching a performance of Gounod's *Faust*, to see the sky blazing sherbet red above the London docks. Since that night his ARP shifts had doubled, and even when he was not on duty Bernard was on the alert, braced for the drone of sirens. He had witnessed horrors, of course—Charles, Dickie's useful friend from the BBC, had been killed when a bomb exploded outside the corporation's music library—but all the same there was something insanely thrilling about the blitz. Bernard sensed that nothing in his life to come would equal the drama, the camaraderie, of surviving from day to day upon the very brink of danger.

This morning he was traveling north, on the first leg of his journey to the Isle of Man. He was going there to report on the island's internment camps to his refugee welfare committee. Since the *Arandora Star* disaster there had been a shocked change in the government's policy on internment. Ministers grudgingly recognized that in the pressure of the moment mistakes had been made—deplorable mistakes, the home secretary called them. Even Churchill airily remarked that he thought the danger from the enemy within had been exaggerated. New tribunals were set up to reexamine the cases of those who had been imprisoned, and already ten thousand internees had been released. As for the men who had been deported to Canada and Australia, the government had dispatched a couple of officials to look into their cases. Bernard had had dinner with one of them, Major Julian Layton, an old comrade from his refugee work in the 1930s, shortly before Layton had set sail for Melbourne.

The porter, a bandy-legged man in his sixties, opened the carriage door and hauled Bernard's suitcase inside.

"Thank you," said Bernard, reaching into his pocket for a tip. Before leaving for the station he had rung Olivia in Sussex. Her voice on the telephone was breathy and uncertain.

"Are you all right, my darling? Not feeling sick?"

"Bernard, I haven't felt sick for weeks." He heard her sigh as she shifted in her chair, trying to find a comfortable position for her unfamiliar bulk. "Did you have a raid last night?"

"No, it was pretty quiet. I don't suppose it will last, though. Adolf won't let us off that lightly." Bernard prodded his leather overnight bag with his toe. "I can't talk, darling, I've got to walk to Euston and catch my train. I just wanted to make sure that you were all right."

"I'm perfectly all right." Olivia sighed and shifted once again. "Don't worry about me."

"Well, I'll come and see you as soon as I get back. Take care of yourself and the little one."

This conversation ran through Bernard's mind as he heaved his suitcase onto the luggage rack. How like Olivia, he thought tenderly, to become pregnant in the middle of a war. In the past months there had been a shift in Bernard's marriage. Perhaps it was the fear of invasion, perhaps it was the shock of Antonio's death, but—quite suddenly, it seemed to Bernard—he and Olivia had rediscovered their passion for one another. More than once he had come home to find her in his study, eyes wide and seductive, and although until that moment he had thought himself too tired to breathe, he found he could not keep his hands from her. My siren, he thought, my mermaid wife. When she told him about the baby he had wanted her to go to Cheshire, to live with his family, but she had insisted on staying in Sussex. Nowhere in the country is safe, she said, and at least in Dickie's house I feel settled. That has to be best for the child, surely?

The train began to chuff rhythmically away from the platform, with a whiff of burning coal. Bernard settled into his corner seat. In his pocket he had the latest letter he had received from Herr Fischer, who was in Hutchinson Camp, one of the barbed wire enclaves on the Isle of Man. The musician wrote every fortnight or so on the army-issue notepaper they gave to internees, twelve lines spaced wide, no writing across the lines allowed. All his letters asked the same thing: Do you know when I will be released? Well, I have no news on that score, thought Bernard, but surely it will cheer Herr Fischer to see a friendly face. The thought of his own beneficence soothed him, and he allowed the waltzing sway of the carriage to lull him into sleep.

A FLOCK OF rooks flew across the iron-gray sky, cawing as they landed in the beech trees beyond the orchard. Olivia was standing on the terrace where once, on a sunlit evening, she had drunk juniper-scented Negronis with Uncle Dickie. She was huge and stately in a loose crimson dress, her hair knotted untidily at her neck.

"Filomena! I've made some tea."

Filomena straightened up. All morning she had been working in the garden, breaking the clods of chalky earth with her hoe. The grounds of the house looked very different now. The lawns had been dug up—Fred the gardener had done it, before he enlisted—

and they were divided into neat plots where Filomena was preparing to plant vegetables. This was happening across the country, as the wartime government urged householders to turn their flower beds into allotments.

"How are you feeling today, Mrs. Rodway?" asked Filomena, wiping her earth-smeared hands on her trousers.

"Like a cow," said Olivia. "Very fat and very stupid. I hope I don't get my wits back after the baby comes, life is so much easier without them." She handed Filomena a mug of tea. "Aren't you cold?"

"Yes, but it's all right when you're working. Go indoors, Mrs. Rodway. There's no sense catching pneumonia."

Olivia hunched her shoulders, wrapping her long cardigan as best she could over her swollen body. She knew that Filomena was right, but she did not like being on her own in the house. There was something about Filomena's presence that kept the ghosts at bay.

Filomena took a mouthful of hot weak tea. She could sense Olivia's longing for company. It dragged upon her as the moon drags upon the sea. You could feed that longing every hour of every day, and still it would not be satisfied.

"Only another hour," she said gently, "and then it will be lunchtime. Go indoors, Mrs. Rodway, please. I won't be long."

FILOMENA HAD NOT, in the beginning, wanted to go to Sussex. Soho had always been her home; now, when so much had been snatched from her, she did not want to leave its bustle, its familiar streetscapes. The blitz did not frighten her. In the daze that is bereavement she felt immune to bombs and to fires.

It was Bernard who persuaded her. "I would be most grateful," he said, a harassed expression on his plump, tired face. "Olivia has set her heart upon staying in my uncle's house, and I do not like to argue with her in her present condition. We have waited a long time for a child, Filomena. It would put my mind at rest, to know that you were there to take care of her."

Filomena liked the way Bernard spoke to her, as if she were an equal, almost as if she were a man. She also knew that she owed him a debt of thanks. After Antonio's death he had intervened in her family's life with the transforming touch of a magician. How he had done it Filomena did not know, but he had rescued the kiosk from the grasp of the Custodian of Enemy Property, which had taken over several Italian businesses, including some of the city's best restaurants. Mauro was now running the kiosk. Confectionery was in short supply, but he made enough from selling cigarettes and soft drinks to support Renata and her baby. The child was a boy, christened Luigi after Renata's late father.

As she marched back toward the vegetable plot, Filomena thought how glad she was that Bernard had convinced her. The simplicity of life in Sussex had slowly begun to heal the terrible wounds of loss. All day she worked hard in the open air, the hills serenely cradling her; at night she slept beneath the eaves of Dickie's house, between expensive white sheets that smelled of lavender, with no sides-to-middle seams to gall her. From time to time the screech of an owl would waken her in the night, and she would remember Antonio, or her father, or Stan lying dead in icebound Norway, but then physical exhaustion like a blessing submerged her once more.

ON MARCH 8 the Café de Paris in Coventry Street was bombed. Eighty people died, including the manager, who had boasted that the café was the safest restaurant in the city, protected beneath four stories of masonry.

Three days afterward the Paradise Ballroom took a direct hit, with nearly two hundred casualties.

"Look!" Olivia pointed indignantly to the newspaper. "One small paragraph. Because it's only shopgirls in ten-and-sixpence frocks nobody cares. It's not a chic expensive place like the Café de Paris, Lord and Lady Mountbatten don't go there and order a dozen oysters."

"You can't blame the papers. The Café de Paris is famous, of course they are going to write about it. And it is consoling for some people, to learn that the wealthy and the glamorous have not escaped the blitz." Filomena paused. "I think my brother Antonio used to sing at the Paradise Ballroom. I remember the name."

These last weeks Filomena had made a deliberate effort to speak of Antonio. I have my whole life in which to remember him, she thought, I do not want that memory consigned to some shadowland of silence. Olivia looked as if she had been stung, pressing her hand to her swollen stomach. It irked Filomena. What right did this rich unhappy woman have to claim intenser grief than Antonio's own sister? Folding her lips she marched to the closet and took out her coat and hat.

"Where are you going?" asked Olivia.

"It's Thursday, Mrs. Rodway. My afternoon off. I'm going to bicycle into Lewes and see what's on at the cinema. Do you need any shopping while I'm there?"

Olivia's face was so stricken that Filomena thought she would say, Don't go, please don't leave me. This had never actually happened, but Filomena was constantly afraid it might.

A moment later, though, Olivia turned her head coolly away. "No," she said, "no, thank you, Filomena, I don't need anything at all."

CHAPTER 34

THE STEAMER TO THE ISLE OF MAN SAILED FROM FLEETWOOD, since Liverpool—a regular target for German attacks—was considered too dangerous. When Bernard disembarked in Douglas it was raining: cold, dense rain that whisked under his umbrella and drenched his socks. The air smelled tangily of salt water and of herrings. Oh, joy, thought Bernard, as he trudged along the promenade, his leather bag in his hand.

Bernard had broken his journey for a night in Cheshire, to visit his mother. Penelope was having a miserable war. There had been no bombings in Macclesfield, and although the prospect of air raids terrified her she was disgruntled at being excluded from the drama of the blitz. She was also bored, since she could no longer indulge in her favorite activities: shopping, flirting, pushing expensive food around her plate. When Bernard suggested that she take on some war work she was appalled. Even the government doesn't expect women of my age to get our hands dirty, she said. Nobody over sixty has to register with the authorities. Bernard smiled, to think of his mother's indignation. It was the first time he had ever heard her confess to being more than fifty years old.

THE ISLE OF Man had become a prison island when mass internment began in the spring of 1940. Now whole settlements were swathed in barbed wire. Hutchinson, the camp where Herr

Fischer was interned, was formed of a cluster of houses behind the promenade. In fine weather the inmates played bowls upon the lawn, using the gilt knobs from their bedsteads. Bernard waited for the musician in the front room of the house to which he had been assigned. It had been a boardinghouse before the government commandeered it, and it had the self-conscious gentility of seaside lodgings, with yellowing lace curtains and antimacassars on the armchairs. Through the window, beyond the barbed wire, Bernard could see the gray March waves lash and swell. A guard stood at the door, to ensure that Herr Fischer did not plot treason or smuggle out uncensored mail.

Bernard's first thought when he saw the musician was how he had aged, his hair scant and brittle, his skin the color of parchment. Then Herr Fischer caught sight of him, and his face was transfigured.

"Mr. Rodway," he said, sitting eagerly in the chair opposite Bernard's, "have you come to fetch me to London?"

"What?" said Bernard, startled. "No, I'm afraid not."

"But there are new tribunals in London now, examining the cases of men like me, writers, musicians, men who have made a contribution to the arts." Herr Fischer leaned forward, his eyes bright with hope. "Several of the men here have been set free, to continue their life's work."

"Yes, I know. Indeed, I have been pressing for them to reopen your case—"

"The composer Ralph Vaughan Williams is chairing the musicians' panel. I have written to him three times, although I have not yet had a reply. I am sure that if he could hear my work—if he could hear the song that I wrote for your wife—he would urge the authorities to release me."

"Yes, I am sure that he would, Herr Fischer. I am sure that in time he will. But you must be patient, you know. The panel has many cases to review."

Herr Fischer stared. "So that is not why you have come?"

"Not this time," said Bernard. "This time I have come to be sure that they are treating you well, Herr Fischer. It is not so bad here, is it? The camp commander seems a decent enough fellow, and I hear the men themselves organize plenty of activities. Lectures and concerts. I understand that last summer there were performances of Schubert and Puccini. You do not lack kindred spirits."

There was a wheedling note in Bernard's voice. He had intended to play on Herr Fischer's discontent, to prompt criticism of the camp officials or the internees' food to add ballast to his report. Faced with this despair, though, he could not do it.

"Oh, yes," said Herr Fischer, "there is music here. Some of it to an acceptable standard."

"The camp commander tells me that the BBC news bulletins are broadcast every day," Bernard went on. "You will know that London has taken a drubbing from Hitler's bombers. Liverpool, too; I daresay you have glimpsed the fires across the water. At least it seems that we are no longer at risk of invasion. The Jews in this country will be safe from Nazi persecution, which must set your mind at rest. And there is good news from North Africa. Our troops have pushed back the Italians."

Herr Fischer gave a flick of his hand, as though success in Africa meant nothing to him. "So you do not know, Mr. Rodway, when—or if—my case will be reopened?"

"Not yet, no. As I say, Herr Fischer, you must be patient. I am doing all I can on your behalf, you must believe that."

Herr Fischer nodded three times. Then, abruptly, he rose from his chair. "Thank you for coming to see me, Mr. Rodway. I am very grateful. I hope that your visit here will be a pleasant one."

And before Bernard could protest he was gone, vanishing soft-footed into the shabby depths of the boardinghouse. It made Bernard feel foolish. He hoped that the soldier at the door had not been paying attention. He got to his feet with a bluff, devil-may-care expression.

The guard, though, looked at him and shrugged. "Don't take it to heart," he said. "They all ask that question, all the time. When am I going to be released? It's the boredom, sir. Doesn't matter how cushy it is here, they can't stand the boredom. It eats their souls like rust."

TWO DAYS LATER, before he left the island, Bernard went to see Bruno, who was interned in Palace, one of the camps for Italians. A former hotel above the sea front, it was notoriously overcrowded; the inmates had been segregated into two groups, fascists and antifascists, to stop their constant fighting. Bernard did not want to waste his time on a supporter of Mussolini, a man who had fought in Abyssinia for God's sake, but Filomena had asked him especially, her face luminous with concern. She had taken a snapshot of Renata and the baby for Bernard to give to Bruno. He has never seen his son, she said, and Bernard, thinking of his own soon-to-be-born child, had relented.

The photograph was not a very good one. The baby had refused to sit still on Renata's lap, and its face was no more than a blur of grayish light. All the same, Bruno stared as though by staring he could step into the picture's margins and touch his son. He was a ratty sort of man, Bernard thought, with the questing desperate expression that all the internees had.

"I wanted him to be called after Antonio," Bruno said. "My letter was held up by the censors, though. It did not arrive until after the christening, and by then it was too late."

"You swapped papers, I believe, so that Antonio could stay with his father?"

Bruno nodded. "We knew that Enrico was dying. All three of us knew, me, Antonio, his friend Peppino."

"Peppino? The fellow who worked with Antonio at La Rondine?"

"That's right. He sailed on the *Arandora Star* too, though I hear on the grapevine that he survived the wreck. He was picked up by a Canadian destroyer." Bruno's mouth twisted ruefully. "And then they shipped him off to Australia, with two hundred other survivors."

"Dear God," said Bernard. He wanted to add, There are times when I am ashamed of my own country, but he would not voice those words to a fascist.

"Filomena is well, is she?" Bruno asked.

"Yes. She is living in Sussex, as a companion to my wife, Olivia. Your wife is well too, I believe. Her uncle is running the Trombettas' kiosk, she no longer has to worry where her next meal is coming from." Bernard expected Bruno to recognize his cue and express gratitude; grudgingly, perhaps, but gratitude all the same. Instead he gazed at the picture of his son, as though he had not been listening. It annoyed Bernard.

"It is just as well that your wife has her uncle to support her. It seems to me, my friend, that you are destined to be here for a long, long time. As a man who has fought for the fascists they will be in no hurry to release you."

Bruno closed his eyes. "Mr. Rodway," he said, "I do not think about such things. I am a good Italian, a loyal Italian. Once upon a time I would have given my life for the *duce*. Now all I want is for this godforsaken war to end, so I can go home to Lazio with my wife and child."

PRIVACY IS A rare commodity in an internment camp. After supper, on the night that Bernard left the Isle of Man, Herr Fischer slid quietly away to the laundry that served Hutchinson Camp. It was a narrow hut with a row of slatted shelves and a copper for boiling the linen. He took with him a pencil and a sheet of notepaper, with its twelve well-spaced lines. He had intended to write to his sister, Brigitta, but he found he could no longer visualize her face. All he could see was the photograph he had of her, grainily fixed in time upon the banks of the Danube. Leaning against the copper he wrote to Bernard instead, in English, thanking him for his kindness. When he had finished he folded the paper and tucked it into his shirt pocket.

There were hooks in the ceiling, from which the airing racks were suspended. If you stood on a chair you could reach them easily. Herr Fischer chose a dirty sheet so as not to make more work for the men assigned to laundry duties. The hem was stoutly sewn, but once it had given way it was easy to rip the cloth. Herr Fischer tore two long strips and knotted them carefully together. Then he pulled, hard, to be quite certain that the rope would bear his weight.

CHAPTER 35

THE AIR IN THE DE LUXE CINEMA WAS WARM AND THICK WITH cigarette smoke. Filomena, nestled in her sixpenny seat, tried to quash the anxiety bubbling inside her. I'm entitled to an afternoon's freedom, she thought, I shouldn't feel guilty, it's not my fault that Mrs. Rodway can't stand to be alone.

The afternoon's main feature was *Waterloo Bridge*. Filomena had started watching it in the middle, just as Vivien Leigh lost her job as a dancer and began her shady double life. That was how it worked at the De Luxe. The programs ran continuously from half past two until ten o'clock, and you went in whenever a seat became free. Filomena had seen Rhett Butler abandon Scarlett before he kissed her, she had seen Manderley burn before understanding Rebecca's malignant power. You got used to it. Narrative was less important than a three-hour respite from the war. Sometimes, in the comforting fug of the cinema, Filomena found herself daydreaming of what might have been: Stan returning from the war, getting married, setting up home together in Soho or in Bermondsey. Mostly, though, she pushed such thoughts away and allowed herself to be swept along by the images before her.

On the screen Vivien Leigh, in a low-cut satin dress, was touting for business at Waterloo station, welcoming soldiers as they came back from the trenches. There was something troubled about her beauty, which made Filomena think of Olivia: the same fragility, the same air of drama. All at once she remembered how Danila had gone into labor, without warning, just as they were arguing about Bruno. She tried to stifle the memory—it was her afternoon off, for glory's sake, the only time she had for herself—but it was no use. I'll have to go back, she thought, and seizing her coat she began to squeeze along the row of hunched knees. Two or three people tutted as behind her Vivien Leigh glimpsed the lover she had thought was dead.

Outside on School Hill it was already dark, with a silver wedge of moon in the clear cold sky. You're a fool, Filomena said to herself, as she retrieved her bicycle. You'll get there to find that nothing has happened, it'll just be Mrs. Rodway all fey and weepy. Nevertheless she pedaled as fast as she could, down the steep hill toward the river and on into the blue-black, encompassing hills.

OLIVIA GUESSED WHAT was happening as soon as the pain began. She had had pain before, rumbling through her body like thunder, but this was different: fiercer, more urgent. For thirty seconds it seized her in its fist, and then, just as suddenly, it released her. Olivia's brain, which for months had been fogged by grief, became perfectly clear. Filomena would be away for hours yet; she had better ring the doctor.

Dr. Croft lived in the nearby village of Firle. It was his wife who answered the telephone.

"He's at Mrs. Hobden's, she's had another attack. If the pains have only just begun it'll be a while yet, Mrs. Rodway. I'll tell him as soon as he gets home."

Olivia sat on the stairs, beside the telephone. Bernard will be cross, she thought; he wanted to be here for the baby's birth. Another contraction gripped her, twisting like a blade in the small of her back. They were coming more often now. She had a sense of her child's impatience, kicking and wriggling to get out into the world. It pleased Olivia. She would have liked to go to bed but if she did there would be nobody to let in the doctor, and so she fetched a cushion from the green drawing room and lay on the hall rug. She could feel the tiled floor hard against the knobs of her spine.

That was how Filomena found her when she came back from the cinema. She gave a yelp of alarm; then she crouched beside Olivia and took her hand.

"Mrs. Rodway, are you all right?"

"The baby's coming." Olivia struggled to sit upright. "I rang for Dr. Croft but he was visiting another patient. Maybe you should cycle to Firle and fetch him."

Filomena's competent palm was inching across Olivia's pelvis. "I think it's too late for that," she said in a careful voice. "How often are you getting the pains?"

"I haven't been counting. Every five minutes?"

"Let's put you to bed." Gently Filomena helped Olivia to her feet, one arm laced about her shoulders. "Don't be afraid, I have done this before. I helped the midwife deliver my brother Antonio's son."

"I'm not afraid," said Olivia, and Filomena could see that she was telling the truth. There was a brilliance in her face, as if she had just woken from a long stupor.

Upstairs Filomena opened drawers and cupboards, gathering towels, a nightdress, a ribbon to keep Olivia's hair from her hot damp forehead. She hoped that she would remember everything she had learned from the bossy Tuscan midwife: when Olivia should breathe and push, how to clasp the infant's head so its shoulders did not tear her flesh.

The baby was born an hour later, just before midnight.

"It's a girl," said Filomena. The child had dark tangled hair, plastered wetly over her head. She was squalling with a kind of thwarted rage, as though this was not in the least what she had expected.

"Let me see." Greedily Olivia stretched out her arms for her daughter. "Oh, she is beautiful."

"Yes," said Filomena, "she is very beautiful."

"She looks just like her father," said Olivia, and she began to laugh.

Filomena looked at her. Their eyes met and held, laden with knowledge, but neither of them said anything at all.

Bernard arrived at lunchtime the following day. He had returned to London the night before and rolled into bed, unwashed, unshaven, only to be woken by Filomena with the news that the baby had come early. At Lewes station there were no taxis and he had to cadge a lift from a market gardener on his way home from delivering a van load of spring cabbage.

When Filomena opened the door he kissed her on both cheeks. "Filomena, you are an archangel. What in the world would we have done without you?"

Filomena blushed. "It was Dr. Croft who cut the cord," she said, "and he made certain that everything was—well, as it should be. Which it is, of course. They are upstairs, Mr. Rodway: your wife and the baby."

"My wife and my daughter, you mean, Filomena," said Bernard, and he bounded up the stairs into the bedroom. The baby was lying in a small wooden crib, drowsy and blissful from her feed. Bernard scooped her into his arms.

"You caught us napping, little one, didn't you? We weren't expecting you for another month at least." He glanced across at Olivia, who was propped on a heap of pillows. "My clever sweetheart. Well done."

Olivia's eyes were sparkling. Her face against the white pillows was tired, but he had never seen her so alive; not even when she danced the tango, not even when she made love to him.

"Nina," she said, "I want to call her Nina."

Bernard leaned across the bed and kissed her, still cradling the baby. "Oh, my darling," he said, "we can call her whatever you like."

TEN THOUSAND MILES away a bull-necked figure was standing outside a corrugated iron hut. The night was very cold. He could smell the eucalyptus trees that surrounded the camp. Above him the stars glittered. One of the camp's inmates was teaching him to name them: Corvus, Centaurus, Hydra, Crux.

Peppino had arrived in Australia in September 1940, with two hundred other survivors from the *Arandora Star*. The ship on which they sailed—the SS *Dunera*—was overcrowded, with sewage flooding the decks, and the guards were brutal and thieving. German U-boats still prowled the seas. Once Peppino heard the rasp of a torpedo striking the ship's side, although this time the explosive failed to detonate. On his arrival in Melbourne he was transported a hundred miles north to Tatura. The camp was a cluster of tin huts upon a hillside, with a barbed wire fence to separate Italians from Germans. Peppino had been set to work as assistant to the camp's carpenter. He was one of the only inmates strong enough to saw through a length of Australian hardwood.

The door of the hut opened and a man stepped out, dressed in dungarees. "What are you doing, Peppino? The night watch will be patrolling soon."

Peppino pushed his hands into his pockets. The seams were lined with dust, which got in his fingernails. The dust in Tatura drove you to despair, whisked into gritty stinging clouds by the slightest hint of wind.

"I'm looking at the stars," he said.

The other man stood beside him, tilting his face toward the sky. It was a handsome face, or at least, a face that had once been handsome, before it was ravaged by hunger and hardship. His black hair was beginning to turn gray.

"They see different stars in England, don't they?" he said.

There was a note of longing in his voice. Peppino put an arm about his shoulder. "That's right. They see different stars there."

From beneath the trees there was the crunch of boots, the flash of a torch. It was the night patrol, enforcing the curfew, a tedious job that could make the guards spiteful. Last month Peppino had been docked sixpence from his wages, paid in the camp's own currency, for leaving his hut after nightfall.

"Come," he said to his companion, "let's go inside."

The other man was still gazing hungrily at the sky. Peppino touched his shoulder once again.

"You won't change anything by staring," he said. "Come inside, Antonio. Come inside, my friend."

SPRING 1947

CHAPTER 36

THE TADPOLES HAD GROWN SINCE SHE LAST CAME TO THE pond. Nina lay on her stomach and poked at them with a stick. Several were half-frogs now, short legs sprouting from the buds of flesh along their bodies. She watched as they winnowed clumsily through the scum at the pond's edge. The water smelled thick and dank.

"Nina! Where are you?"

It was Aunt Min. She was calling in English, which meant that she was cross. Nina hesitated. She was not supposed to go near the pond by herself. She could come out right away and be scolded, or she could stay here and pretend she had not heard. If she hid for long enough Aunt Min would get anxious, she would think something bad had happened, and when she found Nina she would be too relieved to punish her.

"Nina! You can hear me, I know you can. If I have to come and hunt for you there'll be trouble."

This time there was an edge to Aunt Min's voice. Reluctantly Nina clambered up. She had got green pond slime on her dress, viscous against the yellow stripes. It was on her legs too, a great streak of it next to the rubbery white scar where she had fallen in some gravel when she was three.

Aunt Min was standing on the terrace beside the back door. She wore a flowered cotton overall, her dark hair tied up in a scarf.

"Just look at you. I thought I told you to keep away from the pond. You're as grubby as a Gypsy."

"Gypsies are really called pikeys," Nina said, trailing her stick behind her. "Fred the gardener told me."

"Not in this house they're not." Aunt Min threw the stick aside and hustled Nina indoors. "Now, into the bath with you, and then you can have supper in your pajamas. It's early to bed tonight. We've got a long day tomorrow."

"Why?" said Nina. "*Perchè, Zia Mena?*"

"You know why. We're going to London to see your father."

The bath was very deep, with ornate feet like claws. Sometimes Nina imagined that it was a giant bird and she was riding it, like the roc that carried Sinbad the Sailor.

"I don't want to go to London," she said. "I'd rather stay here. Can't we stay here instead?"

Aunt Min took no notice, but whipped Nina's dress over her head. "At least you haven't got pond muck in your hair. That's one thing to be thankful for."

Nina's hair was dark and curly, inclined to tangle. Whenever it was washed she screamed like a banshee. It's just as well we don't live in Soho, Aunt Min used to say. The neighbors would think I was beating you. Aunt Min often talked about Soho: narrow higgledy-piggledy houses, the smell of cigarettes and fried onions, music and chattering late into the night. She had taken Nina there once, excitedly pointing out this doorway, that little café, but to Nina it seemed just an ordinary row of closed-up houses, not a magical place at all.

The enamel of the bath was scratchy with lime scale. She thought of her father, his mustache that tickled when he kissed you, the gentle wheeze when he spoke. He was a writer, quite a famous one, he got his picture in the papers. Whenever he saw Nina his eyes would skew sideways, as though there was something wrong with her face and he could not quite bring himself to look at it.

Nina watched the slime on her legs dissolve in the bathwater. "Aunt Min," she asked, "why doesn't Papa like looking at me?"

Aunt Min did not answer, but reached for the flannel and the cake of Pears soap. Nina thought the question must have been rude, or else impossible. She was always being told that her questions were impossible.

In silence Filomena dunked the flannel in the bathwater. "It is because you remind him of your mother," she said at last.

THERE HAD BEEN no sense of foreboding about Olivia's departure, that day in July. If anything, she had been excited about going to London. Filomena had helped her pack, fetching out the smart clothes she hardly ever wore in Sussex, the chiffon blouses, the well-cut suits, a couple of evening dresses.

"Perhaps we'll go dancing," Olivia said, holding up one of the dresses. It was of damson satin, subtly reflecting the light. "I haven't set foot on a dance floor for months."

Filomena smiled. They led a quiet life, punctuated by occasional visits from Bernard; it was not surprising that Olivia got restless. Sometimes she would push back the chairs and wind up the gramophone, and she would dance the tango in the sage-green drawing room. Filomena and Nina used to watch her enraptured as she twisted and spun across the floor. It was not the same as dancing in public, though; Filomena could tell that from Olivia's face.

"Do you think Nina will miss me?" Olivia said suddenly, clutching at the dark red dress. Filomena took the question to mean, Is it wrong of me to leave her?

"Nina will be all right," she said as she tucked some rolled-up silk stockings into the open suitcase. "It's just for a few days, Mrs. Rodway. She'll hardly notice that you're not here."

A flicker of relief crossed Olivia's face. "You're right, Filomena. She's only three, she won't notice I've gone. And I'll be home again before she knows it."

It was Bernard who had asked Olivia to go to London. Penelope was coming to stay. He had told her he would be too busy to entertain her, but she had insisted, and now Bernard was afraid that she would feel neglected.

"I'll only make it worse, Bernard," Olivia said when he telephoned. "You know that. She'll sulk because she hasn't got you to herself."

Bernard harrumphed. He still disliked it when his wife criticized his mother. "Well, perhaps, but at least you can keep an eye on her. Penelope thinks that now the Allies have invaded France the war's as good as over. She doesn't understand that London's a dangerous place. I don't think she believes that doodlebugs exist."

That summer the Germans had unleashed a new weapon upon southern England: flying bombs, or V-1s, known as doodlebugs. Several had landed in Sussex, and they were wreaking havoc in the capital. They struck by daylight when the streets were crowded; the engines would fall silent, and moments later a ton of high explosive would descend.

"Besides," Bernard said, in a different, wistful voice, "I want to see you, my darling. I haven't seen you for weeks."

On Olivia's first evening in London they went dancing, not to the Golden Slipper but to another nightclub close to Piccadilly. Bernard tipped the bandleader to play "Dark Eyes," so that Olivia could dance the tango in her plum-colored dress. She danced more wonderfully than ever, Bernard thought, as though she were making up for lost time. Nobody in the nightclub could keep their eyes from her.

The following day Penelope arrived. Just as Olivia had predicted, she was annoyed to find that she would not have Bernard to herself, and she sniffed and pouted, complaining about the food, the stuffy weather, Olivia's poor housekeeping. To keep the peace, Bernard took them both for lunch at the Savoy, Penelope's favorite. In the taxi to the restaurant Penelope would not stop needling Olivia. Why on earth was she spending so much of her time in

Sussex? She had a nanny for the little girl; surely her place was with her husband? That was what Penelope would do, in her situation. Olivia grimaced. She knew perfectly well that if she had decided to stay in London Penelope would be sniping at her for neglecting her child.

"Filomena has war work to do, she cannot always care for Nina," she said, with careful serenity. "Besides, she is my daughter. I want to watch her growing up . . ."

They had reached the Savoy now. Bernard paid off the taxi and led them toward the hotel entrance, set back from the Strand. He was halfway there when he heard the drone of a V-1 in the sky.

"Quick!" he shouted, as he swung behind a sheltering pillar. "There's a doodlebug. Take cover!"

Penelope, on the pavement, was fussing with the seams of her stockings. "What? Don't be so silly, Bernie—"

Olivia plunged toward the pillar. As she dived she grasped Penelope's elbow, trying to drag her to safety. Penelope resisted, her high heels braced stubbornly, like a horse.

"For God's sake, Mother," snapped Bernard. Leaping forward he seized her arm and hauled her against the wall. The violence of his lunge threw Olivia off balance. She felt a terrible lurching, struggling to save herself, knowing she must fall. Above her the V-1's engine cut out. There was a flash, a crash; then silence.

Olivia was killed at once; probably, Bernard said, she knew nothing about it. That was what he told Filomena, in an unnaturally calm voice. Filomena asked what to do. Should she bring Nina to London, or did Bernard intend to travel to Sussex, to tell his daughter what had happened? There was a silence on the telephone as though Bernard had not thought about this at all. Oh, he said, I think you should talk to her, Filomena. It will be better coming from you.

Filomena had watched her own mother die, but she had no idea how to break such news to a three-year-old child. In the end she took Nina on her lap and explained that Olivia had had an accident, she had been hurt, too badly hurt for the doctors to help her, she would not be coming home again. Nina sucked her fingers, as she always did when she was thinking.

"Has she gone to heaven?" she asked at last.

Filomena seized gratefully on the question. "Yes, that's right. She's gone to heaven. And she's watching over you, Nina, to keep you safe."

Nina gave her a slow thoughtful look, and Filomena did not know if she believed this comforting vision or not. Afterward she did not talk about her mother. Instead she would tiptoe through the empty rooms in Dickie's house, peering behind the sofa, pulling back the curtains. Sometimes she would say, tentatively, *Mama?*, as though she did not quite dare to hope for a reply. She began to wet the bed, a habit she had outgrown months before, and often she would wake in the night, howling and shivering, unable to speak. When this happened Filomena took her into her own bed, until warmth and company lulled her to sleep once more. Those nights gave Filomena a primitive sense of satisfaction. Surely you could not do anything in your life more worthwhile than to comfort a bereaved child.

She remembered it now, as she poured herself a whisky and soda in the sage-green drawing room. She had put Nina to bed, and she was savoring the peace before the onslaught of their trip to London. It was a pity, she thought, that Bernard had not seen his daughter in the months after Olivia's death. He sent Filomena money, generous amounts of it, and every week or so he telephoned, but it seemed there was no question of a visit. By the time he finally came to Sussex the damage had been done. Bernard was a stranger: "that man," Nina called him, no matter how Filomena corrected her. As for Bernard, he had tried to hide it, but Filomena had seen him stiffen when he first glimpsed Nina's face, thin and beaky, with Olivia's eyes.

She took a mouthful of whisky, feeling it burn pleasurably against her throat. Nobody in Frith Street would have allowed her to drink whisky: not her father, not her brothers, not Bruno, if she had married him. Bruno had gone back to Lazio after the war, with Mauro and Renata and the baby. As for the kiosk, the lease had been sold to a returning Cockney in his demob suit, and the money shared within the family.

Filomena looked around the drawing room. Over the years she had come to think of it as hers, with its russet curtains, its chrome-tipped decanters, the gaudy stage designs upon the walls. She had her nest egg of money, she had her job caring for Nina; after the havoc and grief of war her life had apparently righted itself. Even the loss of Stan Harker had grown easier to bear. She could remember his face calmly, tenderly now, without having to push the memory away.

Yet tonight she felt uneasy. It seemed to her that uncertainty stalked the house, sniffing warily at the corners, like a fox. Nothing lasts forever, thought Filomena. You ought to know that by now.

CHAPTER 37

THE REPORTER FROM THE *TATLER* WAS A BUXOM YOUNG WOMAN in a powder-blue suit. She sat demurely upon the sofa in Bedford Square, scribbling in her shorthand notebook.

"And there is another book on the way, I understand, Mr. Rodway?"

"Oh, yes. That is, when I can find the time to finish it."

The *Tatler* reporter stopped writing and gazed with the earnest expression of a fan. "I'm so glad. I loved your first book, I can't wait for the next one."

Bernard smiled. "Thank you. It's kind of you to say so." He leaned forward and poured more tea from the silver pot. "Do have another biscuit. I'm sorry I can't offer you anything more exciting. We've used up our sugar ration."

"So when can we expect the second book?" the reporter asked, still with that ardent fan-club expression.

"Oh . . ." Bernard raised his china teacup with a vague flourish. "I do a great deal of refugee work, you know. Everyone supposes that because the war is over the refugee problem has gone away, but of course it hasn't. There are thousands of displaced people in Europe, trying to find new homes, new jobs. Thousands, too, who are looking for the relatives they have lost. That is what is taking up my days, helping to trace those who vanished during the war."

The reporter nodded rather glassily. "Goodness. Yes. One simply can't imagine what that must be like." She took another biscuit from the plate. "I believe that you began the first book between shifts as an air raid warden?"

"It was a good way of passing time. You can always keep a notebook and a pencil in your pocket, even when you're running for shelter. And then, later in the war—well, let's say it helped to keep the demons at bay."

"Of course," said the reporter quickly, respectfully. She glanced toward the photograph upon the mantelpiece. "Do you mind my asking—is that a picture of your wife?"

Bernard did not need to look. It was the picture that Dickie had loved, taken on their honeymoon.

"Yes," he said, "that's my wife. That's Olivia."

WHEN THE REPORTER had gone Bernard crossed to the fireplace and picked up the photograph of Olivia. While she was alive he had never paid it much attention. It was a picture of his wife, that was all, the kind of picture any man would display if he were married to a beautiful woman. Now the photograph had acquired the half-sacred status of an icon. There was something inscrutable about Olivia's face, mysterious, out of reach. It made Bernard wonder if he had ever really known her. Perhaps I should hide it away, he thought, if I cannot see it then it cannot harm me, but he could not bear to think of consigning Olivia to the darkness of a closed drawer.

Turning away he examined the business card that the *Tatler* girl had left behind. Bernard's first novel had been published two months before. It was a murder mystery, set in the Cambridge of his student days. His hero was rich, humane, stupendously clever. Women adored him, but some deeply buried grief prevented him ever accepting their love. Privately Bernard thought the book frivolous, not like the futuristic novel he had written before the war. He had begun it as light relief, to distract him during the blitz; then, in the bleak, blank days that followed Olivia's death, he had found that writing numbed the horror, blotting out the visions that spooled inexorably through his head. The last chapters he had written in a frenzy, surfacing from the page to find that it was three in the morning. He had been astonished by the book's success. Already there was talk of a second edition, despite the shortage of paper.

The tea things were growing cold upon the table. Once Avril would have been quick to collect them, but since her return to Bedford Square she had been mopey and distracted. Avril had joined the Wrens during the war. She had been posted to Egypt, where her heart was soundly broken by a married naval officer. Bernard could not help thinking less of her, for turning what should have been the great adventure of her life into a cliché from a cheap romance. He was about to call her to take the tray away when the doorbell rang. Filomena, he thought, Nina. There was a flurry of noise in the hallway, and then footsteps scrambling up the stairs. With an effort he composed himself to greet his daughter.

"Come along, Nina," said Filomena's voice on the landing. "Don't be silly, go inside, say hallo to your papa. He's waiting for you."

The door inched cautiously open. Nina was wearing a Viyella dress of Black Watch tartan. It was too small for her, and with her wild hair and beaky face it made her look like some feral creature, a lynx, a pine marten, forced into human clothes.

"Hallo, sweetheart," said Bernard. "Come and give your old father a kiss. No, not like that, sweetheart, don't screw up your face like that. Give me a proper kiss. That's better."

IN MELBOURNE IT was a bright winter's morning, with a crisp wind blowing from the ocean. Antonio was sitting in the café near the harbor where he and Peppino lodged. In his hands there was an unopened letter with a London postmark. He kept turning the envelope between his fingers, twice, three, four times, as though the act of turning might change the message written upon it.

Peppino, who worked in the café, was preparing to open up, wiping down the counter, flicking dust from the tables. They were mundane tasks but as he performed them Peppino felt the peppery invigorating sense of his own liberty. He and Antonio had been released from Tatura shortly after the bombing of Pearl Harbor. Manpower was in short supply; it seemed suddenly absurd to be squandering the energies of a captive workforce. They joined the Employment Company of the Australian army, and were sent to pick fruit—peaches and ripe yellow pears—in the orchards of Victoria.

Crossing toward his friend, Peppino took the envelope gently from his hands. It was the second letter Antonio had sent to his sister in Frith Street. Like the first it had been returned: *Not known at this address.*

"You could write to your wife in Lazio," said Peppino.

Antonio shook his head. "Filomena is the one who haunts me. Even my son—well, he was always his mother's child. I don't suppose he remembers me at all. But I hate to think that Filomena still believes me dead. And if I cannot find her, maybe it would be better if I stayed lost. I have a good life here, a successful life, I am doing what I love. Perhaps I should be content to leave the past alone."

Two months after joining the Australian army Antonio had taken part in a community concert at Melbourne Town Hall, organized to raise public morale. His performance had caused a sensation. The concert had been broadcast by the local radio station, and before he knew it Antonio was in demand across the state. He sang in army barracks and workplace canteens, the sentimental songs that everyone knew: "I'll Be Seeing You," "We'll Meet Again." Now that the war was over his career was flourishing. He regularly performed in Melbourne, and an executive from Columbia's Australian company wanted to record a disc, although so far nothing had come of it.

Peppino frowned. "I do not know, Antonio. It is different for me, I have no ties with the old world. There is no reason I should not settle and be happy here. But you . . ."

The previous month Peppino had applied to become an Australian citizen. There would be no revolution in Italy now: Togliatti, the bespectacled communist leader, had squandered the opportunity by joining the postwar coalition government. It would do him no good, said Peppino; the Christian Democrats would chew him up and spit him out like gristle. Meanwhile in Australia the summers were warm, and there was a newness about the country that made all things seem possible, not like hidebound world-weary England. Besides, his two sea voyages had left their mark upon Peppino. He could only sleep beside an open window, and even then he woke at night, sweating and screaming.

"I could be happy here too," said Antonio, faintly mutinous. "Why not? I have my career, and nothing in my life means more to me now."

"What about the Englishman? The one who paid for your singing lessons. I remember him, he was a man who liked doing good. He may be willing to look for Filomena."

"I cannot write to Mr. Rodway, Peppino. I slept with his wife. Worse than that: I was in love with his wife. How in God's name can I ask for his help?"

Peppino grinned. "You are too scrupulous, Antonino," he said, and then, more seriously: "The war has changed many things. What does it matter if you loved his wife? He may not know, he may not care. He may be glad to learn that among so many dead you are still alive." Peppino strode across the room to unlock the door of the café. "Besides, aren't you curious to find out what has happened to the beautiful Mrs. Rodway? She too may want to start a new life in Australia. With or without her husband."

Antonio was silent. Even now, after seven years, he could hardly bear to think about Olivia.

"She is a rich man's wife, Peppino," he said at last. "It is not possible. What kind of life could I offer her?"

"You cannot forget her, though, can you, Antonio?" Peppino's voice was matter-of-fact. "I see how you are with other women, in the nightclubs, here in the café. They gaze, they flirt, and you smile sweetly back at them, but you cannot forget her."

Antonio looked across at his friend. "No," he said, "that is true. I will never forget her."

CHAPTER 38

IT WAS A BEAUTIFUL DAY IN JUNE, AND FILOMENA WAS SITTING at her desk beside the window, overlooking the garden. Above the house Firle Beacon lay like a sleeping giant, lush and primeval. A shrill cloud of swifts wheeled through the sky.

Nina, on the lawn, was dancing. It was a clumsy, self-absorbed, dervishlike dance, her limbs flailing to and fro. Lying on the grass was her favorite toy, a cloth rabbit, now grubby and threadbare. Bernard had bought her several expensive toys—a celluloid doll that cried, a rocking horse for her bedroom—but the rabbit was the only thing to which Nina had become attached. Filomena could see from her lips that she was singing under her breath, and a desperate wave of love washed through her.

She turned away to the letter on her desk. It was from her sister, Paolina. Since the war had ended, Paolina had written from Lazio every two or three months, screeds of gossip and grievance in badly spelled Italian. Her husband had enlisted early in the war and he was killed soon afterward, somewhere in Russia; Paolina did not seem to know exactly where or when. He had left her with a tribe of children who ran half-wild around the village. Paolina was always recounting their misdemeanors: stealing figs from the neighbors' trees, pushing each other into streams and spiny myrtle bushes. According to her last letter her oldest son had broken his brother's nose, cracking a water pitcher over his head.

Mostly, though, Paolina complained about Danila. Some of

those complaints were familiar to Filomena. She tells me how to cook spaghetti as if I had not been doing it all my life. She thinks that because she has one docile son she can lecture me on controlling the behavior of my children. She believes she is better than I am, cleverer, more refined. Lately the complaints had grown vaguer and more hostile. Danila had become Valentino's *housekeeper*—the word was underlined—which was not respectful to the memory of their dear brother Antonio. She had moved into their grandmother's house in the village, and possession, Paolina said darkly, is nine-tenths of the law. When Filomena asked her sister what she meant her reply was more enigmatic than ever. It was not Valentino's fault, she wrote, he would always do right by his family. The trouble was that he had never been able to say no to a pretty woman.

Filomena shook the pages from the envelope. She had expected another baffling lament about Danila's behavior, but this letter was short and matter-of-fact. Paolina's eldest daughter, Giulia, was getting married: a good marriage, Paolina said, to a young man named Franco Rossi, the son of Valentino's employer. It had all happened very quickly, but that was the war for you, it had changed so many things. Filomena tried to think how old Giulia was. Sixteen, maybe seventeen? Probably she was pregnant, only Paolina did not want to say so. The wedding was taking place in July, in the village. You should come, wrote Paolina, you are Giulia's aunt after all, and it is over ten years since you traveled to Italy. If you leave it much longer you will have forgotten what your family looks like.

"Tcha," said Filomena, pulling a face. It is impossible, she thought, I cannot drop everything, I have responsibilities here. Paolina does not understand that. Through the window she could see that Nina had wandered into the vegetable garden. She was standing among the runner beans, climbing her rabbit up the bamboo wigwam that supported the plants. Filomena looked at the letter once more. At least Paolina had not invoked the memories of their father, of their brother Antonio; that was something to be thankful for. Even as she thought this, Filomena saw Enrico's face, stony and reproachful, his mouth rigid beneath his coarse gray mustache. Oh dear God, she thought, the ghosts. She tucked Paolina's letter into one of the desk's cubbyholes; then she got to her feet and called Nina in for her tea.

IN THE DRAWING room at Bedford Square Bernard was mixing gin and Its. He handed one to Filomena, who was sitting opposite him in a brown leather armchair.

"Chin chin," he said, raising his glass.

Whenever she stayed at Bedford Square, Filomena's behavior was impeccable, Bernard thought. She made sure that he was not disturbed by Nina during his working hours; trickier still, she contrived not to offend Avril, who was touchy about her status in the household. Filomena would eat her supper early with Nina, fetching the tray herself so that Avril would not have to serve her. Then, when Nina had gone to bed, she would have a drink with Bernard. He looked forward to these occasions. In theory they gave him an opportunity to discuss Nina, but in practice he and Filomena talked about much more: Bernard's progress in tracking refugees, Filomena's childhood in Soho, how the world had changed since the war's end. There was something infinitely reassuring about Filomena. Over the years she had grown stouter but it suited her, it made her look handsome and sensible. She was the thread that linked Bernard, innocently, to so much—deeper, less innocent—that he had lost.

Tonight he felt he had earned his gin and It. That afternoon they had taken Nina to the zoo. It was not an excursion Bernard would have chosen, traipsing around the enclosures in Regent's Park, and having made the sacrifice he had been disappointed by Nina's response. She stared at the giraffes and the sleek tigers in silence, sucking her fingers.

"Well, a long day," Bernard said in a jovial voice. "I expect Nina will sleep like a log."

Filomena nodded, but she did not answer. There was a preoccupied expression on her face.

"Is anything the matter, Filomena?" asked Bernard.

Filomena hesitated for a moment; then she said: "I have had a letter from my sister, Paolina. Her daughter Giulia is getting married next month in our village in Lazio. Paolina has asked me to come to the wedding." She lifted her face candidly toward him. "I would like to go, Mr. Rodway. It is years since I saw my family. And I will not be gone for long, two weeks, maybe three."

"Oh," said Bernard, nonplussed. "What about Nina?"

"I thought that maybe she could stay here in London. She is shy and awkward with you, Mr. Rodway. You can see it for yourself, you must have noticed it today, at the zoo. She hardly said a word, which is not like Nina. If she spent more time in your company I'm sure that she would overcome her shyness."

"Well, perhaps." The prospect of being alone with his daughter for two weeks, without the buffer of Filomena's presence, filled Bernard with a kind of blunt panic. "Perhaps you're right, perhaps I ought to get to know the child better. But now is not the best of times, Filomena. I have my refugee work, I have my second book to finish. And Avril would not be able to care for Nina, she would not be willing to care for Nina, we would have to engage a nanny . . ."

He waited for Filomena to interrupt and say, Ah, well, I will not go, if it is not convenient. She was silent, though, looking across at him from the armchair. Her steadfastness took Bernard by surprise.

"Well," he said, "I can understand that you want to see your family again. Of course you do, I should have thought of that before, it was inconsiderate of me." He took a mouthful of gin and It. "I have a suggestion, Filomena. Why don't you take Nina with you? A holiday abroad will be good for her. I'll pay your expenses, naturally. Then when I have cleared my desk a little I can come and join you. We can have some days in Rome, I can spend time with my daughter there."

Filomena frowned. "It will not be very interesting for Nina. The village where my family lives is very quiet, and I will have to spend most of my time with my relatives—"

"Oh, Nina won't mind. All new things are interesting to a child, don't you agree? Besides, I would like my daughter to see Europe, I would like her to see how people in other countries live. I don't want her to grow up as a prim little English girl." Bernard swallowed the last of his drink and rose to mix another one. "Of course, I'm assuming that you intend to come home again, Filomena. You're not secretly planning to run away to Lazio and abandon us?"

He had intended the remark as a joke—a clumsy one, admittedly—but Filomena looked stricken. "I would never do that. I would never abandon Nina." She paused, her cheeks flushed with distress. "I will be happy to take her to Italy, Mr. Rodway, if you will trust me with her."

"Oh, Filomena. There is nobody I would trust more, you must know that. Now, let me refill that glass of yours. And tomorrow we will start to make the arrangements for your journey."

"WELL, I FEEL honored," said Lionel, in his bluff facetious way, "it is not often that I dine out with a celebrity."

Bernard signaled to the waiter to bring more bread. "Don't be absurd," he said. They were having dinner at Rules in Maiden Lane. The restaurant was Lionel's choice. Beneath its gilded glass roof it served the traditional English food that he favored: jugged hare, steamed game pudding, treacle tart.

Lionel was in London to negotiate new orders from the expensive shops of Jermyn Street. The silk business, like so many industries, had changed during the war. With silk supplies from the

Far East cut off, there had been a rise in synthetic fibers like rayon and nylon. Now, in an age of austerity, those cheaper materials had taken over the mass market; silk, it seemed, was an indulgence destined only for the wealthy.

"Do you think it will be successful, concentrating on luxury goods?" asked Bernard. "Times are hard. Nobody has money to burn."

Lionel shrugged complacently. "There are always people prepared to pay for something special, even with rationing. That is one of the things I love about England. The poor may always be with us, but so are the rich, thank God." He ate some potted shrimps and glanced up at the baroque lyres and laurels on the glass ceiling. "It's such a shame Mother can't share in your success, Bernard. She'd have loved to see your picture in the papers. Poor old girl. It's a living death, don't you think?"

The doodlebug that killed Olivia had been too much for Penelope. Within a year her memory had begun to disintegrate. At first Lionel's wife, Caroline, managed well enough, retrieving her when she went wandering along the lane, placidly replying when she asked the same question twenty times. She lost patience, though, when Penelope started to roam the house at night, leaving lighted cigarettes on the sideboards. She's a danger to everyone, Caroline said. What about the children? What about the dogs? Penelope had been installed in a very expensive care home where she sat drugged and passive, her hair immaculate with lacquer.

"She always said that you were going to be a great writer, she would have been thrilled to bits." Lionel speared his last brown shrimp and ate it. "Of course, you must be thrilled too."

Bernard grimaced. "Dust and ashes, Lionel," he said, "dust and ashes."

Lionel put back his head and laughed. "Nonsense. You can't fool me, Bernard, you're loving it. Did you say that you've finished the second book?"

"I finished it last week." Bernard leaned back in his chair to allow the waiter to remove their plates. "I wanted my publisher to have the manuscript before I leave for Rome."

"Ah, yes," said Lionel, "the holiday in Rome. Nina's there now, is she? With what's her name—the Italian girl—Filomena?"

Bernard let out a sharp sigh. "Spit it out, Lionel. I can tell you don't approve of my domestic arrangements."

"I think you should send Nina to a decent boarding school, that's all. Rightly or wrongly, there's a lot of prejudice against Eyeties still. At the very least you should prevent this girl of yours from talking to her in Italian. Young children shouldn't speak two languages, it hampers their development. Besides, it will make Nina different, which is never a good thing in my opinion. She's a bit of a changeling as it is. A boarding school would knock off the rough edges, help her to fit in. I'm sure she'll be grateful when she's older."

"Nina's very attached to Filomena," said Bernard. "She's already lost her mother, I don't see why she should lose Filomena too."

The mention of Olivia shut Lionel up. She had not been a suitable wife, there was no denying it, but he knew she was the kind of woman who got under your skin. It was not surprising that her death had thrown poor Bernard into chaos.

"And before you ask," Bernard said, "there is nothing between Filomena and me. She's a very capable woman, that's all. She's had a difficult life and she's survived it with great credit. I admire her."

"Of course there's nothing between you," said Lionel blandly. "I wouldn't dream of suggesting it. Ah, goody. Here comes the waiter with my liver and bacon. What could be more scrumptious?"

CHAPTER 39

"*BELLISSIMO!*" CRIED NINA AS FILOMENA THREW OPEN THE shutters, and she scrambled out to lean over the balcony. Below her, catching the late morning sun, was the shallow basin of the Fontana della Barcaccia, its ornate ship's prow rising from the water.

"Be careful, Nina, please," said Filomena.

She too was smiling, though, as she stepped into the brightness. She had forgotten how glorious the sunlight was in Italy, transforming all things with its heat, its glitter. It seemed to Filomena that she had been living in the twilight for years, cramped and bleary. Now she could expand, now she could relax.

They had arrived in Rome early that morning. Bernard had told Filomena to book herself and Nina into the best hotel she could find, but even with money in her pocket she found herself incapable of crossing the marble thresholds of the Via Veneto. Instead she chose a serviceable *pensione* overlooking the Piazza di Spagna, a stone's throw from the tawny house where Keats had died in 1821. Filomena did not know Rome well. To her it had always been the place where you got off the train, hot and tired and thirsty, and traipsed with your luggage to wait for the bus. Once, as a child, she and Paolina had been taken to St. Peter's by their mother, but all she could remember was the hot swell of panic as the cathedral loomed above her, dripping with gilt and porphyry. It made her feel so small, so insignificant, a pinprick upon an infinite canvas.

Filomena stepped back into the coolness of the room and began to unpack their clothes. Her plan was to spend a day or two in the city recovering from the journey before they set out for the village. In England she had been excited at the thought of seeing her family once more, but now that she was in Italy she felt anxious about the reunion. She was accustomed to her own independence: it would be irksome to have to bite her tongue at Paolina's foolishness, Valentino's arrogance. And she was afraid that it would stir up the memories of Antonio, of her father, which had at last begun to lie quietly in her heart.

Nina was standing beside the window. "I don't like that picture," she said, pointing. Above the bed there was a picture of Jesus, doe eyed, soft haired, his heart glowing with a fleshy orange flame. Filomena kicked off her shoes, climbed onto the white cotton bedspread and unhooked the frame.

"There," she said, as she slid the picture behind the wardrobe, "it's gone. Now, wash your face and hands, Nina. We're going to send a wire to your father to tell him that we've arrived safely, and then we'll explore."

ROME HAD ESCAPED the mighty devastation of London or Dresden, but it had been battered nonetheless by both German and Allied bombers. In July 1943, after a string of military disasters, Mussolini had been toppled by his own supporters. To the last they were fearful of his famous rages. Dino Grandi, once Italy's glamorous ambassador in London, secretly took two hand grenades into the meeting of the Fascist Grand Council, and slid one under the table to his colleague Cesare de Vecchi, like schoolboys passing notes.

Caught between the two sides in the war, the new government, led by the aging Marshal Badoglio, dithered. By the time they signed an armistice with the Allies in September it was too late to stop the Germans seizing Rome. For two more years the fighting continued as the Allies inched their bloodstained way along the peninsula. Mussolini, daringly rescued by Nazi paratroops, became the leader of a puppet state in the north, the Republic of Salo. As the Germans retreated, though, they had no further use for him. In April 1945, a week before their surrender, he was captured by Italian communists fifty kilometers from the Swiss border. The next day, he and his mistress Clara Petacci were shot and their bodies strung up by the heels above an Esso petrol station in Milan. Afterward it was whispered that the British had ordered his execution so that he could not reveal his secret wartime correspondence with Churchill in a public trial, but nothing was ever proved.

THE GEARS OF the bus strained and whined as it climbed the steep hill that led to the village. Nailed to the trees on the boulder-strewn roadside were signs forbidding hunting. It was late in the afternoon; half a dozen women were standing beside the fountain in the square, filling their bronze water jars and gossiping. They eyed Filomena with curiosity as she descended from the bus, holding Nina's hand. The heat reverberated from the walls of every building, the large ugly town hall, the church where her parents had been married. Filomena had come here for the summer all through her childhood, and the sight of the square was etched into her being, deeper than memory. And yet, she thought, here too I am a foreigner, here too I do not really belong.

Filomena and Nina had spent two days in Rome. They had clambered up the Spanish Steps to the twin bell towers of the Trinità dei Monti, they had taken refuge from the midday heat in the Colosseum, they had visited the fruit market in the Campo de' Fiori, where they gorged on dark red cherries as if they were sweets. Nina's eyes were wide with wonder, drinking in all that she saw. From a shop near the Castel Sant'Angelo Filomena bought her a straw hat with a green ribbon, to protect her face from the sun.

On their second morning there was an argument with the landlady at the *pensione*, who had discovered the sacred heart picture hidden behind the wardrobe. Filomena explained that it scared the little girl, but that appalled the landlady even more. What kind of godless child was frightened by a picture of Our Lord? Time to move on, thought Filomena, pulling their clothes from the musty chest of drawers. While she packed she could feel her shoulders stiffen, as though her body, like her mind, was bracing itself to meet her family once more.

THE HOUSE WHERE Paolina lived was on the outskirts of the village, beside the cindery road that led to the cemetery. A grubby flock of children, the oldest in his teens, the youngest about six, milled in and out, squalling. Their feet clattered in their *zoccoli*, rough wooden soles held on by a strap.

When Filomena last saw her Paolina had been plump, her waist marked only by her apron strings. Now it seemed that the flesh had melted from inside her skin, leaving her with loose wrinkled skeins beneath her upper arms, a dewlap under her chin. She wept when she saw Filomena.

"Oh, Mena. It's wonderful to see you at last. You look so like our poor lost Antonio, he might be here in the room, alive."

Filomena knew that this was not in the least true, but she did not argue as she embraced her sister. "This is Nina," she said. "Nina, say hallo to Zia Paolina."

Nina sucked her fingers and said nothing. A puzzled expression crossed Paolina's face. "Who is that child?"

"She's my employer Mr. Rodway's daughter," said Filomena. "She has come with me for a holiday."

Paolina studied Nina for a moment longer; then she called to a couple of the children who were chasing a scrawny chicken about the yard. "Aldo, Laura, go and fetch some water from the well. Take Nina with you. Your aunt Mena and I are going to have a chat."

Filomena sat at the huge ancient table in the kitchen while Paolina heated some coffee. The table was clean but splintery; Filomena had to arrange her knees carefully so it did not snag her blue cotton skirt. "I suppose it was hard for you here, during the war," she said.

"I do not know how we would have survived without Valentino." Paolina poured the coffee into small chipped cups. "He has been a good brother, he made sure we did not go hungry. There was always food on our plates."

"Black market stuff, I suppose?" said Filomena.

"When you have eight mouths to feed you do not care where it comes from. Everything was rationed, potatoes, lentils, milk. I was more anxious that our brother would be found out. You could be shot for hoarding food." Paolina pushed one of the cups toward Filomena. "I hope you don't want sugar because we've used it all up."

Filomena took a mouthful of the coffee, which was burned and nasty. "What is Valentino doing? Is he still in the village?"

"He's working for Guido Rossi, who used to be the mayor here. It's his son Franco that Giulia is going to marry. She's staying with the family now, choosing furniture for their apartment. Valentino was Signor Rossi's right-hand man all through the war, that's how he managed to help us with food and money. Signor Rossi is very well connected."

"I'm surprised that he hasn't been arrested," said Filomena, "or murdered, come to that. Wasn't he the leader of one of those fascist gangs, the *squadristi*? The ones that used to roam the countryside attacking anyone opposed to the *duce*?"

"Oh, nobody cares about that anymore, apart from the communists. Guido Rossi is a man of the future, Valentino says. He's got business interests in Rome, something to do with the reconstruction of the city. Valentino spends a lot of his time there now, it seems Signor Rossi can't manage without him."

"Valentino's still got the house, though, hasn't he? Our *nonna*'s old house?"

Paolina sniffed. "Well, for the moment he has. That house is yours and mine too, you know, Mena. If I wanted I should be able to go and live there."

"What do you mean? Is Valentino trying to take it from us?"

"It's not Valentino, I don't blame Valentino. It's Danila. Don't you read my letters, Filomena? I explained it to you. Danila moved into Nonna's house right after the war, when her mother died. Valentino claims it's because he needs a housekeeper, but I can see straight through that story. Danila's so sly. I swear she had her eye on Valentino even before our poor brother Antonio was lost." Paolina crossed herself in a perfunctory way, as though the gesture had become an automatic accessory to Antonio's name. "And now—well, you know what Valentino's like. He can't resist a pretty face."

"Ah," said Filomena, "so that's the secret, is it?" She remembered how Valentino had revered Danila when they lived in Frith Street, how Danila had listened entranced as Valentino talked to her about fascism. At the time it had seemed quite innocent, the devotion between a brother- and sister-in-law. Perhaps it had been innocent, at the time. We were all so young, thought Filomena, we knew so little of the world.

"Hardly a secret. It's been going on for months." Paolina sniffed. "I'm glad you're here, Mena. You can talk to Danila, you can tell her that she's to keep her hands off our *nonna*'s property. She never listens to me."

"I don't suppose she'll listen to me either," said Filomena, "but yes, I will pay her a visit. I'll go tomorrow. I'll have to see her sooner or later, after all."

Bernard was in his study, looking out at the sunlit trees in the square. It was one of those gilded summer days when it seemed impossible—ungrateful, almost—not to feel joy. A flicker of pleasure touched Bernard's heart, as if from a great distance. Well, perhaps that is all that remains of happiness, he thought, when you are middle-aged, when you have suffered great loss. Perhaps the fires of delight really do burn themselves out.

That morning he had booked the tickets for his journey to Rome. When he first proposed the trip Bernard had only half intended to go through with it; in his mind was the comforting idea that he could send a telegram at the last minute, claiming some emergency. Now, though, he was looking forward to it. To his surprise he was missing Filomena. He often passed weeks without seeing her—she and Nina visited London about once a month—but it irked him to think that he could not see her now if he wished, he could not catch the train to Lewes or summon her to Bedford Square. He thought of what he had said to his brother, Lionel. *She is a very capable woman . . . I admire her.* Then he remembered the confusion in her face when he had teased her about running away. The memory filled him with an unexpected tenderness. There was something disarming about seeing so unruffled a woman thrown off guard.

The afternoon post fell through the letter box with a clunk. Bernard got to his feet. Avril, who usually brought up his letters, was in bed with a sick headache: one of several ailments she had acquired since her heartbreak in Egypt. Bernard wished her misery were not so conspicuous. It was as though her nose were perpetually dripping, and she did not have the wit to pull her handkerchief from her pocket.

On the doormat was the usual clutch of envelopes: three stiff ivory invitations, a typed note from his publisher, six or seven handwritten letters, probably fan mail. I ought to get a secretary, thought Bernard, to deal with this kind of thing. He scooped up the envelopes and took them back to his study. As he dropped them upon his desk he saw that one was an airmail envelope, with an Australian stamp upon it.

CHAPTER 40

FILOMENA VISITED DANILA AFTER SIESTA, ON HER SECOND day in the village. She took Nina, still drowsy from her nap. The little girl had spent the morning roaming with Paolina's wild children, tumbling into the moss-edged springs where they stopped to drink, poking sticks at the chickens and the scrawny local cats.

The house that had belonged to Filomena's grandmother stood at the top of the hill, along the crooked cobbled path that climbed through the village. As they passed, half a dozen people came out of their houses to stare. They did it openly, not pretending that they were doing anything else. Like Paolina they looked thinner and shabbier than Filomena remembered.

"*Ciao*, Filomena," they said, raising their hands in greeting, and they fixed their eyes upon Nina, examining her face, her hair, her clothes.

"Why are they looking at me?" said Nina. "I don't like it."

Filomena tightened her grip on the child's hand. "It's because they don't know who you are. It's nothing to be frightened about."

DANILA HAD LOST her kittenish plumpness but Filomena had to admit that in its place was a piquancy that made her more alluring than ever. She wore a black and white checked dress with a sweetheart neckline, and her hair had been cut and jauntily permed.

"Filomena, at last," she said, as though she had been kept waiting, "come in."

Filomena stepped into the room that had been her *nonna*'s proudly guarded parlor. The brown chenille curtains had been pulled half-shut to protect the furniture from the brutality of daylight. Everywhere Filomena looked, she saw signs of Danila's presence, Danila's taste. On the sideboard there was a battalion of ornaments, gilt-painted china animals, little vases of Murano glass. Among them was a photograph of Antonio, taken on his wedding day. The sight caught Filomena unawares, and brought sudden salty tears to her throat.

"Rico," called Danila from the kitchen, where she was clattering with plates and glasses, "come and meet your aunt Filomena."

A slim, dark boy of ten wandered shyly into the room: Enrico, Antonio's son, named for his grandfather and for the singer Caruso.

"Zia Mena," he said, lifting his face to be kissed. He was beautiful: so beautiful, thought Filomena, that you feared for him, with his long-lashed eyes and his curls like glossy purple grapes. Nina put her fingers in her mouth and gazed idolatrously.

Danila returned with a plate of almond biscuits, the kind you had to dip into coffee or Marsala, or else they would break your teeth. Then she settled herself against the beige plush cushions just as she used to settle into the comfortable chair beside the stove at Frith Street.

"I'm glad you're here, Mena. There is something I need you to do for me. It's seven years since Antonio died"—like Paolina she crossed herself briskly as she spoke her husband's name—"and still I do not have the papers to prove it. There did not seem much sense chasing them during the war, but it is different now."

"I am not sure that I can help," said Filomena. "We have never had official confirmation of my brother's death, not like poor Papa's. I wouldn't know where to begin."

"Oh, not you, Filomena, I know you can't do anything. But this employer of yours, this Mr. Rodway. He's an influential man, isn't he? Surely he can make inquiries, ask the authorities to send the papers I need?"

Filomena remembered, across the gulf of time, how annoying she found Danila. "Why?" she asked ingenuously. "Do you want to get married again?"

Danila flushed. "Of course not. But if I *did* want to marry—well, I have a right to do it, Mena. Your sister, Paolina, may think that I should wear widow's weeds for the rest of my life, but in my opinion I deserve some happiness after all I've been through. You have no idea what it's been like here."

"I can imagine," said Filomena. "Life has been hard in England too."

"Yes, but England wasn't occupied. That's the difference. You didn't have German tanks rolling along the streets. Everywhere we went we saw posters on the walls, threatening to hang ten Italians for every German soldier who was killed. Even after the Allies marched in we didn't know what would happen next, we had to live with the uncertainty. It was terrible."

Filomena said nothing. She was not going to remind Danila that once upon a time she had applauded the Germans as good fascists. She felt a great desire to be at home in England, reading stories to Nina, drinking gin and Its with Bernard.

"And it was so cold," Danila went on. "Do you know, in the winter of '45 there was snow in Rome?"

Before Filomena could answer there was the sound of a key in the door. Danila's face softened in expectation.

"Valentino!" she called. "We have a visitor. Filomena is here at last."

Her brother was the only person Filomena had seen who had actually grown fatter during the war. Once lanky, he had the sleek look of a man who has never been denied oil on his salad or Bel Paese cheese on his plate. He greeted Filomena cheerfully, kissing her hard on both cheeks.

"Well, I've done a good day's work," he said, throwing himself in a chair. "I've managed to find a job for your cousin Bruno, Danila. Not a well-paid job, but it will keep the wolf from his door. Poor old Bruno. He is a broken man after the way the British treated him. He can barely haul himself out of bed to support his family."

Valentino cocked an eyebrow at Filomena as if Bruno's misfortunes were somehow her fault. She resisted the urge to snap. She did not want her first meeting with her brother to break down into a quarrel.

"I am glad that you've helped him," she said. "It is generous of you, Valentino."

"Oh, I am in a position to be generous. You've heard that our fortunes are on the rise, haven't you, Mena? I daresay that's why you've come back to Italy."

"I haven't come back. I'm here on a short visit, that's all. A holiday, with my employer's daughter, Nina."

Filomena gestured toward the couch, where the children were sitting, their bare brown legs dangling. At the sight of Nina, Valentino gaped.

"Good God," he said. Nina, whose mouth was full of sucked biscuit, stared back without speaking.

"Rico," said Danila, "take Nina off to play. Show her your canary, she'll like that."

Languidly Rico stood up. "Come," he said in Italian, and reaching for Nina's hand he led her from the room.

Valentino fixed his eyes upon his sister. His face had turned turkey-cock red. "I always knew you'd disgrace us, Filomena. Ever since that day when you shamed poor Bruno in front of all his friends. But I didn't think that even you would do something so stupid. I suppose he promised you marriage, this employer of yours? Or maybe he paid you, like British soldiers pay the sluts who pleasure them on the Palatine. And now he's chucked you aside like a used rag, and you've come here expecting me to support his bastard."

Filomena snorted. "Don't be ridiculous, Valentino. Nina's not my child. I was there when she was born, I helped to deliver her—"

"I'm sure you were there when she was born. You can't fool me. She's a Trombetta. Look at her hair, look at her nose." Valentino touched his own face as evidence. "It's exactly like mine."

"Oh," said Filomena, "you mean she looks like your friend Claudia's child? He had a big nose too, didn't he? Surely you remember Claudia, Valentino. The one whose husband scared you so much you ran squealing back to Italy."

With a yelp Valentino raised his hand to smack Filomena. It was Danila who intervened, leaping up to seize his arm.

"You should not reproach your brother, Filomena. It is not fair. Valentino may have been wild once upon a time, but he has changed his ways now that he is with me." She laid her small possessive fingers upon Valentino's wrist. "I may as well tell you, Mena, we are engaged to be married. As soon as my papers are in order we are going to fix a date. Isn't that true, Valentino?"

In spite of his fury Valentino could not help giving the rueful grimace of a captured man. Aloud he said: "Yes, my love, it's true."

"Be nice to Mena, Valentino. She has offered to help us when she goes back to England. She is going to ask her employer to speak to the authorities in London. He will persuade them to give me the documents we need, and then we can be married."

Filomena looked directly at her brother, composing her face into sincerity. "Believe me, Valentino, Nina is not my child. Nothing improper has ever occurred between me and Mr. Rodway. I swear it on our mother's grave."

Grudgingly Valentino met her gaze. They were both conscious that neither their father nor Antonio had a grave on which to swear. From the bedroom came the sound of a boy's high, bittersweet voice: Rico, singing a snatch of the Neapolitan song "Funiculì, Funiculà."

"Well, Filomena," said Valentino, "I will give you the benefit of the doubt. Since you swear such a solemn oath. You have to admit there's a resemblance, though."

Filomena did not answer. "I congratulate you on your engagement," she said. "Is Rico pleased?"

"Oh, Rico adores Valentino," said Danila at once. "He's been like a father to him. Paolina won't like it, but it is nothing to do with her. She's jealous, that's all. And she's convinced that I want to lay claim to this house, when nothing could be further from the truth." She looked scornfully around the little parlor. "Valentino and I wouldn't dream of staying here. When we're married we'll move to Rome, to a proper apartment with running water. I'm not spending my life traipsing to the fountain twice a day like a peasant. It may be good enough for Paolina, but it's not good enough for me."

"Of course it's not." Valentino patted Danila's hand, smiling down at her. "Now, fetch the prosecco, my angel, we'll have a drink to celebrate. You'd better stay for supper, Filomena. You're in for a treat. Danila makes the best gnocchi in Lazio. With a big pinch of black pepper, just the way our poor dear papa liked it."

CHAPTER 41

IN ROME THE MORNING WAS HAZY, THE DULL MILKY HAZE THAT presages a hot and unforgiving day. Bernard was passing through one of the *borgate*, the shantytowns at the city's edges, on his way into the countryside. These settlements had sprung up in the 1930s, to house those who had been displaced by Mussolini's grandiose reshaping of central Rome. The tenement walls were covered in graffiti, scrawled in angry red. Half a dozen men were hauling at their bicycles, ready to go to work.

Bernard had not been to Rome for more than twenty years, since his great journey after leaving Cambridge, and in his eyes the city was gilded by the memory of that momentous time. Returning now he was shocked by the shabby streets, the air of destitution. He felt glad that he had not come here for a holiday, frivolously, as he had originally planned. I have a purer motive now, he thought. I am that sacred thing, a messenger, I bring news that will change lives.

The drab suburbs were receding, giving way to sun-scorched hills. Instinctively Bernard touched the pocket where he had put Antonio's letter. He thought of how Filomena's face would be transfigured when he told her. A sense of excitement grew within him, building and swelling as the heat of the day built and swelled.

Filomena was in the kitchen, wrapped in one of Paolina's ancient stained aprons. It was the day of the wedding, and she had risen early to take charge of the food for that afternoon's feast, a task for which she had somehow acquired total responsibility. Paolina herself was upstairs with her daughter Giulia, helping her to get ready. Giulia had returned home two days before: a pretty, lazy, sloe-eyed girl, who spent most of her time squabbling with her siblings and trying on makeup. Her gown, made by the village dressmaker, was carefully pleated to disguise her pregnancy.

On the splintery kitchen table Filomena marshaled a pile of mismatched plates. Half the village was coming to the wedding, and they had all lent crockery and glasses for the feast. That morning vast quantities of food had arrived from Guido Rossi, soon to be Giulia's father-in-law: pale ham and mottled pink salami, round creamy slices of straw-colored cheese, white bread from a Roman baker, olives, pickled artichokes. His largesse annoyed Filomena, who had spent the previous day toiling in the heat, trying to stretch a tiny panful of *ragù* across four dishes of lasagna. Gathering up the plates she carried them through the yard. Valentino had taken one of the doors from its hinges and mounted it on a pair of trestles behind the house, overlooking the mountainside. A checkered cloth was laid across this makeshift table, weighted down with stones so it did not blow away in the wind.

Paolina's children were supposed to be helping Filomena, but they had soon grown bored and wandered off. Now, buttoned into their Sunday clothes, they were throwing a ball around the garden, leaping and pushing to catch it. Nina in the middle was squealing with delight. Her cries were as loud as the shrilling of the cicadas. She wore a green and white striped dress that had been Olivia's, cut down to fit.

"Nina," said Filomena, "you're going to ruin that dress. Come inside and sit down quietly, please."

A mutinous expression crossed Nina's face. All the same she was about to obey when she caught sight of a man approaching them along the cinder track. He was wearing a cream linen suit and a Panama hat. The bridge of his nose was already pink from the sun.

"Papa," said Nina. "Zia Mena, it's Papa."

"Hallo, Nina." Bernard laid his hand upon the child's head like a benediction. He was wheezing a little after his walk from the village.

Filomena stared. "Mr. Rodway. I did not expect you so soon. In fact, I did not expect you here at my sister's house at all—"

"Yes, I know, Filomena. I changed my plans at the last minute."

For a moment Bernard held her in his gaze. Filomena wished that she were not wearing Paolina's grubby pinafore, that her face were not pink and greasy from her efforts in the kitchen. "Nina," she said, "come, we will take your father indoors—"

"No, let her play, she's having fun, aren't you, Nina? And it's you that I've come to see, Filomena." Bernard pulled an envelope from his breast pocket: a creased airmail envelope with an Australian stamp. "I have brought you some good news."

THEY HAD TO find a quiet place to sit before Filomena fainted. Bernard put his arm about her and guided her toward a crumbling stone wall, beneath a white oleander tree. The noise of the cicadas seemed suddenly deafening.

"I have replied to Antonio," said Bernard. "I replied at once, by telegram. Your brother has been doing well in Australia, he has made a name for himself as a singer. In fact, he has earned the money to pay for his passage home."

"So he is coming back? I will see him soon?"

Bernard smiled at the radiance in her face. It was just as he had imagined it; better, if anything, warmer, more rapturous. "Oh, yes. He is coming back. It is a long voyage, but it should not take more than—what?—six, seven weeks."

"Oh, Antonio." Filomena pressed her palm against her mouth. "I cannot believe it."

"Of course, you must decide what to tell your family. It was you Antonio wanted to find, not his brother, not his wife. He was very clear about that."

"Oh, I will tell them he is alive," said Filomena at once. "It would be unkind not to tell them."

Gently Bernard took Filomena's hand, cradling it in both his own. "As you wish, Filomena. Everything will be as you wish."

There was a clamor from the house as Paolina began to round up her children to walk to church. Filomena scrambled to her feet. "I must change my clothes, we will be leaving in a moment, I cannot go to Giulia's wedding dressed like this." She turned shyly toward Bernard. "Perhaps, Mr. Rodway, you would like to rest here while we go to the church? And then—if you would not mind—perhaps afterward you will stay and help me to break the news?"

"Of course," said Bernard, "I will be delighted."

"I should warn you. If you stay for the wedding feast, people will stare at you. They will stare and they will whisper. It is how they—how we--do things in the village."

Bernard laughed. "I am a man of the world, Filomena. I have survived Rugby School, I have survived the blitz. I think that on your account I can endure a little staring."

FILOMENA WAS RIGHT. Everyone at the feast stared at Bernard. He had chosen what he thought was an inconspicuous place to sit, at one corner of the table, but that only made matters worse. The guests kept leaning forward and twisting their heads to look at him, ignoring the groom and the young bride at the table's head. Filomena's family had greeted him politely but warily; none of them, it seemed, knew quite what to say to him. As for Nina, she had run off to join the other children. He could see her now, in her green and white dress. A dark-haired boy of about ten was whirling her about so her bare feet flew through the air. Her beaky changeling's face was alight with bliss.

Bernard poured himself more wine from the jug. It was a local white wine, brackish but refreshing. He felt stupefied by the heat. From the mountainside he could smell the healthful scent of pine trees. He watched Filomena as she glided from one end of the table to the other, fetching bread, refilling glasses, clearing plates. There was an unconscious grace in all her movements. Perhaps I will move to Italy, thought Bernard. I can write here as well as anywhere; better, maybe, away from the hubbub of London. I will find a house in the countryside where I can live with Nina and with Filomena. I will start again. It is not too late, after all, to start again.

For Filomena the wedding passed in a daze. She had watched the luscious black market food vanish without being able to eat any of it. All she could think of was Antonio, impatient for the moment when she would tell her family he was alive.

The guests were beginning to relax now, some pushing back their chairs, others strolling across the garden to stretch their legs. One of the neighbors had begun to play his accordion, accompanied by another man with a violin. Guido Rossi, a hawklike man with hooded eyes, was handing out cheroots. Valentino puffed extravagantly at his, blowing smoke rings just as he used to do in the yard at Frith Street.

"Finesse, that's what it takes," he said to Franco, the bridegroom, who was pursing his lips without success. "Some men have it, my friend, some men don't."

Franco shrugged. Tossing aside his cheroot with the negligence of a rich boy, he wandered off to talk to one of the village girls, a plump girl in a yellow dress. Rico, his stiff wedding suit rumpled, was singing the Neapolitan song "O Sole Mio." His voice, which had not yet broken, was high and sweet and raw.

Bernard in his expensive linen suit picked his way toward Filomena. "Who is that boy? I saw him playing with Nina just now."

"It's my nephew Rico, my brother Antonio's son. He's a nice boy, he's been very good with Nina."

"Good lord. I'd forgotten that Antonio had a son. Well, he has his father's looks, that's for sure, lucky fellow. His father's voice too." Bernard paused and said more softly: "Will he remember Antonio, do you think?"

Filomena shook her head. "He was only a baby when he and his mother left England. Antonio will be a stranger to him. Mr. Rodway, I cannot bear to wait any longer. The wedding is nearly over, I must talk to my family now . . ."

Before Bernard could answer there was a shrill wail from the corner of the garden. It was Giulia, her dark sloe eyes wide with rage.

"Don't lie to me, Franco. You were kissing her, I saw you kissing her. On your wedding day, too."

Franco sidled away from the girl in yellow. "No, I wasn't," he said, sticking out his chin, "and even if I was, well, it was only meant in fun—"

"You were kissing her. And I've been your wife for what? Five hours. Your wife, Franco, and the mother of your child—"

"Shut up, Giulia. You're behaving like a peasant," said Franco, and he tapped Giulia on the rump. She let out a shriek.

"How dare you call me a peasant?" she said, diving for his face, her nails out. Guido Rossi stepped in, grasping her by the wrist. He spoke a few rapid words, too low for anyone else to hear. Giulia's face changed at once. She fled toward the house, half-stumbling over her long white dress. Paolina ran after her, calling her daughter's name.

"Oh, glory," said Filomena, "the poor girl."

"Not such a poor girl." Valentino had sauntered toward them, still smoking his cheroot. "She will have a very comfortable life, once she learns how to conduct herself. Don't waste your sympathy on Giulia." He turned to Bernard with a wheedling expression, fueled, thought Filomena, by a great deal of white wine. "Mr. Rodway, we have a favor to ask you when you return to London. You were always so kind to my dear brother, Antonio, I hope you will help us. It concerns Danila, my brother's widow—"

Filomena clutched her brother's arm. "Oh, Valentino. Don't say any more, everything has changed. I have news for you, news from England. Fetch Danila, fetch Rico, we will go inside where it is quiet. There is something that I have to tell you all."

Valentino burst into tears when Filomena gave him the news. It took her a moment to realize that they were tears of pure joy.

"What? So Antonino is not dead? He was rescued after the ship went down?"

"Yes," said Bernard, "a Canadian destroyer picked him up. He was taken to Scotland, and from there to Australia."

"My God, Filomena." Valentino embraced his sister, throwing his arms about her; then he hugged his nephew. "You have a father after all, Rico, your papa is still alive. Oh, Danila, my love, isn't it wonderful? Antonio wasn't lost at sea with Papa, he survived. At this very moment he is sailing back to England."

Filomena looked at Danila, who was sitting at the kitchen table. Her face had turned cheese white, all its charm, all its piquancy, quite gone.

"But it is seven years. For seven years I thought he was dead. He can't just come back like this, it isn't fair—" She began to cry. Rico, his huge eyes wide with trouble, inched toward her.

"What is it, Mama? Why are you crying? Aren't you glad that Papa is alive?"

"Yes, I am glad—of course I am glad—but why couldn't he have kept quiet? Why did he have to tell us? He has ruined everything."

Valentino stared. Filomena could see that it had just dawned upon him what his brother's resurrection would mean for Danila. He licked his lips uncertainly.

"Don't cry, my angel," he said at last. "I know my brother, Antonio. He will not stand in our way, he will want us to be happy. Marriages can be annulled, can't they?" He turned to his sister. "You will have to talk to him, Filomena. Explain the situation, tell him that he has to set Danila free."

"I think that when he returns to England Antonio will have more urgent things on his mind," said Bernard drily.

Valentino opened his mouth to argue and then closed it again. "Of course, you are right. I am being selfish. It is the shock—" He pulled out a large white handkerchief to wipe his eyes. "I have always loved my brother, Antonio. I love him with all my heart. You know that, don't you, Mena?"

"Yes," said Filomena, "I do know that."

Danila was still sobbing. "And I suppose you'll tell Paolina, and she'll never stop gloating. She was sick with rage when Valentino and I fell in love, she will do anything in the world to prevent our marriage—"

"Don't cry, my love, don't cry." Valentino sat beside Danila, making soothing throat noises as he clasped the nape of her neck. "It will be all right, I promise. We will find a way . . ."

From the far side of the table Rico fixed his eyes upon Filomena. His beautiful face was pale and tense. It was the face of a child who has been pushed before his time into the adult world. Filomena had a glimpse of what it must have been like for Rico: the loss of his father, and the war, and then to see his mother's attention purloined by Valentino. She hoped he would not ask if Antonio had sent a particular message for him.

"Zia Mena," said Rico, "will you be seeing my father soon?"

"As soon as I can, yes," said Filomena. "As soon as he arrives in England."

Rico's taut forehead relaxed. "When you see him, tell my father that I will meet him wherever, whenever he wishes. And, Zia Mena: tell him that I want to be a singer too."

OUTSIDE, IN THE dusk, the musicians were still playing. A few of the wedding guests were dancing in loose relaxed embraces. Franco, the bridegroom, was slumped at the trestle table, blearily trying to blow smoke rings once more. There was no sign of Giulia.

Filomena hauled Nina from a tangle of children and took her upstairs to bed. While he was waiting for her, Bernard had another drink, feeling the alcohol percolate exquisitely through his limbs. He gazed out at the expanse of hills that stretched toward Rome, fold upon bluish fold. Lamps like stars were beginning to come out in the distant villages. The warmth of the night was thrilling.

When she returned Filomena had a frown on her face. "I hope you do not mind, Mr. Rodway, I have made up a bed for you in one of the attic rooms. I am afraid it will not be very comfortable, but it is too late for you to return to Rome now, I am sorry—"

"Hush, Filomena, hush. You're not responsible, you know, for everything that happens in the world." Reaching out Bernard took her hands: capable hands, he thought, hands that have pulled up cabbages, delivered children, dug the chalky Sussex earth. "And now, will you dance with me? Nobody will notice us, and if they do, well, they'll be too drunk to gossip."

"Oh!" said Filomena, startled. Then she stepped forward, and he felt her body relax trustfully in his arms. There was a solidity about her which filled him with delight. More than delight: a sense of rightness. He breathed in the smell of pine trees, the sun-scorched scent of Filomena's hair. It was as though he had spent weeks, months waiting for this moment, and now at last it had come.

"There is a question I want to ask you, Filomena," he said. "You don't have to answer at once, I know what you are like, you will want to think about it. But I would be so honored—and so grateful—if you would consider becoming my wife. Human beings are not meant to live alone."

CHAPTER 42

THE DRESSING ROOM AT THE GOLDEN SLIPPER HAD NOT changed at all. It was still cramped and airless, with a glaring row of lightbulbs around the mirror. Antonio breathed in the sweetish, faintly stale smell of makeup as he laid his brush and comb upon the little table. This afternoon he had come to the nightclub to rehearse; tomorrow he would sing in public for the first time since his return to London. The club's manager had been delighted to hear from him. You were one of our greatest stars before the war, he said. We'll give Hutch a run for his money now that you're back.

Antonio turned toward the chrome rail to put on his suit. The movement made him momentarily giddy. Three weeks had passed since his return, and still he could not trust the ground beneath him, expecting it to buck and sway under his feet. He thought of Peppino, who had come to the harbor front in Melbourne to see him off.

"Well, Antonino, good luck," he had said. "We will see each other soon. You will return to Australia, I am sure. And who can say? Perhaps one day I will come back to London."

Antonio had nodded as he embraced his old friend. They both knew that Peppino would never again set foot on an oceangoing ship.

In the nightclub the musicians were tuning their instruments. Antonio pulled on his jacket. He remembered how he used to stand in the dimness of the wings, waiting for the moment when he would step onto the stage. And at that moment he would look for Olivia, scanning the lamp-lit tables, the glimmering bronze chairs, hoping that tonight she would be there. Bernard had broken the news of Olivia's death in his first long eager telegram. *My beloved wife is dead but she has left me a daughter.* What will it be like? thought Antonio, as he straightened his collar. What will it be like to step into the light knowing that I will not see her, knowing I will never see her again?

The call boy knocked on the dressing room door. "Ready for you now, Mr. Trombetta," he said.

Antonio cleared his throat. He could feel the familiar thrum of stage fright fluttering against his breastbone. It will pass, though, he thought. It will pass as soon as I open my mouth to sing. This is what I was born to do.

FILOMENA WAS WAITING on the quayside in Southampton when Antonio's ship docked, standing tense and eager eyed in the drizzle. Afterward they traveled together to the house in Sussex. It was Bernard's idea, to give Antonio a few days of peace to recover from the voyage, and to be reunited with his son. Rico had arrived the week before; he was staying in Sussex with Nina and with Bernard himself. It will be easier for the boy, Bernard said, to have other people present, it will not matter then if he is tongue-tied or embarrassed. And Nina will be thrilled to see him.

"You have never been here before, have you, Antonio?" Filomena said, as the taxi wound through Lewes, past the De Luxe cinema, over the river Ouse. The sky had cleared; it was a golden rain-washed afternoon, with the sharpness of autumn in the air. Filomena kept gazing at her brother as though she could not believe he was really present.

"Once," said Antonio. "I came here with Mrs. Rodway, just after war broke out. Mr. Rodway asked me to accompany her—" He paused, staring hungrily at the curved green hills. "So you have been living here, Mena, with Mr. Rodway's daughter? I am glad that he has been good to you. And I expect you were a comfort to him, after his wife died."

"I hope so," said Filomena in a sober voice. She did not want to talk about Bernard—at least, not yet. Since their return from Lazio they had been living in a curious, vaguely pleasing kind of limbo. There was the warmth of an understanding between them, although the actual words—*Yes, I will marry you*—remained unspoken. The only change in their behavior was that sometimes, after their evening drink together, Bernard would kiss her lightly on the lips when they said good night.

The taxi had turned along the lane that led to the house, lined with hawthorn bushes. "We are nearly there, Antonino," Filomena said, clutching her brother's hand. "Mr. Rodway must have heard the car, he's come outside to welcome us. And look, Antonio! There is your son, waiting for you. There is Enrico."

As BERNARD HAD predicted, the reunion of father and son was ecstatic but awkward. Once they had embraced, fiercely, they did not know what to say to one another. Even Filomena was struck dumb. It was left to Bernard to ease the situation, ushering them indoors, pouring drinks, chattering. He was shocked by the sight of Antonio, with his gray hair, his harrowed face, but he thought—hoped—he had managed to hide it.

"Rico has a wonderful voice, did you know, Antonio?" he said. "I heard him sing in Italy, at your niece Giulia's wedding. We ought to find him a school where he can train properly, in Rome maybe, or else in London."

Antonio nodded. He had a dazed air as he looked all about him, at the russet velvet curtains, at the stage designs upon the walls, at Filomena, at his son.

"Is your daughter here too, Mr. Rodway?" he asked at last. "I would like to meet her."

"Nina? Oh yes, she's playing in the garden. She and Rico get on famously, they've been having a marvelous time, romping about and climbing trees." Bernard refilled Antonio's glass, squirting soda into his inch of whisky. "And Nina's very excited about having dinner with the grown-ups tonight. Roast chicken and plum tart with cream, just the kind of food my dear old uncle Dickie used to love. You remember Dickie, don't you, Antonio?"

"Of course." Antonio moistened his lips with the whisky and soda. "How old is she, your daughter?"

"Six. That's right, isn't it, Filomena? She was born during the war, Filomena here delivered her. Your sister is remarkable, Antonio, I do not know how I would have managed without her. It seems there is nothing she cannot do."

"Oh, yes," said Antonio, "my sister has always been remarkable."

Briskly Filomena stood up. "It is nearly time to eat," she said. "I'll go and call Nina."

"No need," said Bernard, "here she comes now."

The door clattered open and Nina burst into the room. She looked wilder than ever in her tartan Viyella dress, which had split at the shoulders. Her dark untidy hair was ragged as a broom.

"I'm hungry," she said, "and I couldn't find Rico—"

"Good lord," said Bernard amiably, "what a little ragamuffin you are. Nina, say hallo to Signor Antonio. He is Rico's papa, he's come to stay with us."

Nina did not answer. She put her fingers in her mouth and stared at Antonio. He stared back. He could not take his eyes from her. Nobody spoke. Silence quite suddenly filled the room, sharp as electricity.

It was Filomena, in the end, who broke it. "Come along, Nina, upstairs with you. You can't sit at the dinner table dressed like that. Your father's right, you're a ragamuffin. And, Rico, I expect you'd like to wash your hands before we eat. Come along, both of you, we'll leave your papas to finish their drinks in peace."

Holding out her arms she shepherded the children away. Antonio turned his head to look at Bernard. He could feel his heart thump in his throat. "She is my child," he heard himself say, "isn't she?"

"Ha!" Bernard let out an abrupt forced breath. Rising to his feet he walked across the room. As he walked he touched his fingertips to the chrome-edged decanter, the stone mantelpiece, the lead-lighted window. Then he said: "Yes. She is your child."

"Did you—" Antonio paused, swallowed, tried again. "How long have you known?"

Bernard smiled. "It is curious, don't you think? How you can know a truth and yet deny it, even to yourself? I think I realized when I first saw her, in Olivia's arms. And then, after Olivia died—well, that was like a madness, I would have believed anything. I did believe anything, from one day to the next. But it was seeing her in Italy, with her cousins, with your son, Rico—"

"And Filomena? Does she know?"

"Ah, Filomena," said Bernard. "Filomena is the wisest woman I have ever met."

Antonio's hands were shaking. He had to set down his whisky glass before it fell from his grasp. "You must have hated me," he said, his voice very low.

"No. Not at all. Is that surprising? Of course, when I look back I think what a fool I must have been, how could I have failed to notice? But it was a different world. We were different people in it."

Tears came to Antonio's eyes, hot and stinging. "Oh," he said, "I do not deserve your generosity, Mr. Rodway."

"It is not a question of generosity," said Bernard. "It is a question of survival. We have endured a great deal, you and I, and we have survived. Nothing else matters." From the sideboard he took the photograph of Olivia, in her oyster silk dress. "She was a beautiful woman. Look! Do you remember how she danced the tango? Nobody could resist her when she danced the tango."

Antonio took the photograph in both his unsteady hands. His eyes devoured it. So did Bernard's, leaning over his shoulder. And that was how they were when Filomena returned to call them in for dinner: two men engrossed by one lost, desired, unreachable face.

IN THE DAYS that followed Filomena could not get the memory of what she had seen from her mind. It surfaced at unexpected moments, as she was laying the table for breakfast, as she was brushing her hair at night. She could not name the expression on Bernard's face; all she knew was that she had never witnessed it before.

After a week in Sussex they took the train to London. Bernard had work to do: his writing, his committee papers, his letters from refugees. As for Antonio, he had to prepare for his first night at the Golden Slipper. For the present he was living at Bedford Square with Filomena and the children, but once Rico returned to Italy he intended to find a place of his own.

"It's a pity that Antonio's first engagement is in a nightclub," Bernard remarked. "Otherwise we could have taken the children to hear him. Nina is a little young, perhaps, but Rico would have loved it. I do hope his mother lets him come to England again. I'm afraid that once she gets her way over the annulment she'll be difficult."

"Well," said Filomena, "it would be like Danila, to make life difficult. But perhaps my brother Valentino will persuade her to be amenable."

They were having coffee after lunch, while upstairs Rico and Nina were resting. Later that afternoon Filomena was going to Soho with the children. Rico wanted to see the house in Frith Street, the house where he was born, and today was his last chance: in the morning they were taking him to Victoria, to begin the journey home. They had decided not to tell Nina about her true parentage. Best for the child to get to know Antonio first, Bernard had said, before baffling her with such a shock.

Filomena put the empty coffee cups on the tray, ready to take it to the kitchen. She still felt ill at ease in Bedford Square, uncertain of her own status, employee or future mistress. Bernard glanced up from the newspaper he was reading.

"Don't do that. I'll ring for Avril. She'll have to get used to fetching and carrying for you once we're married. If she wants to stay on, that is." Bernard flicked at the newspaper, turning the page. "I've been meaning to ask you, Filomena. Do you have anything to wear for Antonio's first night?"

"Oh," said Filomena. "I've got a lilac coat and skirt. I thought I'd wear that."

Bernard shook his head. "You need a proper evening dress. It's an elegant place, the Golden Slipper, all the women will be dolled up to the nines. And it will be our first public appearance together. There may even be photographers there. Have you got enough clothing coupons to buy yourself something?"

Pulling out his wallet Bernard peeled off some white five-pound notes and passed them to Filomena. In her hands they felt leathery and well thumbed. She thought of the yearning expression on Bernard's face as he looked at his dead wife's photograph. She thought of the real Olivia, pampered and beautiful and unhappy. Gently she laid the notes upon the table, next to the coffee tray.

In that moment Bernard guessed. "You're not going to marry me after all, are you?"

"No," said Filomena, "I'm not. I am very grateful to you for asking me, and I know you would be the kindest husband in the world, but I cannot do it. I would never be your equal, even in your eyes. I would always be the Eyetie girl from Soho . . ."

Bernard opened his mouth to argue. Then he stopped and said: "That's not the real reason, is it, Filomena?"

Filomena bowed her head, searching for the words, and the courage to say them. "I saw you looking at her picture," she said at last, "Olivia's picture. I saw your face. You do not love me, Mr.

Rodway. What you want is companionship. And I may be thirty years old, I may be past my prime, but I'm not ready to settle for that."

Bernard gazed at her, so serious, so composed. He felt overwhelmed by regret. "You would lack nothing, you know, if you married me."

"I would lack passion." Filomena said it quietly, without any suggestion of reproach. Bernard was silent. He knew that it was the truth.

"Besides, you are a successful man, a famous man. You will find someone cleverer and more glamorous than me, someone far better suited to be your wife—"

"Oh, Filomena. Nobody could be better suited than you." Reaching out he took her hand and kissed it. "You will stay with me, though, won't you? You are like my family, you and Nina and Antonio. I could not bear to lose you from my life."

Filomena's cheeks had flushed crimson with the relief of speaking out. "Of course I will stay," she said. "I could never leave Nina, and besides, you have been so kind to us, so generous. How could we not repay that kindness now?"

WHEN HIS REHEARSAL had finished Antonio set off to meet his family, walking through Piccadilly Circus toward Charing Cross Road. Soho now was a dream landscape, familiar, half-forgotten buildings interspersed with empty spaces. Newport Dwellings, once home to scores of Italians, had been destroyed by a mine, plummeting from the sky in broad daylight, suspended from a parachute. The jumbled ruins had been colonized by rosebay willow herb, the whiskery plant nicknamed fireweed because it flourished upon bomb sites.

Filomena and the children were waiting for him in Ricci's café; or rather, what had once been Ricci's. During the war, while Carlo Ricci was interned, his wife had brought in a shrewd young manager who secretly renegotiated the lease in his own name. The café was called the Blue Grotto now, with Formica tables and a glossy espresso machine behind the counter.

"What's wrong?" Antonio said to Filomena. "You look flustered."

"Nothing's wrong," said Filomena, "nothing at all." Briskly she gathered her belongings, snapping shut her handbag, buttoning Nina's velvet coat. "Let's be off. I think it's going to rain."

The house in Frith Street looked as it had always done, tall and narrow, the door opening directly onto the pavement. The curtains were drawn at all the high windows. It made the house seem shrunken and secretive, shutting them out.

"We used to live there, your *zia* Mena and I," Antonio said. "My papa, Enrico, and I ran a little sweet shop. And *zia* Mena used to work in a laundry, washing sheets. When she came home her clothes always smelled of starch."

"Soho," said Nina, "we're in Soho, aren't we?"

"That's right." Antonio glanced at his son. "Do you want to go inside, Rico? We can knock on the door if you like, see if the new tenants will let us in."

Rico had screwed up his eyes, tilting his neck back to look at the upper window of the house. "I do not remember it," he said. "I do not remember it at all." His voice was thick with distress, as though the not remembering were somehow his fault.

Gravely Antonio put his arm about his son's shoulders. "It does not matter, Rico," he said, and he gestured along the street toward the square, with its patch of lawn, its graceful trees. Their leaves were beginning to curl and fade in the autumn chill. "We'll go, shall we, and sit in the park? Then we can find somewhere to have tea. Nina? Do you want to go to the park?"

Nina had been distracted by a figure on the opposite pavement. "Aunt Min," she said, pointing, "why is that man staring at us?"

Filomena turned. The man was stocky and wide faced, with straw-colored hair. He stood quite still, his feet planted upon the paving stones. Her first giddy thought was that he had not changed, except that in one hand he carried a stick. Then he stepped out to cross the road, rolling his weight clumsily forward to get started.

"Frostbite," said Stan Harker. "I lost three toes to it, out there in Norway. Made life in a German prison camp tricky, I can tell you." He fixed his pale blue eyes upon Filomena. "I'm surprised to see you, Filomena. I came to look for you, but the new people said you'd moved on."

"I have—I did—" Filomena's mouth was loose and sticky as glue; she could not get the words out.

"I've got lodgings around the corner," said Stan. "Easy for walking to Bow Street. They've given me a desk job with the force, but it won't last. I can't stand it, not after being on the beat. I'll have to learn a trade, carpentry maybe, or mechanics." He looked at Nina. "Is this your daughter? She looks like you."

"No, it's not my daughter, I'm not married, it's my—my niece, we've been living down in Sussex, she and I. And this is my nephew from Italy . . ."

Antonio, hearing his competent sister dither, stepped forward. "Constable Harker," he said, putting out his hand. Stan smiled.

"It's Antonio, isn't it? Well, I'm glad to see that you got through the war."

"Yes," said Antonio, "I got through the war." The two men looked at one another. Each could read the memory of hardship and imprisonment in the other's face.

"What about your mother?" asked Filomena, finding her voice.

Stan shook his head. "Air raid. The house was flattened. And she wouldn't use the shelters. She always said that if she was going to be killed she'd rather it was in her own bed. Well, she got her wish."

Filomena was going to say, I'm sorry, but her mouth had turned to glue once more. Beside her Nina was growing restless, turning her toes in and out, fidgeting with her belt.

"Are we going to the park, Aunt Min? Rico and I want to go to the park."

"We are going to Soho Square, Constable Harker," Antonio said, "and then to have some tea. Would you like to come with us?"

"Thank you," said Stan. "That's very civil. I will, if you don't mind."

The square was in shadow but the sun was glinting upon the top of the trees. Antonio took one of Nina's hands, Rico the other. From time to time Nina gave a gawky unexpected skip, jerking at their arms. Stan and Filomena followed. At first Filomena kept pausing, concerned he could not keep up, but then she and Stan fell into step, and they walked on in silence, side by side.

ACKNOWLEDGMENTS

SEVERAL BOOKS HAVE BEEN INVALUABLE TO ME IN WRITING THIS novel. *'Collar the Lot!'* by Peter and Leni Gillman offers a definitive account of the internment and expulsion of so-called enemy aliens during the war, while *Island of Barbed Wire* by Connery Chappell paints a vivid picture of the lives of internees on the Isle of Man. Both Terri Colpi's *The Italian Factor* and Claudia Baldoli's *Exporting Fascism* provide detailed insights into the Italian community in Britain, especially during the 1930s. Of the many books that exist about wartime Britain the one I found most useful was Philip Ziegler's *London at War 1939–1945*. Any historical errors are, of course, my own.

Thanks go to my wonderful agent Maggie Hanbury for her belief in me and in this book. I am also grateful to Jenny Parrott, Philippa Pride, and Sheila Thompson for their advice on the text, and to Robin Straus and all the team at Crown, especially Rose Fox and Kim Silverton, for their hard work on this U.S. edition. Finally, thank you to my parents, Elinor Winifred Luxton and Don Love, for their lifelong encouragement, and to Barry MacDonald for his constancy and support.

The GIRL *from the* PARADISE BALLROOM

A READER'S GUIDE

1. Antonio and Olivia, as a singer and a dancer, are both able to captivate and hold the attention of an entire room but neither possesses the same confidence and authority in their daily lives. How is this contradiction reflected in their relationship?
2. Discuss their first meeting and its repercussions throughout the novel.
3. Antonio and Olivia are both outsiders to the glamorous world of high society London; do you think this is what brings them together?
4. Do you think the statement, "Maybe some women aren't meant to be tamed. Maybe they just need to run free until they find someone just as wild to run with them" applies to Olivia? Do you think this is why she pulls away from Bernard and is drawn to Antonio?
5. Did you respect Antonio for his sense of duty to his family, or did you feel that he put undeserving individuals before himself and his dreams?
6. The women in the novel, especially Olivia and Filomena, have to find ways of dealing with the social or family restrictions that limit their independence. How far do you think restrictions like these still apply to women in the twenty-first century?
7. Fascism is a theme and source of conflict throughout the book on both a global and familial scale. Discuss how, despite An-

tonio's resistance, his family's connection to the fascist cause ultimately results in his downfall.

8. Discuss the roles that lineage and heritage play throughout the generations in the novel.
9. Discuss the relationship between Filomena, Nina, and Bernard in their unconventional family structure.
10. How did your opinion of Bernard change throughout the book, as a philanthropist, husband, and widowed father?
11. Filomena and Stan have a very different kind of relationship than Olivia and Antonio. What does the resolution of the novel say about passionate versus unhurried love?
12. Why do you think this time period in London is so enthralling and captivating to Americans?
13. If you were to write the epilogue, what would you envision happening to all of the characters?